Ruth *AND* Naomi

OTHER BOOKS AND AUDIO BOOKS
BY TONI SORENSON

Ruth AND Naomi

Whithersoever Thou Goest

a novel

TONI SORENSON

Covenant Communications, Inc.

For Nedra Dee

1

THE MIDWIFE WRAPPED THE JUST-BORN baby in a shred of clean linen and put her to her mother's breast.

"Hurry! Feed the child to make her quiet. It's the only way to save her."

Sakira trembled in terror and pain. A woman barely graduated from girlhood, she offered the squirming baby a swollen breast.

The child turned away, her little pink mouth open, screaming so loudly the sound bounced off the walls of the palace, piercing the mandatory silence the king so savored. The midwife feared that the child's lungs were so strong her wails might be heard all the way down the long stone corridor and into the great hall where King Eglon, ruler of Moab, sat ripping great hunks of bread to sop up the grease from the leg of roasted swine he also savored.

Bowing her head, the midwife prayed aloud. "God of all Israel, look down with mercy on this baby girl and guide her to her mother's milk. Silence her before her father does."

Great tears tumbled down Sakira's cheeks. "Do you really believe Eglon will destroy his own child?"

In a quivering whisper the midwife replied, "If he discovers he has fathered yet another girl, yes. But, then, you *are* the king's concubine, so you know his capabilities when his mood is foul."

The midwife's words pierced Sakira's heart. "Pray again; please pray to your god. For your god is merciful, unlike Chemosh."

The midwife prayed with renewed fervor, her words whispered and desperate. She continued to pray even as the other servants gathered around her, looking shocked by the reckless courage of such an act. A servant of the king of Moab praying to the God of Israel! The penalty could be death—or worse.

"What is your name?" Sakira asked.

Hesitantly, the midwife said, "In the Hebrew language of my people my name means *friend*." She continued to beg her God to spare the child, until, finally, a miracle was granted for all to witness. The baby turned her red face toward her mother and began to suck.

When the baby was fed and asleep in her mother's arms, Sakira looked at the midwife with unspoken gratitude. Silence had never been so welcome.

Unaware that Eglon had requested to be disturbed only if the child born was a male, a manservant walked into the great hall with a smile on his face, his footsteps echoing on the hard floor.

Eglon gulped down a goblet of cream sweetened with apricot nectar and swiped the back of his hand over his mouth. Cream and grease clung to the whiskers on his knuckles. "So I have another son!" He returned the servant's smile.

"A daughter, sir, healthy and whole, I am pleased to report."

The king's fat fingers squeezed the cup, but the grease made them slip. In a crash the royal pottery landed on the stone floor and shattered.

The distraught servant fell to his knees to gather the pieces while another servant, standing in the archway with a band of ready men, ran to fetch a new cup for the king's wine.

"You dared disturb me for news of another daughter?" the king hissed. "Take this man off to the grove! Have him shackled and imprisoned until the harvest."

The band of ready men stepped forward at the order.

The manservant was still on his knees. With shards of pottery cupped in his hands, he began to weep. "Please, sir, no! I meant no harm. Please. I have a family, sir, a wife and three young sons. They need me."

The king's elbows slammed the table so hard it rattled. "Off!"

They dragged the man away, cleaned up the mess, and set fresh bread and wine before the king, a father who would not bother to view this infant girl, his twenty-seventh daughter.

And so the twenty-seventh daughter of King Eglon, the first and what would be the only daughter of Sakira, was named in honor of an Israelite midwife. The girl was called Ruth.

* * *

Across the valley, on a white stone hillside, another mother listened as her four-year-old twin sons played with rocks and sticks and pretended to battle King Eglon, the man who stole their food and kidnapped their neighbors.

"They are good boys, Naomi," one well watcher said. "Thin, but not deformed like so many of our children."

"God has been merciful and we are grateful," Naomi said, trying not to count the ribs of Chilion, the frailest of her twins. "Soon, our land will be returned to us and our people will heal."

"Not soon enough," the well watcher said. "Already it is too late for so many."

"We must be grateful for all that we have and not dwell on those things for which we want."

"Oh, sweet Naomi, you are a bright soul like your mother, Anna. Oh, how Bethlehem misses her!"

Naomi smiled. No one missed Anna more than Naomi—Anna's only daughter, her only child. As Naomi walked over to a bench near the well and sat down, she thought that if she could acquire just a part of her mother's goodness and faith, she would also become a woman to be honored.

Though Anna had been dead for years, her reputation lived on. She was a humble shepherd's wife and a renowned midwife, said to have the love of God in her heart and the power of God in her hands, hands that could rub life back into a baby born blue.

Anna was also an artist. Whenever she held a sharpened stick, the splinter of a jawbone, or, on rare occasions, a metal blade, something of beauty was created. Her lasting legacy was the bench where Naomi now sat watching her boys play. It was a long-shared seat where everyone who came to the common well sat to rest. Anna had crafted the bench from a hewn olive trunk with years of loving labor, and those who sat there felt no hurry to leave.

When Bethlehemites sat on the bench, carved smooth and even, they let their fingers glide over the nooks and ridges of lovely carved vines and blossoms. Anna had also carved the laws of God into the wood. Even those who could not read still felt the power of this inscription, a visual reminder of the laws Father Moses brought down from Sinai.

In a way, Anna had created a place of worship without even realizing it.

Anna herself never learned to read, but she was meticulous in her artwork, and the best scribes in all the land deemed her renderings flawless. She did not have to read the laws to understand them; they were carved into her heart.

Memories of her mother were like tiny pebbles that sat at the bottom of Naomi's heart, each one heavy and hard. Anna was dead. Her humble shepherd husband, Lowell, Naomi's father, was dead. Even Ruth, Naomi's humble apprentice midwife, had been taken by force to serve a king that did not care to know the God of Israel, the God who had been everything to Anna.

The sound of approaching voices brought Naomi back from her melancholy memories. Another family had arrived at the well. It was a woman from the highlands with a daughter and a son near the age of Mahlon and Chilion, the twins of Naomi and Elimelech, her husband.

"Have you heard?" the other mother asked. "The news is tragic."

The well watcher moved closer and tilted her good ear to better hear. "What is it? Did someone else die during the night? Abel, the potter's son, has been so sick. Did he die?"

"No," the woman said, sobbing. "My husband has decided we must leave Bethlehem. If we stay, we will starve like so many others."

A twinge of fear entered Naomi's heart. Her husband, Elimelech, had talked of moving too. But leaving Bethlehem, her mother's sacred bench, the only home and people she'd ever known . . . the thought was too much. A tear trickled down Naomi's cheek.

"My husband says that everyone who chooses to stay in Bethlehem will die, either at the hands of a deaf god or by the sword of a filthy Moabite."

Naomi was instantly on her feet. "Your husband is wrong, Sister. Our God is not deaf, only slow to hear us because we are slow to obey Him. My own husband has faith that our hard times are about to end."

The well watcher's eyes narrowed. "This is Naomi, wife of the swordsmith Elimelech."

"I know who she is," the woman said, unveiled bitterness in her tone. She looked at Naomi. "I also know who your husband is—a betrayer to his own people. Elimelech works for King Eglon, crafting the very swords the Moabites use to torture and kill our people."

Naomi lifted her water jug. She wanted to defend Elimelech. She wanted to explain to the woman that Elimelech had no choice but to accept the king's commissions. His work did not betray his people; it helped to bond the Bethlehemites to the Moabites in a way that made Elimelech privy to enemy war strategy. More than once, his insightful information had been used to save lives. She wanted to say these things, but she could not.

The wail of a child turned the women's attention back to the playing children. Apparently, Chilion had whacked the woman's little girl across the shoulder with his pretend sword.

The woman opened her arms to her daughter and, at the same time, her eyes sent Naomi a message of the harshest judgment.

On the walk back home Naomi allowed her sons to run ahead. She wanted to spend time alone with her troubled thoughts. Elimelech's work did cause more problems than it solved. But it wasn't like he had a choice in the matter. Since childhood, his gift had been to design weapons. This gift used to be a blessing to his father's humble but profitable blacksmith shop. Then one of the swords was confiscated, and when King Eglon saw the unique craftsmanship, he ordered that Elimelech's talent be used only for the benefit of Moab.

Elimelech wasn't the only craftsman in Bethlehem to serve the king; there were potters and farmers and tanners and wine makers too. As she walked the dusty path up to their home, Naomi passed a wine press. Its wine also went to tables of Moab. So did the grain that she watched being sliced to stubble each year.

A hard place inside of her turned harder. Was it hatred she felt? Perhaps. Why would she feel anything else? The Moabites were Israel's plague, as sure as locusts had been.

A friendly faced neighbor from down the street passed by, and Naomi could not look away from the woman's swollen belly. Next month she was due to give birth.

Once their greetings had been said and the woman had continued on, Naomi set the water jug down and rested in the shade of a stone wall. Her hand touched her own belly. It was empty—empty of food and empty of life. Her own baby, a daughter too tiny to breathe, had died a few months before, and her sorrow for the infant's smallness and perfection was something that followed Naomi as sure as her own shadow.

"*Ama*! Are you coming?" Mahlon's bare feet rounded the cobblestone corner at the top of the walkway. His big brown eyes stared down. "Are you all right, *Ama*?"

"I'm fine, Son. You go ahead and keep an eye out for your brother. I'll be along."

Mahlon hesitated. "I don't want to leave you alone. I can help carry the water."

Naomi waved. "No. I'm enjoying the shade. I'll meet you back home in a few minutes, and we'll have our morning cakes."

Chilion called for his brother, and Mahlon disappeared.

The fact that both boys were alive was a miracle, one for which Naomi gave thanks every day. When the time had come for Anna's grandsons to be born, the famed midwife was already dead and there was no one qualified to take her place.

The memory flooded back now as Naomi leaned against the coolness of the stone wall. In a few moments the sun would breathe down and the shade would disappear, but for now Naomi did not move as she remembered the day her twin sons were born.

Elimelech had been more nervous than Naomi. He'd paced back and forth across their small courtyard, being more in the way than helpful.

Berta, Elimelech's only sister, was there, although she had made it very clear that she did not want to be. It was her cries, not Naomi's, that had finally brought a spattering of neighbor women to help.

"She's too thin," someone had whispered, but not so quietly that Naomi did not hear. "The baby will have no strength."

"How can she have strength when she has no food?"

The women scolded Elimelech.

"Let go of her hand! Can't you see she's in agony?"

"This isn't a place for a husband. Go for a walk. We'll send for you when it's over."

"Better yet, bring Naomi a cup of porridge to give her nourishment."

"Do you have honey?"

Elimelech bowed his head. "No."

"Fruit? The sweetness will aid her."

Again, all he could say was, "No."

Reluctantly, Elimelech let go of his wife's hand and limped across the courtyard to his sister.

"Berta, please, I beg you, spare us some food."

"How can you ask such a thing?" Berta burst out. "We have sufficient only for our needs. I have two daughters to feed."

"Your daughters are plump, Berta. Surely they can skip a meal."

"You ask me for food even as you insult my children!" Naomi flinched as Berta flew into a rage.

"I'm sorry, Sister." Elimelech's voice cracked.

"Yes, you *are* sorry, and I am too. But I must take care of my own before I take care of yours."

"I understand. But, Sister, you have more than sufficient for your needs."

"And I have a husband with the appetite of a working man."

Elimelech flinched. "I work."

"You work with Father and live off only the allotment of food from your Moabite overseers."

"You judge me now, Sister, and punish Naomi in her time of need? You might not approve of my work or of my choice of wife, but you cannot deny that Naomi has been nothing but kind to you. She has cared for your children and worked hard to keep this household running."

Berta's doughy face trembled. "Fine. I'll spare enough to make porridge, but only for Naomi. You, Brother, can work for your own meal."

"Thank you," Elimelech said.

Naomi would have spoken out if she had had the strength, but she did not. As soon as the watery soup was put to Naomi's lips, she attempted to gulp it but only choked.

She felt Elimelech pressing his lips to her hot, damp forehead before the women pushed him back.

The rest was a blur for Naomi: The searing pain. The unfamiliar screams that must have come from her own lips. The pungent scent of vinegar brought to wash the newborn baby.

Then she saw only blackness.

Naomi's eyes fluttered open when she smelled the sprig of sage being burned to clear the air of evil that might otherwise attach itself to the new child.

She begged to hold her newborn baby.

"You're confused, Naomi. Your baby is not yet delivered."

Strong hands held her down.

Neighbors had been kind enough to bring a bit of cloth and even fresh water from the well. No one had brought food because there was none to spare.

Two women brought bowls to catch the afterbirth.

Someone asked, "Aharon has a blade, has he not?"

"Yes," Naomi whimpered. Her father-in-law, Aharon, was the only blacksmith the Moabites allowed to practice in all of Bethlehem. Theirs was also the only family allowed to possess a blade forged from iron; everyone else made do with sharpened bone or stone or wood.

Berta affirmed, "Yes. Father has a blade."

"Fetch it now!" the woman hissed.

Berta hesitated.

"Go! We'll need a sharp blade to sever the cord."

Naomi's mind surged with a terrifying darkness. She was surrounded by Bethlehemites, among them Pharisees and Sadducees.

"Pray for my child!" she cried, but Kezia, wife of Salmon, high priest and Elimelech's uncle, put a damp cloth to Naomi's lips.

"You don't know what you're saying. You are delirious."

"Pray," Naomi said.

When no one prayed, she prayed for herself and for her stubborn baby. After a while Naomi felt stronger and more clearheaded.

"Shhh," Kezia said. "Your son will arrive soon enough."

"But I want a daughter," Naomi managed to say, repeating what her heart had secretly prayed for so long.

Kezia's hands went high into the air. "Why a daughter? That is outrageous. A daughter steals your heart—and after you have raised her, trained her, and loved her, she leaves you to offer all she has to a man and to *his* mother."

The other women noised their agreement.

"So it is," Naomi said between great pants of pain. "But in those first years together, I will find my reward."

"Girl children are weak and frail. You want a son if he stands any chance at all of surviving in a land without food."

Naomi retreated, easing back down onto the bed. The day passed slowly and torturously, like feet trudging through desert sand.

The next time Naomi opened her eyes she found herself looking into the face of Edna, one of Berta's young daughters.

"Is Auntie going to die?" the child asked.

"Perhaps," Berta said, pulling Edna back. "It certainly looks that way."

The next morning it was impossible for Naomi to open her eyes, though she managed to squeeze Elimelech's fingers in response to yes or no questions.

"Are you hungry?"

No squeeze.

"Are you thirsty?"

A faint squeeze.

Normally, a woman giving birth would have been taken to the red tent on the outskirts of town, but Naomi's water had broken without warning, and there had been no time.

"Something is very wrong," she heard Kezia say.

"What can I do?" Elimelech asked, desperation evident in his voice. "I'll do anything."

"You can get her honeycomb."

"Yes," she heard Aharon say. "Bring her honeycomb. When your mother was in childbirth, only a taste of honeycomb helped her relax so you could be born."

Naomi winced. Aharon and Berta had made no secret of their disapproval when Elimelech had chosen to marry Naomi. They both had felt he could marry someone more suited, someone better positioned in society. They had a specific "someone" in mind, but Elimelech had chosen Naomi.

Now that she knew Aharon was near her, she felt as though his eyes stared at her with disapproval. She tried to turn on her side, but Naomi was too weary to turn, and the pain was so great it rocked her mind back into nothing but shadows and muted voices.

Soon, the honeycomb came, and its warm sweetness wet her lips. She reached to touch her husband's hand and found his fingers swollen. Her heart warmed. Had Elimelech suffered bee stings to bring her a taste of sweetness?

How she loved him! How she wanted to bear healthy children for him.

That was when she recognized uncle Salmon's voice. "Moabite soldiers are watching. They are concerned about the size of the crowd that has gathered to help your wife in her time of need. I'm sorry, Elimelech, but these people must disperse."

"I will stay," Kezia said.

"I will *not*," Aharon said, "and neither will you, Berta. Take your own daughters to your husband, Uriel. Stay in—until this has ended."

"Father, I will stay with my wife. You should all leave," Elimelech agreed.

And that quickly, Naomi heard their footfalls fade away as family and neighbors placed their own safety above their worry for Naomi.

The room was silent, and Naomi had no way of knowing how long it was before Kezia told Elimelech, "Every woman of age knows how to deliver a baby, but this child is stuck. It no longer moves. And look at your wife, Elimelech. She's barely breathing. We need a physician."

Naomi knew that the physicians who had once served Bethlehem were long ago taken by force, uprooted and moved to serve the people of Moab. Even their families were either relocated or killed. It was just one more tactic the Moabites used to oppress the people of Judea by leaving them unable to heal their own. So Naomi knew that no physician would come to help her or her struggling baby.

The birth did not occur until the next morning after Aharon had returned for his morning meal.

"When Naomi dies," her father-in-law said, not trying to keep his voice down, "you will not bury her in our family plot. She must be buried with her parents in the tombs of the shepherds."

"What is wrong with you, Aharon?" Salmon scolded. "Is this your way of comforting your grieving son? You're as caring as a serpent. Look at Elimelech. He's a wreck; his wife is dying, and *this* is the comfort you bring him!"

"My son has brought this sorrow on himself. He should have married the woman he was meant to marry. Perhaps God will right that wrong now."

Naomi did not have a personal recollection of how the father and son had come to blows, but she heard about it afterward, and from plenty of witnesses—how the men had scuffled, voicing long-pent-up resentments, especially about Aharon's infidelity to Elimelech's mother. It ended only when Aharon stomped off toward the blacksmith shop.

It was no proper atmosphere in which to bring a baby, yet the commotion had stirred Naomi, and the child was born, his skin purple and his head far too large for his tiny, wrinkled body.

"He's dead," someone said, and Naomi's heart nearly stopped.

"Rub him!" Naomi cried, recalling her mother's reputation for being able to rub life back into a lifeless infant. "Rub his back, his front—rub his little body until he breathes!"

They obeyed. When the baby whimpered, someone placed him in his mother's arms and Naomi continued to rub him, to tug gently at every twig of a finger and tiny toe until the baby drew shallow but steady breaths.

"Call the boy Mahlon," someone suggested, "for the child has emerged sickly."

And then Kezia looked down in astonishment. "There is another baby! *Another* baby is coming!"

The second baby was even smaller than his brother, but this child was born pink, and his lungs cried with the sound a newborn baby *should* make. Naomi's mind could barely grasp the reality—two boy babies!

Kezia said, "Call him Chilion, for he will pine for his brother when the first boy dies."

"What about my wife?" Naomi heard Elimelech ask in desperation.

That was when Naomi realized the first baby had been taken from her arms and when she realized that the warmth she felt surrounding her was from a pool of her own blood.

"Pray!" she cried, but no one heard her, so Naomi had to pray for herself.

Only Elimelech remained with Naomi. The babies were given to wet nurses. Berta and her girls remained in Jericho. An exhausted Kezia went home, and Aharon had gone again, sulking, back to his blacksmith shop.

"Pray," Naomi pleaded again and again.

The second night a shadow had appeared at their gate.

The law stipulated that one must wait until an invitation was extended to enter another person's courtyard, but this man walked into their courtyard uninvited. His form became easy to recognize when he stepped into a waning shaft of moonlight.

"Uncle Heber."

"I feel your anguish, Nephew," she heard Heber say. Then, in a whisper, he added, "Take this. It will bring you strength and comfort."

"Baal?" Elimelech said.

"No!" Naomi tried to cry. "No!" She guessed that Heber had pressed into the new father's hand one of the small, smooth idols many people secretly carried of a lean figure with features that were muted except for its raised arm and pointed helmet.

"He is a god you do not have to imagine, a god of strength and fertility you can feel. Baal, the son of El, will bring you power as you serve him. Of this I know."

Naomi reached her hand out to stop her husband but gripped only darkness.

Elimelech hesitated.

Heber persisted. "He is only one of many gods secretly worshipped in the land of promise. You know that better than most, nephew. Accept Baal as your secret god and watch as your wife recovers and as your sons grow into men."

It was not the first time Uncle Heber had given his nephew this idol, but it was the first time Naomi had heard Elimelech consider accepting it. Would he simply tuck it away, thinking his wife was unaware?

"I will pray to Baal," Elimelech whispered, "if he will keep my family alive."

Heber's smile was probably fleeting, but his enjoyment of this decision was clear.

2

TWO YEARS PASSED WITH MOAB growing stronger while the people of Israel continued to suffer and starve.

On a day when the country was strong and at peace, the palace felt stifling and the air felt sticky. Even the royal cats were curled up in patches of shade.

"I'm in pain!" King Eglon bellowed. His cheek was swollen and his breath more foul than usual. "Keep those children quiet or I'll send them all to the work fields!"

His personal servant darted a look toward the two maidservants standing at the door. They ran quickly to silence the king's youngest sons and daughters, the ones who usually had free rein in the palace.

A clap of hands and a stern look calmed most of them down immediately. But one little girl, the child called Ruth, giggled even louder and ran faster. Her bare feet slapped the stone floor of the great corridor, causing everyone, including Ruth's older sister, Orpah, to look up.

"I'll get her," she volunteered, and Orpah ran to keep up with Ruth's plump little legs.

But Ruth ran faster.

"No! Not in there, Sister!" Orpah wailed. "Do not disturb Father."

It was too late. Ruth had already skidded through the entryway into the king's private chambers.

"What are *you* doing in here?" The king's black beady eyes narrowed to slits.

Ruth stopped and gave a wide-eyed stare. King Eglon *was* her father, but she was hardly allowed to see the man. He was always locked away behind massive doors or gone from the grounds, pulled away in his massive carriage by a team of giant horses.

Ruth grinned fearlessly as she approached the king.

King Eglon seemed as shocked as his servants.

"Lap," Ruth said and made her best attempt to climb onto her father's knee. But the man was lapless; his bulging stomach covered any hope of a seat.

"You're fat," Ruth said, "really fat."

The air seemed to disappear out of the room. Orpah, who had followed Ruth into the room, could see that the servants feared that the king would have the insolent little girl punished—or worse. Orpah, not quite three years older, was also terrified that the king would send her sister away. Born of a different mother, she still could not bear the thought of being separated from Ruth, and her love for her sister drove her forward, though she avoided looking into the king's gaze.

"Please, Father, don't hurt Ruth!"

Orpah snatched her little sister's hand and pulled her back from the wide shadow of the king.

"Go!" The king waved his hand. "And keep quiet. If I hear you again you will be sorry."

"Yes, Father," Orpah murmured, pulling at Ruth, who dragged her reluctant feet across the stone floor.

"I don't want to go!" Ruth cried.

One of the maidservants grabbed her from Orpah, slapped a hand over Ruth's mouth, and fled down the corridor to safety. Orpah followed, lingering for a moment just outside the king's chamber to hear his decision.

"What is that child's name?" she heard the king ask about his own daughter.

"The small one is Ruth," a servant replied.

The king winced, probably from the pain of his sore tooth. Then he attempted what seemed to be a smile.

"She has my tenacity," he said. "Now bring me a beer to help ease my pain."

Orpah left, smiling now too.

* * *

In the high white hills of Bethlehem the household of Elimelech held a secret. Naomi knew that it was a secret many other Israelite households also hid, often from their own families.

Though she never mentioned it, Naomi knew that her husband secretly prayed to Baal. Ever since that night when she lay so close to death, when their newborn sons were still able to fit in the palm of Elimelech's hands, Baal and his power to save had been invoked.

Their sons were saved and were now stronger than most children in Bethlehem. Did that have anything to do with Elimelech's furtive devotion to a god so small it too could fit in the palm of a hand?

"I worship no god but the God of Israel," Naomi told herself, often saying it aloud so it would sound more convincing.

Just past the setting of the sun, when the sky was swirled in purples and golds, Naomi ducked her head and emerged from the small room attached to her father-in-law's sprawling property with a three-room house, a fenced courtyard, and a back orchard. She climbed up to the rooftop, where Mahlon and Chilion were sleeping.

Her heart turned over in her chest. Her sons were safe, unlike many of the children of Israel. Most of them were weak and sick. Some had been kidnapped to Moab or faraway lands where their young lives were spent in slavery or abuse.

Naomi looked up at the sky, just starting to be sprinkled with stars. "Thank you, God."

The boys slept back-to-back tonight, but Naomi remembered how, when they were first born, the brothers would sleep only if they were so close they could wrap their arms and legs around each other like they had in the womb. More than once they had fallen asleep sucking each other's thumbs.

Elimelech and Aharon were still at the blacksmith shop, so Naomi wrapped her shawl around her and sat down on the roof, looking out over the land. The Lord told Moses this land was "promised" to him. It didn't feel like He kept this promise. The land felt cursed. Neighbors and friends starved or had to abandon the barren fields of Bethlehem for greener pastures elsewhere.

Naomi looked beyond the stone walls, walls built and rebuilt so many times to protect the people of Bethlehem. The scene did not seem right and certainly did not seem fair. While the land of promise was dry and barren, its fruit withered and its animals riddled with disease, across the valleys and rivers and gorges rose a land lush and strong.

A man on swift foot could make the journey from the one land to the other in four days; that was all that separated Moab from Bethlehem, yet one thrived while the other clung to life with a desperate will and hope born from having ancestors who once survived in the desert by eating nothing but manna for forty years.

Was it any wonder that people were fleeing for something better?

The night breeze turned warm, and Naomi lay back, rolling her shawl into a pillow. She stared in wonder at the stars spread out above her. Naomi had a foreboding feeling. It had followed her like a shadow, stalking her for days.

Was it because she held a secret of her own, one she was keeping from her husband and sons? She had known for more than a month now that she was with child again. But twice before, this good news had ended in bad news. This time she was determined to hold the secret safe, to let it grow and to reveal it only when she knew hunger and thirst could not steal it from her.

"Let it be a daughter," she prayed aloud to the God of the heavens above, to the God of the commandments, to the only God she would ever worship.

She thought she heard Elimelech's footfalls below, so she sat up. But it was only a lone jackal hunting in the rising moonlight.

Naomi lay back again and closed her eyes, picturing Elimelech's soft brown eyes. They still held the same kindness she'd seen in them when he was a boy. Memories of a younger Elimelech darted through her mind and she pictured him burdened with armloads of cabbages, carrots, and cucumbers for his sick mother's stew. Naomi remembered Elimelech running through the marketplace, dodging in and out of legs, trying to get away from his older sister's grip. Since then the years and the hardships had made him a man, but there was also a tenderness in him that she knew was rare, and it was something she treasured.

"Ishi."

She opened her eyes and spun around at hearing the name.

"I didn't hear you come home." Naomi scrambled to her feet. "I have soaked some figs in honey and the fire is still going. I'll make you a warm cake."

"No. I'm not hungry. I'm too tired to eat. Let me rest here beside you," he said. And he curled down and closed his eyes.

"Where is your father?" Naomi asked.

"He left the shop long before I did. I suppose he's taken rest in the city again."

Naomi bit her tongue to keep from saying anything negative about her father-in-law or the places he chose to take comfort. It was just as well that he wasn't around. Aharon's disapproval of Naomi had only grown with time. It didn't matter that she cooked and cleaned for him, washed his clothes, and raised his grandsons—he still wished that Elimelech had chosen the chief judge's daughter, Jael, as his wife.

Naomi wished that the widower would take a wife. It wasn't normal that a man should remain widowed. Yet, Aharon gave little heed to tradition or even to law. He did things his own way.

Elimelech's breathing soon fell into a steady rhythm and Naomi snuggled down in his arms, grateful he was more like his dead mother than like Aharon. She'd never known her mother-in-law but had heard of the woman's kindness and how Aharon's brutality wore her down.

A burst of morning sun rose over the white crest of Bethlehem, bathing the entire village in a honey hue. The coo of mourning doves, perched on the branches above them, drowned out a growl from Elimelech's empty belly.

"I'll hurry down and make you food," Naomi said.

Elimelech grinned, looking over at Mahlon and Chilion, still asleep. "The boys will wake hungry too."

"They always do."

Naomi had backed partway down the stairs when she looked back at her husband. "Why are you so happy this morning?"

"I have all the things a man could want: you are my wife, they are my sons, and the work I do brings me great satisfaction."

"It should. The Lord blessed you with a talent that no one else has. You're the only swordsmith in Judea."

"Yes, but my best work goes to that overfed imbecile, King Eglon!"

"Shhh. You mustn't talk so loud, Elimelech. There are ears all around."

"Yes, yes. I am very aware of the spies that infest our land. They wait to have something to report back to Moab so that another Israelite can be punished for trying to survive in this land, which has become unfit for anything but suffering."

"I'll get those honeyed figs for you. You'll feel better after you eat."

She was saddened at how quickly her husband's happiness had faded. But that was how things were. The enemy's hand quickly hewed down any sprout of joy.

"Naomi?"

"Yes."

Elimelech followed her down the ladder and into the orchard. The rising sun cast long, crooked shadows over the hard, gray earth. "We cannot continue to live like this," he said, touching a barren branch. "This land yields one failed harvest after another. The scarce food we do manage to grow is either snatched for Moabites or destroyed before our own people can harvest it. Did you smell the smoke in the air yesterday?"

She nodded as her uneasy feelings returned with a vengeance.

"It was from the burning fields. The Moabites would rather set fire to what's left of our crops than see us glean from our own labors."

Naomi looked at the brittle leaves in their own small orchard and wondered how quickly it would burn should a Moabite set it aflame.

"You were so happy earlier."

"I cannot be happy for more than a fleeting moment, Naomi, not when reality is so bleak. Every animal, every foul, every fish and fruit and vegetable is levied with a tax that leaves our land weak and starving. This is supposed to be the Lord's land, yet how long has it been since we won a single battle?"

"I know that there are rumors of resistance, Elimelech. I hear of them in the whispers at the well."

"Women's talk. But yes, there are those of us joining with Chief Judge Ehud."

"Please, Husband, keep your voice low."

"Talk is nothing new. But words only tighten the tether the Moabites have around our necks."

Naomi moved into her husband's arns, let her head rest against his chest, and felt his heart beat faster than usual. "None of this is new.

We've been living this way most of our lives. What is really troubling you, Elimelech?"

His voice cracked. His eyes looked heavenward and then down at the hard, cracked ground. "When will the Lord honor us as His people?"

"Perhaps," she said in a low, sad voice, "when we honor Him."

His spine stiffened. "We have honored Him. I have honored Him. But what do I get in return? My wife is too hungry, too frail to bear more children. Our sons are so thin I can count their ribs."

Naomi fought back bitter tears. "I was going to wait to tell you, but your words are so hard."

"They are also true." He moved a strand of hair off her forehead. "You were going to wait to tell me what?"

"I am with child."

She did not dare look into his eyes for fear she would see something there besides hope. Elimelech said nothing—not a single word.

She waited and finally begged for a response. "Say something, please, Elimelech. I fear what you're thinking."

She felt his gaze as if it bore into her soul. "I am thinking that we cannot bear another loss. Twice since the twins were born your body has given us promises that it's not capable of keeping."

The weight of his words was like a pile of stones on her back. She stared at him in shock.

He pulled her closer. "I'm so sorry. I do not blame you. I blame this land. I blame God for turning His back on us."

"No, Elimelech." If there was ever a time when she wanted to tell him that she knew about him worshipping Baal, it was at this moment. But she could not because she had known about it for years and had entertained the idea that perhaps there was power for good in it. All she could do was melt into his arms and let his strength hold her up.

Someone coughed, and they both spun in unison. It was Salmon, Elimelech's uncle, standing at the gate.

"Peace, my children." If Salmon was aware how upset Elimelech and Naomi were, he made no indication. The man was a head taller than Elimelech and looked drab this day. His usually colorful priestly garments had been replaced by the drab grays and browns of the earth.

"Blessed be the man who enters through this gate, Uncle. What can I do to aid you this morning? I can wash your feet or offer you wine."

The man cleared his throat and spat on the ground. "You can fetch me water to quench my thirst."

Naomi went quickly to fill a cup for Salmon.

The boys climbed down from the roof and were greeted with an abrupt embrace from first their father and then Salmon.

"Why, are you only now rising? There are chores to be done."

"We have but a few animals for my sons to herd, Uncle. It's best to let them sleep as long as they can."

Salmon waved a dismissive hand. "Where is Aharon? I went to the shop to talk to my brother, but he was not there."

"My father has made it a habit to spend time in the city."

Salmon's cheeks reddened. "My brother is a shame to this family."

As Naomi poured the water she saw neighbor women hurrying by, empty jugs atop their heads. They pretended not to hear Salmon's loud voice, but they slowed their feet as they passed the gate. She blushed, wishing she did not share the same house and land as Aharon. She did not wish to be associated with his ways, though she did appreciate the living he provided for them by allowing Elimelech to take part in the blacksmith shop.

"Is Berta here?" she heard Salmon ask.

"No. She and the girls are in Jericho," Elimelech explained, "where Uriel is working."

"Why are you not at the shop this morning? There is a great deal of work to do, I'm sure."

"I worked into the night, Uncle. What is troubling you and bringing on all of these questions?"

Naomi brought the water, and Salmon gulped it thirstily.

"We have sweet figs, Uncle, if you are also hungry," Elimelech volunteered.

"Yes. Sweet figs will do fine."

Reluctantly, Naomi offered the figs to Salmon—the ones she'd made and saved for her husband, the same figs Elimelech had said to save for their hungry boys. She had to fight back her resentment, knowing that Salmon owned land, so he had money and food, more money and more food than anyone else in the family. Yet he ate their very best offerings almost absentmindedly, sitting in the shade of the courtyard olive tree, devouring the figs, then licking honey from his fingers.

Chilion and Mahlon stood by waiting for their mother to offer them food too.

"Milk the goat," she told them.

"She's almost dry," Chilion complained, making his narrow face seem even more pinched. "I hate milking her when she's dry."

"Take what she offers, and I will bake you a cake with the meal we have left."

"I'll look for eggs," Mahlon said. "Yesterday we found two."

Naomi smiled at Mahlon, grateful for his ever-positive approach to life.

"Just be careful, children. Watch out for snakes."

The boys went off while Naomi busied herself preparing the last of the meal for the cakes she would make. She purposefully moved very slowly, hoping Elimelech would not invite his uncle to stay and eat, though she knew it was breaking the hospitality commandment. Salmon had food back at his house. Besides, he was aware of how scarce food was for Elimelech's household.

Salmon must have felt sure Naomi was not paying attention to their conversation when he lowered his voice and turned his tone even more serious. "There is a matter we must discuss, Nephew."

"If it is about Father, I have nothing to say."

"No. What my brother does is bad enough, but what I hear you are doing is worse."

Naomi's heartbeat quickened.

"Uncle, I mean no disrespect. I honor you as a priest and as my elder. But if you are going to chastise me for the work I do, save your breath."

Salmon spat again. "It's true, then? You have accepted another commission from King Eglon?"

"It is true."

"To design a sword that kills more efficiently?"

"I am a swordsmith. If I reject the commission, I will be punished, perhaps put to death."

"Better to die a martyr for the Lord than to be the one who puts a fiercer weapon in the hands of our enemies. It's treason, I tell you."

"It's how I provide for my family. What would you have me do, Uncle? Let my wife become a widow and my sons go fatherless?"

Occasionally, Naomi stole a glance out at the men through the open kitchen door.

"I would have you remember who you are—a Hebrew!"

"I know who I am," Elimelech said, standing before his uncle. "I am a Hebrew vulnerable to the king's royal orders. They are not something I sought. They came to me when Eglon took control of Father's blacksmith shop and saw my talent as a weapon maker."

"It would have been better for our people if you had continued designing scythes and sickles. At least all you did then was give our people tools to provide food for our enemies. I am telling you, Elimelech, as your uncle and your priest, this alliance with Moab has become something very dangerous—to all of us."

"Why are you so upset now? Nothing has changed in years. It's the same as it's always been."

"Is it? When was the last time you passed along any information to Ehud?"

Naomi was surprised to hear her husband sputter. Hadn't he just told her that was what he had been doing—using his inside position with the Moabites to aid his own people?

She wanted to tell Salmon so, to rush out into the courtyard and stand up for Elimelech. But if it was true, wouldn't Salmon already know that?

"What would you have me do, Uncle, become a beggar—or worse, a slave?" he asked.

The bench Salmon leaned his back against was a small version of the bench Naomi's mother had carved, which stood by the town well. But this one was a poor imitation, carved with an iron blade Naomi wasn't supposed to have. She was not the artist Anna was.

"I would have you stay loyal to your people and to your God. Speaking of which, I've received word that you spend no small amount of time in the high hills with my younger brother—your uncle Heber."

"It is true."

"It is also true that he keeps a shrine to Baal. Like your father, your uncle Heber brings shame to our family."

"Uncle, it seems you've come to chastise me. If you have nothing else to add, I must get to the shop. There's work to do."

"Work!" Salmon looked up and saw Naomi listening in on their conversation from just inside the house. "Naomi, what would your father, Lowell, think of the way idol worship has wedged its way into your life and into the lives of your family?"

Naomi nearly dropped the cake she was patting. Her mouth opened in defense, but Elimelech shot her a look that made her remain silent.

Salmon licked the last of the honey from the corner of his mouth. "Your father was a kind and gentle man, Naomi. I knew him well. Lowell provided wool and, once in a while, meat for this family. He and Anna honored the God of Israel, even in their poverty. They would not be pleased with all that you tolerate."

Naomi knew that she did not possess her mother's faith. Anna never would have tolerated idol worship, even if done in secret.

Elimelech's face went red. His fingers curled to fists.

But at that very second, a boy came through their gate, his dark curls bobbing and his smile as bright as the morning sun.

"Boaz!"

Boaz was Salmon's youngest son, but he did not rush to his father's embrace. Instead, he raced right for Elimelech, who lifted him high into the air, even though Boaz was nearly twelve, twice the age and size of Elimelech's own twin sons.

"Why are you here?" Salmon demanded.

"Mother says that your morning meal is ready," Boaz said. Then he turned his attention back to Elimelech. "What have you made for me, Cousin? You promised to make something special."

Elimelech patted the boy's curls and went to a shelf that stood against the house. He lifted a panel trap and produced a small wooden sword.

"Just for you."

The boy's face beamed in delight. "It's better than most of the others you've made for the village boys."

"I made this one just for you, Boaz."

Boaz swung his blade through the air quickly and decisively.

"I will kill the Moabites and take back our land of promise."

Salmon shook his head sadly. "This is what we are permitted: sharpened wooden sticks? This is all we have to defend ourselves against enemies that come at us with blades of iron and coats of mail and helmets of brass? We have wood that breaks and burns. When will we learn that the Lord God will not honor us until we honor Him? Until then Moab's fist will always be tightly wrapped around our throats."

Naomi watched Elimelech shift his feet uncomfortably, but his mood was hard.

"My wife tells me that the Lord will honor us only when we honor Him and keep His commands, but there are 613 laws according to the Pharisees. It is impossible to keep them all." This was the first time Naomi had seen him stand up to Salmon with such strength.

"Impossible? God's commands are not impossible."

"Tell me of the first garden. Adam was first given the law to stay away from the tree of knowledge. But he was also given the command to multiply and replenish. How could he keep both?"

"Ahh! You make an old man's head hurt."

"I am moving to Jerusalem," Boaz announced. "Next month, I will shadow the scribes there, and one day I will become a great scribe."

Elimelech smiled. "I have no doubt that you will make a great scribe, Boaz. You are the most intelligent member of our family."

Boaz beamed.

"Perhaps you will teach your aunt Naomi to read and write. She has always wanted to do that."

"Nonsense!" Salmon said. "It is a waste to teach a woman such things."

Naomi blushed, more from anger than embarrassment.

"One day," Boaz interrupted, "I will use the money I earn as a scribe to return to Bethlehem. I will buy land and become the richest man in town."

"And what will you do with all of your money?" Elimelech asked Boaz.

"I will raise crops that the Moabites cannot destroy. I will feed our people until they are as fat as King Eglon."

Everyone chuckled—even Naomi.

Then Elimelech bowed at the feet of his uncle. "I want to make this very clear. I am an Israelite. I am a Bethlehemite. My heart is loyal to the God of Israel. I only serve the Moabites because I love my family and must provide the best I can for them. Please do not accuse me of less, Uncle."

Naomi watched Salmon's upper lip twitch. He probably had more to say, but he said nothing.

3

Naomi heard the sound of running feet and then the piercing screams of a woman calling, "Help! Someone please help me!"

Naomi raced to the front of the yard where Elimelech, Salmon, and a small crowd of onlookers had already frantically gathered. In the midst of the chaos, a woman knelt in the dirt on her bloody knees. Naomi recognized her. It was Gila.

She wore the veiled shroud of a widow, a shred of black-dyed linen that was in tatters.

"Help, please! I beg you, help!"

Naomi knelt beside her. "What's the matter?"

"Tell us!" Salmon urged. "You're causing a scene."

The look of desperation in her bloodshot eyes was beyond anything Naomi had seen. Gila once had a pretty face; now it was twisted in horror. "My daughter was taken by Moabites—my little daughter, Abella!"

Salmon's fingers made fists that he pounded through the air. "When? Where?" Then, under his breath, he murmured, "Not again."

Elimelech helped the suffering mother stand, scooped up her fallen veil, and gently handed it back to her. He glanced at Naomi, exchanging a conversation without words, and led Gila to the gate.

"You know the law!" shouted Salmon. "If you invite her through your gate you are obligated to care for her."

"I know the law, Uncle."

"And you know that you have insufficient means to care for your own, let alone for strangers."

Gila sobbed.

"You have no family of your own to aid you?"

Her chin dropped as tears dripped from it. "Before my daughter was born, my husband was captured and taken by Philistines."

"What about your parents?"

"Dead. Their home was burned when the Moabites set fire to the high hills."

"That was years ago."

"I beg you, please, sir, save my daughter. Someone must help me find her."

"And you have no one else?"

"No one."

"She has us," Naomi said as she and Elimelech helped lead Gila through their gate and into the family courtyard.

Salmon took hold of Boaz's collar with one hand and shook his fist at Elimelech with the other. "When your father, my brother, finds out about this, he will be livid. You cannot know what you have just done."

"I have obeyed a commandment, Uncle. Now go and round up help. We must form a search party to help find this woman's daughter."

"If she has been taken by Moabites, we can do nothing to save the child."

Gila cried harder at hearing these words.

Salmon looked at her with contempt rather than compassion. "For all we know, your story is a lie. For all we know, you could have sold your child like so many other poor mothers do."

"No! I would never sell my daughter!"

"Why are you attacking this mother?" Elimelech asked Salmon. "Uncle, be of use and go gather a band of men."

But a band had already gathered. Many neighbors and others had come to see what all the commotion was about.

Naomi held a dipper of water to the woman's dry, cracked lips. It was hard for Gila to swallow. She laced her fingers behind her head, brought her elbows in front of her face, and began rocking hard. "I chased after them—down the highway, through the turns, and all the way to the river—but they were gone. My little Abella vanished."

"We have no time to waste," Elimelech announced, spinning in a circle, searching for faces he knew would support him. "We must form a party and leave now if there is any hope of rescuing the child."

His cousins were there, men he'd grown up with. They all stepped backward instead of forward. These were men of faith, priestly men, elders and servants of God, but none of them was willing to risk his life to save a girl.

"She's probably already dead," Salmon said.

"No!" Gila wailed.

"They won't kill her right away," Elimelech said, trying not to think of what they might do before killing her. "If they truly are Moabites, pray to our God that they are not taking her to the grove."

"It *is* festival time," Salmon said in a flat, cold tone.

"I beg you for your help," Gila sobbed. She was on her feet now, standing beside Elimelech.

"Beg all you want," Salmon said. "As high priest, I assure you that we will not risk another uprising because you failed to take care of your child."

Gila's face went ashen. Naomi put her arm around Gila. Gila was not large by any measure, yet her weight leaned heavily against Naomi. The cruelty of Salmon's words cut Naomi's own heart. How could a man of God be so cruel to a mother in distress?

"Uncle!" Elimelech cried. "The mother is anguished."

"As she should be."

"But to allow you to be unkind to my guest is unlawful."

"No," Gila sobbed, "your uncle is right. I *am* responsible. I was gleaning after the reapers. There was nothing left, really, but I was on my knees searching for scraps while Abella slept beneath a tree. I had turned away for only a moment when I heard her scream. Three men had hold of her and she was kicking like a wild cat."

"How do you know they were Moabites?" Salmon asked.

"Their girdles were dyed orange."

The air went still.

"The color of Chemosh," Salmon said with bitterness.

At the mention of the name a ripple of fear went through the crowd. Naomi felt it and understood why. Chemosh was the god that not only demanded a child's virtue but also incinerated the purest and most innocent in his big, hollow belly filled with fire. Every year a festival was held where Chemosh demanded such horrible tributes and that time was now.

Naomi spoke with urgency to the sobbing mother. "Maybe they've taken her to sell as a slave girl and not as a sacrifice to Chemosh." Naomi wanted her words to bring comfort, for the idea of Abella becoming a slave seemed somehow easier to bear than the thought of her being sacrificed to an iron god. Naomi considered the unborn child in her belly and felt a deeper compassion for this mother's horrific plight.

Salmon ranted on—not to Gila, but to the swelling crowd. "Those who worship the God of Israel, pray mightily for the child. Those who worship Chemosh or Baal or the goddess Ashtoreth, beg that the sacrifice be made quickly, so that she does not suffer more than is necessary."

At these words, Gila collapsed, her knees buckling and her head falling back, her eyes closed.

Elimelech caught Gila and laid her on the bench beneath the shade of the ancient olive tree.

"What are we to do?" Naomi whispered to her husband.

"She's our guest now; we will care for her," Elimelech said. He folded his own outer cloak to make a pillow for the woman. "I wish we had food for her."

"I haven't even fed our sons yet, and your stomach has growled all morning."

"I'm fine. But I must do something, Naomi. I can't let another child just vanish from Bethlehem."

"You know many of the Moabite soldiers, Elimelech. Can't you talk to some of them?"

"I can try."

"No!" Salmon said, leaning against the waist-high stone wall. "I'm not a heartless man, but this woman has invited her own hardship. We have enough problems and cannot afford to take on hers."

"We must move to recover the child," Elimelech said. "We can't stand around and do nothing."

"Don't think such a thought, Nephew! It's neither brave nor noble. As the presiding elder, I forbid anyone from attempting a rescue. Do you understand? I forbid it!"

Elimelech cast his eyes over the swelling crowd. Among the people were the leaders in Bethlehem. Still, no volunteers stepped forward. Naomi was terrified by the determination on her husband's face. If he had to go alone, she knew he would.

"Your obligation is to Aharon," Salmon said. "He needs your help with the royal commission. You cannot neglect him for this."

Elimelech protested. "But this woman, no matter how lowly her station, is a mother in Israel."

Salmon jerked at the bottom of his own beard, saying nothing.

"Uncle, a moment ago you were angry with me for accepting the royal commission. Now you oblige me to honor it. You clearly have something more to add. Go ahead and say it."

Salmon pulled Boaz to him. The man's nostrils flared. His mouth opened, then closed. Finally, he asked, "What of your own sons, Elimelech? What of your wife? If you go after the Moabites, they will surely go after your family."

Naomi's hand covered her mouth. She had not thought that far ahead.

"If I have to go alone, God will go with me, and His hand will protect my family."

Salmon scoffed. "You speak of God as if you know Him. It's no secret to this people—I'm certain not even to your wife—that you worship more than one god. So tell us, Nephew, which god will protect Naomi, Mahlon, and Chilion?"

Naomi felt a cold fear squeezing at her heart. Salmon was doing the unthinkable. He was shaming Elimelech in front of his own people.

Elimelech held his breath and spoke not a word.

Salmon laid a heavy hand on his nephew's shoulder. "You inherited your mother's caring heart and your father's stubborn will. Do not entertain the thought I know you're thinking, Elimelech. If you go after the child, you will lose your life, and you may well incite the Moabites to retaliate against the rest of us."

The people roared their agreement.

Evenly, Elimelech asked, "What will the Moabites do to us that they have not already done, Uncle? Raise taxes? Our levy is already more than we can bear; they steal our food, rob our stores, and abuse our women. Now they even kidnap our children, and we stand by and do what— pray?"

The crowd began to argue among themselves.

Taking his role as high priest seriously, Salmon stood at the gate and spoke as much to the people as to Elimelech. "They can bring war down upon us. They can use the swords *you've* designed, Elimelech, the blades your own father has forged for our enemies. Your actions could be the start of another war. Is that what you want for our suffering people?"

The crowd grew noisy. Several men shouted warnings.

Naomi laid a damp cloth over Gila's forehead. She moved Elimelech's cloak and sat down, resting the woman's head on her thigh, brushing the hair away from her bruised face, wiping blood and dirt away and pouring drops of water through her parched, parted lips.

Salmon frowned at the sight of his younger brother, a black-bearded man at the back of the crowd, who smirked at him, having come down from the high hills, where he kept a herd of goats. Heber was wiry and swift and had the habit of sniffing the air like a rodent.

"What is it you wish to say, Heber?" Salmon asked.

Heber smirked again as he cast his eyes around the crowd. "The only real difference between Bethlehem and Moab is that, in Moab, false gods show their faces in the light of day and aren't hidden in homes, carried in purses, or prayed to in secret."

"You are the only man who worships Baal in this land, where the God of Israel reigns."

Heber walked up to Salmon and shook a long finger in Salmon's face. "Not true, and you know it, Brother. But I worship Baal so that his power might oversee all of Bethlehem and keep my people and my family safe from harm. Baal has done a better job, I daresay, than your invisible Lord."

The crowd sniggered.

Heber shouted, "Tell me, priestly brother, how many of these people here now hide idols in their homes or carry them on strings around their necks so that the idols are next to their hearts?" Heber grabbed the front of Salmon's tunic and yanked.

A long broken string dangled from Heber's hand. On the end of the string was a small statue of Baal. But instead of turning their outrage on the humiliated priest, Salmon, the crowd closed in on Heber.

"We are a God-fearing people, innocent of your accusations!" one man shouted.

"Then you won't object to having your home inspected for idols?"

The man pounded his fist in the air. "You come near my home, Heber, and I will beat you to death."

Heber only laughed and cried out, "Hypocrites!"

Salmon made a huffing noise and cuffed his brother so hard that he knocked Heber easily to the ground. "Get out, and don't show your face here again. You're nothing but a disgrace to our family."

Heber slithered off, sniffing and laughing all the way up the street.

Salmon wrenched his focus back to Elimelech. His anger boomed. "Go! Craft swords for our enemies, but do not bring their wrath upon us for no reason."

"No reason?" Elimelech seethed with defiance. "A child's life is at stake!"

The crowd chanted doom. "She's already dead."

Salmon whirled away from the doubters and faced his nephew with fury. "Listen to me, Elimelech, as your priest and your elder, I tell you that God has raised you up for a divine purpose. He's given you a good and faithful wife. He allowed your sons to live. You may well be the most skilled swordsmith in all the land. Do not jeopardize such blessings. No part of Moab is safe for a young, foolish Hebrew."

Elimelech shifted nervously. He seemed to Naomi like a cornered animal, contemplating how to escape.

Salmon went on. "There is good exchange between our people and theirs."

"Exchange! Uncle, earlier you cursed the Moabites for oppressing us, stealing from us, and murdering our people. Now you talk as if they are our political allies."

"We are not at war."

"Only because we allow them to kidnap our children without trying to stop them."

"But you, Elimelech, are in business with the Moabites."

"So are most of the people here. The wheat farmers, the fruit farmers, the olive growers, and the tailors—we are all in business with the Moabites! They eat the bread we bake and wear the clothes we weave."

Naomi felt the sun begin to prick her crawling skin. Elimelech clenched his fists and would not stand still.

"How many of you have actually been to Moab?" Elimelech shouted.

A few murmurs sounded. Naomi knew Salmon could not say that he had ever set foot in Moab.

"I have been there," Elimelech explained, "with my father, Aharon. I have seen how their god, Chemosh, blesses their land with an abundance that Bethlehem does not enjoy. Moabites do not worship the God we worship, but they are our kinsmen. Have you all forgotten that?"

A vein in Salmon's forehead looked ready to burst.

More warnings, progressively stronger, rose from the gathering crowd, a crowd that now contained some men wearing orange loincloths and carrying swords designed by Elimelech.

"We mean no harm," Salmon assured the soldiers. Then he approached Elimelech and whispered, "You cannot go charging into the land of Moab, Nephew. No matter how valiant you believe the cause."

Naomi heard her husband say, "I did not say that I'm going."

"But you did not say that you aren't."

* * *

Ruth, Orpah, and a dozen of the king's other children splashed with abandon. The royal pools glistened in the sparkling sunshine, the water appearing almost purple because the tiles beneath it were stained in indigo. Six servants, three on each end, waved giant paddles to make the surface ripple like a slow-moving sea.

The laughter of the children chased the birds from the trees. The king lounged beneath the shade of a linen canopy, watching them and wincing.

"Why must they make so much noise?" he asked.

"They are children, sir."

"Silence!" the king bellowed. "You all be still!"

All of the children went quiet and motionless except one girl with her hair in a long, thick braid down her back. She climbed out of the pool and marched over to the king.

"We can't have fun if we have to be so quiet," she said.

Ruth was small and young but stout and audacious, and was the most precocious of the king's daughters—and no one doubted that she was also his most favored.

A servant reached out to draw her away from the king, but he wiggled his fat fingers, motioning Ruth forward.

"I hate noise," he told her.

"I know, Father. It gives you a headache. Maybe you should lie down while we play. You can watch us when we study. We are quiet when we study."

The king smiled, but he grimaced as he smiled.

"What's the matter?" Ruth asked, wondering if another toothache was pestering him.

"My tooth hurts."

"You always have a toothache. Open up and let me see inside your mouth," she insisted.

Ruth marched up to her father, stood on her tiptoes, and peered into his open mouth.

"It stinks in there," she said.

The king blew a puff of foul breath toward her face. She lunged backward and fell on her bottom, making the king laugh.

"You aren't the loveliest of my daughters. You do not have your mother's beautiful hair or your sister Orpah's curved eyelashes, but you do have my bravery. Perhaps one day you will be queen of Moab."

Ruth stood up, resting her hands on her hips. "I never want to be queen."

"Oh, and why not?"

"Because I want to work in the market with Mother, weaving baskets."

Sakira, Ruth's mother, had been given a basket shop in the best section of the market, just west of the great temple. Ruth was allowed to stay with her at night, but the king insisted that the child stay in the palace during the day so he could summon her anytime he wanted to be entertained by her antics.

"Ruth, you are destined for something greater than basket weaving."

"I like weaving, and I like splashing," she said, and away she ran back to the water, where Orpah quickly took hold of her and tried to make her be still. Ruth splashed water in her sister's face and giggled loudly.

Later, a small band of soldiers appeared at the edge of the grounds. One of the men moved hesitantly toward the king.

"I do not wish to be disturbed," he brayed. "My mouth pains me."

Another man, Lemuel, the king's chief priest and captain of his personal army, confronted the men and engaged them in a whispered conversation. King Eglon was nearly asleep by the time Lemuel knelt to whisper the news.

"Sir, a Bethlehemite has been captured crossing the river. He has been held prisoner for some time, but at the time that was to be his execution, he made the claim that he was on your errand."

The king tried to sit up but could not get around the massive flap of his stomach. Immediately, four strong men were there to help pull him forward.

"A Bethlehemite! On my errand? Who is this man, and what is his claim?"

"He is called Elimelech. He is the son of Aharon, the blacksmith from the white city. It is true that he and his father have been in your service now for most of a generation."

"I know Aharon." The king squinted his puffy eyelids in the sunlight. "His son is here—now?"

"No, not here. He is in the lowland prison. Your officers feared executing him if he is indeed on your errand. They tell me the Hebrew is quite persuasive."

The king touched his swollen cheek and flinched. "It's hot, and I am feverish. I could die from this bad tooth. Peasants die from such things every day. Why do I not have more wine? And where are my pain powders?"

"Right away, sir," said two men, scampering off to meet Eglon's demands.

Lemuel waited.

The king lay back and closed his eyes. Then he opened them again. He focused on Ruth, splashing in the water, her laughter thudding in his already aching head. Slowly, he rolled his eyes at Lemuel. "I have no recollection of business with a Bethlehemite. Tell my men to go ahead and kill him."

Lemuel looked overly pleased. "Right away, King Eglon."

4

ON THE SAME AFTERNOON, WHILE King Eglon nursed a toothache and watched his precocious daughter splash in the palace pools, a Hebrew wife wept, not knowing if her husband was alive or dead. Naomi was sheltered on the outskirts of Bethlehem in a red tent that stood out against the white rock and brown, dead grass. The tent was dark red like the dirt in Jericho—like blood gone old.

Inside the tent, Gila held Naomi's hand and wiped the sweat from Naomi's forehead.

"Sorry, it's boiling in here," Gila apologized. "I wish I could do more to ease your pain."

Naomi turned her face toward the side of the tent and stared at the patchwork seams fashioned from animal hides. Places where the tent had been crudely mended and the bottom flap let in both unwanted sand and much-wanted air.

"It reeks of death," Naomi whimpered, pulling her hand free of Gila's grasp.

In the agonizing weeks that had passed since the two women met, they had bonded. Now they were as close as any two sisters could be. Naomi had been there to comfort Gila while she ached for any word about her missing daughter. Gila had also comforted Naomi when no word came from Elimelech. For all the women knew, Abella was dead and so was Elimelech. "Gone forever," people had told them.

"God has heard my prayers," Naomi avowed. "He will bring Elimelech home to me and to our sons. He will return Abella to you."

While Naomi said those words, they were not her deepest feelings. In the caverns of her soul, she spoke other words—words of fear and doubt. And now Naomi lay writhing in agony, her body unable to bear the tiny baby who demanded too much from this half-starved mother.

"Tell me the truth," Naomi begged Gila. "Was it a girl? Did I lose the daughter I have always wanted?"

Gila choked back her own tears. "Yes, the baby was a daughter."

At that very moment the sound of a newborn infant breathing its first breath came from the far end of the tent as the baby gurgled then wailed. A chorus of women sang praises to God. Later, however, the baby died.

The tent felt crowded. Women moaned and cried while babies were born and died in this gathering place of women.

Naomi lifted the flap a bit wider and tried to breathe. It wasn't easy. The air was tinged with the scent of blood, both old and new. A part of her did not want to draw this air into her lungs. A part of her wanted to stop breathing altogether.

Gila touched her shoulder. "Your husband's aunt is here asking after you."

Before she could protest, Naomi heard Kezia say, "It will get better, Child. There will be other children."

"How can I have other children when my husband is gone? I may never see Elimelech again."

"You must not lose your faith now, Naomi. What would your mother think of you?"

"She would weep with me. Of that, I'm certain."

Kezia placed a round of bread into Gila's hand and nodded toward Naomi. "Make her eat. She's nothing but skin and bones."

Gila took the bread and thanked Kezia.

"You have no right to thank me. It is your fault that Naomi lies here suffering without the daughter she longed for and without the husband she so desperately needs."

* * *

An hour later, Ruth crawled out of the pool and ran toward her father again. No servant stopped her approach this time.

"Father?" she said, spraying him with tiny drops of water. "Father!"

"What, Child?"

"Does your mouth still hurt?"

"Of course it does. Worse than ever."

"Then you should do something kind for someone."

"What are you saying? You make no sense."

"Mother says that when we ask for something for ourselves, we should do a kindness for someone else."

"Your mother teaches you such things?" His voice sounded irritated.

"Yes. It works. I asked Chemosh to make your mouth better. Now I will do a kindness."

On her tiptoes again, Ruth leaned up and pressed her lips to King Eglon's sore, swollen cheek.

Then she was gone again, back into the pools to play.

The king actually smiled—slightly, but undeniably.

"Lemuel!"

"Yes, sir."

"Call those soldiers back. Call them back now and tell them not to kill the Bethlehemite, but bring the man to stand before me."

"Sir, the soldiers are already gone to carry out your order."

"Find them and stop them! And do it now!" he yelled at Lemuel. "I no longer wish this brazen Bethlehemite killed." Then, as Lemuel left, the king said to himself, "At least for now I will show him kindness, and, in return, Chemosh may grant me the same."

Elimelech lay curled up in the mud. He felt half-crazed with fear of starvation and of his imminent death. He wasn't afraid to die as much as he feared leaving Naomi and his sons. Aharon would not be kind to them.

His uncle Salmon had been right. Elimelech knew he had been prideful and selfish in his attempt to save a child that could not be saved. He had gone blindly after the girl, based only on her mother's description—this girl with the same black hair as every other girl in Bethlehem, the same dark eyes, the same slight frame.

"Abella," he whimpered aloud.

The Moabite soldier standing nearby kicked him hard, causing a sharp pain to pierce Elimelech's already bruised and broken ribs. He opened his eyes to see the tip of the soldier's javelin.

"Go ahead," he told the soldier, staring with a blank gaze. "It will be a quick death. I know because I designed that blade."

The solider laughed. "You lie," he said, kicking Elimelech again, this time in the head.

Then everything went black.

* * *

In the days following the birth, Gila left Naomi's side only to care for the twins and to cook whatever food Aharon supplied for the day. He was not like the monster that many made him out to be—at least not with Gila. With her, he had shown more compassion than his brother Salmon, the priest.

"Do you blame me for Elimelech's disappearance?" Gila asked Aharon one evening.

"My son was born a fool," Aharon said. "He should have known that your daughter could not be saved. Elimelech went because he wished to be the hero. But there are no heroes in a war that cannot be won."

"You could go in search of Elimelech. You know the king. Perhaps Eglon will aid you."

Aharon's laughter was both bitter and sad. "King Eglon uses me as little more than a slave. To him, I am a filthy Hebrew, a nuisance."

"Why do you work for him then?"

"I have no choice. He commandeered my shop when he shut down every other blacksmith in Bethlehem. I am not a farmer like my brother Salmon or a charlatan like my brother Heber. Blacksmithing is the only trade I know."

That night, Aharon had brought home enough wheat to grind for cakes. He had also delivered a handful of small, dried fish and a bit of honeycomb that the twins had stayed up late to devour.

"You still mourn for your dead wife, and now, because of me, you have lost your only son."

Aharon said nothing but sat before the fire, staring into the flames.

Gila stood and went to the rooftop to make sure Mahlon and Chilion were sleeping. It was too hot for a cover, but she rolled up a matt for their pillows.

When she came back down the ladder, she saw that Aharon was still staring into the fire.

"Elimelech could still be alive," Gila said. "Your son could still return."

Aharon's face looked ragged and deeply grooved in the flickering light of the flames. "What about with your missing daughter? Do you still believe that the two of them will return home safely?"

"I believe in a God of miracles."

"Believe all you want. I used to believe too. I believed that God would make my Rachael well. I believed He would honor my hard work with gold. I believed that He would give me a son who would honor me and a daughter who would tend to me in my old age." Aharon raised darkened eyes to look at Gila. "Now my wife is dead. I work for a king who pays me next to nothing. My daughter spends most of her time in Jericho, and my hardheaded son, as gifted as he is, is lost to me. He could have married Jael, the daughter of Ehud. Our families could be united. Do you know what that would have meant to me? But no, Elimelech defied me and married a lowly shepherd's daughter. When Lowell died, his inheritance was little more than a few sheep and hungry goats."

"You are so disappointed with life?"

"And you are not? You are a woman with no husband and no child. What is your life worth? At least I have a home, some property, and a skill. Gila, you have nothing."

Aharon slid over to make room for Gila on the small courtyard bench that Naomi had attempted to carve.

Gila did not hesitate at the invitation. She sat next to Aharon and the two of them remained silent, staring into the fire until it had burned to nothing more than ashes.

* * *

The next morning, the king was more miserable than ever. He was on his third jug of wine when a band of soldiers led by Lemuel entered the judging chambers, a great echoing hall made of white stone transported from the hills of Bethlehem.

The soldiers came with bare feet, but Lemuel wore sandals equipped with an arch of brass beneath his toes. Every step he took echoed off the walls of the chambers.

"Your sandals give me a headache," the king complained.

"Forgive me." Lemuel stopped. The soldiers stopped. Between two of the soldiers was Elimelech, half dead and barely conscious.

"We have brought the Hebrew spy before you to be judged," Lemuel said.

"Spy? You said he claimed to be on my errand."

Two soldiers, one on each side, propped up Elimelech.

"Yes, that was the Hebrew's claim."

"How do you know he is a Hebrew?"

"He had this in his pocket." Lemuel produced a small wooden carving of Baal.

"So, he may not be a Hebrew," the king said. "He could be from any of the outlying tribal lands."

"He made it no secret that he came from Bethlehem," the soldier next to Lemuel said.

"That's right," Lemuel confirmed. "He is the son of the blacksmith."

"Look at me, prisoner!" King Eglon ordered, but Elimelech did not have the strength to raise his head. "You've tortured him for days?" the king asked.

"I understand it's been weeks, sir. He would have been executed, but the man kept vowing he was on your errand. He has been very stubborn."

"And did he have a royal bulla with my insignia?"

"Not that we could find," Lemuel said.

Elimelech could picture Aharon's bulla, stored safely in the blacksmith shop in a hidden box. The royal bulla was an orange cylinder no longer than the span of his palm, crafted of hardened glazed clay. But when it had been fresh and wet, the clay was rolled over the insignia of Moab. Whoever bore the bulla carried the authority, heralding him as one on Eglon's errand. Elimelech asked himself, *Why didn't I think to bring Aharon's bulla? It would have allowed me passage across the river and into Moab.*

"Bring him closer so I can inspect him!" the king said.

The guards dragged Elimelech forward.

"He's as thin as a starved dog. How am I to recognize such wreckage?"

The guards had no answer.

"Was he armed?" the king prodded.

"Besides the idol, his only weapon was a wild claim that our people had wronged his and that he had the right to your audience, King Eglon. He was very defiant."

"It is difficult to imagine such a wasted man would dare to brave my army."

Lemuel agreed. "It has been reported to me that he was like a man possessed, making wild claims about our soldiers kidnapping a child from Bethlehem."

"A child?"

"A girl, I'm told," Lemuel said.

"The claims, are they true?"

"Perhaps."

"What is this man called?" the king asked.

"Elimelech. His father is the blacksmith from Bethlehem."

"Yes, Aharon. I know him. Has he not served the palace for years?"

"Yes."

"Without incident?"

Lemuel huffed. "Sir, one less Hebrew cannot be a bad thing."

"Hebrews may be our enemies, but they are also our brothers. Do not forget that, Lemuel."

"No, sir."

"You know more than you're telling me. Hurry up! Out with it! I'm in pain."

Lemuel considered telling the king that this was the artisan whose talents had caught the king's attention and that Elimelech designed the very sword in the sheath at the side of the throne. But Lemuel did not want to give the king any reason to keep the prisoner alive. Instead, he said, "I believe such defiance is a threat to the palace. This Hebrew should be punished as an example for all to see, so others will be deterred from such brazen behavior."

King Eglon felt as if his mouth was on fire. His ear ached and his throat was nearly swollen shut, so he was in no mood to show any sort of kindness.

"Prisoner, look at me!" Eglon demanded. "You claim to be on *my* errand?"

Elimelech tried to reply, but his tongue was dry and twice its normal size. One soldier supporting him put a hand beneath his chin and lifted it. Elimelech stared, his bloodshot eyes meeting the king's. All he was able to do was blink.

"What was your so-called errand?" the king demanded.

Abella! Elimelech thought. *Your soldiers stole her, and I came in search of her.* But these thoughts were wedged so far back in Elimelech's mind that he could not give them voice.

"He's worthless like this!" the king bellowed. "And he's filthy. His drool is puddling on the palace floor. Get him out of here!"

"He will be executed within the hour, sir."

"Don't look so pleased, Lemuel." The king waved them away, then changed his mind. "Better yet, take him to the temple dungeon. Wait until the fires of Chemosh are lit again. He can be a pittance offering at the next festival."

No! Elimelech pleaded silently. *Please do not kill me now. I have two young sons and a wife who is with child.*

But the reality of his fate drained the last drop of hope from Elimelech. He realized how foolish he'd been. His body went limp and he fell, his sweat-drenched hand slipping through the grip of the soldier on his left.

Elimelech crumpled into a heap, his blood and saliva smearing on the tiled palace floor. Immediately, Lemuel ground his metal-toed sandal on top of Elimelech's fingers. The cracking, crunching sound infuriated the king.

Angry, Eglon tried to raise his fleshy arms above his head. When he couldn't do that, he pointed a fat, trembling finger at the soldier who had failed to keep a tight grip on Elimelech, saying, "And have this worthless guard imprisoned with the Hebrew!"

5

NAOMI DIDN'T KNOW WHETHER HER husband was still alive. She knew only that there was an unending emptiness inside of her. For the first time in her life, Naomi wondered where her God was and why He had gone so silent.

"Ama, what's wrong?" Mahlon asked, kneeling before Naomi.

It was a windy day, and dirt and sand swirled in the air, gathering in her son's curls. Tiny grains of sand sparkled on the tip of his nose. She brushed them away and kissed his offered cheek.

"Come now, Brother!" Chilion called. "Uncle Heber said we can take the goats to graze in the high fields today."

Naomi frowned. "You stay away from Heber's shrine. He does not worship the God of Israel."

"We know, Ama. We know."

The boys tore off through the back orchard, herding two sheep and four goats—hardly enough to supply a family with sufficient milk, wool, and meat.

Now that she had returned from the red tent, Naomi should have her strength back. But she felt as weak as an orphaned lamb—too weak to go out and glean whatever the Moabites allowed. That was why Gila had gone.

Gila, suffering her own griefs, had done all she could to lift Naomi out of hers. Naomi could not help but notice how Aharon changed around Gila. He spoke with patience to the twins and stayed home at night instead of looking for comfort where no man of God should seek comfort.

It was no use sweeping with all the wind. So Naomi lay down inside on the main floor where the animals bedded. She did not mind the musky scent or the trapped heat. It felt good to her cold soul.

Then came the sound of voices she knew.

Naomi closed her eyes and wished she could disappear.

"There you are!"

"Hello, Berta. You've returned from Jericho?"

"Yes, Uriel thought it was best. His work as head architect on the wall there keeps him so busy we hardly see him."

Berta's daughters, Edna and Jola, both older than her twins, ran to embrace Naomi, leaving their donkey at the gate.

"Auntie!" they cried. "We've missed you."

"I've missed you too," Naomi said truthfully. She hugged and kissed each girl in turn. Apologetically, she said, "I would offer you a cake or a drink of wine, but we have nothing right now. The boys have gone to the high hills, and I was just about to glean."

"I thought gleaning was forbidden," Berta said, leading the donkey into the shelter. Berta was speckled with dirt, and her hair was wild from the wind.

"Now that the Moabites have harvested and burned the main fields, we are allowed to take whatever we can find," Naomi explained.

"How generous of them," Berta said, her voice sour with sarcasm. She motioned to her daughters. "Girls, undo my pack and bring the goatskin. There's wine for all of us."

Naomi stared at her sister-in-law. Berta was more like her father—hard most of the time but capable of kindness.

"I can tell from the haggard look on your face that you have received no word from my brother."

"Nothing, but I hold out faith."

"How long has it been?"

"Twenty-seven days."

"If he was alive, Elimelech would have found a way to get word to you. Surely my brother is dead, and it's all *that* woman's fault. How dare she bring her troubles to our home!"

"It's not Gila's fault. She's lost a daughter. And she has been doing what she can to offer her support and strength."

"What do you mean? Has something else happened that I don't know about?"

Naomi chose not to mention her own lost daughter. It wasn't something she wanted to talk about, especially not with Berta.

They drank wine and ate warm cheese. Naomi knew she was being greedy and felt Berta's judging eyes on her, but that did not stop Naomi from having a second helping.

"Father is at the blacksmith shop?" Berta asked.

"Yes."

"And that horrible woman is gone? Tell me Gila is gone."

"I'm right here," Gila said.

They turned to look at her. The woman's arms were laden with wheat. Next to her was Aharon, a curious smile playing beneath his beard. But his joy wasn't directed at his returned daughter and granddaughters. Aharon was smiling at Gila, the kind of smile that could mean only one thing.

* * *

The temple of Chemosh was a large, flat area of concrete, decorated with palms and flowering shrubs. Each flower petal had been dusted orange with the chalk brought from the red hills of the desert. Around the temple, a grove of trees had clearly been planted in tight, even rows as a curtain to protect temple patrons from curious eyes.

Atop a square altar at the front of the temple stood a likeness of Chemosh larger than any nightmare. Made of stone and iron, the statue was tinted the color of blood when burned. Behind the temple, a rocky hill concealed a cave that wound into the depths of the hill and eventually into a dungeon, where Moab's prisoners were kept—at least the ones assigned to work the temple grounds.

Here Elimelech and his fellow inmate, the former soldier, were thrown together and locked away. In the darkness and filth, the two men formed an unlikely brotherly bond.

The soldier's name was Daniel, and he was the husband of two wives and the father of seven daughters.

Their first days were impossible. Prisoners were given nothing but water and old bones—but that was more than Elimelech had been given in the weeks previous. Daniel boiled the bones, held a cup of this broth to Elimelech's lips, and helped the man drink.

Daniel used the bone shards and any vines that ventured into the darkness as braces to set Elimelech's broken fingers. Having been in many battles, Daniel knew how to tend to wounds and did his best to help Elimelech.

Eventually, Elimelech was able to ask, "Why are *you* helping me?"

"I watched you and heard your claims. I saw your bravery."

"But you wanted to kill me."

"I never wanted to harm you at all. I was following orders. Besides, it wasn't me who beat you and starved you."

It was true. Daniel had sneaked bread and fresh water to him. "I have to escape," he told Elimelech, "and you have to help me."

"How can I help you when I cannot help myself?" Elimelech asked.

"Wait. The opportunity will come."

"I'll be dead before then."

"No. I swear by the power of Chemosh, if I do not die, you will not die."

Some of the guards were acquainted with Daniel and knew he had been incarcerated on the king's whim, not because of any act against Moab. No one except Daniel paid much attention to Elimelech; he was just a broken Hebrew waiting to be consumed in the fires of Chemosh. They did not care about him.

When they could, the guards threw Daniel bones that still had gristle on them. After a while, they began giving him meat and moldy fruit and vegetables.

After a week, the two men, among others, were dragged out of their filth and into the light. The first thing Elimelech saw other than the grunting face of a guard was a beehive on a low-hanging branch. Immediately, he remembered how he had brought honeycomb to Naomi when she was giving birth to Mahlon and Chilion. The thought prompted both comfort and pain. Who was taking care of his family now? Surely they must think he was dead.

But he wasn't dead, and no matter what he had to do, he would not die here, not in Moab, and not as a sacrifice to an iron-bellied god.

The main guard—a man as big as a bull—looked Daniel and Elimelech over. "You won't be much good, but clean yourselves and then clean the temple. The king is coming to prepare for the festival. All prisoners need to work to make things ready."

And so Elimelech became less than a slave. He was a prisoner, shackled to Daniel. His broken fingers were swollen, bruised a deep purple. His ribs were bruised and broken, making it hard for him to breathe. But the two men spent their days cleaning the grounds around the temple, washing the walls of the temple, and, finally, polishing the idol that would consume them unless they came up with a sure plan of escape.

The opportunity for escape arrived later, after the king's carriage approached the temple. Six large horses and twenty-four men accompanied Eglon.

Eglon was as big as twin bulls. His flesh was gray and slick with sweat. He groaned, holding a cupped hand over his clean-shaved cheek.

"He looks as sick as I feel," Elimelech whispered.

"It's his teeth. They're always bothering him. I'm surprised he has any left," Daniel replied.

They were out in the field but had a view through the archway as the king bowed (as best his massive stomach would allow) before the giant idol and uttered a prayer. There was an exactness, a cadence and rhythm almost chant-like, in his words:

> Great Chemosh,
> We bow before thee, god of all gods.
> May this festival fill your stomach,
> Warm your loins,
> And bless you with protection and abundance,
> That you might do the same for those who worship you
> devotedly.

The prayer was repeated over and over until the king let out a loud belch and the people rose from their knees.

Elimelech started in astonishment and understood now why Moses had brought down the command from Mount Sinai: *I am the Lord thy God, which have brought thee out of the land of Egypt, out of the house of bondage. Thou shalt have no other gods before me.*

Elimelech was glad to be rid of his own false god. The little statue of Baal had become a pest that refused to let him be. For years, it had been there, hidden away, demanding to be worshipped, even if only thought of or prayed to silently. He did not miss Baal, and he could not imagine what drove the Moabites to worship Chemosh, an idol that demanded the virtue and lives of the innocent.

"Isn't that what the Hebrew god demanded of Abraham?" asked Daniel.

"What do you mean?"

"Didn't God demand the innocent life of Isaac?"

"Not in the end," Elimelech said.

"But sacrifice is not new, Brother. Every tribe sacrifices."

"Perhaps, but I do not intend to sacrifice myself to your god, Daniel. Not now. Not ever."

As Elimelech carted wood, he tried to avoid using his injured hand. Would he live long enough to craft another sword? Would he ever caress Naomi's cheek again with those fingers or pluck grapes from the vine to toss into the open mouths of his sons?

Yes, he told himself. Whatever he had to do, Elimelech would find a way back home to his family. He would renew his faith in the true and living God. He would return a changed man, changed for the better.

"You're smiling, Elimelech."

"Am I?"

After the prayer, King Eglon lounged on a special throne built wide enough to hold his bulk. On his head, he wore a narrow crown of gold inlaid with jewels and feathers dyed orange to honor Chemosh. Even his beard had been pruned and dusted orange, as were the tufts of hair in his ears and the long tentacle-like nostril hairs that quivered when he breathed.

"Where are my pain powders? Someone bring me wine and pain powders. My mouth is killing me."

Elimelech looked into the black, hollow eyes of Chemosh. Then he closed his own eyes and begged his God for a way to freedom.

An idea came to him like sunshine over the morning horizon.

"Now you're smiling so wide one of the guards will think you're up to something."

"I am, Daniel. Soon we will both be free. Trust me."

"I do."

They continued working, doing whatever was ordered. All the while, Elimelech continued praying and planning.

Moabites arrived, dressed in their best orange. Food was cooked over great fires, and the air smelled of roasting meat and baking bread. But no morsel was thrown to the prisoners. Only once were they allowed a swallow of water.

Just before dusk, the procession began. The king's clouded eyes brightened as they roved over the girls paraded in front of the royal table— young girls. Some of them had been raised in Moab and were marked to be sacrificed for the greater good of the kingdom by their own parents. Others had been taken from enemies on all sides. There were Philistines and Edomites and Ammorites and Hebrews. Each had a different look.

Elimelech searched each face. Was Abella among them?

Daniel explained, "The same way in which I was sent to prison for a slip of the hand, Eglon's mood will determine which of these girls live, which will be burned, which will go back to work in the palace, and which will be sold into slavery."

Having confided in Daniel about the kidnapped child, Elimelech asked, "Do you see any girls that could be Abella?"

"Any of these girls could be your missing Hebrew."

"No. I will know Abella when I see her."

"But you've never seen her before."

"Her mother described her to me. And if Abella is here, God will show her to me."

Unexpectedly, the overseer guard untethered Elimelech and Daniel so they could work better. He warned with a growl, "If you try to run, I will kill you."

There was no doubt in Elimelech's mind that the man meant what he said.

Lemuel sat on the king's right hand. Elimelech particularly hated this tall, sinewy man with a high forehead and a bird's beak for a nose. It was Lemuel who had encouraged the soldiers to mistreat Elimelech. It was Lemuel who told King Eglon a Hebrew's life was worthless.

Lemuel and the other priests watched the king's moves to see which way they should turn. When Eglon laughed, they laughed. If he laughed louder, they also laughed louder.

King Eglon allowed an older, haggard-looking woman to dance around him and to whisper in his ear. But when the woman stooped to kiss the king's sore cheek, he bellowed in pain and declared the woman "too old and ugly to be a priestess" and ordered her removal. A younger woman quickly took her place. She came bearing grapes, which she plopped into the king's mouth. But it pained him to chew even something as soft as grapes, and he spit them back into the woman's face, angry and frustrated.

Elimelech almost smiled at the thought that was now forming in his head. He moved forward on his hands and knees to clean from the floor the grapes, other food, flowers, and garbage tossed wantonly across the tiles. He crept closer so he could have the best view of the king.

Never once did he stop looking for Abella.

"You've got an idea," Daniel said, working alongside Elimelech. "I can see it turning in your head."

"I will need your help."

"I'll do anything."

A company of young male dancers provided the next phase of entertainment. Part of their dance included stopping to massage the shoulders of the king and priests.

To the woman still feeding him grapes, the king shouted, "Smash them first! Can't you see it pains me to chew?"

Lemuel leaned over and had to shout to be heard. "Are you pleased with the refurbishment of the temple, sir?"

The king was busy spooning a mixture of rice swimming in cream and honey into his mouth. "What is the spice on this? It is delicious."

"Cinnamon," Lemuel said.

"Lemuel was in charge of the temple refurbishment," Daniel explained. "He's anxious to know if the king approves of the newly grouted walls and tiled floors, and of the vines guided to grow along those walls in such a way that they create portraits of the faces of Eglon's favorite concubines. Lemuel has worked hard cleaning and polishing the great idol, and he's overseen the creation of bright new costumes. Lemuel is a man who cares about the smallest details. Even the pink-and-yellow flowers were planned and planted a year ago."

But Eglon was not looking at the refurbishments. He was watching the dancers, enjoying the soft foods set before him, and moaning with pleasure at the hands that rubbed his massive neck and shoulders.

Lemuel looked disappointed and angry that he was not receiving the praise he'd hoped for. By now, Elimelech was so close he saw what others did not: Lemuel stared daggers of pure hated at the king as Eglon guzzled wine and drank an entire pitcher of cream.

An entire roasted pig was then brought to the table and set before the king. Around it was an array of grilled fish and roasted chickens. Next, a row of baskets was brought in filled with breads of every shape and kind.

Daniel could not take his eyes from the food, while Elimelech watched only the king. Just as he had silently predicted, the king grew furious after a few mouthfuls. He demanded more wine and stronger pain powders.

Then the fire in Chemosh's stomach was lit, and the already sweltering temple grew even hotter.

"You realize they could call for you any moment. You could end up in Chemosh's belly *tonight*, Elimelech."

"But I won't. My God has given me an escape and, as a result of your kindness, one for you too, Daniel."

A new parade of girls entered through the door. They were adorned in orange dresses and had orange flowers in their hair. They were younger—and more terrified—than the first group. The last girl to enter did not look that much different from all the other girls, but a warm feeling in his gut told Elimelech she was Abella, Gila's daughter.

Elimelech wanted to act then, but his impatience had once nearly cost him his life. He would not make that mistake again. So he waited, pretending to be busier than he really was. Finally, the king's pain powders and wine took effect. He began to eat again, gnawing great handfuls of warm bread, chomping on greasy slabs of meat.

Elimelech waited. He prayed.

Then it came—the king's cry. He screamed, and the temple went quiet except for the raging fire.

"Help me! I'm in agony!"

Servants ran to aid him. Lemuel stood up and motioned for all the other priests to get out of the way.

Everyone watched as the king flung his forearms across the tables in a fit of rage, splattering platters of hot meat and bread in every direction.

Then Elimelech made his boldest move ever, a move that would either free him or destroy him.

"King Eglon! I can ease your tooth pain," he shouted with a voice louder than the roar of the growing flames. "I can take away your pain. I am trained in such matters."

Lemuel protested, but the king ordered him to be silent.

"You? Who are you?"

"I am Elimelech, son of Aharon. You sentenced me to prison, King Eglon, but I can ease your toothache pain. Do you recall that I am a swordsmith?"

Lemuel fumed. "What does a swordsmith have to do with a sore tooth? We need a physician! Not you!"

Elimelech ignored Lemuel and kept his gaze on the king. "I know how to repair what is broken. I can repair your tooth if you will allow it."

The king did not hesitate. There, in front of unbelieving stares, his great jaw dropped and his mouth opened.

Elimelech turned to his friend. "Run, Daniel. Run to the tree by the dungeon entrance. Knock down the beehive and bring me a fat chunk of honeycomb."

Daniel looked at Elimelech like he was crazy.

"Do as he tells you!" the king ordered Daniel.

Lemuel slapped a heavy hand on the king's shoulder and whispered something in Eglon's ear, but the king pushed him away and ordered, "You too, Lemuel, do what this man says. If he can ease my pain, do whatever he tells you to do."

"Clear off the table," Elimelech ordered Lemuel. "Lay the king flat, but prop his head up with your rolled-up cloak for a pillow."

Lemuel stood stone still.

The king saw Lemuel's defiance and spit in his face. "Do what you're told, or *you* will feed the fires of Chemosh!"

Lemuel stepped back, removed his cloak, and handed it to someone else to roll up into a pillow. The table was quickly cleared. Close to forty men lifted the king onto the table and made him as comfortable as possible.

"I will not forget this," Lemuel whispered as he passed Elimelech. "One day you will pay for what you've done this night."

Elimelech ignored him and set about inspecting the king's mouth.

His mouth was foul and swollen. Green pus oozed from bright red gums. The offending tooth had a gaping hole that was stuffed with gray food remnants.

"Pain powders!" Elimelech called.

Pain powders were brought.

"Wine!" Elimelech called.

Wine was brought.

Then Elimelech leaned down and told the king. "I need your blade—the small dagger you keep laced to your thigh."

Eglon's pig-like eye widened.

"I know, sir, because I am the artisan who crafted that blade. Remember me now?"

"Yes."

"King, I would never think to harm you. I came to Moab to rescue a kidnapped child; that is all. Your priests and priestesses surround you. You are protected by guards armed with blades I fashioned and my father helped to forge."

The king nodded. The blade was brought out. Its tip was sharp and small, just right for freeing the larger pieces of food from the king's teeth.

"That girl! I need her also!" Elimelech ordered, confidently pointing at Abella. "Bring her to me."

Though no one understood why, the terrified girl was brought before Elimelech.

"Is your name Abella?"

She swallowed. Tears swelled in her horrified eyes as she looked at the dagger and feared the worst.

"Don't be afraid."

Elimelech lifted a lock of Abella's long, dark hair, bringing the blade down quickly, cutting the strands. He used the strands to clean out the foul food matter caught between the king's teeth.

Daniel approached with welts on his face and arms, holding a hunk of dripping honeycomb. Elimelech mixed pain powders into the comb. The sweetness and softness eased the king's squirming, and he relaxed while Elimelech took his time packing the king's cavity. The honey itself, Naomi had taught him, served to ease the heat and swelling.

After Elimelech had worked for an hour, the king sat up, declaring himself much better.

Elimelech did not hesitate. "Sir, we have served you, and we ask now that you serve *us*," he gestured, meaning Daniel, Abella, and himself.

"What is it that you want?"

"Our freedom, sir, nothing more."

"No," King Eglon said. Lemuel smirked behind him.

"No?" Elimelech had felt that his inspired plan would absolutely work.

"I will let *him* go." The king nodded toward Daniel. "And I will allow the child to return to Bethlehem. But you, you are needed here in Moab. What if I have another bout with my tooth?"

Elimelech's head throbbed.

The king continued, "You are in no position to refuse me. You have found a small amount of favor in my eyes, so I'll allow you to return to settle your affairs and to gather your family, but only on the condition that you vow to return to Moab to work for me in my armory. I want you available when I need you."

Elimelech gulped.

Lemuel seemed both outraged and contemplative.

The king was unyielding and impatient. He wanted to get back to eating now that he felt better.

"A band of guards will accompany you to Bethlehem, of course. They will see that you return to make Moab your home. Now go!"

Eglon turned his attention back to a new platter of steaming meat set before him.

6

A FUNERAL PROCESSION RODE DOWN Bethlehem's narrow, winding, cobbled street that led from the town's well up to Aharon's house. Listening to the mourners' wails, Elimelech held his breath, praying that these cries were not for one of his own.

"He's returned!" the wizened well watcher, a woman without a name, shouted, pointing at the four Moabite soldiers, the girl dressed in orange, and the limping Elimelech.

"He's returned and the girl is with him!"

Elimelech wiped sweat from his brow. The funeral procession moved faster, until the line of faces was before him. He recognized his astonished kinsmen, including his uncle Salmon, who walked in front of the coffin.

Salmon's face was stoic.

Elimelech searched desperately for Naomi . . . Mahlon . . . Chilion. But he did not see them, and his heart tightened into a ball.

"Uncle."

Salmon looked at Elimelech. His dark eyes rolled upward in indication that he was neither surprised nor pleased to see Elimelech return.

"Someone fetch Naomi to tell her that her husband has returned!" the well watcher cried.

"Whose funeral is this?" Elimelech asked the woman.

"Sarah, wife of Bartholomew, the tanner. No one realized they were without food until the poor woman keeled over yesterday, brittle as straw. She starved to death right in our midst, and we did nothing to help her."

Elimelech remembered Sarah, a kind-faced woman whose husband was crippled with age.

"What of Bartholomew? I don't see him here."

"Someone would have to carry the old man. He's that feeble."

"And my wife?" he managed, asking the question he most wanted answered. "How is my Naomi and my sons?"

Just then a child's cry rose above the mourners' laments. Then another shout came, and Mahlon and Chilion flew down the path, straight for their father's open arms.

The Moabite soldiers reluctantly stepped back.

The girl, Abella, burst into tears.

"Who are you?" Mahlon asked.

Abella did not answer. She had not spoken a word since they had left Moab. One eye hid behind a thick lock of black hair. The other eye scanned this way and that.

Where is her mother? Elimelech thought.

"This is Gila's daughter," he told his sons.

"Gila? You're our new grandmother's daughter?" Chilion asked.

Elimelech blinked. "Your new *grandmother*?"

The boys were already getting bored of their father's embraces but seemed anxious to tell their father about how brave they'd been when venturing in the high hills and how helpful they'd been to Aharon at the blacksmith shop.

"Why are you crying, Father?" Mahlon asked.

"I am so very happy to see you. Where is your mother?"

"She's home with Gila."

"Why did you call Gila your grandmother?"

"Because she married Grandfather."

Abella heard all of this and now looked as confused as Elimelech.

Once the tail of the funeral procession moved on, Elimelech tried to pick up his pace—he had so many questions and so much to tell—but he didn't have to wait long because he soon saw Naomi charging toward him.

"You're home," she wept, falling into his outstretched arms.

Yes, he tried to say, *but not for long.*

Three days later, the joy Naomi had felt turned into something else, a sort of numb feeling she could not name. To Naomi, even the skies, clouded over and threatening rain, seemed to mourn. Naomi hoped that it *would* rain so that her tears wouldn't be so visible to everyone who came to bid her family an unexpected good-bye.

"Can't you tell the soldiers that we can't leave today? It's the Sabbath. We're forbidden to carry anything, yet they have us packing everything."

"We have no choice," Elimelech said, "not if we want our family to live."

"Isn't it better to die here than to live there?"

Elimelech grabbed Naomi by the elbow. "Don't ever let them hear you say such things. Moabites don't understand."

"I don't understand, Elimelech. I don't understand any of this. You return home. You bring Abella back to her mother. This should be a time of thanksgiving and rejoicing, but then you announce that the boys and I have to return to Moab with you—to *live*."

"We won't have to stay there forever."

"You don't sound so sure of that. How long are you going to have to be in the king's employ?"

"I don't know. You are so upset, and I understand why, but what do you want me to do about it? I told you what happened," he said. Then, in a softer voice, he added, "I would be dead if I had refused the king."

She buried her face in her hands. "I'm sorry. I am very grateful to God that you're alive and that Abella is back with her mother. But I don't want to move away from my home, the only home the boys have ever known. It feels so wrong."

"It *is* wrong. But, please, do not make a scene or show me any disrespect. Please, Naomi. Be my wife and support me through this. I swear to you that it isn't any easier on me than it is on you."

Because she loved Elimelech, Naomi put on a brave face, something she was used to doing. She even allowed a baffled Berta to hug her.

"My brother has lost his mind. He left it back in Moab."

"Please, don't say such things about my husband."

Berta wailed and wept like someone had died.

That's how it felt, Naomi realized—like a death. She fought back her own tears, determined not to embarrass Elimelech or to let the soldiers imagine that she was weak.

Aharon and his new family, Gila and her daughter, Abella, stood in the back of the courtyard, beneath the shade of the olive tree. Tears streamed down Gila's cheeks, but the gentle grip Aharon had on her arm kept her from rushing forward to embrace Naomi. He had now prevented them from embracing for what seemed like the hundredth time.

Salmon and Kezia were formal—cold, even—in their good-byes.

Young Boaz, just returned from Jerusalem, held a rolled-up leather scroll beneath his arm.

"I was going to teach you to read and write," he said with regret to Elimelech.

"Reading and writing would be wasted on a man like me," Elimelech said, trying to lighten the mood of this very heavy moment.

"Perhaps one day you can teach *me*," Naomi said, kissing Boaz's cheek. "I hear that in Moab women are encouraged to learn such things."

"I will teach you too, Auntie. I just don't want you to move away."

Elimelech ruffled Boaz's thick, black locks. "I will miss you, Cousin."

Then Boaz reached into his purse and pulled out two small wooden tops, both painted indigo. These he gave to Mahlon and Chilion.

"Think of me every time you spin them," Boaz said.

"We're too old for toys!" Mahlon said.

"No, we're not," his brother said.

Edna and Jola clambered forward to see if Boaz had brought them any tokens from Jerusalem.

One of the soldiers raised a lance and gave Elimelech a hard look.

"It's time," Elimelech said.

Their small family, surrounded by four Moabite soldiers, walked away. Naomi kept her eyes on Elimelech, who looked back at the home where he had grown up, where she had given birth, and where his mother, Rachael, had died with her eyes fixed on his. He wasn't a man who showed public emotion, but she saw tears in his eyes as he vowed, "We will return."

No one echoed his sentiment.

"At least there's food in Moab," Chilion said, loud enough for everyone to hear.

Naomi looked at all of the gaunt faces. These people were their kinsmen, their neighbors. In their eyes she saw the anger and betrayal they felt at being left behind.

"You're leaving behind your Lord and your people," someone told Elimelech. "You cannot think that you'll be blessed for abandoning the holy laws."

"I will keep the laws of Israel no matter where I am," Elimelech said.

Naomi looked at her husband and wondered at all he had suffered in the weeks he was away. His fingers were crooked and bruised. An angry red scar replaced his right eyebrow. His chin had been dashed and still bore a scab. His eyes seemed vacant, and he winced when he walked from the pain of his unhealed ribs.

She felt like she and the twins were following a stranger into a strange land.

Jola and Edna ran to them for one final hug from Naomi.

"Why are you moving away, Auntie?" they asked.

"So Father can work in the palace," Chilion answered, "and we can swim in the pool and eat meat and drink cream every day."

Berta caught up with them, and the girls were pulled back into their mother's arms.

Naomi didn't know if Berta had even said good-bye to her brother.

She didn't expect sentiment from Salmon, but Naomi was hurt by the coldness Kezia showed her. "You don't have to follow him there," she had told Naomi.

"Yes, I do. He is my husband," Naomi had replied.

Heber was absent. The rumor was that he had gone to Edom in search of another wife. Would that make his fourth or fifth? But it didn't matter. Naomi knew that Heber was the one person she would not miss.

When they reached the end of the road where the turn would not allow them to look back and see their home, Aharon stepped away from Gila and came forward, dragging the reins of Berta's donkey.

They clopped their way through the crowd, and he handed the reins to Elimelech.

"You can't be expected to carry everything you possess on your own backs."

"But Father, the donkey belongs to Uriel and Berta."

"I will pay them for it. Take it and let the beast bear your burdens."

"Its name is Chamor," Jola said.

Elimelech stepped forward to embrace his father in gratitude, but Aharon backed away.

"I still think what you did was foolish. It will cost you everything. But I am grateful that you returned alive and that you brought Gila her daughter."

"And I am grateful, Father, that you are no longer alone. Gila will make a good wife to you."

Aharon cleared his throat and stepped away, saying, "Peace be with *both* of you, and peace be to your house, my son."

Some neighbors and relatives wished them well, but a few following them shouted insults at their family.

"Traitors!" one called out.

"You will suffer for your choices," another said.

Elimelech looked at his kinsmen and said simply, "I have already suffered."

"You honor Chemosh," one replied. "Because of you, every Hebrew pays a backbreaking tribute to the king."

At the mention of the king, one of the soldiers drew his sword to separate the small family from the rest of the people. But Salmon would not be held back. His angry red face growled at Elimelech, "Choke on the scraps from the king's table. They'll be all you get in the end."

Boaz pulled his father back, then he turned. "Cousin," he shouted, "one day I will own fields in Bethlehem, and no one will go hungry. Then you can return—to your home and to your family."

"I had my dreams when I was your age. Dreams are for fools, Boaz. If I could spare you the pain of broken dreams, I would," Elimelech said. Naomi was shocked at his sad response.

Then, as if waiting for exactly the right moment, four drops of rain fell in the dust—like four teardrops—and that was the end of the promised storm.

In the evening, at their first resting spot, the boys were happy to take Chamor off the beaten path, where he could snatch a few mouthfuls of dried grass. Chilion gathered a small mound of sticks and dried bones that he turned into weapons. Mahlon searched for food.

Later, Mahlon stayed beside his mother, helping her grind the little grain they had brought and boil the few roots they dug up along the way.

Elimelech bought a cup of camel's milk for Naomi. "This will help you with your strength."

That night Naomi slept next to her husband and sons, none of them waking early by the grumble of their empty stomachs.

After they were farther into their journey, Elimelech seemed more at ease. When they arrived at a well to fill their water skins, he put the dipper first to his wife's lips. It was a kind and gentle gesture that she had not expected.

"Please stop weeping, Naomi. I can't stand to see you like this."

"I can't stop my heart from leaking," she said. It was difficult for Naomi to swallow. The lump in her throat would not go down—not with the memory of good-byes so fresh. At Bethlehem's common well, she had slid her palm over the bench carved by her mother's knife. How could she make Elimelech understand that she felt like she was losing her mother all over again?

She smiled. "I do not mean to complain, but this move is so difficult. I don't understand how fixing the king's tooth led our family into this situation."

"What I did to the king's tooth worked, and because it did, King Eglon wants me at his disposal, in case he needs it done again."

"Anyone can fill a tooth's hole with honeycomb," she argued.

"It was more than that. Can't you see? The king saw me as brave and innovative. Can't anyone else understand?"

"I'm sorry," Naomi said. "I can't."

He put the dipper to his own lips, then said, "In Judea, our days are spent surviving. When we arrive in Moab, you'll see—our sons can grow up to be men of importance. Mahlon might be an architect like Uriel or a physician or even a farmer like Boaz and Salmon."

"And Chilion?"

"He can become the swordsmith I never was."

Naomi ached to assure Elimelech that there was still hope for him, but she couldn't—not when she saw how his hand could not even hold the donkey's reins.

In the palace, King Eglon had been feeling better. His mouth was still sore, but his pounding headache was gone, and he even felt well enough to entertain an embassy of Egyptians passing from the desert to the Nile.

The king peppered these men with questions about their pharaoh and how the government in Egypt was run. After answering his questions, one of the men asked Eglon, "Why is your palace as quiet as a snake's den? Are there no children?"

"I have about forty children, but I no longer allow them here. I can't stand the noise they make. Why? Is this an issue worth questioning me about?"

The man dared to speak boldly. "The Pharaoh is very fond of his children and has them educated in all things."

"What do you mean?"

"The Pharaoh is not fond of *all* children, only his own. He believes his reign is strongest when he has his own children educated and trained in everything from architecture to wine making."

The king rubbed his stomach and asked, "What of letters and numbers?"

"Yes. By all means, yes. The Pharaoh's children even study the stars. He has teachers and experts tutor his children so that they speak the languages of their enemies. They all understand culture and history and weaponry, even his daughters."

"Daughters too! The only thing my daughters know how to do is shriek and run through the great halls of my palace as if they are being chased." He laughed, but the Egyptians did not even smile.

The next morning Eglon called for Lemuel.

"Bring my children to the palace," he told him.

"Which children, sir?"

"All of them," Eglon said. "Line them up and let me have a look at my posterity."

"Sir, you have scattered them throughout the kingdom. The young ones are returned to their various mothers, and your eldest sons are in military training."

"I don't care! Locate them all and let them stand before me. I have an announcement to make."

Lemuel eyed him. "What announcement would that be?"

"You'll know when I tell my children. Now bring them before me and do it without delay!"

Lemuel rubbed his face and stammered. "You . . . you want all— all—all of your children brought to the palace?"

"No. No. Not here. Bring them to the temple. That's where we will start."

As the afternoon heat gathered, forty-one children were summoned to the temple, ranging in age from eighteen years to only a few months—two infants still depended on their mother's milk. Only a few of the children came with their mothers, including Ruth with Sakira. Sakira was also taking care of Orpah since Orpah's mother had been sent back to the lowlands along the river, and no guards had been able to locate her.

Orpah attempted to hold tight to Ruth's fidgety hand. "Stay still," Orpah whispered. "The king has an announcement to make."

"He's ugly," Ruth whispered not so quietly.

Sakira was forced to stand across the way, so she put a straight finger to her lips and shot her daughter a warning glare.

"Well, he is," Ruth said. "He's fat and ugly, and he scares me."

One of the maidservants slapped the back of Ruth's head. "Never speak of the king with such dishonor," she said.

"I'm not talking about Father," Ruth said more loudly than before. "I'm talking about Chemosh."

Even the king heard Ruth this time. It was the first time the king did not seem amused by Ruth's antics.

He frowned at her and his disapproval stilled her shuffling feet.

"I have brought you here," the king bellowed, turning from Ruth to look around at them all, "to embark on a program of learning. You will learn of Chemosh's all-powerful ways and the language of our people, both how to read and to write." He paused. "Even my daughters. You will each learn everything there is to know. If Pharaoh's children know the art of masonry, then you will too. You will study the stars, the languages of our enemies, and their false and foolish gods. You will learn how to grow grapes to make wine and olives to make oil. You will learn to tan hides, slaughter beasts, and cure meat. You will learn how to be farmers, soldiers, physicians, artisans, and craftsmen. My children will learn everything!"

The king then called for one of the high priests of the temple, and a short man stood up; he resembled a boulder that had been dyed orange.

"Today, you will learn of Chemosh," the king said.

With that, the king leaned back on his throne and motioned for the priest to take over.

The priest began a jittery sermon on all the ways Chemosh demanded to be worshipped and on the horrors that would come upon Moab if the people failed to pay proper tribute.

Ruth freed her sweaty hand from Orpah's grip.

"Where did Chemosh come from?" she asked the high priest.

The priest looked puzzled as Ruth stepped forward and pointed at the smoke-stained figure. Her young voice was high and confident. "Did Chemosh come down from the heavens? Did he sprout from the earth? Appear out of a lightning bolt? Father wants us to learn all about Chemosh, so please tell us where Chemosh first came from."

The question made King Eglon scratch his beard in wonder. "Answer my daughter," he ordered the priest.

Tiny rivers of perspiration ran down the priest's forehead, striping his face where the orange powder was washed away. "I am not used to answering such questions from a child, but I will tell you that our god is related to other gods. This particular idol was forged in the fires of our grandfathers. It has been here for generations."

Ruth took another step forward and lifted her voice even louder. "So our grandfathers made Chemosh from metal?"

"Yes."

"So if a great fire burned the temple, Chemosh would turn back to melted metal?"

Lemuel leaned down and whispered in King Eglon's ear. "Perhaps there has been enough instruction for the day, sir."

"Let him answer my daughter's question!" the king bellowed.

But the priest struggled to choose his words. His answer came slowly and with uncertainty: "Chemosh has power . . . to command the elements, and he *instructs* your father how to defeat our enemies."

Ruth marched right up to Chemosh and pointed high at his gaping mouth. "Chemosh's mouth is made of metal. How does he speak to my father?"

Instead of answering, the priest looked to King Eglon.

Ruth also turned. "How does Chemosh speak to you, Father?"

The king's face reddened. "I'm tired, and I'm hungry. Your questions can wait."

7

Now on the opposite side of the river, Elimelech's family had stepped into a different life. Entering the land of their enemies was, nonetheless, like entering the land of their family, extended and estranged, but family still. Elimelech tried to explain to his wife and sons that like Hebrews, the Moabites were also the children of Israel through the loins of Lot, Abraham's nephew.

"But they all wear orange," Mahlon said.

"It is the color of their god."

"It's the shade of an angry sun," Naomi explained. "I will never wear it."

"You won't have to, Naomi," Elimelech said. "And the languages are hardly different."

The boys showed more excitement than hesitation now that they were on their way. They moved like they had been reborn. Once past the gates of Bethlehem, they felt an energy come back to them. Out on the King's Highway, they joined caravans and traders and people with dusty faces whom they had never seen.

There were also donkeys and a few desert camels, and lots of merchants were selling the same goods that were made and sold in Israel.

As they climbed upward from the river, they paused so that Elimelech could point out the mount of Ephraim—the burial place of Joshua—on the north side of the hill Gaash.

"Is this what the land looked like when Joshua finally crossed over?" Naomi asked.

"Little has changed."

As they climbed upward from the river, Elimelech recounted Moabite history aloud, telling them about when God destroyed the cities of the plains and sent Lot out of the midst. "Lot took his daughters out of Zoar to live in the mountains, but they thought they were the only people left on the face of the earth."

Elimelech paused to gaze up at a ragged overhang. He asked the Moabite soldiers if they thought Lot had ever stood there, looking out over the flatlands.

They only shrugged.

"Look out at the caves in the rocks," Elimelech said. "Lot and his daughters took refuge in one of them. They believed they were alone in all the earth and decided to get their father drunk so they could bring forth the seed of their father. And that is how Moab was founded."

Naomi turned away. "I want to go home," she said.

"And you will—in time."

Another group of travelers passed. Naomi noticed one woman with a long necklace dangling from her throat. At the end was a carved likeness of Chemosh.

"There is no hidden idol worship here," Naomi said.

Elimelech cringed, remembering the years he had completely hidden a likeness of Baal from her—or at least he thought he'd completely hidden it.

That night they lay on their backs looking up at a sheet of white stars. They were beyond exhausted. The highway was unsafe to travel at night, even with armed Moabite soldiers.

"Let me tell you about my mother, your grandmother Rachael," Elimelech said to the boys. "She died before you were born, but my memories of her are soft. Everything about her was soft—her voice, her skin, the lips she pressed to my boyish cheeks—those were soft back then too."

"Grandfather said she suffered a lot before she died," Mahlon said.

"That is true." Elimelech flinched, remembering how his father had increased his mother's suffering when he might have lessened it. "Mother used to lay in the shade of our courtyard and tell me stories of our prophets. She also used to sing to me."

"Why don't you ever sing to us, Ama?" Chilion asked Naomi.

"I have sung to you many times," she replied.

"I don't remember," Chilion said, "but maybe you'll sing more as soon as we have a new home and plenty of food."

That night the soldiers had eaten grilled meat they bought earlier from a roadside vendor. All Elimelech had to offer was dried fish and thin cakes. He lifted his voice so the soldiers would hear. "Back when I was a boy, the markets in Bethlehem were stacked high with pomegranates and figs and olives. There was plenty of oil for cooking and even meat for those with money."

"Now the markets are empty," Mahlon said.

"And only the Moabites have money," Chilion added.

After a long silence Mahlon suggested, "Abba, you should sing to us."

In that moment, under a night sky of white stars, Naomi heard a sound from Elimelech's mouth she'd never heard before. He sang the songs his mother had sung to him. These songs warmed the chill of the night air and made the stars somehow shine more brightly.

Later, when the boys were asleep and the soldiers had separated themselves somewhat from the family, Elimelech told Naomi things he'd never talked about before.

"When my mother was so sick," he said, "my father stayed away. When she needed him, he found things he wanted to do more than be with her. I understand that it was difficult for him to tolerate the sounds and smells of her sickness—it was hard on Berta and me too—but Father resented it all. He blamed Mother and called her weak."

"I can't imagine having to live with him back then," Naomi said, her head against Elimelech's chest.

"Even Berta scolded him," Elimelech explained, "telling Father that our mother needed him, that we *all* needed him. But he didn't care. He murmured about how Mother's moaning in pain kept *him* from a proper sleep." He sighed.

"It didn't matter how hard we begged or how many times I clung to his leg and he dragged me halfway down the street as I cried for him to stay with us. Father always left. He left for work, for other women, or for time with the elders, who felt pity for his plight."

Naomi said nothing and just listened to Elimelech pour out what had been pent up for so long.

"Father used to tell me that I was too young to understand how important of a man he was, important to all of Judea. He and Uncle Salmon thought they were prophets and esteemed themselves that highly. Father said he forged more than weapons for the Moabites. He claimed that he forged bonds with the enemies and that one day, Ehud would be able to use those bonds to free our people."

Elimelech wiped his face with his palm. "I suppose I have made the same claims. When I received my first commission to design a sword for King Eglon, I felt so important. I didn't even care if he used that sword on someone I knew. I was full of pride."

"You only wanted your father to be proud of you, Elimelech. I've seen that same want ever since I first met you. And now he is. Aharon might not be able to say it, but I believe he approves of you."

Elimelech sniffled. "And now it's too late. I might never see my father again. I don't know how to feel about this life I've dragged you and our sons into."

"I feel terrified," she blurted.

"Maybe you should," he said, then turned away from her and stayed on his side. She wondered whether Elimelech was still awake, until the sound of his snoring joined that of the Moabite soldiers.

* * *

On that same night in the palace, King Eglon was restless. He'd awoken from a disturbing dream, shivering.

"Lemuel!" he called. "Are you there?"

"Yes, sir." His chief priest and captain of his personal army was on a seat just outside Eglon's sleeping chambers. "I never leave until you are asleep for the night."

"Were all my concubines sent back to their sleeping quarters?"

"Yes. Should we summon any particular one back tonight?"

"No. I'm tired. Only, I had a dream that the lower palace, the queen's palace, was attacked by Edomites."

"It was only a night terror, sir. I assure you that the queen's palace is secure."

"I dreamed that our soldiers could not fight the Edomites because our swords were too heavy and too bulky. I dreamed that the queen stood in front of me, laughing, telling me that I was a fool and not much of a commander."

Lemuel said nothing.

"How long has it been since I've seen the queen?" Eglon asked.

"Since last year at the festival, sir."

"She did not come to this year's festivities?"

"No. She did not. It was as you wished."

"I do not wish to ever see her again. She should stay where she is. If that palace is attacked, so be it."

"Sir."

"I did not choose her," Eglon argued. "Our fathers arranged our union. She is not beautiful, she spends too much time in the sun, and she is forever trying to get me to eat less."

"Is there anything else I can get you before you retire, sir?"

"My tooth still hurts. When is that swordsmith from Bethlehem returning?"

"They are on their way now, sir."

"Have him brought to the palace as soon as he arrives."

"As you wish."

The king tried to fall back asleep. But, in spite of the heat, the king felt cold and demanded Lemuel send for sheepskin covers to be heaped on him.

Lemuel also sent for others to help him with the king's fever. Servants rubbed the king's feet, maids rubbed his arms, and the palace physician brought pain powders and a compress of river mud and crushed spearmint to lay over his forehead.

The king drank cream to ease his burning stomach pains. But he also ate cold roasted fowl and boiled figs. So the physician administered ginger tea; it made Eglon belch over and over until the air in the room was foul, even though the windows were wide open.

"Stay beside me," he ordered Lemuel.

Reluctantly, Lemuel pulled a chair up next to the bed so that he could stay awake and watch the king finally fall into a fitful slumber.

In his next dream, the king saw his Moabite armies, fierce as rows of flames in their orange loincloths and feathered headgear. Their shields were made of brass, their swords of heavy iron, and their protective arm and leg bands of animal hides.

From his high tower at the lower palace, Eglon looked out and saw that they were moving. The armies marched forward, but the king could not tell in which direction. Were they headed toward Judea? Israel? Edom? Or were they marching toward Egyptian or Ammonite territory?

"Lemuel!" he cried out.

"I am here," a groggy Lemuel said.

But Eglon was not awake. He was still sleeping and still dreaming.

"Where are our armies headed?" the king asked.

"To fight the enemies of Chemosh," was Lemuel's only answer.

The army slowed because they were lugging swords too heavy to lift and armor too heavy to carry.

"We need better weapons," a woman at his side said.

The king recognized her voice.

"Ruth! What are you doing here?" he asked.

She was no longer a child but a grown woman, dressed in the armor of Moab.

"What are you doing?" he repeated.

"I'm doing what you commanded me to do. You wanted your children to learn everything. I did what you asked, Father, and my specialty is warfare."

"No, Ruth! If you go into battle, our enemies will slaughter you."

"So be it, Father. I am your daughter, the child most like you."

"No! What can I do to help you? I do not wish you to die, Daughter. I wish you to go to the marketplace, where your mother works as a weaver. Weave with her. Do not fight for the armies of Moab."

Ruth's expression was as serious as death. "Moab controls the metal resources of the land. Our enemies fight with wood and bone while our soldiers use swords forged of brass and iron."

"Yes," the king said confidently. "Our weapons are superior."

Ruth shook her head, and Eglon saw for the first time what a beautiful woman she was. She showed her determination in the firm set of her jaw, but she also had her mother's soft eyes and full lips. "Our weapons are *too* heavy and wear out our soldiers before the battle even begins, Father."

This argument resonated with him; he'd heard it before.

"They will be redesigned, Ruth," he promised. "Do not go into battle until you have a sword you can wield against our worst enemy."

"I already have such a sword, Father," Ruth said, smiling. She drew a sword from her sheath. He recognized the sword and tried to get it back, but Ruth held it with both hands high above her head.

When she brought it down with all the fierceness in her, King Eglon cried, "No! No, Ruth, no!" For the enemy she attacked was Chemosh.

King Eglon awoke to his own screaming, with the sound of Ruth's sword clanging against the metal heart of Moab's most feared idol still ringing in his ears.

* * *

As Elimelech's family moved toward their new home, Elimelech had to stop at one point to catch his breath. They noticed a sleeping sea, stretched out like a shimmering blue carpet in the dawn.

"It's beautiful," Naomi conceded. "The land is also beautiful. Maybe we can make a home that won't be as lonely as I feared."

Elimelech turned on her with a hard look in his eyes. "You're already changing. I never wanted you to change," he said.

Naomi could see that he was disappointed in her, but over what? Saying that the sea and the land were beautiful?

He continued. "I never wanted to bring you to Moab to live. Oh, Naomi, this is Canaan. Every parcel is soaked with blood. All it's ever known is war."

"Hurry along," a soldier ordered them.

They obeyed, fearing what the soldier might do if they continued arguing. Chilion had made fast friends with the soldiers. There was one man in particular who let the boy hold his sword and play with his dagger and who fed both boys more than their parents could.

"I will find a way for us to return home soon," Elimelech said quietly. "I will fix the king's sore tooth again and design his best weapons. I will find favor with him and get him to grant our return." He paused. "Look at me, wife. I vow to you that you will not have to make Moab your home forever."

"I believe you," she said. Then she looked away and walked on in silence.

* * *

Just after sunrise the king lay sprawled on his bed, barking orders.

"I had a wretched nightmare," he told his servants. "I can't remember the details now, but it left me feeling miserable. Bring me food. My head hurts. My tooth hurts again, and my stomach. Oh, my stomach. Perhaps, if I ate a little something . . ."

Soon a tray appeared from the kitchen. Boiled quail eggs and a slab of roasted swine were laid before the king.

"Where is the cheese?" he demanded.

"Coming, sir. Here it is now."

"And cream."

A pitcher, thick with cream so fatty it was yellow, was soon placed in the king's grip. He drank directly from the pitcher, leaving his beard and moustache coated with cream.

"Pain powders," he said. "And where is that Bethlehemite?"

"Soon, King Eglon."

"Lemuel," he called, but no one answered. "Lemuel should be here."

"He is on his way," the servant said.

The king made a horrible face, then shouted, "Out! Everyone out now!"

The scrambling servants knew this routine. They left all they'd brought into the king's sleeping chambers and scurried out.

When Lemuel arrived later to go over the morning report with the king, he found the servants waiting outside the chamber doors.

"He is relieving himself," one of the men explained.

"Is the king ill?" Lemuel asked.

"It's his stomach again."

Lemuel frowned, muttered something under his breath, and walked away, saying, "Send for me when he's done and the air has cleared."

* * *

An hour later, King Eglon was dressed and able to make it down the corridor to his resting room, an area with a wide chair and a view of the palace gardens.

Lemuel came and reported the state of the armies. Other military officers reported about different parts of the kingdom.

"And how are the lessons for my children?" Eglon asked. "I want to engage only the finest teachers. I think they should all learn to cook. Cooking is important. Even my sons should know how to roast and season meat. Have the children brought to the palace kitchens. Yes. They can cook for me, and then I will be sure that no one poisons me."

"Sir, you have tasters who are willing to die to save you from being poisoned."

"That's true, I do. And have any of them ever died?"

"No. No one would dare poison you, King."

"All this talk of food . . . Perhaps if I eat something—just a little something on my stomach—I'll feel better. Lemuel, tell the cooks I want a roasted goat—the whole thing—and corn. Is there corn to be had?"

"Yes, sir. There is fresh corn brought from Judea."

Eglon lifted one eyebrow. "After we reaped, we burned the corn fields so the Hebrews could not gorge themselves. Tell me we did this."

"Burned to stubble," Lemuel assured him.

"Good. Better to be wasteful than to feed a hungry Hebrew."

* * *

On the third day of their family's exodus from Bethlehem, the twins were oblivious to everything except for their new surroundings.

"It's like they've been reborn," Naomi said. "I've never seen them bound around with so much energy."

"I pray this move will be a blessing for them," Elimelech said.

A few minutes later, they came to a bend in the road. Elimelech and Naomi watched as the Moabite soldiers confronted a lone traveler that they found suspicious.

"I am a Moabite," the man assured them. "My daughter was chosen as one of the king's concubines. She's very young and very afraid. I am on my way to visit her in Dibon."

"I don't believe you," one of the soldiers said.

Then, as Mahlon and Chilion watched, the soldiers stripped the man. When they found a small dagger concealed in his turban, they brutally beat him, then stoned him. Then they abandoned his lifeless, bloody body in the road.

"It'll be a deterrent," one soldier said.

Naomi felt horrified and could not stop herself from weeping.

"Please, Naomi, stop," Elimelech said. "You must not cry in front of them."

"I can't help it," she sobbed. "Any hope I had that we might be able to make a life in Moab is dashed." Then, more quietly she said, "Our sons will grow up to become enemies to our own people. We've left our God behind, Elimelech."

"No, we haven't," he insisted. "The God of Israel can't be hung from a string or hidden in a pocket. Our God must be carried in our hearts, Naomi. Never forget that."

He wanted to put his arms around her and hold her until her tears stopped, but the soldiers shot them angry looks that encouraged them to hurry on their way.

Just beyond the bend, Naomi turned around to see the white sparkling hills of Bethlehem, but a rugged ledge of red rock blocked her view and stopped her heart. She tried to run back, but one of the soldiers grabbed her elbow.

"I just want one last look at my home!" she cried.

"No," the soldier said. "There is no looking back now!"

8

As they moved closer to the city of Dibon, the twins grew happier, while Elimelech and Naomi grew more sullen.

"Maybe you and the boys should return to Bethlehem," Elimelech said. "I will go to Moab alone."

"Never. We are a family, and we will live as a family," Naomi told him, but her words seemed forced.

Elimelech dragged his feet, thinking back to how this had all really started. He knew it was his faults, his dreams, that had brought his family here. When he was a boy only a few years older than his sons were now, he had worked alongside his father in the blacksmith shop. By that time, King Eglon had shut down every other blacksmith in Bethlehem. Aharon had been singled out, which made him favored by Moabites but despised by his own people.

The king had posted guards to watch over Aharon to see that his farm implements or weapons did not end up in the wrong hands.

"What is that?" asked the guard, a hook-nosed man named Wendell. "What is that you are looking at?"

Elimelech remembered how his young heart had hammered. He had been showing his father a design he'd carved into a piece of goatskin. It had been the design of a sword with a blade barely rounded, thin on both sides of the tip so it would pierce faster and deeper. The hilt would be made of inlaid jewels with a scalloped grip to fit a man's hand more securely.

"My son's a dreamer," Aharon had said, tossing the skin aside.

Wendell had picked it up, rolled it, and tucked it away.

That might have been the end of it, but later, Wendell returned with the design.

"Can you actually make a sword like the one your son drew?" he asked.

"No," Aharon said. "We lack the iron and the jewels and the proper tools."

"I can make it!" he remembered himself saying, rushing forward with arrogance. "If you supply me with all the things I need, I know exactly how to make such a sword."

Aharon had scoffed. "He's only a boy."

"He's worked here beside you all of his life. Let the boy attempt it. And you, you help him, Aharon. The king's chief commander would like to see such a sword."

His first attempt had failed, and so had the second. But by the third, Wendell wasn't the only Moabite interested.

That was the beginning, he remembered, and now Dibon was in sight. Elimelech wondered if the king would keep his promise. Would Elimelech finally become the swordsmith he had always hoped and dreamed he would be? Would his family have their own home and sufficient food to eat? Would he be able to earn the respect he'd always wanted?

Elimelech slapped Chamor on the backside, eager now to hurry the donkey along.

* * *

Working in the warm afternoon sunlight, Sakira moved her long braid out of the way.

"You girls stop playing and come over here and help me move these baskets."

Ruth's mouth was wide open. She dipped to the left and to the right as Orpah tossed grapes at her. The sisters laughed when one bounced off her lip and landed in the dirt.

"Don't waste a morsel," Sakira scolded. "You don't know when Chemosh will frown on us and make the grapevines wither."

"Why would he do that?" Orpah asked. "We've been learning all about him, but Chemosh makes no sense to me. Where does his power come from?"

"The sun," Sakira said.

"Even his giant belly isn't big enough to hold the sun, Mother," Ruth said, giggling and plopping the fallen grape into her mouth.

The sunlight caught Sakira's hair and Ruth realized that it made it look gold.

"My mother—your grandmother—taught me that Chemosh, like some of the other gods, is the sun personified."

"What does *personified* mean?" Ruth asked.

"It means Chemosh has the power of the sun. He can make things grow."

"He can burn them up too," Ruth said.

Orpah nodded. "Chemosh is always angry."

"So don't make him angrier by wasting the food he's blessed us with," Sakira said.

Ruth cocked her head. "I don't think a god should always be angry. I think he should care about us."

"Chemosh does care about us," Sakira said. "Look around. Moab is green while the other lands are wilted and dry. Trust me, my daughters, we are blessed by the power and mercy of Chemosh."

"Once, I saw a little girl blessed by him," Orpah said, frowning. "We were at the festival. Ruth, you were too little to remember. But I remember how the priests bound the child and placed her in Chemosh's burning hands. She screamed and wiggled and Chemosh let her roll free."

"Wasn't she all burned?" Ruth asked, her eyes wide.

"Yes," Orpah said, "but Chemosh let her go. She did not have to die that night."

Sakira didn't know how to respond. But then she didn't need to after all because a guard appeared at the shop's entrance.

"Pardon me, but King Eglon has requested your presence in his private chamber."

Sakira thought the king was requesting Ruth or Orpah. But when she realized he wanted her, Sakira gasped. "*My* presence?"

"Yes. Right away," the guard answered.

She moved a stack of baskets out of the way and brushed the dirt from her hands.

"I'll come with you, Mother," Orpah said.

"Me too," Ruth said.

The color drained from Sakira's face. She looked at the servant. "Are you certain it's *me* the king wishes to see?"

"Yes, quite certain."

"I haven't spoken to King Eglon since Ruth was born. What can he wish of me now?"

She realized it was a foolish question. She knew the answer. She also knew that, as one of his concubines, no matter how long it had been or how far away he had sent her, she had no other choice but to go to him.

"Follow me," the servant said, "and we will prepare you for presentation."

"My daughters—I cannot leave them here alone."

"They will be fine," the guard said.

"I'll look after Ruth, Mother," Orpah said, sounding sure.

"I won't be gone long," Sakira said, her voice trailing off, thin and unconvincing. She knew not to inquire how long she would be gone. It could be hours. It could be days. And when he was done with her, King Eglon would banish her again. That was fine with Sakira. She much preferred weaving in her small shop, making baskets and being with Ruth and Orpah, to being in the palace with the great, greasy king.

* * *

Elimelech and his family could not see the palace yet, but the city that spread before them felt very different from Bethlehem. For one thing, the ground was red and brown, not dusty white and gray. Also, the trees here had green leaves, and green shoots sprang from earth that was not hard packed and barren.

It was difficult for Naomi to comprehend how God could send so much rain to such people while He allowed His children of the covenant to suffer. The more abundance she saw, the more bitter the taste became at the back of her mouth.

"Look around, Elimelech. These people are happy."

"And you resent their happiness?" he asked.

"I would want all people to be happy, but they aren't."

Elimelech smiled. "My hope is for your happiness, dear wife."

Mahlon and Chilion were like young frolicking bucks. They wanted to stop at every vendor along the roadside, but the only place their father agreed to stop was at one shop, where they could buy their first real meal in Moab.

"Can we afford it?" Naomi asked. "We have so little money."

Elimelech smiled at his wife. "I will soon earn plenty of money. We might as well have a decent meal now."

They bought warm bread and some plump figs sweetened with a drizzle of honey. They ate cucumbers that were sliced right before them and dipped in vinegar. And they ate goat cheese, rich and thick, that felt both sour and soft on their tongues.

The soldiers ate grilled goat and bread, and they drank wine.

"We want wine too!" Chilion called.

"Soon you will have all the wine you can drink," one of the soldiers said. "Soon your father will be employed by the palace." The soldiers exchanged knowing looks, and one held out a wineskin for Chilion.

Later they walked on toward the palace through a maze of colors and textures Naomi could never have imagined. "Everything is so bright." She sighed.

"Would you like to buy a basket?" a girl standing in the doorway of a weaver's shop called to them. "Our mother weaves the most beautiful baskets in all of Moab."

"Yes, she does!" a smaller child cried. "Buy a basket today!"

Naomi looked past them into the shop. Where *was* their mother? She stopped walking.

"Are you alone?" she asked.

"Yes," the smaller girl announced proudly. "I am Ruth, and this is my sister, Orpah."

"We sell our mother's baskets," Orpah said.

"Can I pet your donkey?" Ruth asked, and before her sister could grab her back, Ruth's hand was cupped over Chamor's nose. "Is he yours?" she asked Mahlon.

He looked to his father for permission to answer the girl. He wasn't used to a girl being so forward.

Elimelech nodded.

"Yes, Chamor belongs to our family," Mahlon said.

"We are new," Chilion announced. "My father has an important job working for King Eglon."

"King Eglon is my father," Ruth announced.

Naomi smiled at the girl's fantasy. "Are you hungry?" she asked.

One of the soldiers stepped forward and eyed the girls with suspicion.

"You are the daughters of the king?"

"Yes!" they both cried. "Buy a basket from us, sir."

"Where is your mother?"

"Father summoned her to the palace," Orpah said.

The soldier bought a basket for bread and paid twice what the girls had asked.

"Go buy yourselves some food," he said. "And do not stand out here and call to strangers. Tell no one that you are without your mother. Do you understand?"

Naomi was shocked that the daughters of a king would live so humbly, here, where they would be so vulnerable. "Can we just leave them here, unprotected?" she asked the soldiers.

"We do not interfere in such matters."

Naomi leaned down and looked first into Orpah's and then into Ruth's eyes. "Do you girls need anything?"

"No. Ruth has me to take care of her." Orpah pulled Ruth back into the small hut. "Thank you."

Ruth stared out from the shadows at Mahlon and Chilion. They stared back. And then the soldiers made the family move on toward the palace.

* * *

An hour later, the soldiers announced their arrival at the palace, and a servant ran to inform King Eglon that Elimelech had returned from Bethlehem. Chamor was tethered outside while the family was led farther into the belly of the palace.

At twenty times the size of Bethlehem's threshing floor, it was more than Naomi's eyes could behold. It was lavish, made of smooth, bone-colored stone and gray concrete. Every pillar was covered with green vines that grew purple flowers. The bottoms of its many ponds were dyed indigo so the water looked beautifully blue. Slaves with foreign-looking facial features she did not recognize wore flowers in their hair. Even the men dressed in costume.

Elimelech had told Naomi once that each male servant was charged with the task of keeping the grounds free of leaves and keeping the water churning. Several men stood in the hot sun with huge paddles and bulging muscles.

Naomi noticed that her boys were mesmerized by the frogs that leapt in the marsh around the ponds.

"I've never seen this much water," Mahlon said.

"Except in the sea," Chilion said. "The sea is bigger."

"But it's not blue like this."

Once the soldiers had announced the arrival of Elimelech and his family, they were treated as royal guests and shown hospitality so grand Naomi could scarcely fathom it all.

Elimelech leaned down and whispered to her, "Here I am no simple blacksmith. Here I am an artisan."

In spite of her fears, her resentments, and her alternating feelings of hope and despair, Naomi felt happy to see Elimelech treated with such respect.

"You will come with me," a woman with a veil over her face said to Naomi. "You must be washed to be presented at the table."

Naomi could tell something was wrong with the woman—the way her arm was twisted and the way she dragged her foot and walked like a rag freshly wrung. When the sunlight caught her veil, Naomi gasped. Her face looked as though it had been plunged into boiling oil.

"I am Driann," the woman said. "It is my duty to make all the king's guests welcome."

"I am Naomi. My husband is Elimelech, the swordsmith."

"Yes, we know who your husband is."

Elimelech and the boys were being taken in a different direction. Naomi looked toward them with concern, but they did not even look back at her.

Naomi was not escorted into the palace, but was led to a garden within the walls to bathe separately. The garden was divided from those surrounding it by a wall made of white stone that might have been hauled all the way from Bethlehem.

Naomi's assigned mikveh, or bathing pool used to restore her purity, was more of a pond, bigger and deeper than any she had seen in Judea. It was large enough to cleanse her entire body. The experience was all so overwhelming that panic tightened every muscle in her body. She felt as if her throat were closing shut.

"Are you all right?" someone asked.

Naomi spun around to see another servant, a round, short woman with charcoal lining her eyes holding out clean orange robes for her. Naomi's breath caught in her throat. Her heart pounded, and the servant's face went blurry.

"I was separated from my husband and sons," Naomi cried. "I don't know where they've been taken, and I can't go see them."

The servant rushed to her, a look of distress on her own face. "You must not lift your voice. The king demands the grounds to stay peaceful."

"Elimelech!"

"Please, be silent. Please."

"Mahlon! Chilion!"

Driann limped toward Naomi with an unexpected fierceness.

"Do you wish your husband to lose his favored status with the king?"

Naomi shook her head, feeling embarrassed and ashamed but still panicking that she was so alone.

Driann spoke out of the side of her mouth, where her lips were not scarred together. "Your husband might have astonished the king once, but that does not mean he can't fall out of favor just as fast. Do you understand?"

All Naomi could do was nod.

* * *

Later, when Naomi had bathed and dressed in a new garment the color of a camel instead of orange, Elimelech and the boys reappeared. They too wore clothes that were not their own. Their feet, faces, and hands were no longer coated in dust and grime.

They seemed oblivious to what had happened to Naomi in the women's quarters. Their smiles were wide, and the hospitality feast set before them held more food than Naomi had ever seen in one place.

"All this is for our small family?" Elimelech asked, astonished.

"Enjoy," a manservant said.

Chilion and Mahlon ate until their bellies ached. They had meat and sweet cakes and baskets of bread and dried figs and apricots coated in thick, rich cream.

"This wine tastes sweeter and richer than any I've ever tasted," Elimelech said, clearly savoring everything about their welcome.

It was the first time in their marriage that Naomi was allowed to sit and dine at the same table and at the same time as her husband. She was used to watching the men eat before she took her first bite.

Servants with large feather fans adorned each end of the table to wave away the flies.

Elimelech extended a cup for Naomi. "Customs are different here, Naomi. Please enjoy this. Accept it as your new way of life. A *better* way of life."

Chilion groaned with stomach cramps. "I don't care how bad it hurts," he said. "I never want to leave this place. Moab is wonderful!"

Mahlon laughed and smiled at Naomi. "He's right, Mother. I don't know why you were so afraid to come here."

She nibbled a morsel of date bread and accepted the wine her husband offered. Silently, she thanked God to see her family so happy, so full. Had she been wrong about Moab?

As soon as they could eat no more, a few boys not much older than Mahlon and Chilion came with bowls of shiny pink grease to rub on the family's hands and feet. Its smell was foreign to Naomi, but far from unpleasant.

A maidservant she had not yet seen knelt before Naomi and began to massage the strangely pungent grease into her dry, cracked heels. Another woman took her hand and rubbed the ointment between her fingers, pulling at them, massaging each knuckle with a healer's touch.

Elimelech moaned with pleasure when his shoulders were massaged. At first the twins were shy, but once they relaxed, Naomi had to smile at the way they both closed their eyes, laid their heads back, and stuck their feet out while their sore muscles were massaged.

The treatment ended for the men. Mahlon and Chilion were escorted on a tour of the grounds while Elimelech was taken away to meet with King Eglon.

Panic rose inside Naomi again, and she sat up from the lounge where she was being massaged.

"You have nothing to fear," a tall, lanky man with a clean-shaven face and uncovered head told her. "I am called Lemuel, and I am the chief priest and captain of King Eglon's personal army."

Immediately, Naomi was suspicious of him.

"Your husband will return shortly. The king merely wants your husband to tend to his bothersome tooth again."

Though Elimelech had told Naomi all about how he had packed the king's mouth with honey and honeycomb, it sounded strange to have Elimelech summoned to attend to anyone's tooth—especially that of a king.

"Thank you for your hospitality," Naomi told Lemuel. "Please inform the king of our gratitude."

"Lie back and relax. Enjoy it while it lasts."

What was it about the man that was so unlikable? Did it matter? Instead of fearing the worst like she was prone to do, Naomi relaxed her shoulders and allowed herself to feel a level of pleasure she had never felt. The massage moved to her scalp, where peppermint oil rubbed out the pain she'd been holding for so long. The same fingers quickly braided Naomi's hair into four long strands that were then woven together and pinned up in a fashion she'd never even imagined.

Next, Naomi's face was oiled, including the insides of her ears. Her teeth were cleansed with a mixture of sand and honey. She was not allowed to spit on the royal grounds, but was instructed to spit into the cup a servant held for her. The final touch was a dab of pink salve to color her lips and cheeks.

Even the most stubborn part of her realized that it would not be difficult to get accustomed to this daily treatment.

"It must feel strange to you," the servant whispered, "to be touched like this, but Moab is a land of the senses—unlike Judea."

Driann was back and she was visibly upset. "This woman is a Hebrew!"

The servants drew back.

"Are you not allowed to touch a Hebrew?" Naomi asked, realizing just how little she knew of Moabite culture.

Driann scoffed. "If you're a Hebrew, you shouldn't touch this."

"This?" Naomi asked.

Driann pointed to Naomi's glistening skin. "Swine fat."

Naomi reeled back, mortified. "It's for-for-forbidden," she stuttered.

"To eat it is forbidden," another servant said. "I know your laws because I used to live under the yoke of Hebrew law. But you and your family are no longer under those laws."

"We are still Hebrews!" Naomi insisted. "The law will always bind us." She frantically tried to wipe the pig fat from her face, her arms, and her feet.

"It is seeped into you through your pores," one servant said.

"I am unclean now!" Naomi declared. "Please—please allow me to bathe again."

"No," Driann said, looking almost pleased. "Moab is your new home and it is time you accustom yourself to the laws of pleasure instead of pain."

Elimelech returned angry that evening. Naomi could see his frustration in the tensing of his jaw and the shifting of his eyes.

"Did you see the king?" she whispered as they wound through a great garden of sweet-smelling blossoms and vines, of red rock hedges and flowering fields. The buzz of bees vibrated in the air. She could see the twins laughing and playing with other children across a field.

"Yes," Elimelech finally answered her, keeping his voice low so the servants around them would not hear. "I cleaned rotten meat from the king's foul mouth and stuffed wax in his crumbling tooth."

"What about your job with the royal armory?"

"He has put his chief priest and captain of his personal army in charge of my work."

"The man I saw earlier, the lean one with cruel eyes?" Naomi asked.

"Yes, Lemuel. He despises me and thinks I cannot do the work I came here to do because my hand has not healed properly. He told the king as much."

"But you can! Prove to him you can."

He held out his right hand. The fingers were curled, almost claw-like.

"Can't you straighten them?" she asked.

"If I could, I would."

Her fear was back, its fingers gripping her throat. "If you are not going to be treated with the respect you deserve, if you're not going to have the work you wanted, let's leave now," she said. "Let's turn right around and go back to Bethlehem. This may be our only chance."

"We have no chance! Eglon will kill us all if I defy him. Look behind us. Lemuel already has people watching us." She realized now that servants were on every side, their eyes and ears taking in everything.

"They report back to Lemuel, and he's just waiting for me to make a mistake so he can have me punished."

For a second Naomi thought Elimelech was going to weep.

"I'll prove him wrong," he said. "I'll show the king the kind of work I'm capable of, and it won't matter what Lemuel says or does."

Naomi touched her husband's elbow, but he drew away quickly.

They stopped and watched Mahlon and Chilion running and playing with a band of other boys.

"The one good report I can give you is news that our sons will be included in a learning program the king has just started. He wants the children associated with the palace to learn alongside his own children."

"What kinds of things will they be learning?"

"I understand he is setting up a broad range of opportunities. He's assembling teachers to instruct them in reading and writing and mathematics and astrology. He wants the children to learn architecture and agriculture and even skills like pottery and weaving."

"Only the boys?"

"No. Girls will be included," he said.

"I've never heard of such a thing."

At that moment two military guards motioned for Elimelech to join them while another servant said to Naomi, "I will escort you and your sons to your new home while your husband conducts his business."

That quickly, they were separated again.

"What about Chamor?" Mahlon asked. "We must fetch our donkey."

"He will be brought to your new home," the servant assured them.

The boys were too old to have their hands held, but Naomi's stern looks kept them in line as they moved from behind the palace walls to an area of the city that spread both down the slope and up again. Bethlehem had streets and rows, but nothing as organized as Dibon. There were rows and rows of tiny houses crafted of brown mud, separated by short walls of river stone set with more mud. But the yards attached to each house were hardly roomy enough to grow cucumbers.

Swine and chickens ran together, slopping up the streets. Children chased each other, laughing and shouting, wearing little more than strips of orange cloth.

Orange, Naomi thought, *the color of an angry sun.* This color set Moab apart. It was a reminder tied to waists, wound around arms and foreheads, and waved from posts like flaming flags made to wave away the great God of Israel. Naomi had never known such a storm of emotions. One minute she felt terrified, the next sad, the next hopeful, praying that some good would come of this change. And now she was angry.

"Ama, you're walking too slowly," Chilion complained. "Let us run free and explore our new home."

"No."

"Please, Mother, let us enjoy this day," Mahlon said.

She grabbed hold of Mahlon's shoulder. Her tone was as sharp as it had ever been. "Listen to me! You are no longer safe to run free! And you are no longer little boys. You'll soon be grown. Show proper respect to me and do as I tell you!"

The brothers looked at each other and fell into line like scolded pups.

"We're sorry," Mahlon said. "We just wanted to be happy."

A group of squealing children ran past them, chasing each other, laughing and darting in and out of courtyard gates.

Naomi had to admit to herself that Dibon didn't appear to be a place where children feared being consumed in the fires of Chemosh.

She paused and whispered to her sons, "I am sorry. I'm just afraid."

Chilion's face was purple from the grapes he'd eaten. "What are you afraid of, Ama?"

His eyes were innocent and joyful. Trusting. "I'm afraid of losing you, my sons," she admitted. "You and your father are my world. I could not bear it if anything happened to you."

The boys chuckled. Mahlon took his mother's hand and squeezed it. "Don't be afraid; this is our new home. We're safe here, Mother."

Safe. The feeling was as foreign to her as Moab.

They traveled past street after street: pottery row, basketry row, carpet weaving row, and carpentry row.

"Look how bright everything is," Chilion said, twirling in circles, pointing in all directions.

"Yes," Naomi admitted, "people here value color."

"Especially orange," Mahlon said.

Each step Naomi took felt heavier than the last.

The air was clouded with smoke and the scent of cooking meat. Onions that were rare in Israel were abundant here, hanging in strands from vendor stalls. The aroma made Naomi hungry even though she'd just eaten.

"This is the artisans' row," their guide told them. "You will live in house number 18."

"What's that, Mother?" Chilion asked, crooking his finger at the likeness of a creature with curved horns and bulging eyes and a belly so round it looked as if he'd swallowed an entire basket of grain.

"That is Chemosh, he who subdues our enemies," the servant explained.

Naomi felt sick, realizing that Hebrews were the ones being subdued.

Their escort pulled out a small spear with the head of a woman welded to the top. He thrust it deep into the earth so that it stood in their courtyard like a sentinel. "This is Astarte, who some call Ashtoreth," he said, "the goddess of fertility to Molech."

"Who?" the boys asked in unison.

"These are things your sons should know," their escort scolded. "Molech was the idol that Canaanites worshipped when Joshua brought your people into our land."

Chilion stepped toward the man. "Don't you worship Chemosh?"

"Yes. Here Chemosh is worshipped, but that does not take away the power of other gods."

"We worship Yahweh, the God of Israel," Mahlon said, pronouncing the name with strength. Even though Naomi was afraid, she was also proud of her son.

The escort smiled. "Yes, I know of your god."

"Our uncle Heber worships Baal," Chilion added. "He dances and sings and feeds Baal corn and beer."

"Enough!" Naomi said, motioning for her sons to settle and be still.

The escort gave Naomi a kind look. "Do not be so disheartened, Sister. If you serve her well, the goddess Astarte will bring forth more sons to your family."

Naomi's face went hot, and she clasped each of her sons' hands with a firmness that made them struggle for freedom.

That night, they settled in their new home and put their few possessions away. While the boys tended to Chamor and while Elimelech was still away, Naomi knelt on the unfamiliar earth and touched her forehead to the soil.

"I cannot live here, Lord," she prayed. "To honor my husband, I will stay here, but I will not *live* here. Moab will never be home to me," she promised. "And their gods will never be mine."

9

Yet, Naomi *did* live there. In a matter of days, a routine was established that seemed to please the boys and Elimelech, though it left Naomi feeling half crazed with boredom.

Elimelech was mandated to report at the armory while the boys were mandated to attend the king's ever-changing learning program. Some days the children studied at the temple of Chemosh. Other days they learned to draw letters and numbers in the soft wet sands along the river.

But the twins' favorite lessons were in the military fields, learning to fight and conquer.

A guard came to escort them every morning before the sun rose. Mahlon and Chilion were elated at the chance to train with "real weapons" made of iron and brass.

Naomi felt bitter and angry with this focus on studying warfare, and this resentment she turned on Elimelech. "You told me our sons would learn letters here. You said they would get an education. You did not say they would be training to starve and murder their own people!"

"I don't choose the king's methods. Besides, they're being taught how to fight, not how to fight the people of Judea."

"Those are *our* people, Elimelech. Have you forgotten that already?"

He raised his hand as if to hit her, the first time he'd ever done so. She cowered away from him, tears welling up in her eyes. "We've only just arrived, and everything has changed."

"Changed for the better," he said. "Your belly is full. Our sons aren't just learning how to wield a weapon—they're also learning from scribes and artists and craftsmen in every field. If I had received that kind of learning, I would not be where I am now."

Naomi sat down at a small wooden table and rested her head. "Perhaps it's not too late for you to learn to read and write," she said. She knew this was a sensitive matter with Elimelech. His younger cousin Boaz had made arrangements to teach Elimelech once he became a scribe. But when they moved to Moab, those dreams were dashed.

"I have to leave for the armory," he said without emotion. Then he walked out the door before she could even hand him the bread and cheese she'd packed for his daily meal.

People employed by the king were given an allotment of food that was delivered to their small courtyards each morning. The baskets' contents varied, depending on what fruits and vegetables were in season, and the amounts were meted out according to the number of people in each home. Growing sons were allotted more food than most.

Naomi felt grateful for every mouthful her family had to eat. Despite her gratitude, she still felt lonely and terrified and bored.

Gleaning was not permitted, and it took her hardly any time to sweep and straighten the house. She did plant a small garden and had two trees to tend, an apricot and a fig. These trees grew behind the house, where the communal sewage system ran downhill into a gathering hollow, a breeding ground for the flies that launched a nonstop assault on the small artisans' village. On the hottest days, the stench made her realize just how little King Eglon really valued the people who lived in their community.

The only animal for Naomi to tend was Chamor, and he was a gentle beast that required little care. With a loose rope around his neck, the donkey followed her up and down the steep narrow streets of Dibon as Naomi explored, hoping to make a new friend. But the Moabite women were not eager to associate with a Hebrew.

Naomi *tried* to be friendly. She washed the family's clothes alongside the other women at the washing bins. She shopped in the same markets and watched the same sunrises and sunsets. She even greeted the women in her neighborhood as friends but seldom got a similar response.

Day after day, the schedule never deviated. Naomi felt the same emotions from one day to the next, while Elimelech's moods ascended and descended like the steep steps carved into the mountainous walls of the city. Some days he came home happy and spent time talking with his sons, showing them the work he was doing. Other nights he dragged himself in, seeming worn and angry. It wasn't long before his angry moods became stronger and lasted longer. What made matters worse was that, in time, his bent fingers still refused to straighten.

"At least the king still has you tend to his teeth," Naomi said, "so he still holds you in favor."

"He's not getting better. His mouth is always swollen and sore."

"Surely he doesn't blame you."

"Lemuel whispers in his ear and controls the king in ways I can't explain," Elimelech explained. "Lemuel holds a grudge against me. He refuses to acknowledge my talent and has me do the type of work Father had me doing in Bethlehem back when I was the age of Mahlon and Chilion. I'm little more than a servant here."

She rubbed his sore hand, trying to find sympathy for him.

"Please don't be angry with me, Elimelech. All these months that we have been in Moab while you've been working as hard as a slave, and our sons have been learning skills they never imagined, I have been left alone. It has given me time to think."

She continued rubbing his hand, easing out the stiffness in his crooked fingers.

"I believe I know now why the Lord has not blessed Bethlehem, why He's withheld His favor and protection. I think I maybe even know why we ended up here in Moab, tied to the king's whims."

"Why?" asked Elimelech, learning forward, seeming genuinely curious.

"Because we did not honor our Lord wholly," she said. "Here, the people live and breathe their allegiance to Chemosh. They wear his color and speak in fear and reverence of his power. They also put out idols to remind them of Chemosh during the day. Their prayers sound powerful, and even the women and children know the words and rhythms. Everyone is allowed to worship at the altar of Chemosh," she said, then paused, worrying how Elimelech might react.

"Continue, Naomi," he said. "I can tell you've given this a great deal of thought."

"Well, we Hebrews know prayers. We know the stories of the scriptures. We each hang our mezuzah to remind us of our obligations toward God for His mercy on our people. But are we reminded? Our sons walk by the doorpost and pay no more mind to the mezuzah than if it were a fly."

"I pass the temple here every day," she continued, "and see the likeness of Chemosh. Each time there is a throng of worshippers. Maybe they worship out of fear, but they still do it. Even women and children are allowed to touch the idol, to pray at the altar.

"I have never seen the ark or the commandments or the holy things Moses made available to our people, and I have never been allowed inside a temple," she said, looking down. "The priests and holy men rule our religion, Elimelech. Your uncle Salmon once discovered me alone on my knees, praying in our orchard. Do you know what he said to me?"

"I can imagine."

"He mocked me and told me I had no authority to pray. He said God would never hear such prayers and that I was mocking God by trying to communicate with Him."

"My uncle is an arrogant man," Elimelech admitted.

"He is a priest, yet he secretly wears Baal around his neck. How many other priests do the same?"

Elimelech squirmed, perhaps feeling uncomfortable with his own memories of worshipping Baal. "Your point is clear, Naomi. And it is sadly vivid."

That night they lay on their small rooftop, looking up at the same stars that their own people in Bethlehem could see. Naomi nestled herself against her husband and closed her eyes. Remembering, it was as if she could feel her mother's carved bench, could hear the well watcher's gossipy voice, and could see the street that she'd walked up a thousand times to enter the gate that led to home.

"You're quiet tonight," Elimelech said.

"I was wondering what is going on back in Bethlehem," she said. "I wonder how your father and his new family are doing, and I wonder about Berta and the girls." She sighed. "Do you think Uriel is still working in Jericho? I wish we would receive word from them," she admitted. "And what about Boaz and Kezia and Salmon? We live here with food in our bellies and flesh on our bones, and I wonder how our loved ones in Bethlehem are doing. I fear for them," she said. Then she asked, "Don't you?"

But Elimelech answered with no more than a snore.

* * *

After that night, Elimelech did something that surprised Naomi. He brought home pieces of leather and forged instruments for writing. The tools were thin but heavy, crafted out of iron scraps with tips sharp enough to drive into the leather. Elimelech seemed to become a boy again, excited about learning, and Mahlon was his teacher.

"Each one of these symbols represents an idea," Mahlon explained. "When you put them in order, they tell a complete story."

"I never thought I could learn this," Elimelech said, leaning over Mahlon's shoulder. He stared in wonder at how careful Mahlon's fingers were, how they gripped the pen just so.

"It's not forbidden for women to learn letters here," Mahlon said to Naomi. "In Judea you would have been punished, Ama. But here you will be admired for knowing how to read and write."

Elimelech gave her a nod and a smile. "I think it would be good for you, Naomi. Your mother could only replicate the letters; you will be able to read them."

So the three of them sat around the table while Mahlon took turns guiding their hands, helping them to bury the pen's point and showing how to draw it back into a line or a curve.

After an hour, Naomi could write her own name. Elimelech had trouble gripping the instrument but did not give up until he too could scrawl his own signature.

"All my life I've felt inadequate because I did not know the letters," Elimelech said. "My father knew them but did not see fit to teach me. My uncle Salmon and his son Boaz are expert scribes. Heber never wanted to learn."

"Abba, whatever I learn, I will teach you if you wish."

Elimelech gave Mahlon a long embrace, one that swelled Naomi's heart with a love for her husband she had not felt in a long time. She felt now a sense of the pain and hardships he'd been enduring silently. She vowed then that she would show him more patience, compassion, and support.

But Elimelech's enthusiasm for learning letters did not seem to last. He always came home bone tired. His fingers dropped the pen again and again. And the easier it was for Naomi, the less Elimelech wanted to try.

"I'm making a fool out of myself," he said one day.

"No, Abba, you can do it. You can draw the trickiest designs in your weapons—"

"Not anymore! These fingers are worthless."

Mahlon was a patient teacher.

"Don't try to hold it so tight, Abba. Picture the letter in your mind, and then let the pen take over."

Elimelech tried but tired quickly. When his feeble fingers failed to obey him and his efforts ended in frustration, Naomi took over and made the curves and swirls and lines just like they were meant to be.

Mahlon heaped praise on his mother's developing skill. "Ama, you have a gift. The scribes praise me, but if they saw how accurate your letters are, they would hold your work up as the example."

Her cheeks blushed with pride. "My mother never learned to read or write, yet her depictions of the commandments, the ones she carved into the bench back home, were accurate. Even Salmon said as much."

"I remember that bench," Mahlon said.

"I should hope so," Naomi said. "We haven't been away that long."

"Why don't you carve a bench like that here in Moab, Ama?"

"I will never be the artist my mother was," she said.

"That doesn't mean you can't try."

Naomi decided not to tell anyone, but during her long, boring days, she began to practice writing letters. She wrote the words from the mezuzah in the dirt, only to erase them before anyone could return home and see the scratches of her budding efforts.

* * *

One unusually cold and rainy night, palace guards came for Elimelech, saying, "King Eglon has summoned you."

He followed their torch lights out into the narrow street.

"When will you return?" Naomi called, but the only answer was the howl of the wind.

A whole day passed.

Then another, and another. No word came to inform her of her husband's whereabouts or what he was doing. The sun came back out and the ground turned hard and dry again. The twins were also away at a military training camp. Naomi felt so nervous and bored that she was driven to dip into the collection of coins Elimelech had been saving behind a loose brick in the back wall.

With Chamor's rope in her hand, she led the donkey through the marketplace. It was difficult to believe that they'd lived in Moab so long she'd already made this trek hundreds of times. The vendors all knew her and were pleasant but far from friendly.

She decided to buy onions, garlic, and an armload of leeks so she could make porridge for the night's meal; it was Elimelech's favorite.

The coins he brought home were few in number, but they had added up over time. Naomi had enough money to buy hairpins or new sandals or pottery for the house. But she didn't. She saved their money, hoping it would soon buy their way back home.

Only one shop consistently caught Naomi's attention. It was the first one she'd stopped at on that first day in Moab. Today she stepped into the shop and thought of actually buying a basket.

"Peace, Sister," someone said.

Naomi turned and looked into the face of a woman. Her face was gentle, her eyes so golden that Naomi could not help but stare. In the woman's arms was a baby boy.

"Peace. Are you the weaver?"

"I am."

"I'm awed at how you dye your reeds such brilliant colors and how your designs are so intricate. You've woven the body of a dove in flight right into this basket."

"I am an artist first, before I am a weaver. Forgive me, I am called Sakira."

"I am called Naomi. My husband and sons and I come from Bethlehem."

Sakira smiled and moved her son to her hip. "Yes. I've seen you stroll past here many times."

"I stopped here on the day we first came to Moab. Your daughters were here."

Sakira looked thoughtful. "Yes, I recall that day. It was the only time I've left them alone." She looked at her plump-cheeked baby boy. "My son is called Nathaniel."

"He's a healthy boy, no doubt," Naomi said. "May I hold him?"

Without hesitation—in fact, with a look of relief—Sakira passed the child to Naomi's outstretched arms.

"This is your husband's shop?" Naomi asked.

"No. This is my shop."

"Oh, I have never known a woman proprietor." Then Naomi chuckled. "That day when I spoke with your young daughters, they told me that they are the children of the king."

Sakira blushed.

"Oh, forgive me," Naomi said.

"I should be proud," Sakira said, moving her work from a small tabletop to set out nuts and sweet cakes for the two of them. "There is no shame in being the king's concubine. It is an honor. *I* should feel honored."

Naomi was quiet for a long moment, taking in the fact that this kind woman and her sweet children were Moabites. They worshipped a god that the God of Israel despised. Yet they were also kind and accepting.

"You have a worry etched across your brow, Naomi," Sakira said.

"My husband was summoned by the king's men," she replied. "It's been days, and I have heard nothing from him."

"If anything had happened to your husband, you and your family would have been evicted from your house. King Eglon is known for selecting people, using them, growing bored, and abandoning them, only to do it all again whenever he feels like it."

Naomi sighed. She believed Sakira. Clearly she knew what she was talking about.

Nathaniel's little fingers explored Naomi's face. When he suddenly leaned in to kiss her cheek, she laughed. The sound of her own laughter surprised her; she realized that she hadn't heard it in so long.

The cakes vanished and the mint water ran out. Naomi offered to take Nathaniel with her to go pick more mint by the stream that ran behind her home. That day, an unlikely friendship took root. It didn't matter, Naomi realized, that Sakira wore a likeness of Ashtoreth around her neck or that she wove baskets with Chemosh's image bulging along the sides. Sakira was the kind of friend Naomi would have chosen no matter where she lived.

One evening, when she returned home, Naomi was relieved to see the fire already burning.

"Elimelech!" she called. "You're home. Tell me what happened to you!"

He lifted hollow eyes. "I have become a slave to the palace. The king summons me for odd tasks: fixing his aching tooth, showing his artisans how to set jewels, explaining to Lemuel the exact armor of a solider of Israel."

"He's asking you to be a spy?"

"He's asking me to turn my soul over to the palace, bit by bit," he replied.

She tried to embrace him, to offer her support and concern, but Elimelech brushed her aside. Instead, he hunched by the fire, refusing to eat or sleep, and then got up and left again without saying anything more.

* * *

Soon, mornings found Naomi hurrying through her chores so she could get to Sakira's shop. The shop bustled with life while Naomi's own little courtyard felt empty and lifeless.

"Our children know each other!" Sakira gushed one morning when Naomi appeared with a fat, red pomegranate. "Orpah and Ruth talk all the time about two boys, but I had no idea they were your sons, Naomi!"

Naomi thought for a moment and her lips curved upward. "Mahlon and Chilion talk often of two sisters who are both beautiful and bright."

"Maybe one day we will be family," Sakira said.

The smile slipped from Naomi's lips. *My sons will never marry idolworshipping Moabites*, she thought. *Never.* If they did, there would be no returning to Bethlehem.

Naomi decided she could never allow her true feelings to show. She cared for Sakira, and she grew to love Nathaniel in a motherly way that almost frightened her. The first night the girls were allowed back from their royal schooling, Naomi was astonished at how big they'd grown. Had it really been that long since she'd first laid eyes on them?

Sakira was overjoyed to see her daughters. She embraced them and kissed them and wept at their return. Though it had been only weeks since Sakira had seen them, it had been years since Naomi first laid eyes

on Ruth and Orpah—two years. To Naomi, the two years had passed in
a blur of sand and time: two years of living in a dark dream, doing the
same things over and over and finding no meaning in anything except
seeing her sons grow—and now, in watching Nathaniel take his first
steps.

Orpah, the eldest, reached out to take Nathaniel from Naomi's
arms. He went to her with a squeal of delight and the two danced by the
threshold, sunlight and dust sparkling in the air.

Ruth, the youngest, was an oval-faced girl now whose fingers could
weave almost as rapidly as her tongue could talk. "Oh, Mother," Ruth
said, "we are learning the power of the stars. Father has hired Egyptian
teachers who believe we can predict the seasons by the shifting of the
skies."

"Your father believes many things," Sakira said with a flatness in her
tone. "Now, don't be rude, girls. I want you to meet my friend, Naomi.
Her sons are your friends. They attend the royal school with you."

Ruth said nothing, but her mouth stayed open, and her honey-
colored eyes went wide.

"Who are your sons?" Orpah asked with a shy smile.

"The twins, though they do not look exactly alike," Naomi said.

Ruth dropped the reeds she was braiding and asked, "Mahlon is your
son?"

"And Chilion?" added Orpah. "We know them. They like to tease
us, especially Chilion."

Naomi smiled. "Yes, I can imagine."

After that, the girls pelted Naomi with endless questions about
Mahlon and Chilion. They wanted to know everything about them,
from what foods they favored to what they used to do back in
Bethlehem.

Later, when Naomi was at home with her sons, she told them about
the girls.

Mahlon shrugged his shoulders. "They are the king's daughters. Ruth
is his favorite, and she knows it."

"Orpah is different," Chilion said. "She's more serious. We talk
about what Lemuel could do to strengthen Moabite borders."

"You talk war strategy with a girl?" Naomi asked.

"Orpah's very smart. She listens," Chilion said. "Ruth only talks."

Mahlon made a face. "Ruth is full of life, Ama. She talks because she has a lot to say. She knows something about everything, and she's fearless—especially around her father."

"They seem like very nice girls," Naomi said.

"They are nice," Mahlon said, "—for girls."

"You know," Naomi said, "you could never marry Moabite women, don't you?"

"Why not?" Chilion asked.

"Because we are God's covenant people. We marry those of our faith and our beliefs."

"That's nonsense, Ama," Mahlon said. "That's what Grandfather tried to make Abba do. He tried to make him marry someone he didn't love. He loved you and chose you."

"Our son makes a good point," Elimelech said, grinning as he came inside. "Now, what's for supper? I smell porridge."

* * *

By the time Nathaniel was running around and jabbering his first words, Naomi and Sakira knew each other as well as sisters. Through the throngs of people who came to Sakira's shop, Naomi met other Moabites. Most were kind and friendly, but some were not.

She also met other Hebrews living in Moab. She tried to befriend them, but they showed no more interest in her than did the Moabites.

Most who bought baskets were women who talked of husbands, of neighbors, of food, and of how to make themselves more beautiful. Sakira was an example of beauty. She oiled her hair and wore it with combs made of seashells. She cut and cleaned her nails, she dyed her lips and cheeks with flower petals, and she brushed her teeth with sand grit. Unlike Naomi, who wore the same two dresses over and over, Sakira wore skirts and robes and scarves dyed different colors with unique patterns.

There was once a time when Naomi would have judged such a woman with a cold heart. Now she loved Sakira as the sister she never had.

"I was barely thirteen when the king's men first saw me," Sakira explained one day. "I had no choice in the matter. I was dragged from my father's house and taken to the palace. Then I was prepared and paraded before the king." Sakira nearly wept when she told Naomi this part of the tale. Then she smiled. "But I have a good life," she said. "I have Ruth and Nathaniel."

"And Orpah," Naomi added.

"Yes, and Orpah. She is a wonderful daughter, but I am not her mother."

"You aren't?"

"No. Her mother was also chosen as a concubine. Then, when King Eglon grew bored, he sent her away from the palace like the rest of us. I am fortunate; he set me up with this small shop. But I know that I am not free. Anytime the king summons me, I have to go."

"What became of Orpah's mother?" Naomi asked.

Sakira shrugged. "No one knows. She simply vanished from the palace and left Orpah behind. There was a search, but she was never found."

"Do you think she escaped?"

"I don't think anyone escapes King Eglon's grip for long," Sakira said.

Naomi chewed nervously on her bottom lip, realizing what Sakira was saying. "Tell me about King Eglon. I've seen him from a distance a few times, and my husband still tends to his sore teeth once in a while. But I know little about the man who holds us captive here."

"He's many men in one," Sakira said. "And I don't just mean because he is so fat. There are many sides to him. He can be kind, but he might also have a guard executed for making the smallest error. He despises your people, yet he invites you to live among us because he believes such arrangements will make better relations between our people and yours. He favors Ruth and tolerates Orpah but ignores most of his other daughters."

Nathaniel sat by their feet playing with a pile of reeds, which made Naomi smile.

"What about his queen?"

"She never comes to Dibon, so we've never seen her. There are some rumors that say he had her killed and only pretends she lives in the lower palace. There are other rumors that suggest she is in alliance with the Hebrews and that one day she will help your chief judge bring an end to our peace and plenty."

Naomi had never heard of that. She broke off a small piece of bread and fed it to Nathaniel. "I'm so sorry to hear about Orpah's mother," she said. "But I am so grateful you have taken her in as your daughter."

"She and Ruth are as close as two sisters can be," Sakira said.

* * *

One morning, months later, Naomi stopped in her tracks before she reached the shop. Lemuel and Chilion were standing in Sakira's doorway.

"I thought you were away at military camp," Naomi said as she approached. "What are you doing here, Son?"

"We are on official business," Chilion said. There was a chill in his voice.

Lemuel stepped out of the shop. Behind him came a pale-faced Sakira, holding Nathaniel tight in her arms. "The king has summoned Nathaniel," she said to Naomi. "He's never even seen Nathaniel, and now he wants my son at the palace."

Naomi ran toward her, but Lemuel held a staff out to keep them separated. "This child is the king's son."

"Nathaniel is still a babe." Sakira choked on her words.

"He can walk," Lemuel said. "He is no babe."

Naomi looked to Chilion for help, but the only person he would help was Lemuel; he held the captain's cloak.

"You should be proud of your son," Lemuel said to Naomi. "Chilion has found favor with me. I have taken on the boy's training as a personal challenge."

Naomi wished she could ask Chilion, *When did this happen? When did you become an apprentice to Lemuel?* But she kept silent.

Chilion took Nathaniel, while Sakira grabbed a small basket and shoved a few of her personal items in it. "If I must go, I'm ready," Sakira said.

Lemuel smirked at her. "The king did not request your presence— only the child's. He wants to see his son."

Terror twisted Sakira's beautiful features. "King Eglon has never shown the slightest interest in Nathaniel," she argued. "I had to give birth to him in the back of my shop instead of at the palace. In all this time, he's simply ignored us. And now he summons this child!" Angry and fearful tears glistened in Sakira's golden eyes as Chilion kept Nathaniel away from his mother.

"When will he be returned?" she demanded.

"Perhaps later today," Lemuel said. "Perhaps not."

Naomi walked over to Sakira and put her arms around her shaking shoulders. She had to hold Sakira back as the mother lunged forward after Nathaniel.

"Please, Chilion, give him back!" Naomi pleaded. "Don't take Nathaniel. Can't you see the child is frightened?"

Chilion glared at his mother with eyes so cold and hard she did not recognize them. She watched in shock as Chilion turned his back and took Nathaniel away.

"No!" Sakira screamed.

Nathaniel began to cry. Chilion kept walking, but Lemuel turned around and raised a fist to Sakira. "Silence!" he ordered.

"Silence!" Chilion repeated, looking back at Naomi.

And Naomi saw then what she had refused to see. Her own son was now the spitting image of Lemuel. He carried himself, shuffled his feet, and snarled his lip like the chief captain of the king—enemy to their family.

10

FOR SEVERAL WEEKS, THE SOUND of strange drums and chanting came from the great temple. Naomi was used to the noise, but this night every drumbeat felt like it was thudding against her soul.

How had Naomi ever imagined that her family could live among the Moabites and not become like them? How could she have let an idol of Ashtoreth reside next to the mezuzah that her own mother's hand had written? How had Naomi allowed her writing, her friendship with Sakira, her own full stomach, to push aside her faith in the true and living God?

In the meantime, Mahlon was mastering his letters. But Chilion was closer to Lemuel than ever before. Naomi suspected that the chief captain had selected Chilion not based on the young man's military merits but because selecting him was a way to injure and infuriate Elimelech.

Naomi didn't even recognize her own husband anymore. He seldom spoke, and he vanished for days on end. When he was with them, he was impatient with her and distant from their sons.

This night, Naomi stooped by the fire, feeling more alone than ever. She put her hands over her ears to try to muffle the drums, chants, and screams coming from the temple.

"What's wrong with you?" someone asked.

She spun around to see Elimelech. His eyes were bloodshot and half-crazed with frustration.

"Are you drunk again?" Naomi asked.

He wiped his face with the back of his hand. "No."

Naomi pulled out the bench by their small wooden table, saying, "Sit. I have food for you."

He sat down, and his shoulders began to shake.

Naomi's heart went still. "What is it, Elimelech? Has something happened to one of our sons?"

"God forbid, no," he said. Then he raised his sad eyes to hers. "King Eglon has given me to Lemuel's charge, and *he* has relegated me to chief idol maker."

"*What?*"

"He has taken me away from the armory and has me working in a blacksmith shop, casting idols of Chemosh."

"Oh, husband, I am so sorry. If the king doesn't value your work as a swordsmith, will he allow us to finally leave this forsaken place?"

Elimelech used his good hand to make a fist and brought it down on the table in such a fury that the wood splintered. Naomi lurched back.

"I have designed swords, Naomi. You've seen my sketches. Every design that is accepted by the king is one that Lemuel takes credit for. Since we moved here, the swords of the soldiers are lighter, swifter, and better, but I get no honor. I haven't had an audience with the king in months. Lemuel is my overseer, and he's deemed my talent worthy of nothing more than idol making."

"Let's leave," she whispered. "If we can't run back to Bethlehem, perhaps we can head toward Egypt. Any place would be better than Moab."

He trembled in anger. "You say that, but you do not mean it. I see your cheeks. They are full and healthy. I know that you spend your days with your weaver friend, and you practice your writing, Naomi. Sometimes you forget to wipe the dirt clear after you've sketched your letters." He swallowed. "Our sons are educated. They want for nothing here."

"Chilion is Lemuel's shadow," she protested.

"Yes, and there is no safer place for him. Lemuel is surrounded by guards, even secret guards, watching him night and day. As long as Chilion stays in his favor, he's safe."

"I didn't know, Elimelech."

"There's much that you don't know, Naomi."

"Tell me, then, I plead. Tell me what I don't know that I might be able to help and comfort you better."

"You do not know," he said, "that I am not the traitor to Israel that you think I am. You do not know how truly brave your sons are."

"How can I know such things when no one tells me?" she asked. "Tell me now what you're talking about."

"I can't tell you," he said. "You've become a stranger to me. You judge me. I see it in your eyes. You treat me like I'm a Moabite, like I'm separate and less than you."

"No," Naomi protested, "that's not true."

"It is true. But change is coming," he said. "Those drums you hear tonight are war drums. Chemosh is thirsty for blood."

Elimelech stood up, pressing the heels of his palms against his temples. Fat tears dribbled to his chin then splashed onto the tops of his dusty feet. He turned toward the door.

"Please don't go, Elimelech. It's dark and dangerous out there. You're not safe on the streets."

He paused.

"Maybe if we prayed together," she said urgently. "Maybe if we asked God to forgive us for allowing ourselves to be poisoned here in Moab. Maybe we can repent and turn our hearts toward Him again."

Elimelech looked at her. Light from the flames reflected in his dark eyes, making them seem a terrifying orange. "You do not understand, Naomi."

What did Elimelech mean? Would Mahlon and Elimelech be forced to fight against their own family? Such thoughts had worried Naomi, but she had kept them to herself and had kept on doing her best to worship God in a land where He was most unwelcome.

Before she could beg him to stay, Elimelech was already gone back out into the night.

King Eglon returned Nathaniel after only two torturous days and nights. Then all seemed right again with Sakira and her household.

Mahlon spent most of his time in the palace schools, and Chilion stayed in Lemuel's shadow. When he was at home he showed his parents kindness, but there was a distance between them, a slight disdain.

Finally, Naomi asked, "How can you be so loyal to a man who is ruining your father's life?"

"If Abba's life is ruined, it's his own fault. He is weak," Chilion said loudly enough for his voice to drift up to the roof, where Elimelech slept. "If he was strong, he would stand up for himself. Instead, he allows

Lemuel to push him down time and time again. I've seen it. Everyone has seen it, how he cowers before Lemuel. He came to Moab because he'd found favor with the king, but the king doesn't remember Abba is even alive."

"Never speak of your father with such disrespect," Naomi demanded. "Have you forgotten the fifth commandment?"

"Moses's commandments don't apply here, Ama."

Naomi felt her fingers ball into a fist. She wanted to strike her own son—something she'd never done. "They're not Moses's commandments— they are *God's* commandments."

* * *

Winter brought something unfamiliar to Elimelech's household: snow. There were colder seasons in the high hills, but those were remedied with wool clothes and sheepskin blankets. This new dusting of white power that melted at the touch was something Naomi had seen only from a distance, when she was back in Bethlehem looking across the rivers and valleys to the hills she now called home.

The thought made her shiver.

Shouts of laugher came up the street, and Chilion and Mahlon ran through the gate like little boys again, dancing and laughing and playing in the snow with Orpah and Ruth and dozens of other young people.

"How is your mother?" Naomi called to Ruth.

"Well. She says she hasn't seen you in a while." Ruth's nose was red from the cold.

"And Nathaniel?"

Naomi dropped her shawl, but Ruth was right there to pick it up and brush off the snow. "He's growing. You should come visit us soon."

At that moment, balls of snow flew through the air and pelted Ruth on the back. She whirled around, laughing.

"Chilion!" Naomi scolded.

Chilion, the warrior, shadow to the chief commander, was once again like a little boy. His face was happy, his eyes bright. From the corner of her eye, Naomi saw Elimelech standing at the gate, watching the two brothers laughing, chasing, and enjoying each other, having fun with friends and neighbors like neither had a care in the world.

Moments later Elimelech came inside and found Naomi kneeling in a corner of their small house, asking God to let this day never end. She finally looked up at Elimelech, shyness washing over her face.

"It is so rare to see my family this happy," she explained. "I begged God to let it go on and on."

"I am not like Salmon. I am not telling you not to pray, but I wonder why some prayers are never heard."

Later, as if to prove him right, the gray skies parted and let pale yellow sunlight through. The air remained cold, but the snow soon melted into nothing but mud and memories.

* * *

In the spring when the days grew longer and warmer, Naomi began to venture farther and farther from the house. It seemed like nothing more than a cave now, small and cramped. When she was alone in it, which was most of the time, she felt like a solitary prisoner.

Some days she climbed the winding path above their house, up through other neighborhoods, where the military families resided. She kept climbing until she could see out over the land, until she could spy the glittering white rocks of Bethlehem.

Then she fell to her knees. "Oh, God of Israel, bring me home again. Bring me back home to the land where Your spirit is felt, where Your words carry truth, and where Your promise gives hope."

When she came back down from the hill, Naomi went straight to Sakira's basket shop. Her mouth fell open at the sight that met her this time.

The king's carriage was parked in front of the shop. At least a thousand people must have been gathered around, gawking while the doughy-faced king encouraged Orpah to come take a ride with him, saying, "Hurry now, Daughter. This is your only chance to ride with your father on review."

Naomi could not see how such a thing was possible. The king's rolls of flesh, his yards of fabric, and his entire being took up almost all of the room in the carriage.

"Go ahead," Sakira said. "It's an honor." And she bowed as the king watched.

A guard hoisted Orpah up, and she wedged herself between her father's great thigh and the wall of the carriage. She stuck her face out into the cold wind and wore the expression of someone who had smelled a foul odor.

"Keep a smile on your face," Eglon told her loudly enough for everyone to hear. "This is a prime opportunity for you to attract interest from a potential husband."

Lemuel and Chilion were nowhere in sight, so as soon as the king was gone, Naomi slipped into the shop.

"He's taking her to look for a husband?"

"She's almost of age." Sakira looked down at her trembling hands. "When the king's carriage appeared, I feared he was here to take me away again—or worse, to take Nathaniel."

"Did he say anything to you?"

"No. He only stared at me and said something about Nathaniel to one of his guards. Oh, Naomi, living like this, at the king's mercy, is no way to live."

"I understand," Naomi said, believing she did.

"I fear that Eglon will force Orpah to marry one of her half-brothers. They are too much like King Eglon, aggressive and gluttonous. Orpah would prefer to marry your son—the funny one who stuffs his mouth with grapes and pops them into the air like hurled rocks."

"But our children seem so young."

"I was not much older when the king's men first chose me as his concubine."

The wind stirred up, bringing the smells of wood smoke and baking bread, of cardamom and roasting pig and rosemary.

"Is that your stomach growling?" Sakira asked. She immediately called for Ruth to come out of the back, where she was tending to Nathaniel. Sakira put a few coins in Ruth's hand and sent her out into the market to buy a meal for all of them.

* * *

Later, Naomi was teaching Nathaniel to draw letters in the sand when the carriage returned with Orpah. Inside, the king was fast asleep, his head back, his mouth wide open.

"He was like that for most of the ride," Orpah said to Ruth. "But while I was riding in the royal carriage, I found the sights were different than they are just walking the streets." The girl seemed so strong and steady, but suddenly, Orpah burst into tears and threw her arms around her sister's neck. "He told me that he might give me to a Philistine prince."

"No!" Ruth squealed. "He will never separate us. I won't allow it."

"Stop it, Ruth. There are some things even you can't control."

"You must tell Father that you refuse."

"He'll have me killed. You know he will."

They looked to Sakira, whose mind seemed far, far away. She spoke in a whisper. "I will not be separated from my daughters. I will take you both and run away before I will ever let that happen. Perhaps we can hide in Bethlehem. Naomi, what do you think?"

Naomi tried to imagine how the people of Bethlehem might welcome King Eglon's concubine and her children. "There has to be a better way," was all she could say.

* * *

Time turned over. Some days brought hope. Others were so bleak that Naomi stayed on the roof all day alone.

Then, one day Elimelech was in a rare pleasant mood. His face was flushed, and his step seemed quicker than usual. He even brought home a piece of fresh meat for cooking.

Naomi greeted him at the gate. "Are the boys around?"

"No. Mahlon is still at the school, and Chilion has gone to the west barrier with Lemuel. I saw a familiar face today," Elimelech announced, splaying the meat over the stone closest to the fire and then taking his place at the table.

Naomi set a bowl of broth before him and brought him some bread ground from hearty wheat with bits of rosemary baked into it.

"You've worked hard," he said, noticing the special bread.

"I work hard every day, like you, Elimelech. Tell me, whose familiar face did you see?"

"Ehud came to pay tribute to the king."

"The chief judge was here?"

"Yes. We spoke for a long time."

"Tell me," Naomi said eagerly, "is there any news from Bethlehem?"

"The famine continues."

"But it snowed here in the winter. The streams are full."

"Judea has not been so blessed."

"What more? What of our family and friends?" Naomi asked, turning the sizzling meat over, sprinkling it with some of the chopped rosemary. Because it was pork, she would not touch it, but she held it with a sharpened stick and served it that way to her husband.

"Kezia is not well," he said. "Salmon has taken her to Jerusalem to have her stomach treated."

"I'm sorry to hear that."

"But Boaz is apparently doing very well. He bought the highland property from Heber."

She sighed. "He said he had a plan to buy up every parcel he could. Who did Boaz choose to marry?"

"If he is married, I did not hear," Elimelech said.

"Surely by now he's taken a wife."

"All Ehud told me of Boaz is that he uses the money he makes as a scribe to purchase parcels as others make their exoduses from Bethlehem."

"Who else has forsaken our land?"

Elimelech frowned, his good mood souring. "Is that how you see what I did . . . what we did? You believe that I have forsaken my land, my family, and my God?"

Naomi muttered an apology. "If others have left Bethlehem, to where did they flee? If not here, then where?"

"I don't know." He lowered his voice and motioned for Naomi to lean in closer. "I can tell you one thing Ehud told me: the days of Moabite reign are coming to a close. Our people are ready to revolt."

Naomi drew back. "This is the war news you spoke of before? Because if it is, it is long overdue. All this time, the Moabites have been growing fat on our grapes, on our grain, and on our tribute."

"You are bitter?" Elimelech asked.

"Yes, I'm bitter. I'm angry, and I don't know whom I am more angry at: King Eglon, for his horrible neglect of you; Lemuel, for his cruelty towards you; Chilion, for betraying us; or Ehud, for promising to free our people but cowering before Eglon when he brings him tribute."

"Naomi, you have no knowledge and no right to say such things."

They were about to engage in one of their all-too-common arguments when Chilion came in through the gate.

He was alone and smiling. "I have news."

Elimelech sat back from the table. "Tell us, Son."

"I have earned the king's approval."

"Approval to do what?" Elimelech asked.

Chilion's smile blossomed into a full grin. "To marry his daughter."

"What?" both of his parents cried at once.

"Do not be upset. I know you want me to marry a Hebrew woman. But since the first day we arrived in Moab, I have watched Orpah, and now the king has approved me as her suitor."

Naomi sighed.

"You should be happy for me, Mother. You know what a fine woman Orpah is."

"The last I heard," Naomi said, "the king wanted her to marry a Philistine prince."

"Lemuel made my case. He made the king see how a marital alliance between Moabites and Hebrews will strengthen ties."

Elimelech said nothing.

"You are too young to marry," Naomi said.

"Not now. But soon. In a year or two, maybe three."

"Much can happen in three years," Elimelech said, finishing his meal.

"Why can't you support me? I am happy. I have done extremely well for myself. I am blessed. You should rejoice with me."

"Would you like bowl of broth, Chilion?" Naomi asked, holding out a steaming bowl.

Chilion sat down across from his father. "I know I am talking of dreams. The idea that a simple Hebrew could marry the king's daughter seems hard to believe. But you don't understand. Orpah and I are friends."

"If you marry her," Elimelech said, "the girl by law will become an Israelite. Is she willing to do that?"

"I know the law, Abba. But I don't care about such things."

"You *should* care," Elimelech said. "Our people may be friendly enough right now, but an uprising is coming. And then what will become of a family with a Moabite for a wife and a Hebrew for a husband?"

Chilion looked at him with hard eyes. "Israel doesn't stand a chance of obtaining freedom. Even if the rains come, Moabites will keep Judea in a famine. The Moabites will take what they want, provide only the bare essentials for Hebrews, and destroy the rest. Judea will never be free of famine as long as Moab reigns. You know how strong their army is. Even the Amorites fear us."

Elimelech's eyebrows lifted. "Us? Did you just refer to yourself as a Moabite?"

Chilion laughed nervously. "They've taken us in. They've provided work for you and training for Mahlon and me. One day I will marry Orpah. When that happens, I will be a Moabite by adoption."

Naomi froze as Elimelech drew in a deep breath and let it out slowly. "No. By law, Orpah will become an Israelite."

"Does it matter?" Chilion asked.

Elimelech pushed himself back from the table. "You are a young man now, and I am proud of your accomplishments. I am glad you dream, Son. But yes, Chilion, it matters very much."

11

FOR DAYS, ELIMELECH STEWED. Wasn't it enough that King Eglon had refused Elimelech his freedom? Now that all of his teeth had been pulled, Eglon ate only cream and meat that was ground into fatty gray mush, and he no longer called for Elimelech at all.

Elimelech was forgotten.

Forsaken.

Cast among the slaves of Moab's royal regime.

And wasn't it enough that Lemuel tormented Elimelech or that he played Chilion against him like a pawn in some game? Now the king had gotten it into his head to write the history of his reign on a large black stone so that elements and time could not corrode his glory. So he called for his best scribes, and Mahlon's teacher suggested that Mahlon be considered to work on the project.

"It is an honor, Ama," Mahlon told his mother one cloudy afternoon. "I have studied and worked hard. I have been favored of God, and now I will be part of something that lasts far beyond this life."

"If you want to record the history of Moab," Naomi said, "you will need to record the cruelty, the idol worship, the innocent sacrifices—"

"Stop!" Mahlon interrupted. "Do not taint my blessing, Ama. I am happy here. I have risen above a slave, a servant, or a common laborer. I have even reached a status that lifts me higher than a military officer."

"Are you saying that you're now more important than your father or your brother?"

"Ama, don't allow your bitterness to ruin my happiness."

He sounded just like his father, so Naomi said as much. "Your words are your father's."

"No, Ama. You did not want to move here, yet this is where we live. Moab is our home. It has been good to us. I am sorry that you are so unhappy. But I'm not."

"I'm sorry, Mahlon," she said. "I only know that there is one true and living God, and He does not dwell here in Moab. He cannot and will not bless us as long as we dwell where we do not belong."

A clap of thunder sounded and a soft rain began to fall.

"Look around, Ama. He has already blessed us here."

When Elimelech returned home, it was still raining and Naomi was still upset. Elimelech did not enter through the gate, but bid Naomi to come.

"You should be working," she said. "If Lemuel discovers you've left early, he'll punish you."

"Don't tell me what I already know. Come with me now and make haste."

She left Chamor under the awning of their tiny garden while she hurried to catch up to Elimelech, who headed for the rain-slick, high, rugged hills. When she looked back over the valley at the layout of their neighborhood, at the marketplace, and at the ever-expanding temple, she shivered. It was festival time again, and, in spite of the rain, people were flocking to the temple. Soon the incessant drums would beat, and the people would dance and chant and sacrifice. It was the time of year she despised most.

Huffing for breath, Naomi hurried to keep up with Elimelech.

"I've brought you up here so we could talk without ears hearing everything we whisper," he said.

"It's true. Our neighbors are so close that I can hear them sleep." Naomi breathed in the air, laden with the scent of damp cedar. "What is it, Elimelech? You look so serious."

"I won't do it anymore."

"Do what?"

"I will not make another idol for the king."

He unfurled the fingers of his strong left hand to reveal a small bronze statue in the exact image of Chemosh. It was polished and detailed and looked almost like a doll resting in the hollow of his palm.

"This is the work you've been doing?"

"Yes," he said with shame in his voice. "I've made nine hundred of these so far. There will be one soon in every household." He slipped the idol back into his pocket. "I saw him this morning."

She waited, uncertain.

"I saw King Eglon. He came by the blacksmith shop to review the work we're doing."

"And?"

"And he praised my idols. I showed him a sword I have been working on. It's a short sword with a double edge. The hilt fits a man's hand, and the swing cuts through the air sharper than any sword there is."

"I thought you were not allowed to make swords."

"I've made it when Lemuel was not around."

"What did the king think?"

"He thought it was excellent, but then Lemuel showed up and was furious. Lemuel accused me of stealing the materials to make it." He sighed. "It's not difficult to change the king's mind, and his praise for me soon turned into fury."

"What happened then?"

"Lemuel told the king that other men could replicate my design. So the king gave me a commission to design a new likeness of Chemosh. He told me that *I* should be a bond between his people and mine."

Naomi touched her husband's cheek, stroked his beard and thought how gray it looked in the dim light. "What do you think Eglon meant by that?"

"He meant that my gift from our God is fortifying his god's strength. He believes that a renewal of Chemosh's power must surge through Moab. So he's commissioned me to help make thousands more of these idols, idols small enough for every Moabite to carry, to pray to at any time, and to sacrifice to at will."

"Isn't that what you've been doing?"

"Yes and no. Not with this new allegiance to Chemosh. King Eglon is afraid. I saw the terror in his eyes. He's heard the rumors about how Ehud's army is building; he knows that our people are readying themselves to retaliate."

Naomi's heart jumped. "Is it true? Is it finally true?"

"It is true. But it is also true that Moabite soldiers in Judea are killing our people at will. Hundreds of lives have been taken so far." He took a deep breath, held on to Naomi by both shoulders, and said, "Naomi, Moabite monsters killed Salmon."

"No!"

"They accused him of being a spy and stabbed him to death in front of Kezia."

"How do you know these things? Maybe the news is not true."

"It is true. I heard it from Boaz himself."

"Boaz is here in Moab?"

"He was. He accompanied Ehud to deliver tribute for the festival. You were right," he suddenly said. "We *are* consumed by this place. Salmon was also right. I have betrayed my God."

Naomi threw her arms around Elimelech and clung to him while they both wept.

He pulled back and said, "I am taking my family back to Bethlehem."

"They might kill us."

"Yes. But it is better to die going home than to live staying here."

These were the very words she had waited for and hoped to hear for years. But now that Elimelech had said them, Naomi felt afraid.

"Chilion and Mahlon won't go," she said.

"I am their father. They will do as I say. I've told you before that war is inevitable. In spite of their strength and their numbers, the Moabites have been losing farming territory to the Ammonites. The Philistines are bringing reinforcements over the great sea, and some of their enemies are never peaceful."

"What about the children of Israel—our people? If they attack Moab, surely *we'll* be killed."

"Eglon announced today that there will be no more school for the children of Moab—only military training. He wants to build up his forces as fast as he can." He smiled. "I am not the weak slave to Lemuel that my sons think I am. I am also not the traitor to God that you think I am. One day you will know that."

"I love you," Naomi said. "We've grown so far apart, and yet I love you. You are my husband, and whatever we can do, we will do together."

"We can start with this." He unfurled her fingers and placed the tiny idol in her palm.

They both smiled now as Naomi drew her arm back and flung the statue through the air and watched it splat in the mud.

* * *

For a couple of weeks, Naomi was feeling both fearful and hopeful, until she encountered Elimelech on the road, trembling and drenched with sweat.

"What is it? What's wrong?"

"I got caught stealing," he said.

Naomi's stomach boiled. "Stealing what?"

"My own work."

"I don't understand. You stole something you made at the shop?"

"Yes. I've been working on it for a very long time. I took it so I could pass it along."

"Along to whom?"

"Ehud has spies placed carefully throughout all of Moab. There's so much that I can't tell you because it is safer if you don't know."

"I'm beginning to realize that now," she said. "But why would you steal something you made? Was it the idol you hold in your hand?"

"No."

"Then what?"

He patted a round sword handle wrapped in a piece of leather and tucked into his belt.

"One day you will know that your lowly husband attempted to change the course of the war between Moab and Judea."

She waited for him to go on.

"It turns out that Hebrews aren't the only spies in the land. This morning, one from Moab was placed at the blacksmith shop, and he caught me in the act."

"I don't understand. If you were caught, why aren't you in prison—or worse?"

"Because the spy who caught me is our son, Chilion."

The news cut like a dagger through Naomi's heart.

"If he tells Lemuel that I took the short sword, I'll be killed," Elimelech said as calmly as if he were telling her the sun was going to rise tomorrow.

"But Chilion didn't report you?" she asked.

"No."

"Then he won't. No matter how loyal he is to Lemuel, our son will never betray you, Elimelech."

They were almost back home when a woman careened around the corner in front of them. She slid and nearly fell on the slick stone path.

Naomi rushed to steady the woman.

"Ruth? Ruth! What is it?" Naomi asked. "You're out of breath!"

"It's Mother! Please, you must help her."

"What is it?" Elimelech asked.

"Nathaniel. They've taken him!" The girl's face was red and covered with sweat, and her entire body shook. In her hands was a piece of worn leather.

"Who has taken your baby brother?" Naomi asked.

"Father's men. Soldiers. His captain. I don't know who took him. All I know is that they ripped Nathaniel from Mother's arms and she's gone mad."

Elimelech offered his elbow for Ruth to hold on to until she could catch her breath.

"This happened before. They will return him," Naomi offered.

"No," Ruth said. "You don't understand. This time is different."

"Where's Orpah?" Elimelech asked.

"She went to the palace. She's trying to find Nathaniel."

Elimelech had met Sakira and her children. But now he looked confused. "The king, your father, has taken his own son?"

"Yes. Mother has gone to the palace, but the guard at the gate won't let her in. He's threatening to kill her. Oh, Naomi, please go help Mother!"

"I'll go," she said.

"Wait!" Elimelech cried. "Eglon has a right to his own son."

In the distance the festival drums began to beat.

"You don't understand!" Ruth screeched. "Father isn't interested in Nathaniel's growth or learning. He claims Chemosh has demanded a personal sacrifice from him. He intends to make Nathaniel the first sacrifice of the festival."

Naomi's blood went cold. "He's the baby's father! That will never happen!"

"You're wrong," Elimelech said solemnly. "It has happened before. And if the king thinks that Chemosh is demanding a greater sacrifice to protect Moab, he won't spare even his own."

"What can we do?" Naomi asked, holding a quaking Ruth.

Elimelech stood tall and issued orders with an authority that surprised Naomi.

"You will go to the gate and try to calm the mother before she gets harmed. I'll go see what I can do."

"Thank you!" Ruth cried.

"It will be all right," Naomi said, but her words felt as hopeless as her own heart.

Mahlon came charging toward them, running right for Ruth. "I heard the news from Orpah. What can be done?"

She pulled away from Naomi and sobbed in front of Mahlon. "I don't know. Father may sacrifice Nathaniel!"

"I'm going now," Elimelech announced. "Take this and hide it," he said to Mahlon. He twisted the short sword in the leather and passed it to Mahlon.

"Father, it's not safe for you. Lemuel—"

"Forget Lemuel! The man has caused me nothing but hardship. If the baby can be saved, he will be."

A memory flashed across Naomi's mind of a much younger Elimelech, vowing to save a girl called Abella. Naomi saw her husband's bravery and wanted to embrace him but didn't. She stood alone and watched as he hurried off. Then, as she watched Mahlon comforting Ruth, she realized that this girl and her sister already felt like family.

When they arrived, Sakira was at the gate. Only she wasn't acting crazy. She was on her knees, her forehead against the hard-baked earth.

"Sakira. I'm here." Naomi knelt beside her and looked deep into her friend's swollen, red eyes. They seemed vacant. "Elimelech and Mahlon are doing all they can to retrieve Nathaniel. Come with me now."

An armed guard nodded his encouragement. "Go now. Don't ask for more trouble."

Sakira did not resist. Dragging her bare feet over the uneven stone paths, she allowed Naomi to walk with her all the way back to Naomi's home on Artisans' Row.

The music from the temple grew louder, the festival drums pounded, and people everywhere bustled about, excited for another chance to beg Chemosh for protection and prosperity.

"May Chemosh's blessings be yours, Sisters," a woman carrying purple spring flowers greeted them.

Naomi took Sakira inside and tried to care for her needs. Sakira drank the water Naomi offered her. She fingered the necklace that hung from her throat. Naomi realized that it was one of the idols Elimelech had designed.

"I should be honored," Sakira finally said in a tone that was so void of emotion it was unrecognizable. "I should be honored that my son was chosen as tribute."

"No. Don't think like that."

"His eyes are brown. That's why."

"What do you mean?"

"When King Eglon called me to his chambers after all those years, he told me that he wanted me to bear a son with golden eyes like mine—like Ruth's—but Nathaniel's eyes are common brown like Eglon's. That's why he can lay our baby on the altar."

"No father can do such a thing."

"You don't know the appetite of Chemosh; it's ferocious. That's why Eglon eats and eats and eats; he wants to be like Chemosh, who is never satisfied and who demands innocence, virtue, and blood."

Naomi didn't know what to say. She didn't know what to do. Could anything be done if the king's mind was decided? Then she remembered Abella.

"Once," Naomi said, "my husband rescued a girl from Chemosh's grip."

"And do you know what became of her?" Sakira asked.

"My father-in-law married her mother. As far as I know, they are a family in Bethlehem."

"There is nothing that can be done to save Nathaniel if Eglon's mind is decided."

Fighting back her tears, Naomi said, "I will trade my life for the child's."

"Your life would not be a sacrifice of innocence, my friend. My baby's pure and innocent life is exchanged for a full harvest and armies strong enough to fend off our enemies. I should be honored that my child has been chosen."

Sakira's eyes went blank and she began to rock back and forth, her arms folded around her knees in front of her, as if she were cradling Nathaniel and offering him comfort.

"Hush now, Son," she said to the imagined child. "Don't be afraid. It will all be over soon enough."

By the time the sun went down and the flames rose up, Sakira's mind seemed to have melted. Naomi did not know what more she could do but tend to her anguished friend and pray to a God who had never seemed so far away.

"Forgive us, Lord. We have turned away from Thee. But it is not for us we ask a blessing this night—please, please, I beg, spare the life of Nathaniel."

Naomi paused as she heard the sound of footsteps approaching through the darkness. Someone was at the gate. Naomi rushed forward with the torch and gasped at the sight.

Elimelech lay limp and bloody as he hung over Chilion's back.

"I found him in a ditch by the temple," Chilion said. "His leg is broken and there are angry burns on his back, as if he's fallen into a fire pit."

"Lay him gently on the table, Chilion. Send for a physician. I can't set his leg by myself."

Naomi had to step around Sakira, who was still curled into a ball, hugging her own legs as if they were her child.

"Who did this to your father?" Naomi demanded, struggling to light a torch.

"Lemuel and his men," Chilion said.

You are one of Lemuel's men! she wanted to cry but bit back the accusation. When she set the torch in place, she saw the damage to her husband's face. "It looks like someone crushed his face with a rock."

"It was foolish of Abba to think he could save a child that was not meant to be saved."

Sakira began to hum, rocking as she did so.

"Is her mind gone?" Chilion asked, pointing his chin at Sakira.

"I fear it is. Any mother's mind would rather leave before it could grasp what has happened to Nathaniel. Tell me, Chilion, that the king changed his mind and that Nathaniel is still alive."

"I can't tell you that, Ama. But I have to leave now."

"You can't go!" she said. "You have to stay and help me tend to your father. He needs you!"

"Father will be fine. I'll send for a physician to set his leg."

"Please don't go!"

His eyes narrowed. "I have other duties."

"Duties to Lemuel."

"Yes, to Lemuel. He's the one man who believes I am meant for greatness."

"Your father and I have always believed in you. Take a good look, Son; this is what your father has sacrificed so that you can be a mighty man in Lemuel's army."

"You make little sense, Ama."

"Do you know where Orpah is?" she asked, washing the blood from Elimelech's face, grimacing at what was left of his nose.

Chilion's face went pale. "Why do you ask?"

"She went to the palace to find Nathaniel, but she should be here with her mother while I tend to my husband."

"I will look for her at the festival," he promised, looking worried.

Naomi listened. The drums were still pounding. The songs for Chemosh were still rising in the air. Elimelech groaned, and she put her cheek next to his. "I'm here, husband. I'm right here for you."

"I will send a physician," Chilion repeated.

Naomi measured her words carefully. "No matter how much orange you wear or what kind of sword you wield, no matter what god you pray to, you will never be a Moabite, Son."

Chilion rolled his eyes and spat on the ground by her bare feet, defiling their family courtyard. "You've always been so bitter, Mother. Perhaps if you had given Father your support instead of your opposition, things would have fared better for him here."

Just then Orpah crashed through the gate, alone and sobbing, dressed in orange with purple flowers laced through her hair. She stopped and looked at her mother on the ground before her eyes went to Elimelech, lying limp and broken on the table, and then to Chilion.

Chilion looked into Orpah's eyes, saying, "I swear to you, I did not know about Nathaniel."

She nodded in relief, squeezing his hand quickly as he left. Then she sat down and kissed her mother's forehead and asked Naomi, "Is she all right?"

"Her mind can't take in what has happened."

Orpah stood and gave Naomi a quick hug. "How can I help?"

"My husband's leg is broken. Chilion promised to send a physician. Oh, Orpah, I fear that Elimelech has lost too much blood."

Orpah kissed the small idol around her neck, a likeness Elimelech's talent had crafted. She held it skyward and began to pray, "Oh, Great Chemosh, heal this man with your power."

"Stop!" Naomi screamed, ripping the necklace off Orpah. "I would rather have my husband die than have him be saved by the power of Chemosh! Don't you understand that we are Hebrews? Your god is not our God! It is Chemosh who has caused all of this!"

Orpah reeled back. "I—I'm sorry. But Chemosh is the only god I know."

When the physician arrived later, the smell of wine was on his breath. He examined Elimelech's leg. "I can set it, but it will not heal straight."

"Do what you can, please," Naomi begged. "Help my husband."

Orpah did her best to secure Elimelech's arms while Naomi helped the physician set and splint the leg with bark and rope.

"Can you stop that woman from humming?" the physician barked. "It is distracting me."

Orpah whispered something to her mother, but Sakira did not hear her. She continued to rock and only increased the volume of her humming.

"Do you have pain powders for my husband?"

"No. I have nothing. I'm sorry. If the man lives through the night, perhaps I can send something by tomorrow."

Naomi nodded and thanked the man. Then she pulled her stool close to Elimelech and kissed his battered hand.

Orpah boiled mint tea and ground grain for cakes that no one ate. "You love your husband very much," she said.

Naomi nearly wept as she replied, "Very, very much."

The air became thick with ash and the scent of grilling meat. Music pulsed as thousands of voices chanted their allegiance to Chemosh.

"I think my heart might turn to ash this night," Naomi finally said. "It feels dead."

Orpah kissed Naomi's cheek then sat on the ground next to her mother and sang a lullaby to a baby that was not there.

Mahlon rushed through the gate just as Naomi began to doze off.

"Abba! Who did this to him?"

"Lemuel and his men."

"I will kill them!" Mahlon said, raising the short sword his father had given him.

"Put that away before the soldiers see it. Hide it, Mahlon. We cannot afford any more trouble than we already have."

Mahlon did what he was told. He removed some of the loose bricks and hid the short sword where Naomi kept her few coins.

"How can I help Abba?"

"He's unconscious from the pain. So you can pray for him, Son. Pray that our God will hear and answer our pleas."

Cheers went up from the temple. Thousands of voices called, "Chemosh! Chemosh! Chemosh!" Rumbling from the dancing feet shook the table where Elimelech lay.

And then the terrible cheer that meant a sacrifice had been made seemed to split the air.

For the first time since she moved to Moab, Naomi felt the power of Chemosh. She knew now that the metal idol was indeed powerful, strong enough to reach its way across the temple grounds, up the narrow streets that led to their courtyard, and into her chest until it ripped her heart in two.

Orpah held her mother, who rocked faster, hummed louder, but found no song in the world that could drown out the horror of this night.

Then, through the smoke and blackness came a sound that spun them all around.

"Mother!" cried a little boy's voice.

And there was Ruth in the gateway, holding Nathaniel tight in her arms.

The rescue story Ruth shared was simple, tragic, and heroic. Elimelech had sacrificed himself to distract Lemuel away from King Eglon so that Mahlon and Ruth could reach him and reason with him. While Lemuel and his men were breaking Elimelech's bones, Ruth was on her knees, bowing before the king, begging him to spare the life of her brother.

"What about you, Mahlon? You had the sword."

"But I did not have to use it. I would have, though. I would have killed King Eglon himself if he had not heard Ruth and agreed to her pleas."

Naomi hardly dared to ask, "Was another child sacrificed in his stead?"

"Yes," Ruth said. "Another son of the king from a different concubine."

"Of course," Naomi said without any visible emotion, but inside she felt sick.

Sakira's mind did not return with Nathaniel. She held him. She bathed his cheeks with her tears, but she continued to rock and hum and stare blankly into the distance.

The family stayed that first night, but in the morning, Orpah took her mother and brother back to their home while Ruth stayed beside Naomi.

"I am here for you. Let me know what you need."

"I need camel's milk to bathe the wounds, and I need river leaves to cover them."

"I'll go get those things," Mahlon volunteered.

"No, please, stay here with your father," Naomi said. "You are strong enough to hold him when he stirs."

"I'll go," Ruth offered. She left and came back later with a pitcher of thick yellow camel's milk. She stayed with Naomi and did not flinch at the sight of blood or the raw, angry line of infection.

She also made a porridge of onions and leeks that they could dribble down Elimelech's throat. Then Ruth crushed pomegranate seeds and put the sweet red liquid to Naomi's lips.

"You need strength too," she said.

Naomi saw the looks Mahlon exchanged with Ruth. It was obvious now that the two had an undeniable bond, and something changed in Naomi's heart. If her son wanted to marry a Moabitess with so much goodness in her, Naomi would not be opposed to his choice.

The bread Ruth baked was sweetened with honey. After she saw that Naomi ate, Ruth crept out again. Hours passed before she returned, her basket filled with mud and damp leaves from the river. These they used to bandage the open wounds on Elimelech's face, arms, legs, and especially those on his back.

Chilion came by with swine fat in a jar. "To swab the burns."

"It will only hold the heat in," Naomi argued.

He spoke to Mahlon in whispers and left without saying good-bye.

The second night of the festival was quieter, with the rituals dedicated to Ashtoreth. Naomi hardly paid attention because she was focused on bringing down Elimelech's rising fever.

Ruth stayed beside her while Mahlon fetched a basket of cool mud from the high streams.

"Don't put the mud right into his wounds," Naomi said. "Let it rest on top of the leaves."

"Yes, Ama."

Chilion stopped by the gate at sunrise. "I thought he'd be conscious by now."

"His eyes have fluttered a few times," Ruth said. "He's moaned in pain, but I don't even think he knows we're here."

Chilion held out a small earthen vessel. "This is vinegar the physician told me to bring. He said you should wash the burns with it."

"With vinegar?"

"For the infection."

"I'll try anything."

Ruth helped Naomi soak the leaves in vinegar, then they all wrapped Elimelech like a mummy. But when the leaves dried, they pulled away large bits of Elimelech's cooked skin.

The next day Naomi realized that although Elimelech's head was so bruised, there was little swelling.

The physician returned and brought some pain powders.

Mahlon paid him, and the two talked privately. When Mahlon came back he averted his eyes from Naomi's. She did not ask him what was wrong—she already knew.

For a long time Ruth held Naomi while she silently cried.

That evening, the festival-goers burned crops they'd stolen from Judea. The air smelled of corn and wheat.

Chilion appeared again at the gate, saying, "I've brought you food from Orpah and her mother."

"Don't stand outside like a stranger; come in," Naomi said.

Ruth rushed to help set out the goat stew and almond cakes.

Mahlon tried to make his father sip a few spoonfuls of the broth, but Elimelech choked and had to be patted on his burned back to help him catch his breath.

"When the festival is over and the noise dies down, maybe then your father will get the uninterrupted sleep he needs to heal," Ruth said.

"Maybe," Mahlon said. He himself had not slept since his father had been injured.

That night, a slight breeze suddenly turned into a full windstorm. They didn't dare move Elimelech because of his severe burns. But ash and soot and dirt blew through the air, and it became almost impossible to keep tiny pebbles from sticking to Elimelech's burned and battered flesh. They kept him covered in damp leaves, and the next morning Ruth and Mahlon helped to pick out the gritty pieces of rock and dirt.

Suddenly Elimelech's eyes flew open.

"*Ka'lah*," he said.

Naomi was at his side. "Yes, yes, I'm here, my *ishi*."

She dipped her fingers into her best olive oil and rubbed it onto Elimelech's parched lips.

"I am not worthy of you," Elimelech said.

"I'm here for you. What do you need?"

"We're all here for you, Abba," Mahlon said.

Elimelech seemed to look around him, but his eyes did not fix on any one thing or on any particular face.

"Mahlon?"

"Yes, Father. I'm right here."

"Chilion?" His gaze darted about.

"Chilion was here, but he's not here right now."

"Tell him that I forgive him."

"Forgive him for what?" Naomi asked. "He's the one who found you beaten by Lemuel's men." In that horrifying instant, she realized again that Chilion *was* one of Lemuel's men. But he couldn't have had anything to do with his own father's beating. No. The thought was absurd, and she drove it from her mind.

"I defied my God. I turned my back on my own people."

"No. No, Elimelech, you did not. Now stop struggling and use your strength to heal."

He battled to sit up, and Mahlon held a cup of water to his lips. It was impossible for him to swallow.

Ruth stayed between Naomi and Mahlon, fetching water, a damp cloth, fresh leaves, or whatever they needed.

Elimelech's eyes fought to stay open, but he was too weary and the pain was too much. As the day wore on, he became even weaker.

"I have mistreated you," Elimelech told Naomi. "I have not been the husband, the father, not even the son I should have been. Can you bring my father to me? I want to beg his forgiveness."

"No, Elimelech. Aharon is back in Bethlehem, married to Gila. Don't you remember?"

Elimelech's dark eyes refused to focus, and it was difficult to tell who he was addressing. It was a challenge to make sense of all he said.

Later, Chilion appeared with fresh leaves and more pain powders. "I got these from the king's physician. They are very strong."

"Son? Chilion?"

Chilion fell on his knees. "I'm here, Abba. Your entire family is here with you."

"My sons. My wife. My God."

"Rest now, *ishi*," Naomi urged.

"Tell me you forgive me, *ka'lah*. At least send me away with that."

"I forgive you," Naomi said, fighting back tears. "I love you." She laid her lips against his fevered forehead. His left hand reached for Mahlon and his twisted right hand for Chilion. And Elimelech died with his eyes still wide open.

12

KEEPING THE TRADITIONS OF HER people, Naomi tore her dress at the right side. She ripped and tugged until the fabric rent, symbolizing her grief as well as her faith that Elimelech's soul lived on. Naomi might as well have torn her heart, for it, too, was in tatters.

She did not see the worn, broken man who lay there dead: When she looked at Elimelech, she pictured the boy she had fallen in love with—the lad who ran through the markets of Bethlehem, gathering food to make broth for his sick mother. She saw the young boy who had tried all his life to win the approval of his father and died believing he'd failed. She saw the young man who had chosen her over the wealthy, respected, petite, and beautiful daughter of a judge. She saw the husband who had climbed a tree whose branches were filled with bees to bring homeycomb for her parched lips. She saw the only man in Judea willing to risk his life to save a kidnapped child. And she saw the anguished soul, disappointed at life's allotment—her husband, protector, and provider.

Elimelech was all of these and more. And now he was gone.

"God!" she screamed at the heavens. "Why is it you punish the faithful and reward the vile? Why do you let your own people starve while the fat king of Moab stuffs himself? Why do you take a husband when he is so needed?"

Her sons and neighbors let her rant until she wore herself out demanding answers from a silent God. Then Naomi drew in a long breath, leaned over, and gently closed the eyes that had seen only the best in her.

"We have to leave," she said, weeping. "We have to leave *now* for Bethlehem. Your father would want his bones buried with his mother's."

She turned at a sound and saw Mahlon and Chilion rending their garments over their hearts, showing their respect for the ways of their people.

"Oh, my dear sons! You've lost your father."

And her heart broke in another place.

"Mother, sit. You look ready to fall over." Mahlon guided her to sit on their small, unadorned garden bench while he and Chilion eased Elimelech's body from the table, where he had been tended while he lay suffering.

Quickly, she rose, as if she'd forgotten something, and went into their small home. She came out with a folded white cloth. With a billow of linen made for such an occasion, the twins covered their father for the final time.

"You're unclean now," Naomi said. "You've touched the dead."

Chilion shot his mother a harsh and resentful look. "Your laws, your endless laws, mean nothing now."

"No. They only mean nothing to *you*—to me the laws of Jehovah govern my life." Ruth sat beside her while Naomi buried her head in her folded arms and wept as quietly as she could.

In time, some neighbors came who had hardly ever spoken to Naomi. One afternoon, a neighbor she had seen but never spoken to brought a string of fish. "In death we are all one," he said before he hurried off.

A blank-eyed Sakira holding tightly to Nathaniel's hand also came with Orpah. They brought tallow candles to burn next to Elimelech's body. Naomi lifted her head, and Nathaniel climbed up on her lap.

"Oh, little one," she said, "you've been spared—but for how long? This land is so hard and cruel."

"Sad?" he asked in his little voice. He reached up and kissed her cheek.

"Yes," she said, "I am very sad."

"Why?" he asked, but a butterfly fluttered into the courtyard, and he slid down from Naomi's lap and ran to chase it.

"What more can I do for you?" Ruth asked, touching her hand.

"You've been so kind, Child, so very kind." She wanted to stand but her legs would not lift her. After she had talked to so many people, her tongue felt like a blank piece of parchment.

Elimelech was dead, and her sons were young men.

Mahlon leaned down and whispered, "The shomerim are here."

The keepers of the body had come—men who volunteered to stay with Elimelech's body because a corpse could not be left alone. It was the law, even in Moab.

A man called Dan, broad-shouldered and soft-spoken, stood with his hands folded. "I worked with Elimelech," he said. "He was my friend, and I am here to help in any way I can."

Naomi looked up at him and smiled her gratitude. "I wish I had known that my husband had a friend, but of course he did. Please know that you are welcome here."

"You can take a rest now, Mother," Mahlon said. "We will take over from here."

"I will not leave my husband," Naomi vowed, "not even in death."

But after a very long time, her eyes closed, and she slept. She woke later, when she felt a hand on her shoulder shaking her. Only the shomerim remained; the neighbors and Sakira and her girls were gone. There was no soft kiss on the cheek or squeeze from Nathaniel's little hand to comfort Naomi now.

Chilion put a plate of food before her. "Mother, you have not eaten in days. It's important to keep up your strength."

"I have no need for strength."

"But *we* need you to be strong. Do it for us, Mother," Mahlon said. "Chilion and I still need you."

"You're grown now," she said to Mahlon. "Your brother is a soldier, and you will soon be a teacher in the palace. You have no need of a mother who knows nothing."

"That is not true, Mother." Mahlon knelt before her and put his head in her lap. "You know the laws of God, and you are learning your letters. You know much about life that you still need to teach all of us."

"I know only that God is angry with me and has punished me by taking my husband and your father."

"Eat now, Mother," Chilion said with a voice that was still bitter somehow. "None of us can speak for God."

"I will not eat now," she insisted, "not in front of the dead. It would show great disrespect."

"More laws," Chilion said. "It's always about laws with you."

Was Chilion right? The laws around Naomi felt like so many ropes pulling tighter and tighter.

"Are you all right?" a young woman said. "I've brought you mint tea and dried apricots."

"Ruth! I thought you left."

"No. I was just resting upstairs. I hope that's all right."

"Yes! Please, yes. Stay. How is your mother?"

Ruth fought back tears. "We are fine. Nathaniel has been spared—at least for another year."

"You can't mean—"

"I cannot speak of anything that might bring the wrath of Chemosh to our family. We must rejoice that we have been spared—for now."

Naomi held tightly to Ruth's hand. "Mourn with me, then. Be by my side."

"We are not permitted to mourn death," Ruth explained.

"I don't understand, Child. Every loss requires mourning."

"Chemosh is the giver of life and the taker of life. To mourn death means to doubt his wisdom."

"How can an idol fashioned of metal have wisdom?" Naomi asked.

"Please, do not say such things about Chemosh."

"But your people honor Father Abraham—I know they do."

"Yes," Ruth admitted.

"Well, we believe that God Himself comforted Isaac when Abraham died. We share in grief to make the burden somehow less. It is our duty."

"How do you share in grief? Teach me, and I will do my best."

"You have already done it, Ruth, just by being here and by caring. We mourn by doing just what you've done: We sit together. We weep together."

"We are not allowed to show our sadness, not for death."

"I am sorry," Naomi said. "I am sorry for so many, many things, Child."

Orpah brought Naomi more food, though the first meal she had brought was hardly touched.

"Is your mother all right?" Naomi asked.

"Yes, she is with Nathaniel. They are resting."

"Praise be to God," Naomi said.

Orpah gave Naomi a strange look as if to ask, *How can you praise your god at a time like this?*

While Orpah sat with Ruth, Naomi looked at her two sons. Each boy seemed focused on a certain daughter of Sakira. Mahlon quietly kept his eyes on Ruth, while Chilion was bold enough to speak to Orpah outright.

Naomi knew that she was not alone, but she had never felt so utterly alone in all her life. So she gathered her clean clothes and the mourning material and went out back to the small cistern to wash and prepare for the coming days of mourning.

"I am alone," she cried to herself. "Please, don't let me be alone," she prayed, her words echoing back at her off the cistern walls more loudly than she had anticipated.

Hearing sounds from the back of the house and realizing that Naomi was no longer inside, Orpah and Ruth rushed out to help her.

"We do not know your customs, but we want to help you," Orpah said.

"We will do all that we can," Ruth agreed.

"Just do not leave me alone," Naomi said. "I have no mother, no sister, and no daughter in my time of need."

"You have us," Ruth said, and Naomi's pain somehow lessened because she realized how true this was.

Naomi's grief was eased further when she returned to the house and saw Mahlon and Chilion washing their father's body. They had no priest or grandfather, no cousins or uncles to help them. They wrapped Elimelech in a white shroud with the proper and sacred adornments. Then they bound Elimelech's feet and wrapped his face.

Someone had brought them myrrh and aloes to lessen the smell of decay. These were mixed to make a sort of cast over Elimelech's face cloth.

"Father looks like a baby, all swaddled," Chilion said quietly.

"And he will be put back into the womb of the earth to await a rebirth," Mahlon replied.

"Do you believe in an afterlife, Brother?" Chilion asked.

"I do, I suppose," Mahlon said. "I cannot imagine *never* seeing Father again."

"And do you believe like Mother that the Hebrew God has punished Father by taking his life?"

"I don't know." Mahlon sighed. "I am torn between Ama's teachings and all that I've learned and seen here in Moab."

With Ruth on her left and Orpah on her right, Naomi had watched her sons and thought what she often thought—that though they were twins, they were separate men. One had a rounder face and heart; one had a more chiseled face and heart. Mahlon's eyelids drooped, giving the impression that he was tired even when he wasn't. Chilion's eyelids were high and thin, giving him a constant look of astonishment.

Ruth cleared her throat to let the boys know they were being watched, and the brothers looked up and smiled—first, gently at their mother, and then at the girls. Mahlon smiled at Ruth while Chilion's eyes brightened for Orpah.

* * *

The next morning Naomi lifted the veil from her face to sneak one last look at Elimelech's face, already sunken and gray. She lamented, "If only we could bury your father in soil that was his own."

"No, Mother," Chilion said. "He must be buried today."

"But his bones, once the flesh has rotted from them, they can be carried back to Bethlehem."

"And who will carry them, Mother—you?"

"Chilion!" Sakira said through the open window, her blank eyes brightening. "Don't speak to your mother with disrespect at this time."

Naomi was surprised to see her friend. "When did you get here?"

"I have taken my daughters back to school at the palace."

"How do you feel, Sakira?"

"I am restored." She pointed to Nathaniel, who was curled up in Mahlon's lap.

Naomi wanted to smile, but she noticed a man at the gate.

"Lemuel!" Chilion called, hurrying outside.

The king's captain was not alone, but as always, was flagged by bodyguards. Chilion greeted him and swung the gate wide, inviting him immediately into their humble courtyard.

Naomi was relieved to see that Lemuel had the decency to reject the invitation. She was also relieved that Elimelech's body was wrapped so that Lemuel could not lord his superiority over her husband one final time.

"I have come to offer the king's condolences," said Lemuel.

"Thank you, Captain," Chilion said. "Please tell the king that his thoughtfulness is much appreciated."

"Where will your father be buried?" Lemuel asked.

Mahlon lifted Nathaniel to his hip and walked over to stand beside Chilion. "We will bury Father in the lowland cemetery," Mahlon said. "It's all his humble wage can afford."

If Lemuel took offense at the jab, he didn't let it show. In fact, he smiled. "Ah! That's the second reason I've come. Here is sufficient money to honor the work your father was doing for Chemosh. His design of our god has regenerated a loyalty not seen in Moab for a generation. King Eglon was most upset to hear of Elimelech's death. He felt your father was forging a bond between your people and ours."

In a rage, Naomi flew toward the gate. "Your king forsook my husband. You saw to that. And for all I know, my husband died at your hand!" Naomi screamed as she lunged at Lemuel, wishing her nails could claw the flesh from his smiling cheeks.

"Mother!" Chilion yelled, shoving her back so hard that Naomi nearly tripped.

Mahlon handed Nathaniel to Sakira and took Naomi in his arms, cinching her firmly around her waist.

"I hate you!" she yelled. "I curse you, Lemuel!"

Chilion's face was red with embarrassment. "She is grieving," he said to Lemuel. "She knows we have no idea who beat my father and left him for dead. I apologize a thousand times, Captain."

Lemuel rubbed the bridge across the top of his narrow nose. "You are right. Your mother is grieving. I take no insult."

"Thank you," Chilion said.

Naomi lunged again, but Mahlon dragged her away from the gate.

"Stop it, Mother, please," he whispered in her ear. "Do not make matters worse for us."

Naomi stopped struggling, her stiff limbs going limp. Mahlon was right, she thought. She was only making things harder for her sons. Her hatred for Lemuel was nothing. She was nothing. Never had Naomi felt so utterly valueless.

Lemuel looked right at her and smirked. "I have also come to bring happy news at this sad time."

"Happy?" she sneered. "How dare he mention the word at such a time?"

"Yes, happy," he repeated. "King Eglon has approved the union."

"What union, Captain?" Mahlon asked.

Chilion backed away, ducking his chin.

"Don't be shy now, Chilion," Lemuel said. "I had no idea that you haven't told your family. Just as well, you can share your request with them now that it has the king's approval."

Sakira stood beside Naomi; the two women laced their fingers together.

"Tell us, Chilion," Mahlon said.

Chilion lifted his head. He looked pleased. "I sent a formal request to ask King Eglon for Orpah's hand in marriage."

Sakira gasped and squeezed Naomi's hand, which had gone slack.

"Is my daughter aware of such a request?" Sakira asked Chilion.

He nodded. "We have spoken."

Lemuel laughed and reached to grasp Chilion's hand. That's when Naomi saw something that made her blood run ice cold. She saw that the captain's hands were unblemished, even his nails scraped free of dirt, while Chilion's hands were bruised, his knuckles scabbed and scraped as though he'd been in a recent fight.

Chilion approached Naomi slowly. "I want to marry Orpah. Would it be too much to ask for your blessing, Mother?"

Naomi was grateful her face was veiled so her expression would not give away her true feelings of disappointment.

13

THE MOURNING DAYS CAME AND went in what felt to Naomi like an endless night. If she had given in to her own future's bleakness, she might never have emerged.

"Chilion's marriage to Orpah is such a joyous thing to anticipate," Sakira said one day as they sat at the back of her shop beneath the shade of a flowering tree. The air felt cool and smelled of blossoms. Naomi breathed their fragrance in, afraid to tell her friend that she felt no joy in the upcoming nuptials.

"Twist the reed just a little," Orpah said, guiding Naomi's hands. The women had all taken on the task of teaching Naomi how to weave. They felt it would keep her busy and occupy her thoughts.

"I will never be gifted at this," Naomi said. "But if you continue to show such patience with me, I might become skilled."

Ruth had come up with the idea that Naomi could tell the history of her people in basket designs. So she drew images as Naomi told stories, then Sakira and Orpah dyed and cut each reed to fit properly until they had literally woven a story into a basket.

When she turned it around, the first basket they made told the story of their first father and mother in the garden called Eden. Another depicted Noah and his flood. Even the basket was shaped to resemble what they imagined his ark to be like.

Whenever Naomi made a mistake or grew impatient, and her fingers stopped, it was Orpah who patiently unwound the reeds and helped Naomi.

"You will be the daughter that I always wanted," Naomi told her gratefully as Orpah taught Naomi to weave and to hope again for a brighter day.

Days turned into weeks, and the art woven into the baskets began to be appreciated and even sold. Naomi found her faith renewed and began testifying to Orpah and Ruth and Sakira of her love for her Lord. It was done with a boldness she had never known in her life. No matter what had happened, Naomi's devotion to Jehovah only grew.

"Why is Father making me convert to your beliefs?" Orpah asked one day as they worked.

"The king sees marriages between Moabites and Judeans as a way to bond our two peoples," Naomi answered. "We see it as a blessing because you'll turn away from idol worship."

Orpah was quiet, and Naomi feared she'd offended her.

"I don't think Chilion believes in your god anymore," Orpah said.

"Why do you think such a thing?"

"Because of what he shares with me," Orpah answered. "Your unseen god left his young prayers unanswered. He tells me how he used to pray for food and for good things to happen to your family, yet you lost your babies and nearly died of starvation. But here, in Moab, Chilion has grown strong and found favor with the captain. Chemosh has not only accepted Chilion, but he has blessed him."

Naomi cringed. She took a deep breath, then said, "When you get to know the Lord who brought our people out of Egypt on dry ground, you'll feel His mercy like manna fall into your life. Then you will know His power and the love He has for His children. Then you will know that a god fashioned from the metals of this earth has no power except the power it is given."

"How can you believe so firmly in a god who took your husband from you?" Orpah asked.

"Because I believe in the God who gave me my husband to begin with."

For a long time they wove in silence, thinking. Then Orpah admitted, "It all feels strange to me. The god I know is the god I can see, Chemosh. Why must I be immersed to show faith in a god that I cannot see?"

Naomi repeated now what she had always been taught: "Immersion is a purification process. Just as Jews performed immersion at Mt. Sinai to complete the conversion process, converts of every age must also immerse in a mikveh."

Orpah looked at Naomi with the same sort of confused expression as if she'd just bumped her head.

"Oh, Orpah, over time all of it will make sense to you. When you marry my son you will become my first daughter. I will be a mother to you and my God will show Himself to you in ways that you cannot deny."

Orpah said nothing more, only picked up a another reed and began weaving again.

* * *

Chilion did not act like a young man who had abandoned his faith. For the next couple of weeks, he spent any free time he had up in the hills, where the stone was soft enough, carving out a mikveh from a small, trickling spring. Because there was no rabbi to supervise, Chilion was careful with his measurements, knowing the pool had to be deep enough and long enough to cover every inch of Orpah's immersed body.

Naomi followed him, helping where she could. "Son, there are men watching you work."

"They are Lemuel's men," Chilion said.

"*You* are one of his men."

"Yes," Chilion said. Then he waited and whispered a confession of sorts to Naomi. "I think Lemuel has begun to resent me. I think he is growing jealous of the favors King Eglon is showing me."

"What favors?" Naomi asked.

"He's promised me a house and an orchard closer to the highway, and he's appointed me as captain in my own right. Mother, I will earn a wage and have a home to offer Orpah."

"I think that is wonderful," she said honestly. "Why would Lemuel resent such a thing? I'm sure he has even grander privileges."

"Ama, I'm not the stupid follower Lemuel thinks I am. I learned what I needed to from him, but now I am my own man—"

"Be wary of him, Son," Naomi interrupted. "The man carries a spirit of evil in his heart."

"What is evil, Ama? It's only a judgment."

She sighed, breathing in the scent of freshly turned earth, not wishing to debate the definition of evil with Chilion. He was only now beginning to soften his hard feelings toward her and to talk to her with a civil tongue. And she was only now beginning to realize how absurdly foolish it had been for her to even think that Chilion might have been one of the men who had attacked Elimelech on the horrible night that led to his death.

"I'm proud of you, Chilion, for honoring Orpah's conversion," she said, instead of all the things she could have mentioned.

He paused and said, "I'm doing it only because the king believes it will forge our people with his. He's more concerned than ever that the Hebrews are gathering a secret army to attack Moab."

Naomi remembered what Elimelech had told her about Ehud's army and how there were spies in the land of Moab who were helping to overthrow King Eglon. With a wry smile, she asked, "Who is to say they aren't?"

There was a man waiting in Naomi's courtyard when she returned. His back was turned, and she did not recognize him.

"Naomi?" he called her name when he turned around and saw her.

Still, the man was a stranger—tall, broad-chested, with a beard trimmed as close as most Moabites wore, if they wore a beard at all.

"Do I know you, sir?"

"I am your nephew."

"Boaz?" Naomi asked.

"I have come to Moab to accompany our chief judge in paying tribute to the king. I only now heard of Elimelech's passing."

She wanted to run to him, to throw her arms around his neck and weep. Instead, Naomi stood still and said, "Thank you. May I please make you something to eat?"

"It was not right of me to enter your gate and make myself at home," he admitted. "But I'm tired and hungry. The king feeds Ehud but not Ehud's escorts."

She hurried to make him feel welcome, bringing out water and a bin in which his feet could be washed. She cut fresh melon, and while she ground grain, she could not hold back her questions.

"My mother lives with my sister in Jericho, not far from Berta and her family," Boaz was saying.

"Tell me of my sister-in-law. In all these years there has been little word from her."

"Uriel still works to rebuild the city. They have added two sons to their two daughters. I believe they are well."

Naomi felt the slightest jab of envy. Berta—with her money, her important husband, and her stinginess—was blessed.

"Will you be the one to tell her of her brother's passing?" Naomi asked.

"I will."

While Naomi pelted him with more questions, Boaz ate and smiled and even laughed a few times.

"Tell me about you." She worded the request carefully, not knowing on what ground she was treading.

"I am just out of mourning myself," Boaz admitted. "I married a woman from Yafo named Ketrina, and she died last year in childbirth."

"Oh, Boaz!" Naomi cried. "I am so sorry. It seems we all suffer."

"Yes, it has been a very difficult time."

"Tell me more about Bethlehem," she said. "The last time you were in Moab you spoke to Elimelech and told him you were purchasing property."

"The highlands," Boaz confirmed. "I have invested the money I made as a scribe in Jerusalem. Though the crops are now worthless, one day I believe Bethlehem will again be worthy of its name."

"The House of Bread," she said, interpreting. "I hold out hope for such a day."

"Do you and your sons plan to return soon?"

"I would like nothing more, but Chilion has become an important military leader here and will soon marry one of the king's daughters."

"Yes. I heard that from Ehud. It seems Chilion has asked Ehud to officiate at the immersion ceremony before he returns."

"Of course," Naomi said. "Please, have more bread. I am allotted more food than I need."

It probably seemd like a cruel statement, Naomi realized almost immediately, considering that Bethlehem was still plagued by famine. She hurried to cover her embarrassment, saying, "I didn't mean anything by that."

"And I took no offense, my auntie," Boaz assured her. "I am just very happy to see you."

Orpah still seemed nervous as the day of her immersion ceremony approached. Hebrew law was very strict regarding the immersion ceremony. It required at least three qualified witnesses, something Dibon did not have to offer, which made it even more important for the ceremony to be done before Ehud and Boaz returned to Bethlehem. When the day arrived, Ehud was the chief officiating elder, while Boaz and another priest also served as witnesses.

"'To *convert*' means to accept something different, be it an idea or a way of life," Ehud explained to the small group of people, including all the family Chilion and Orpah could gather as well as Lemuel's watchers and a few of Orpah's friends. "Above all else, 'to *convert*' means to change. Orpah, this day you will accept a new God and a new way of life—your husband's."

Orpah smiled nervously.

Naomi tried to hold on to Nathaniel's hand, but he was older and stronger and more curious than ever. He would not stay put, and Sakira had never fully recovered from the trauma of almost losing him. She was watching him move about on the rocks, but was she seeing him?

Ruth slipped her hand into Naomi's. "I wish it was me," she whispered. "After everything you've taught me about the God of Israel, I wish I was the one being immersed."

"Really?" Naomi asked.

Ruth nodded. "I would never tell anyone how I feel, not even Mother. But, please, do not stop teaching me. What you say feels warm and true in my heart."

"That's because it is," Naomi whispered. "There is a living God who hears and answers prayers, who gives commands so that we can prove our loyalty and can be better people."

When it was time for the immersion, Orpah began to weep. Ruth ran to put an arm around her.

"I don't know if I can do this," Orpah said.

Chilion looked both embarrassed and angry, but his eyes focused mainly on Lemuel's watchers.

"Do you want to convert or not?" Chilion asked impatiently. "These men have inconvenienced themselves for you. I have—"

"Yes," Orpah interrupted. "Yes. I am sorry, Chilion. Of course I want to convert. I want to marry you."

After that, the ceremony was simple and unhurried: Words were spoken. Orpah was immersed. A vow was taken. And the ritual cleansing was complete.

"I feel no different," Orpah said afterward.

"You will," Naomi assured her. "In time, you will know the difference between a handmade idol and the true and living God."

"Ama! Be careful what you say. There are many ears listening to us," Chilion warned.

"And their eyes watch us, Chilion. We have done nothing that the king has not sanctioned."

While Orpah was being dried and dressed by her mother and sister, Naomi could not help but notice a private conversation Mahlon had with Ehud. The two men seemed to be sharing a secret. What could Mahlon possibly be telling the chief judge of Israel that was so enthralling?

After the ceremony was complete and as everyone was heading back to Naomi's courtyard to eat the goat that had been roasting all day, they heard the sound of horse hooves clopping up the hill. Lemuel and a half dozen men, all equipped with the armor of warriors, charged forward.

Nathaniel saw the chief captain's horse. "Horse!" he cried, rushing up to the quivering beast. His little hands lunged forward to pet the black, sweaty animal. As his hands caught the flank, the horse reared back, nearly toppling Lemuel. Then, in an instant, the hoof swung back, aimed right for Nathaniel's head.

There was no time for anyone to scream, only time to scramble. With a sickening thud, the horse's hoof made contact at the same instant that Nathaniel was thrown out of harm's way. Ruth and Boaz had crashed together in the same instant and the same effort, landing in a tangled heap. But it was only Boaz who came away bleeding. The hoof had caught him on the forehead and left a deep, gushing wound.

While Naomi ran to help him, Lemuel cursed and moved his horse. "Search them!" he shouted. "There are Hebrew traitors among us."

Boaz held out his hand to help Ruth back onto her feet.

"I'm so sorry about your head," Ruth said.

"I'm all right," Boaz assured her.

"No, you're not," Naomi said, wincing at how deep the half-moon gouge was. "We have to tend to you, Boaz."

"No!" Lemuel said, digging his heels into his horse's side so it moved forward, wedging between and separating them.

In an angry barrage, Lemuel's men dismounted and, joined by those who had already been watching Chilion, demanded to search Ehud and the priests. Naomi was mortified to see the chief judge, Boaz, and the other Hebrew priests knocked to the ground, stripped of their cloaks, and searched.

Sakira's family hurried down the hill, but Naomi stayed to stare daggers at Lemuel. Even so, he looked through her as though she were invisible.

"What were you expecting to find?" Ehud demanded once he was standing and his cloak was back in place. "We've already delivered our tribute to your king."

"Weapons," Lemuel said. "We received a report that you smuggled weapons into our land."

"And how would I do that?" Ehud asked. "It is impossible. We Hebrews have nothing, not even wood, from which to fashion weapons. You've searched us. Now let us return freely to our homes." He spoke with such authority that Naomi wanted nothing more than to leave with them, return to Bethlehem, and live out her days in a land where the men deserved respect and honor.

As Lemuel left, Mahlon and Ehud exchanged one final look. That was when Naomi remembered something she had long since forgotten. Behind some those bricks in her courtyard wall there was a weapon, a short sword made by Elimelech's talent and hidden there by her son.

* * *

Soon, the wedding feast was held in the palace courtyard. As the honored mothers of the newlyweds, Sakira and Naomi were escorted and given a place at a table separate from the king, his men, and Chilion and Orpah. Mahlon was seated on the other side of his brother, while Ruth was set apart at a table with some of the king's other children.

With his ravenous appetite ruling his senses, King Eglon managed to tear apart and eat an entire roasted fowl, despite his missing teeth. Naomi should have been awed by the massive amounts of food spread out on the tables. Mostly, though, she felt empty, sad, and confused.

People wanted her to be happy—this was the marriage of her son to the king's daughter! Part of her was happy, but a bigger part of her knew that this union would forever tie her family to Moab. As long as Chilion was happy here, he would never desire to return to the bone-dry and sunbaked Bethlehem.

It's God's will, she decided . . . this marriage was God's will, and she forced herself to smile when she felt Driann's eyes on her. The royal maidservant had appeared today just as she had Naomi's first day in Moab. Driann did not look any older, but Naomi felt like a lifetime had passed since then. Driann stood near the king, veiled in orange, ready to serve him at the first order.

"How did she get so scarred?" Naomi asked Sakira in a whisper.

Sakira leaned in and spoke in hushed tones. "She was meant to be a festival sacrifice, but either the priests did not bind her tightly enough or an unseen power broke her cords, for she rolled out of Chemosh's hands and landed on the ground. After that, she became a lifetime member of the royal staff."

"How old was she when that happened?"

"It happened long before I came to Dibon, but I've heard that Driann wasn't much older than Nathaniel."

"How horrible," Naomi said.

"Horrible?" Sakira raised her hands in shock. "It's not horrible. It's honorable. She was spared by the mercy of Chemosh. She lives in honor."

The water of the long rectangular pool glistened an unnatural blue in the background. Then dancers that appeared at both ends and splashed for the entertainment of the guests, twisting and turning to a beat that also added heat to Naomi's already smouldering mood. Their immodest dance made Naomi angry, causing her to look away. Even after what had almost happened to Nathaniel, Sakira was incomprehensibly loyal to Chemosh.

Chilion caught his mother's attention and lifted his cleanly shaven chin. He nearly smiled at her, and Naomi was happy that he was happy. Mahlon too seemed like he had emerged from his mourning. His eyes were always watching Ruth.

Naomi told herself to feel some level of joy. Sakira sat beside her, a true friend. Also, she was about to gain a daughter that she already loved very much. But Naomi's heart ached, and she felt as out of place as she had ever felt.

The drumbeat stopped and the air thrummed with anticipation. People went quiet and held still as a likeness of Chemosh was carried in on a litter. Naomi could not help but wonder if Elimelech's talent had been used to fashion the idol. Everyone, beginning with Ruth and including Chilion and Mahlon, bowed before it. Freshly cleansed and converted, Orpah also bowed. A chant was mumbled, a prayer to the destroyer god.

Sakira tugged at Naomi's hand. "Kneel!"

But Naomi forced her knees to not bend.

Naomi saw Driann's eyes, staring as if she would bore hot holes into Naomi as the woman leaned over to whisper to the king. For the first and only time in Naomi's life, the king looked directly at her. His face was so doughy that it was difficult to make out the two black beads he had for eyes, but Naomi could feel his stare, just as harsh and judging as Driann's.

A few nearby guards noticed her resistance but did nothing. Even Lemuel only stared at her with a mocking disdain. She knew when their eyes met that she had defied the god of Moab.

Naomi half expected to be dragged away from the celebration, to be beaten and left for dead. But no punishment befell her as Sakira bowed and pledged her all to the terrifying idol with his rotund gut and outstretched hands.

When the dancing resumed after Chemosh had been hoisted to his place of honor, all the women were called forth to dance and play timbrels. Sakira, much to Naomi's surprise, was among the first to join the weaving line, right behind her daughters. They were smiling and threading their way around the men.

Naomi bit her bottom lip until it swelled. Did Orpah not understand that she was no longer a worshipper of Chemosh? And what about Naomi's sons? They were both soiling themselves with this pagan ritual. But what had she expected—that they would separate themselves? This was the first ceremony she had ever attended with Chemosh. Had her sons and even Elimelech been bowing to the idol all along?

Naomi felt a kind of sadness different from mourning as she witnessed Orpah dancing—not only with the women but also with a string of men who poured forth from the palace arches, naked in honor of the fertility goddess Ashtoreth.

It was a sight that Naomi could not bear. How could Chilion watch his bride do such a thing? Feeling queasy, Naomi closed her eyes and dropped her chin. The music and the images clawed at her very soul.

She bore it as long as she could. She did not want to disrespect Chilion and Orpah's new union. But finally, without a word, Naomi crept out of the wedding celebration and walked to the shut gate.

"I cannot allow you passage," the gate guard said.

"I am the mother of the groom. I am feeling ill and must return to my home," Naomi argued.

The very ground beneath her trembled and swayed with the pounding of drums and the stomping of feet. The air was smoky and heavy with the scent of roasting meat. There were screams of pleasure and pain.

"Please, sir, I beg you, allow me to leave," Naomi insisted.

"Naomi?"

Naomi did not have to turn around to know the voice.

"Ruth."

"We are here for you, Mother," Mahlon said, standing right beside Ruth.

There was confusion and concern in his expression.

"Oh, Children, my children, I saw you both," she said, "dancing and drinking and worshipping Chemosh."

"We were celebrating, Mother, not worshipping," Mahlon said.

"Yes," Ruth was quick to add, "we were only enjoying ourselves. But when I saw you get up and walk away, I knew something was wrong."

"I feel feeble," Naomi said. "My mind thinks dark thoughts, and my body, though not old in years, feels ancient."

Mahlon and Ruth embraced her and she fell willingly into their arms.

"Walk me home," she pleaded.

"Yes, of course," Mahlon said.

But when they turned toward the gate, the same guard said, "I cannot allow you to leave until the king has declared the celebration ended."

"Open the gate," Ruth said evenly but firmly. "I am Ruth, daughter of King Eglon, and I order you to open the gate and allow us passage out of here."

The guard unlatched the gate just wide enough to let them through, then latched it again. As Ruth passed, he bowed slightly to her.

Naomi could never have imagined such a thing. She knew Ruth and Orpah were the king's daughters, but she had never seen them exert their influence—had never before realized just how powerful Ruth could be.

The streets were quiet and dusky. A few street cats slid out of courtyards and from behind fences. A black, shabby feline ran to rub its side along Ruth's ankle.

"They're invading us," she said. "They're coming up from Egypt. I've never seen as many as I've seen lately."

"I heard Queen Zima ordered thousands of cats released in the land."

"Why would she do that?" Naomi asked.

"Because the king hates cats, and she hates the king."

It was the first time Naomi had smiled since they had left the palace.

They walked the rest of the way in silence, wrapped in their own thoughts. They stopped at the well and begged a dipper of water for Naomi. When they reached home, Naomi lay on her bed. Then she asked, "Children, can a person worship more than one god?"

Mahlon lit the courtyard torch. The face of Ashtoreth, the small polished idol lanced into the ground on their first day in Moab, glinted in the flame. "Mother, you're tired. Rest now, and we'll talk later."

"It's impossible," she said, letting her head go heavy against the softness of the tick mattress.

"I will check on you tomorrow," Mahlon said, "before I leave for the winter palace."

"Yes. Yes. The queen's palace," Naomi said. "I remember now. You are going to teach letters to the king's sons."

"I am."

"And Ruth, you will stay with your mother and help at the shop?"

"I will."

Mahlon and Ruth stood side by side in the torchlight, so close their shoulders touched.

"In Judea," Naomi said, "it is forbidden for a man and woman who are unwed to spend time alone together, especially under the cloak of night. It is shameful, and yet you two are free to roam the city together. No one here questions whether you are married."

"Good night, Mother."

14

And so the waiting began.

Each of them waited for a specific blessing.

Naomi waited for her pain to ease. But her back was bent with the weight of loneliness—separation from her husband, her sons, and, most of the time, from the God she begged to stay close to her.

Sakira waited for the king to call her back to the palace, to honor her again as his concubine. But he had new concubines, much younger women, to entertain him and to bear him sons.

Chilion and Orpah waited for Ashtoreth to bless their new union. But every month Orpah emerged from the red tent. She bathed and presented herself to her husband at her most fertile times only to have the cycle repeated the next month.

Mahlon waited for the king's consent to marry Ruth. But he lived far away at the winter palace, teaching letters to the king's son, and months passed with no word from the king's palace.

But Ruth waited most patiently of all. "I trust in what will be," she said.

* * *

After a year of marriage, Chilion was told by Lemuel one morning that the king wanted to see him.

Chilion went, bowed, and was humiliated in front of his fellow soldiers.

"Why has my daughter not borne me a grandson by now?" the king demanded.

Chilion stammered, unable to utter an answer the king was willing to hear.

"I want a private army of only sons and grandsons. Do you understand me?"

They were so close that Chilion's cheeks were spattered with the spittle that flew from the king's toothless mouth.

"I understand," Chilion said.

In the months that followed, Chilion grew angry and hard. One day Naomi brought Chamor to the basket shop so Nathaniel could ride him. When she heard weeping, she went inside and saw Ruth consoling her sister.

"Orpah?" Naomi said.

Orpah reeled back into the shadows, but not before Naomi saw the black eye and the bruises on her arms.

With a tongue gone dry, Naomi asked, "Did my son do this?"

"Please, Mother," Orpah pleaded, "say nothing to him. Not a word. Vow to me."

"It's true," Ruth said. "If you say something to Chilion, things will only grow harder for my sister."

The fear in their eyes silenced the words Naomi wanted to say to her son.

* * *

More time passed, and the waiting went on. Prayers to every god seemed to go unheard. One clear afternoon, Sakira and Naomi sat outside the basket shop, weaving and watching people scour the market for the best bargains.

Dan, the friend of Elimelech who had offered comfort at his death, stopped by and purchased a basket, a small one for carrying small things. His long hair was pulled back, and his freshly shaved faced gave him a younger appearance than Naomi remembered.

"Is this for your wife?" Sakira asked, smiling in Naomi's direction.

"No. I am a widower hoping to remarry soon." He did not take his eyes off of Naomi.

Sakira laughed. "You could not be more obvious, sir."

Red-faced and stuttering, he paid her for the basket and hurried on his way.

"That was rude," Naomi said. "The poor man was only being kind."

"He wants to marry you, Naomi. Do you want to marry Dan?"

"No! I could never marry again. I'm too old to bear children and the Moabite men do not want to marry a woman who prays to Jehovah."

"Well, then," Sakira said, "I've done you a favor by sending him away."

Nathaniel came tearing around the corner. "Mahlon is here!" he yelled. And the boy took off running down the street.

In a moment, Nathaniel bobbed back over the crowd as he rode atop Mahlon's shoulders.

"I have not seen you smile like that in—in as long as I can remember," Naomi said to Mahlon. "What has you so happy, Son?"

He slid Nathaniel down and stooped to kiss his mother's cheek. Then he knelt before Sakira.

"I have heard from the palace. King Eglon has given me permission to marry Ruth," he said. "I have nothing but my heart and my hands to offer your daughter, and I know that she deserves so much more. Still, I will honor Ruth all the days of my life. Please, Sakira, I seek your blessing for our union."

Sakira pressed her lips into a thin line. She took her time in answering. "If you were anything like your brother, I would tell you no."

"I am sorry for the treatment Orpah has received at Chilion's hand," Mahlon said. "I vow to never hurt Ruth in any way."

"I believe you," Sakira said. "But I want you to know that Ruth has truly lived her name's meaning: She is my friend as well as my daughter. She is loyal and loving and will make the kind of wife every good man deserves."

Mahlon eagerly nodded his agreement.

"Her heart has chosen you, Mahlon," Sakira said. "I think you are the only man she has ever considered marrying."

"And I will be devoted to Ruth all the days of my life," he vowed.

"My daughters are women of Moab," Sakira said, glancing at Naomi. "It does not matter whether you immerse them in your mikveh. It does not matter what blessings and prayers your priests pronounce upon their heads. Orpah converted to your faith, and you see the results: Ashtoreth is angry. My daughter's womb is empty because the goddess has not received her proper sacrifices."

"Sakira!" Naomi was shocked at her friend's brazenness.

"I speak the truth, Naomi. Your son refuses to worship as Ashtoreth and Chemosh command."

"They command sacrifices that are impure and immoral," Naomi protested.

"And your god commands you in everything. I do not understand how you can worship a being that parts the sea so His people can cross on dry ground, only to let their promised land go fallow."

"Jehovah does not punish our land. He does not even punish us," Naomi said. "He does not bless us because we do not deserve it. We are disobedient. We hide idols in our pockets, in our flour baskets, and in our hearts."

"Because you know that idols have power," Sakira insisted. "You can see and feel an idol. Your god is where—high in the heavens, looking down from a distance that cannot be bridged? We can see Ashtoreth's power in the big bellies of our women. We can see Chemosh's power in the sun itself."

"It takes great faith," Naomi said quietly, "to believe in a God we feel only in our hearts."

Slowly, Sakira shook her head. "And do you believe as your mother believes, Mahlon?"

He shifted his feet and looked at the ground.

"My Ruth," Sakira continued, "is willing to forsake her religion to marry you."

"I know."

"Then she deserves to know that it is something *you* believe in."

"I do."

Sakira moved aside a pile of leaves and waited for a long time before speaking again. "I have my doubts about that, Mahlon. You do not act as a man of sure convictions. Chemosh is the only god Ruth has ever known. She knows his power and his demands. I don't know how she will ever be able to rid herself of that knowledge."

"We will grow and change together," Mahlon said. "My Hebrew God requires little more than a willing heart."

Sakira's eyebrows rose high on her forehead. "The same cannot be said for Chemosh."

* * *

Eventually, Sakira gave Mahlon her blessing. Joyful preparations were then made for the wedding. Mahlon built a small house not far from the winter temple, where the king had him working to teach letters, something his mother had seldom practiced since Elimelech's death. As part of Ruth's dowry, Sakira, Orpah, and Naomi helped weave, sew, and make things Ruth would need to make her own home: baskets, sleeping clothes, pillows, pots, and, heaven forbid, burial clothes.

Naomi also spent a great deal of time making the same gift she had made for Chilion and Orpah—a hand-painted mezuzah.

Ruth was immersed the next time Ehud came to pay tribute to King Eglon.

"Boaz did not accompany you?" Naomi asked, disappointed not to see her nephew.

"No. He is very busy with his crops," Ehud said.

"So Bethlehem is no longer in famine?"

"Bethlehem is still very much a land of famine," Ehud said, "but Boaz has great faith. He is even now building storehouses and a new threshing floor in the high hills. Your nephew is a man of great faith."

Lemuel's men kept watch from a distance but did not invade the immersion ceremony as they had at Orpah's.

Otherwise it was very much the same, except Ruth seemed different from her sister.

"I know I am asking a lot of questions," she said apologetically.

"Ask all you want," Naomi said. "If I do not know the answers, I will find them."

She asked about prayer, about the prophets, about the commandments, about which foods were clean and which were unclean. She even practiced cooking with Naomi.

"Since Elimelech died and my sons left home, I have not done much cooking," Naomi admitted. "In Bethlehem our food was so limited there were really no choices. Here, there are so many spices and herbs and onions. Oh, I love onions!"

"Mahlon doesn't like them at all," Ruth reminded her.

"That's why I pick the mint that grows by the stream," Naomi said. "Chew it after you've eaten onions and the smell goes away. Your mother taught me that trick."

Ruth also spent a great deal of time in her father's presence. As part of her gift from him, he provided chickens, ducks, two goats, and a small herd of sheep, as well as the land on which Mahlon built their small home.

Naomi helped them prepare and plant their courtyard. She took delight in planting flowers and shrubs that she knew would receive enough rain to grow. She also planted a small garden that she knew would produce well. And while she worked she prayed, "Please bless Bethlehem with rain. Please bless my people with freedom."

Chilion helped his brother build a stone wall around his yard, carrying the rocks up from the river in small loads pulled by Chamor's old, tired legs.

* * *

King Eglon insisted that the wedding feast take place at the temple. He knew that his daughter had converted, but he acted as though it made no difference. She was now considered a Hebrew—but not in his eyes.

So when the music and the drum-beating started, when the women stood to dance, he expected Ruth to join in as she always had.

"I cannot," she announced to all of the guests. "Chemosh is no longer my god. I am the wife of a Hebrew."

The people held their breath, waiting for the king to explode. But he didn't. He did what he had done all those years ago when Ruth had broken into his private quarters and called him fat: He laughed.

And the dancing, feasting, and sacrificing went on.

Orpah and Chilion danced and smiled. To anyone simply watching from afar, the couple looked happy. Naomi knew better.

When the king's hand went up, he called for Orpah to come forward. Naomi feared he would say something to ridicule her because she was unable to conceive. Instead, he simply said, "Sing!"

Orpah opened her mouth and sang a beautiful love song, a prayer to Ashtoreth, for Ruth and Mahlon. When the song was finished the sisters held to each other as tightly as Mahlon and Chilion once had when they were first born.

Sakira reached over and took Naomi's hand. "We are sisters too," she said, and Naomi nodded, a tear forming in the corner of her eye.

Ruth, grinning, rushed to embrace her mother. Naomi watched the two embrace and tried to imagine what it would be like to have a daughter so loving, so devoted, so filled with life. Orpah had not been that type of daughter; though she was kind and loving, she did not have Ruth's vigor for living, especially now that her womb was still disappointingly empty.

When Ruth's lips touched Naomi's cheek, the new bride whispered, "You are now my mother also."

"And now I have the daughters I have always wanted," Naomi said. "My life is not what I expected, but I am blessed. Praise be to Jehovah."

She said it louder than she intended. Heads swiveled, and eyes stared at her in judgment.

That night, after Naomi was in bed, alone on her small rooftop, she heard a scraping sound.

"Who is it?" she called.

"It is Sakira."

"Is something wrong?" Naomi asked quickly as she hurried down the ladder.

"Nothing is wrong. I wanted to invite you to go with me to the temple."

"What? Why?"

"To make the needed sacrifices for our children," Sakira said.

Naomi wiped sleep from her eyes; still, Sakira's request made no sense.

"For fertility," Sakira said, unlidding a vessel that smelled of fresh blood. There was a wild glint in her eyes and a desperate tone in her voice. "There are certain acts we must do, Naomi, please—to insure the fertility of our children. I did not do them for Orpah, and I will not make that mistake now for Ruth. Hurry, we have no time to waste!"

Naomi stepped back. "You are my dear friend," she said, "but I don't know the woman who stands before me. You *know* that I do not worship your idol gods."

Sakira's hand gripped Naomi's wrist, squeezing it tightly. "The realization came while you were talking to me. You said that your god cannot honor your people, cannot protect them from ours, because you fail to do what he has commanded of you."

"That is true."

"Well," Sakira said, "I have failed to do what has been commanded of me and of my daughters. If we do not do as we've been commanded, Ashtoreth will seal the wombs of our Orpah and Ruth. You can already see that it is happening."

"No."

"You must, Naomi. We are sisters. We are family. If you do not do this and do it tonight, *you* will bring a curse upon both Ruth and Orpah."

"I will do no such thing," Naomi insisted. "And you asked nothing like this when Orpah was married."

"I should have," Sakira said. "Maybe I didn't because she did not come from my womb. But now, before the morning sun rises on the eve of the wedding night, we must perform before Chemosh in the grove of Ashtoreth."

Perform? Naomi wondered. "No. I will not do what you ask. Unspeakable things go on in that grove."

Then Sakira's beautiful face seemed to turn into that of a stranger, lined with fear and anger and the age she tried so hard to fight.

"I will go alone," she said. "I will not be the one who punishes our daughters. Naomi, for once, think of someone besides yourself. Do this to ease Orpah's suffering. Do it to bless Ruth."

"I will not."

"Then our friendship will never be as it has been." Her mouth opened wide, and Sakira screamed loudly enough to wake every sleeping neighbor around them. "The sorrow of your sons and my daughters be upon your head, Naomi!"

Again and again, Naomi was haunted by the memory of Sakira's words and the image of her back as she walked down the road in a blood-colored shaft of moonlight, her elbows crooked to hold her basket, the monstrous black orb of Chemosh on the hillside laughing down at them both.

15

IN THE WEEKS THAT FOLLOWED, Naomi's loneliness was like a heavy cloak—and try as she might, Naomi could not remove its weight from her shoulders. It bent her back, and it stooped her spirit. Faith, she told herself, was what she lacked.

She prayed that Jehovah would grant her more faith, sometimes spending a week alone with no one to keep her company except Chamor. She did not ask for comfort or strength; she knew those things would come if she were more faithful.

When boredom and loneliness became too much, Naomi dragged the small wooden bench into her house. It was the bench Elimelech had crafted for their courtyard—the one she had made a few attempts to adorn with her own carving. Inside her home, where no prying eyes could see, Naomi removed the short sword from its hiding place behind the loose bricks. *Had Mahlon forgotten it was even there?* she wondered.

Using its sharp-pointed tip, Naomi carved what she could remember of the Lord's commandments into the back of the bench. Each letter was small and precise. She took a great deal of time and care making sure every curve and line was as perfect as she could make it.

For days she worked.

Then weeks.

Then months.

Finally the entire back of the bench was gouged with carvings deep enough that she could run the tips of her fingers over them—could read them and feel them. As she did so, she could feel the spirit of her mother, Anna—the midwife, the artist, the wife of a lowland shepherd— whisper to her, "Well done, Daughter."

"You are going crazy," Chilion said when he realized what she had done and how many hours she had spent doing it.

"That might be very true," Naomi said.

"Do you still receive your regular allotment of food?"

"Yes."

"Good. As long as I am in the king's military service, you will be allowed to live here and will be given food sufficient for your needs. Is there anything you lack for, Ama?"

"No, just your company, Son."

"I'm here now!" he protested. "Isn't that enough? You know I'm a busy man. We just lost more than a thousand men in our battle with the Amorites. I was captain of that command, Ama. You should be proud of me," Chilion said.

"I love you very much," Naomi said.

"But you should be proud of me. I am brave. I am smart. I am the leader Abba never was."

Naomi took Chilion's hand and saw the scars across his knuckles. She remembered thinking once that he might have been one of the men who helped beat his father. But in her heart, she knew that was not true, and a wave of guilt washed over her for even thinking such a thought about her son.

"I love you," she repeated.

"I love you too."

Those words from Chilion kept Naomi company for a very long time.

* * *

Sakira seemed preoccupied and distant, just as Naomi suspected she would. The distance between them had grown as every new month passed without the announcement of either daughter's pregnancy.

Naomi began to think that maybe it *was* her fault.

"Oh, Ruth," she said one day when the newlyweds had returned from their home at the winter palace, "I am so sorry that I cannot offer you more. As the firstborn, Mahlon was entitled to a double portion of his father's inheritance, but his father left him nothing to inherit."

"We are fine, Mother," Ruth assured her. "I received my father's dowry, and Mahlon teaches for a number of my brothers. Did Mahlon tell you that Father also has him learning the art of concrete?"

"Yes, he's very excited."

"Just as you've carved commandments into your olive-wood bench, Father wants his history etched in stone."

"Concrete is not stone," Naomi said.

"No, but you've seen the big black stone Father had carved when I was a child."

"Yes."

"It wasn't big enough for him," Ruth said. "He wants the palace walls to be like books that tell his history."

"*His* history," Naomi said. "You mean how Moabites have subdued our people for an entire generation?"

Naomi saw Ruth's face flush. "I am sorry, Mother," Ruth said. "Sometimes it is very difficult to be a daughter to both you and to my father, the king."

"I'm the one who is sorry, Ruth," Naomi apologized. "Sometimes I forget where I am—maybe even *who* I am. We won't talk about such difficult things now. Let's bake bread, shall we?"

* * *

A few days later, a shrill voice at her gate made Naomi get up quickly from her knees where she had been working in her garden. At first she didn't recognize the small, stooped man with the black beard and bare head.

"Do you not know your own brother-in-law?" he asked.

"Heber?"

He did not wait to be invited through the gate but stormed in, starving and filthy. He washed with her cistern water, devoured her small allotment of food, and lay in the shade of her courtyard. In exchange, he briefed her on news from Judea. Ehud was gathering forces from every village for his never-going-to-happen rebellion. Trees and people were withering and dying still.

When she told him of Elimelech's death, he barely blinked. But when she told him of her sons' marriages, he seemed particularly pleased.

"This is the life. I don't know why I didn't move here long ago."

"You're moving to Moab?" Naomi asked.

"Not officially. I am just passing through looking for a new wife. I think I'll continue to the Nile and marry an Egyptian. They are beautiful creatures."

"What became of your last wife and the ones before her?" Naomi asked.

"They all left me. The last one got a bill of divorcement."

"Did you abandon her?"

"She claims I did."

"What of your children, Heber? Where are all of them?"

"They are not loyal to me, not even my sons. They've scattered after their mothers, some as far as the great desert."

"I am sorry to hear that, but it is not difficult to understand."

"I wish *I* had children who married royalty," Heber said. "Don't look shocked, Sister. I have heard about your good fortune."

"It is not as you think. Orpah and Ruth are the daughters of concubines. Orpah's mother hasn't been seen since Orpah was a baby, and Ruth's mother, Sakira, runs a modest basket shop at the market."

"Still, King Eglon has been generous with his daughters."

"Yes, I suppose he has. In spite of his capacity for cruelty, he can be kind to his own."

"Do you have any more wine?" Heber asked.

Naomi poured him the last drop.

Heber sat upright and let his eyes roam. "I suppose you'll remarry soon. You don't have much, but it's pleasant enough. And you've got sufficient food, though you wouldn't know it by looking at you. You're no bigger than a twig."

"I have no desire to remarry," Naomi said. "And don't you concern yourself, Heber, with the laws. Here there is no obligation for a man's brother to marry his widow."

He chuckled. "Especially if she's past her childbearing years as you are, Naomi. Honestly, I'm surprised your sons haven't taken better care of you. Didn't they receive a royal dowry or even an inheritance?"

"They received sufficient for their needs."

He laced his fingers behind his head and lay back. "Tell me what that means. Have they homes? Herds? Money?"

"My sons both work very hard."

"They've been given work for the palace, right?"

"Yes, that is true. Chilion is a captain. Mahlon is a teacher, but he is learning to work with concrete."

"Yes, I've seen the high walls Eglon is having erected around the palace. He thinks they'll stop his enemies. But our people can scale walls, Naomi. It's just a matter of time until Ehud's army takes over this land. How do you think you'll be seen then, Sister? As a traitor? That's what they call you back in Bethlehem."

"That's how I think of myself, Heber, so your words neither surprise nor upset me."

"Good, because I didn't mean to upset you. It's just worrisome for me to see you alone like this."

"I have a friend. And I have daughters now who are a great blessing and comfort to me."

"Then why do I find you all alone and looking so downtrodden?"

"I am a widow, Heber. My life is good but not easy."

"And your grandchildren?" he asked. "How many sons have your sons given you?"

"I have no grandchildren—yet."

"That's unfortunate. The king, I've heard, favors grandsons. He intends to assemble an entire army of his grandsons."

"That's true."

"Well, I'm sorry to hear that Chilion and Mahlon have married women without wealth. I thought maybe I could impose on their wealth, seeing my own has been stolen."

"Stolen?" Naomi asked.

"Yes, my own nephew robbed me of my parcel of highland in Bethlehem. Boaz is buying up every piece of property he can. He owns almost every field near the threshing floor."

"I know Boaz. He would not do such a thing."

"He tricked me. He's an expert in letters, and the contract he wrote was nothing but trickery. When I asked for more money, he denied me."

"So he paid you what the contract agreed?"

"Yes, I suppose."

"Then I don't see how he robbed you."

Just then a group of young women passed the gate. They were garbed in feathers and jewels, preparing for the first night of the fertility festival. Heber's head turned so fast Naomi thought it might fall off his shoulders.

"Maybe I'll marry a woman here. Maybe I'll even take a concubine or two."

"Why do you suggest such a thing when you know it's forbidden?"

He flicked a fly away from his nostril. "Oh, my sister-in-law, I thought you'd lived in Moab long enough to realize that nothing is forbidden to the man who lives only by his own laws."

* * *

Heber eventually left and, much to Naomi's relief, did not return. But at the end of the season, Ehud, Israel's chief judge, was back in Moab to pay the harvest tribute. Naomi tried to imagine how much he must hate the king, having to deliver food, wine, and crafts made by his own people only to be claimed by their enemies. She would never admit it to anyone, especially not to Orpah and Ruth, but Naomi hated the fat king with all of her heart. She had dreams that he died and that she had blood on her hands.

When she woke, she prayed for forgiveness—not for the blood but for feeling no remorse at Eglon's death.

This year's tribute was different. It required more priests to bear it because King Eglon wanted to punish the land of promise for the rumors of a rebellion. He doubled the required tribute and invited all of Dibon to come and witness his power over the weaklings.

Naomi intended to stay at home, but when Sakira invited her to go watch the procession, Naomi accepted.

Ehud looked weak and dejected as he led his band through King Eglon's palace gates. Their Hebrew backs and carts were loaded. They brought grain the Hebrews could not do without, along with barley, dried figs, dates, pomegranates, and barrels of apricots. There were rugs and winter coats made from camel hair, baskets and pottery, sandals made of leather and with shoulder pouches designed to match, olive oil and vessels of new wine. And there were even small statues of Chemosh carved from olive wood.

Moabite soldiers armed with shields, swords, and sabers looked ready for war should any Hebrew make a wrong move.

The king lumbered out to greet them, his face glistening with sweat, great beads of it splashing from his jowls and even off his elbows. The very ground rumbled when he laughed.

"Ehud!—judge of the land of Hebrews—greetings, Brother!"

Ehud bowed his head but refused to bend his knees. "Peace, King Eglon."

"You know, I've heard rumors of a rebellion lead by you," the king said loudly enough for all to hear.

"I've come in good faith," Ehud said, "to bring you your deserved tribute."

"And so you have!"

It took the king what seemed forever to make his inspection. There were cattle, sheep, goats, and two young mares matched in auburn hue and identical gait.

"Mother."

Both Naomi and Sakira turned at the sweetness of Ruth's voice.

"Mahlon and I have come to watch the tribute delivery. Father seems pleased."

"He should be," Naomi snapped.

"Don't mind her," Sakira said. "She eats the food of the tribute. She wears the clothes. But she doesn't like to watch."

"You're right, Sister," Naomi said. "This day I realize what a hypocrite I've been. You are absolutely right."

"Please, don't argue, Mothers," Ruth begged.

"Where is Mahlon?" Naomi asked.

"He said he had an errand to attend to. Come celebrate with us," Ruth invited.

"Yes, Naomi, come celebrate the arrival of the greatest Hebrew tribute ever delivered to Moab," Sakira pleaded.

"I don't feel much like celebrating."

Sakira crooked her arm around Naomi's elbow. "Nonsense. You will join us, at least for the feast. It's no day to be all alone."

Orpah had saved a place at the front, permitting them a grand view of the king's table. After King Eglon boasted about Moabite supremacy and the massive tribute was displayed and distributed, they dined. The king ate most of a small roasted swine, the meat swimming in fat. He also ate bread dipped in the grease and drank more wine than Naomi could drink in a year.

Ehud sat on the king's left while Lemuel took the seat to the right. Behind Lemuel was Chilion, who thought himself more of a man than his father, Elimelech, but who stood ready to fill Lemuel's wine cup any time it ran dry. He refused to look out at either his wife or his mother but kept his eyes on the king's chief captain.

The guests were finally fed after those sitting at the royal table were halfway through their meal. Naomi accepted a handful of nuts, but could not even bring herself to chew them.

"Eat, drink, and be merry!" Sakira shouted. She had hardly taken her eyes off King Eglon. It was clear to Naomi that the woman wanted his attention, but the king was surrounded by younger women—girls, really—and he paid no attention at all to Sakira, though her lips were red, her cheeks rouged, and her eyelashes tipped with indigo.

Naomi felt pity for Sakira but would never say it.

The dancers entered and moved up and down the tables, men and women who were willing to do whatever Eglon and the other guests requested. Dances as well as fire and music and sacrifices were paid to Chemosh as tithing.

Orpah and Ruth were whispering to each other. Sakira was in the midst of the dancers. Chilion was still beside Lemuel, trying to anticipate the man's every desire.

Naomi left. When she arrived at home, she found that she had company.

"Heber?"

"No, Ama. It's me."

"Mahlon! What are you doing here?"

He looked nervous, and she saw that he held something behind his back.

"I came by to check on you."

"I was with Ruth at the temple. I couldn't bear to watch another moment."

"I understand," he said.

So did she. She knew what Mahlon was trying so hard to conceal. She just didn't know what he was going to do with the short sword.

* * *

It wasn't until the next morning that she learned the truth as bits and pieces of the incredible story unfolded on a neighbor's wagging tongue, from Sakira's wailing cries, and from Chilion's outrage. It wasn't until she walked with Mahlon to fill her water jug that the whole tale made sense.

"The king ate and drank until he was gorged. You can imagine Ehud's humiliation, being subject to the greasy, greedy king. Eglon actually thought Ehud was savoring the royal hospitality.

"It went on for hours after you left, Ama: the dancing, the sacrifices, and the maidservants. Then the horses came, and they carted the king and our chief judge back to the palace with Ehud, humiliated and subject to the king, pretending to enjoy the royal hospitality.

"Ehud allowed the king to get almost to the door of his sleeping chambers before calling after him, 'A word, good king, and a word in private.'

"'Now?' the king asked, very drunk and clearly annoyed.

"'Yes, I beg you. I should have said something before, but it is a personal matter—highly personal, in fact.'

"'Say whatever you must,' the king bellowed. He grabbed one of the maids by the hair with his slick fingers. 'Be quick, Ehud. I have things to do.'

"Ehud looked toward the closed door of the king's private chambers and asked if they could speak alone.

"Instead of granting Ehud's request, the king asked, 'What is so important that must be said at this hour?'"

Naomi was enthralled with the story. When a group of women came to the well to draw water, she put a straight finger to her lips, telling Mahlon to lower his voice. Once they were alone again, she motioned for him to continue.

"I don't know how you know all of these details, but please continue," she whispered.

Mahlon spoke fast, like he was purging himself of the tale. "Ehud forced himself to tremble as he lifted his head and made his eyes go wide. Very, very soberly Ehud told the king, 'I have a word from the Hebrew God directly to you.'

"King Eglon crossed his arms over his giant belly, then brought his elbows out fast and hard, sending the maids scampering back. 'Leave me for now,' he demanded. 'I'll send for you when I'm ready.'

"'Thank you, good King,' Ehud said. 'I promise that you will be most surprised.'

"Eglon looked at his guards. Lemuel was there. So was Chilion. In fact, it was Chilion who had to search Ehud before allowing him to enter the king's sleeping chambers."

"Search him for what—weapons?" Naomi asked.

Mahlon nodded and smiled. "Yes. Ama, if you could see the king's sleeping chambers you would be astounded. It is a massive room with an idol of Chemosh by the window and a painting of Ashtoreth and her fertility cohorts on the wall. In the center of the room is a gigantic round mattress. The air smells of perfume, but it is not strong enough to mask the odor of sweat and human waste.

"Ehud hurried in, closed the doors securely behind him and said, 'Be comforted, king. The Lord of Israel is mindful of you.'

"Eglon sniffled nervously. 'Yes. Yes. He has rewarded me this day with greater tribute than Moab has ever received. But when you think on it, we are brothers, descended from the same family, Moabites and Israelites. The tribute is rightfully mine.'

"A noise came from the open window, and they both looked out but decided it was the wind that had fluttered the curtains.

"'Yet we are not spiritually related, are we?' Ehud asked, drawing the king's attention back to him.

"The king heaved himself down onto a leather padded bench wide enough for eight normal men.

"'Make your point, Ehud. I'm tired.'

"'When you were born, did your mother tell you what your name means?'

"'No. I suppose it means *king*.'

"'It means *circle*. All these years that I have judged Israel and brought tribute to your threshold, I've thought about that meaning. We go round and round and get nowhere. We have trodden the same circle over and over, until the path is worn down,' Ehud explained.

"'Leave now. You're boring me.'

"'But I'm not finished.'

"'Call for my girls to come back.'

"Ehud moved toward the window and appeared to lean out into the night air. When he turned back around he stood taller, straighter. He went on. 'When we honor the Lord, the Lord honors us. Our people have not honored the Lord the way we should. Did you know we recently cleansed Bethlehem of all idols, finding them hidden in almost every home?'

"'Leave me now, I said!' the king bellowed.

"Ehud stepped closer and grinned. 'King Eglon, this moment is just the way he'd imagined.'

"'Who are you talking about?'

"'Do you know that I am the son of Gera, a Benjaminite? And did you know, King Eglon, that I am a left-handed man?'

"'You have no message.'

"'It is not easy for a left-handed man to wield a right-handed weapon. A weapon must be especially crafted for a left-handed man. The hilt must fit precisely. The blade cannot be too heavy or too long.'

"'You've gone mad, Ehud.'

"'Ehud! That's my name. Do you know what my name means, King?'

"'I don't care what your name means. Get out of my chambers or I'll have you thrown to the dogs!'

"'It means *I give praise and thanks*. And I do.'

"'What is the message from your god?' the king asked as he struggled to raise himself. 'Tell me and be gone!'

"'This is the message: There is only one true God, and He is the Hebrew God, the great and powerful Jehovah.'

"Eglon's jaw dropped and his gray tongue wagged out, but no sound escaped his throat. For, in one smooth swoop, rehearsed so many imaginary times, the double-edged blade that my grandfather, Aharon, and his young son, Elimelech, had designed and fashioned years before—the sword your husband and my father had smuggled into the land of his enemies, the sword that lay in hiding until I crept into the king's sleeping chambers to conceal it for Ehud's taking—came forth out of the shadows and sank deep into the bowels of the king."

Naomi slapped a hand over her mouth to keep from shouting, screaming, gasping in surprise and emotion. What she was hearing was as miraculous as Moses's parting of the Red Sea. Finally, she understood what Elimelech had meant all of those times when he told her, "You know nothing about what is really going on with me."

Mahlon carried the water jug but kept his eyes on hers as he told the story with great animation.

"The guards waited. Chilion shifted back and forth, nervously, as though he was bursting with an inner secret.

"The maidens waited.

"Lemuel came up the stairs two at a time.

"'The king is occupied, Captain,' Chilion reported.

"'What do you mean, he's *occupied*?' Lemuel responded.

"'Can't you hear him grunting?'

"'You mean he's on the chamber pot?'

"Chilion tipped an ear toward the door. Everyone standing nearby heard a horrible grunting sound.

"'Then I will retire for what's left of the night,' Lemuel said. 'You will stand guard, Chilion, you and the others.' His sharp glance was aimed at three other men.

"'Yes, sir.'

"And they waited some more.

"Chilion's heart went cold when he heard the sound of Lemuel's metal-toed sandals clacking over the stone corridor. There were dark bags beneath his eyes, and he yawned.

"'The king's not finished yet?' the captain demanded.

"'We can still hear him relieving himself,' one of the guards said.

"Lemuel huffed, 'As much as he despises noise, he sure makes us suffer with his. I have a report that I'm anxious to give him. I'll wait if I have to.'

"Chilion closed his eyes as if he was praying. Finally, the room went quiet.

"'King Eglon?' Lemuel rapped his knuckles on the door. 'It's Lemuel. I have a report to present. May I enter?'

"When there was no response, Lemuel forced the door open and found Eglon in a heap, excrement leaking into a puddle.

"'How could you leave him alone like this?' Lemuel demanded.

"'He wasn't alone,' one of the guards reported. 'Ehud, chief judge of Israel, was with him.'

"'What?' Lemuel's face became bloodless. His eyes looked ready to pop from their sockets.

"Chilion shrugged and spoke matter-of-factly. 'King Eglon said it was all right. He told us the two had business to conduct.'"

Naomi trembled. "Are you absolutely certain that King Eglon has breathed his final breath?"

"Very certain."

"And the sword?"

"They didn't discover it until this morning. It was encased tightly between folds of stomach fat, so they had to slit his gas-filled belly open and deflate it to get the sword out."

"Can they trace the sword back?" Naomi asked.

"Back to where, Ama? No Moabite has ever seen such a sword. It was as though the weapon was designed just for a certain man to use at a certain time."

Naomi wept as the truth became clear to her, felt as surely as the morning breeze.

"Tell me, son, how can you relate the account in such detail? It sounds as though you were present somehow, which we both know is impossible."

"Oh, Ama, don't you remember what you've taught your sons all of our lives?"

"What's that, Mahlon?"

"That for the God of Israel, nothing is impossible."

16

MOAB DISSOLVED INTO CHAOS. Rumors flew from the palace that Ehud had escaped out a window, aided by someone below who was waiting for him—someone who had slipped in during the festival and had planted the short sword used to murder the king. When that man was discovered, the rumors said, he would be executed for everyone to see.

Queen Zima, a woman whose existence plenty of the people doubted, was sent for from the winter palace. Mahlon was among those dispatched to accompany her to take her rightful place as the king's replacement.

Ehud was said to have fled to Seirah, where he had blown a victory trumpet all throughout the hills of Ephraim. The Hebrews, who had suffered and slumbered for so long, were now rallying, vowing to attack Moab in revenge for a generation's worth of torture, murder, and suffering.

Before the queen arrived, Eglon's many sons all seemed to want to sit on his throne. But Lemuel was faster than them all. Using every bit of his authority, Lemuel took over the kingship hours before the king was laid to rest in a cave that had to be sculpted out by a hundred masons before it was large enough to hold the corpse.

Chilion had quickly switched sides and joined the Hebrew army. Naomi feared that they would not accept him, but he was immediately assigned the rank of captain. He seemed overjoyed to report that Israelites were spilling out of the highlands and joining forces with Ehud. Soon, the fords of the Jordan would belong again to Israel.

While fish grilled over the fire, a late-afternoon sun spread light the same shade as an apricot. Naomi ground grain for bread and the girls crushed olives.

"We're supposed to mourn our father?" Orpah asked. "I never really knew him."

Ruth said nothing. But more than once, Naomi saw the tears she tried to hide. Naomi did her best to comfort her new daughter, but how could she say she was sorry that Eglon was dead when everyone knew she wasn't?

"Feel what's in your heart," Ruth said. "Don't allow anyone to put feelings there that aren't there."

"All I feel is relief," Orpah whispered. "I feared him more than I loved him."

Chilion then came through the gate.

"What's wrong?" Naomi asked. "I can tell by the look on your face that something is wrong."

"It's not safe here for Sakira."

"Why?" Ruth and Orpah asked at the same time.

"Lemuel is like a male lion, claiming his territory by killing off any remnants of the old king."

"That means *all* of us!" Orpah cried.

Ruth gasped. "Where is Mother—and Nathaniel?"

"I've hidden Nathaniel in our own ranks," Chilion said. "He'll be safe. Sakira might be fine. Lemuel might leave her be, but we must watch over her."

Orpah went to her husband, and he put an arm around her shoulder, an act of affection Chilion seldom showed. "I will never let any harm come to my family," he said.

"This is the time we should all pack our things and go home," Naomi said with boldness.

Chilion spun toward her. "Your answer to every problem is to run back to Bethlehem. Ama, there is still no food there. The highways have never been more dangerous, and if you tried to cross the river now you'd be robbed, if not stabbed. The people are crazed in their unrest."

"I did not know," Naomi said, her boldness tamed.

"You must trust me now."

"I do," she said. "More than I ever have."

Ruth touched Naomi's shoulder and pointed. Two strangers were walking toward the gate. One was so familiar lately that seeing him made Naomi's heart drop; the other, a woman, was a complete stranger.

"Heber! Uncle!" Chilion called.

The last person Naomi wanted to see was Heber, but his scrawny legs barged through the gate with the woman following two steps behind him. Unlike the women he usually chose, this one was raw-boned and wore a weathered face. Looking closer, Naomi noticed that there was something vaguely familiar about her.

Heber and Chilion embraced and laughed.

"What happened to the boy I knew?"

"I'm a man. A husband. A military captain," Chilion said.

"And this must be your beautiful wife."

"No. That is Ruth, my sister-in-law. This is my wife, Orpah."

Hasty introductions were made, then Naomi asked, "And who have you brought with you, Heber—is this your newest wife?" It was rude, and Naomi regretted saying it the moment the words were off her tongue.

"No," Heber said. "Lydia is hardly my wife. But she's part of the family nonetheless and deserves a place at the table and a share of the estate."

They waited. The girls looked at Naomi, but she shrugged to indicate that she was unaware.

"Lydia, step forward," Heber ordered.

It was spoken in a manner more fitting Chamor than a woman. Eyes to the ground, the woman shuffled forward at Heber's command. Naomi could see by her vacant expression and by the scars on her hands and arms that life had not been gentle with her.

"It's taken me months to find Lydia. This was not a safe time to make such an arduous journey. Add to that the fact that I had to convince the woman that my claim was true." Then he pointed straight at Orpah and said to Lydia, "Take a hard look. You'll see that I speak only the truth."

"Who is this?" Naomi asked.

Heber half smirked, half smiled. "Why, Lydia is King Eglon's long-forgotten concubine. Lydia is Orpah's mother. Can't you see the resemblance?"

It took a moment for the shock to wear off, but when it did, Orpah let out a wail and ran out the back way, weeping.

"I'll go after her," Chilion said. Then he looked at Lydia. "She's shocked; she didn't mean to be inhospitable."

"Do you think Orpah ran to tell Sakira?" Naomi asked Ruth.

"Sakira?" Lydia asked, her voice hoarse.

"*She* is Orpah's mother," Ruth answered. "And she is *my* mother."

A short while later, Chilion and Orpah marched through the gate with Sakira. Sakira's jaw was set, and her red eyes looked suspicious.

"Mother!" Ruth greeted her, but Sakira walked straight for Lydia.

"I don't believe you!" Sakira said.

For a second, Naomi thought Sakira was going to strike Lydia. "I don't believe that you gave birth to my daughter. I don't believe you ever knew King Eglon. I don't believe anything Heber has said about you!"

"Calm down!" Chilion ordered. "This woman is our guest and will be treated with hospitality."

"Do not speak to my mother like that." Orpah's nostrils flared and her eyes bulged. Naomi was stunned to see this side of her daughter-in-law, but it pleased her very much. "Neither of us believes that this woman gave birth to me," Orpah continued. "She only showed up now because the king is dead and now there is no one left to dispute her claim."

"Her claim to what?" Heber asked.

"The royal wealth," Orpah said. "Rumor has it that Father's wealth will be divided between his wife, his concubines, and his acknowledged children. That's why this woman is here now."

"That's not entirely true," Heber said, holding his palms out toward them to prevent things from turning into an all-out brawl.

Chilion glared at Orpah, then said, "We need to hear the details, Uncle Heber. Tell us how and where and when and why you came upon this woman."

"I have a name," Lydia said. "And I have a voice. I can answer all of those questions."

Naomi's eyes widened at the woman's brashness.

"Go ahead, speak your mind," Heber said. "But first, could we have something to eat?" He appeared amused at the confusion he'd caused.

The meal was awkward, but Heber ate like he'd been summoned. Lydia's appetite, too, was anything but shy.

"The bread's very good," she said, taking her third piece. "I hope you don't mind. I have not eaten in a long time." Her eyes lifted to meet Heber's, but he was too busy helping himself to the last of the olives.

Lydia's eyes fixed on Orpah, and Naomi could see how their noses matched, long and thin. Also, both sets of eyes were almond-shaped. But it was their little fingers that made her concede Heber's claim—both fingers were crooked in the same fashion.

"If what you are saying is true, why didn't you come and find me before now?" Orpah blurted. Suddenly she sounded like a lost little child.

Heber jumped up, jittery as a jester. "Now, now," he said. "All your questions can be answered later. What matters is that you've got a third mother to care for and an uncle who has fallen on hard times. Surely, between you all, there is plenty to spare for a man who has sought to bring you such a wonderful gift."

Orpah's chin quivered, but she said nothing more. Naomi had plenty to say but did not dare voice her opinion of Heber or his actions. Her arm went around a pale and quaking Sakira, who refused to let go of Orpah's hand. Lydia seemed such a solitary figure that Naomi's heart went out to her.

"We will make do and do the right thing," Mahlon said.

"Whatever that may be," Chilion said.

Heber began to mutter, but Lydia cut him off. Keeping her gaze only on Orpah, she explained, "I was sixteen and betrothed to my cousin Daniel. We were to be married in a matter of months, but then Eglon was made king. One of the first things he did was send scouts around the land, looking for concubines. I was doing laundry with my grandmother when Lemuel came by on the biggest, blackest horse I'd ever seen. Right away, he pointed at me and told me that I'd been honored as one of the chosen."

"I believe you," Sakira piped up. "I believe everything you claim. But I will not accept you as the mother of my daughter. Orpah will always be mine."

"I understand," Lydia said.

"So there is no money attached to this woman?" Heber asked in a voice that was more of a squeak. "Tell me that she is worth something. I surely deserve some payment for bringing Lydia here. She wasn't easy to find."

They all turned their eyes on Heber, but no one said a word.

He finished the last of the wine and left Lydia behind.

* * *

Lydia volunteered to live at the shop and work to repay Sakira for mothering Orpah all these years.

Sakira's response was harsh. "No. I want nothing to do with you."

"Don't you have a home and a family to return to?" Naomi asked.

"I have no one."

"Then you will stay with me," Naomi said. "There is room and food enough for two."

Dividing the few chores they had still left Lydia a great deal of time to wander. She liked the same high hills and trails Naomi liked to trek. Sometimes they even went together, sharing small insights about each of their lives.

Lydia claimed she was simply abandoned by the king. "After Orpah was born, the king's maids took her from me. I was allowed to serve as her wet nurse, but I was not allowed to mother my own daughter."

She sighed. "I thought my time at the palace would go on. I thought I would have more children with the king and that I would receive some sort of security, like Sakira, perhaps. Then one day the king's maidservant, a wretched woman called Driann, handed me a small bundle, and I was taken in a royal carriage back down to the river bottoms where I came from."

"The king never sent people to look for you?"

"No. I was left to myself, a lone and shamed girl. You can imagine what my life has been like."

* * *

Day followed day. With a band of soldiers here and a band there, the Hebrew military force slowly invaded Moab. Naomi hid her etchings and kept the bench she'd carved out of sight. She never thought she would be fearful of her own people, but these men were fierce warriors and looked at her as a kind of traitor.

Orpah came to the house in tears. "Chilion is in the great battle between your people and ours."

"What battle? And what people? We are *one* now, Daughter."

"Israel has attacked Moab," Orpah said, struggling for breath. "Chilion's men are fighting along the borders. They are coming in to tear down every idol and to declare Moab a land of peace."

"That cannot be a bad thing," Naomi said.

"Lemuel's armies have banded together and sworn to fight to the death."

Naomi saw the fear Orpah felt for Chilion, and Naomi felt it too. "Lemuel will personally target Chilion," Naomi said.

"I know," Orpah said. "Please, Mother, pray for him. Pray to your god."

"My God is your god, Orpah."

"No. No. You pray, Mother. Now! Please!"

They knelt together and prayed for the safety and deliverance of Chilion.

They had just finished when Lydia came to the gate with an armload of wheat.

"Where did you get that?" Naomi asked.

"From the king's fields," Lydia said. "People are plundering."

Orpah wiped her tears. "It's against the law to glean."

"I wasn't gleaning," Lydia explained. "I was stealing. And I think we all should take what we can before it's gone."

"What kind of woman are you?" Orpah asked.

"I am the kind of woman who has been deceived all of my life. Did you know that Heber lured me here, promising me a life of ease and comfort? He told me that you were searching for me. I came here for my daughter, but all I've found is your cold shoulder and your true mother's wrath."

Orpah did not soften just then, but the next day she sat on the threshold next to Lydia while she was grinding corn. Naomi excused herself, pretending she had work to do, and went out into the market, hoping that it was safe to leave her home.

* * *

The battle never made it all the way to Dibon. Ten thousand Moabite men died along the riverbanks. Naomi did not know the number of Hebrew dead, but when she heard a horrible crash coming from the temple, she knew that the Hebrews had declared victory.

First, the great and powerful idol of Chemosh was brought down and desecrated. The pieces were melted or carted off. Then the mandate came: Anyone displaying a likeness of Chemosh or Ashtoreth would be punished.

"Where is Lemuel?" Sakira demanded of Chilion.

"Hiding behind the palace walls like the coward he's always been."

Gradually, an uneasy peace came to Moab. Lemuel was allowed to remain on the throne, but he lacked the power he'd snatched and enjoyed for only a moment.

"He's only a figurehead now," Chilion said. "A vicious and plotting figurehead."

"My fear is for my sons. But tell me, Chilion, will I be evicted now that you're no longer a Moabite captain?"

"I am no longer a captain at all, Ama. I've been stripped of my command."

"Why?"

"Because I am not trusted by the leaders on either side."

"What will you do to support your wife?"

"I'll join my brother in working the concrete around the palace. Lemuel wants everything around the palace gray with concrete."

"So you are working for Lemuel again? That does not seem safe, Son."

"What choice do I have, Ama?"

* * *

The idols were gone, but Naomi did not feel the presence of Jehovah enter into the land of Moab. All she saw or felt were more laws and more soldiers. And if she wished to continue living where she was, she would now have to pay a small rent.

Naomi wept to Lydia. "I have no money to pay rent, and I can't ask my sons for money. They struggle to support their own families."

"You have shown me kindness," Lydia said. "And you have given me a home. I will pay the rent."

And she did. Lydia sold reeds she plucked from the riverbanks. She sold snatches of herbs and seeds she gathered in the wild. She sold wild nuts and seeds and sometimes kindling. She even sold honey she gathered from the trees in the highlands.

Meanwhile, Naomi wove baskets, but hers were never as tight or as beautiful as Sakira's.

As the months passed working in the shop and no babies came, either to Orpah or to Ruth, Naomi was racked by her doubts concerning the curse of Ashtoreth. Every time she was in Sakira's presence, Naomi relived that night when Sakira had said those words of doom. Finally, Naomi asked Jehovah, "How could an idol goddess—in whom I don't even believe— have the ability to weigh me down with such crushing guilt and fear?"

She was in a fitful sleep one night when she heard Sakira scream, "Help me! Someone help me!"

Naomi hurried down the ladder as fast as she could, but Lydia was already there.

"Lemuel had my shop set on fire!" Sakira cried.

The women grabbed jugs and jars and vessels that they filled from Naomi's small cistern, but by the time they got back to Sakira's shop, it was nothing but ashes. Other shopkeepers and people were there to help, but it was too late. Every basket had burned.

"You will live with us," Naomi said. "You are family."

Sakira said nothing as she dragged herself behind Naomi and Lydia into the night.

The house grew even more crowded a few days later when Mahlon and Ruth had to move in after their house was taken over by Hebrew soldiers. They made their sleeping quarters in the lower room with Chamor. It was humble and cramped, but they did not complain.

A cold wind blew across the hills and brought snow to the red rocks of Moab again. About the same time, a traveling physician came from Egypt announcing that he could make any infertile woman fertile, as long as her years were not too many.

"Chilion will not let me be examined," Orpah said.

"Mahlon is *forcing* me to visit the physician," Ruth explained. "My husband wants sons."

Naomi could not bear to see her daughters so sad. She had suffered the pains of miscarriage, and her own womb had gone barren. But she had also known the joy of motherhood, and she wanted that desperately for Orpah and Ruth.

Sakira glared. "How desperately does he want sons?"

"I will not pay homage to Ashtoreth. Not now. Not ever," Naomi replied.

"Then our daughters will remain infertile."

* * *

When Sakira and Naomi returned with a dejected Ruth, Mahlon was waiting in the street.

"What did the physician say?" Mahlon asked.

"Can we talk about this in the privacy of our home?" Naomi asked.

"No. Tell me now, please. What did he say?"

Ruth's big golden eyes welled with tears. "He said there is nothing wrong with me."

Mahlon's head tilted to the side. He scratched his scalp. "But there *is* something wrong with you!"

"No," Ruth repeated. "He said my body is able to conceive and bear a child."

Mahlon's cheeks turned red and his nostrils flared. "The man is a charlatan. I will go demand our money back," he said, and he left Ruth standing in the street watching her husband grow smaller and smaller in the distance.

* * *

Seasons came and went. They were each different, winter with its snow and summer with its scorching heat, but Naomi did not feel them. She only felt numbness in the face of so much pain—a pain she could do nothing to stop.

"You must drink more water," Lydia said as they hiked up a peak that allowed them to look out over the whole city of Dibon. "You'll feel better with this sweet air. The city air is only smoke and ash."

Naomi looked into the woman's gray eyes. "It's my fault Orpah and Ruth do not bear children."

Lydia laughed. "It is not your fault, Sister."

Naomi's eyes lifted. She looked into Lydia's face, a face now so familiar, and wondered how it had happened—how Lydia, hard-working, solemn Lydia, had turned into a sister. Yet she had, and Naomi was glad for it.

Chilion and Mahlon worked more and more with concrete and less and less at the work that brought them joy. When the neighbor next door died, Chilion and Orpah made arrangements to rent that house. With some remodeling that linked the two residences, they were all living together.

"It's how families should be," Naomi said to her sons. "I only wish your father was alive to witness it. He would be so proud of the men you've both become."

* * *

Over time and without much conversation, the women became five sisters. Sakira never spoke directly to Lydia, but the two would often sit weaving together for hours.

Naomi might have felt left out if Orpah and Ruth had not flagged her, catching her when she stumbled, shading her when she needed it.

"I need you to start singing again," Naomi told Orpah one day. "I miss the sound of your voice."

"Yes," Sakira agreed.

So, reluctantly, Orpah taught the women to harmonize. They sang together so often that people gathered to hear them.

Even Ruth's eyes lit up, at least when there was music.

"Teach me to dance," Naomi said on another day to Ruth. "I never knew how."

"Hebrews don't dance?" Ruth asked.

"Some do, but not like Moabites."

Ruth tried, but even big-footed Lydia had more rhythm than Naomi, and it made the women laugh and forget their troubles, even if just for a few moments. But those few moments turned into memories that Naomi revisited often.

Lydia taught them all, even the men, how to tie a fishing net and to make a haul in the "dark spots" along the river.

One sweltering evening, Orpah came into the yard, her eyes red from weeping. Naomi feared that Chilion had hurt her again.

"I'm sorry, Mother," she said, and all three women turned to her. "I have just come from the street prophet."

"The old man who begs money for a fortune?" Lydia asked.

Orpah looked grim. "He told me that as long as we worship the God of Israel in this home, there will be no children born to either me or Ruth."

"Chemosh is still my god," Sakira said.

"And mine," Lydia said. "They can take away our idols, but I will remain loyal."

The others turned to study Naomi's reaction.

"You pray to Jehovah every day," Sakira said. "We all see you do it."

"I make no secret of my devotion," Naomi responded.

"It must stop," Sakira said. "If there is to be a baby for our daughters, it is time you made a new kind of sacrifice."

Naomi felt as if her life was a pot spinning on a wheel, about to fly off and crash to pieces. Though she did not pray out loud, prayer became her first morning thought. She prayed when she dressed, grateful for her clothing. She prayed when she straightened the house, grateful for shelter. She prayed every time she washed or ate or performed any mitzvah. She prayed at night—and if she woke before dawn, she prayed for the people her mind focused on—always her daughters.

"Why do you punish Orpah and Ruth?" Naomi silently begged to know. "They've done what you've asked, Lord. Now I ask of Thee that their hearts be healed with the arrival of children."

* * *

One rainy winter day when her heart was feeling cold, Naomi put her hand to the gate.

"Would you like me to accompany you?" Lydia asked. She had been replastering the walls—not that they needed it but because she needed to occupy herself.

"No, not today. Thank you, though. Today I need to be alone to clear my thoughts."

From the high place to which she liked to climb, Naomi saw that the famine was finally lifting from the land she loved. Green was growing where nothing but stony gray earth had once been. God was hearing years' worth of desperate prayers. Why would He not hear and honor hers?

When she came back to the bottom of the incline, she saw a small man, his spine twisted. He sat on the ground, leaning against the stump of a tree.

"You carry a burden, Sister."

"I know you. You are the street prophet who spoke with my daughter."

"I am Stephen."

She had seen men like him before. They roamed the streets preaching of the future, promising that in exchange for a coin a prophecy could be had. A *personal* prophecy.

Naomi clutched her basket and tried to hurry past him, but the man's bony fingers reached out and grabbed her ankle—her *bare* ankle. She stopped, and a scream caught in her throat. With the return of Israelite rule, it was unlawful for a man to look upon a woman's bare skin, let alone touch it.

"Sister, I have something for you," he said.

She spun away. "I cannot speak with you." Naomi's eyes darted in every direction; people were around but paying no attention to her and the prophet. "I have no money," she said. But Naomi did not turn and flee like she knew she should.

"Let me see the palm of your hand," the man said as he lifted his dark, hooded eyes, eyes that looked unblinkingly at her. "I will tell you what you wish to know."

"I know all I need to know."

He smiled a wry smile as he batted away a fly eager for the moisture that seeped from his staring eyes. "There is something you have asked of your God, something you desire more than anything you've ever wanted."

She set her basket down. She held out her palm, and, though she knew she shouldn't, Naomi allowed his filthy hand to touch hers. The man smelled of onions. His long fingernail was thick and yellowed. Its point dug into the lines of her palm as his gray tongue poked out between lips as yellow and cracked as his fingernail.

He dropped her hand. "It is simple to read such a simple life."

She waited until a camel had passed by them, led by a trio of laughing boys, then asked, "What do you mean?"

"You are a one-line woman."

"Please, sir, you have my curiosity."

"You are a widow."

"Yes. You've probably seen me wear my widow's veil."

"That is true. I've seen you pass before, a hundred times, maybe more, carrying your basket, keeping your eyes downcast, and hurrying on. But today you stopped and lowered yourself to my level. Your soul is heavy indeed, Sister. Your desire weighs on you like a rock sitting at the bottom of your heart."

How could he know what weighed her heart down? she wondered.

"Be comforted," he said. "In the coming days your desire will be granted. Your God will grant your petition."

She clutched her heart in a sudden burst of joy. "My daughters will bear grandchildren for me?"

The man clucked his tongue.

"What, then?" she asked. "You said my deepest desire will be met!"

"And it will be, for you will be returning to your home."

Naomi's heart leapt in her chest. "Home!"

"Yes, but it will not be the happy journey that you have hoped for."

"What do you mean?" she asked.

The man's head dipped. He crossed his legs and settled himself on the hard ground.

"Are you finished?" she asked. "Do you have nothing else to say to me? Please, sir, explain yourself."

His dark, flat eyes looked up again. They fixed forward and a single tear slipped down from one wrinkled corner. Immediately, the fly was back. In one flash, the man's hand snatched the fly out of the air, his tongue flicked out, and he ate it.

She heard the crunch of the fly's body as the man's teeth ground down.

Naomi gathered her basket and turned for home. Her heart trembled against her ribs. Halfway up the cobbled street, closer to her house, her feet broke into a full run.

17

IT WAS AN UNUSUALLY HAPPY day. The five women, woven now like the fibers of a watertight basket, were in the high meadow picking petals to be crushed into perfume.

"Smell the air," Orpah said, tipping her head back and breathing deeply. "Listen to the birdsong."

Sakira put her hands over her ears. "All I hear is the incessant pounding and shouting from all of the construction around the palace."

"Lemuel has finally gone mad," Naomi said. "He's so fearful of losing his throne that he thinks he can build walls to keep his enemies away. Doesn't he know that they are behind the walls with him?"

Lydia chuckled. "Our most dangerous enemies are always those closest to us."

"All I know," Ruth said, adjusting the shoulder strap of her basket, "is that Mahlon is worn to threads. As soon as they finish building one wall, Lemuel orders it torn down to build a higher one."

"Chilion also drags himself home so tired his eyes sometimes close while he's eating his supper."

"I only pray the peace that has slowly come to Moab isn't upended by Lemuel's insanity," Naomi said. The women all looked at her as she spread a cloth on the ground and opened a basket of grapes, cheese, and bread. "In these last months, I think we have proven that it is possible to live in the same land and worship different gods. It is possible with enough love."

Ruth helped Sakira lower herself to sit on the blanket.

"I wonder how much love keeps peace in the palace between King Lemuel and his new bride."

The women broke into a chorus of laughter.

"To become king, Lemuel had to marry Queen Zima. Imagine that union."

More laughter.

Sakira leaned forward. "I heard that the queen has the ravenous appetite King Eglon had."

Ruth broke a cluster of grapes apart and passed some to each woman.

"It's hard to believe that she's real. All those years she was married to Father, and we never saw her," Orpah said. "I think she was an embarrassment to him."

"Because she is as large as he was?" Ruth asked.

"And for her hair. Chilion told me it is flaming orange."

"I want to see her with my own eyes!" Lydia said. Looking at Sakira, she added, "All those years we were upstaged by a queen on which we never laid eyes. Did you ever hear the rumor that Eglon and Zima were brother and sister?"

Sakira gave a faint nod.

"All I know," Naomi said, "is that she's supposed to be five times the size of Lemuel and ten years older than he is."

"Finally," Sakira said, snickering, "the horrible man has received the kind of happiness he deserves."

The women finished their meal but continued talking and laughing all the way down the hillside.

They were at the corner where the roads divided when Chilion rushed up. His face was slick with sweat, and he seemed in a great hurry.

"What is it?" Orpah asked him.

"I'm looking for Mahlon. The entire front wall of the palace is cracking, and Lemuel has offered triple pay to any man who helps repair it."

"Triple!" Orpah smiled.

"Mahlon is already at the palace working," Ruth said.

"No, I'm not. I'm here," Mahlon said, yawning as he came out of the gate. "I finished my shift and came home to rest. I heard your voices."

"Come back to the palace with me, Brother. Lemuel is in a fury and is willing to triple our wage until the wall is repaired."

Mahlon stood beside Ruth and brushed her veil back with a gentleness reserved for privacy. "You smell like flowers," he whispered.

Ruth smiled and lifted her cheek to her husband's lips.

"Hurry, Mahlon," Chilion argued. "Triple pay!"

"All right, all right, I'll come with you. But first allow me a crust of bread. I haven't eaten since morning."

"There's no time for food," Chilion argued. "You must come now before Lemuel fills his quota. He's called for every Hebrew in Dibon to take advantage of this offer. I think he's trying to make a show of goodwill."

"I don't trust Lemuel," Naomi said.

"None of us trust him, Ama," Mahlon assured her. "But that doesn't mean we won't accept three times our regular pay."

Ruth held out the basket from their picnic. "Take this. There are still grapes, cheese, and bread in the basket."

"We'll have a hearty supper waiting for you when you return," Lydia told them.

Orpah turned to Chilion. "Be safe."

He frowned, saying, "Always."

And the brothers hurried off to work.

A memory from long ago—a clear image, despite the passage of time—crossed Naomi's mind. She saw her twin sons hurrying through the orchard in Bethlehem, side by side, rushing off to herd their small flock of sheep.

I love you both! she wanted to call after them but did not, for fear of embarrassing Mahlon and Chilion.

* * *

The porridge was steaming, and Lydia and Orpah were husking corn when the world seemed to come crashing down. The sound was one of thunder clapping and people screaming.

"What has happened?" Naomi asked. "Are we at war?"

"It's best to stay safe behind our gate," Lydia said.

But Orpah and Ruth rushed through the gate and out into the street, where mayhem was unfolding. People were rushing to discover the reason for such a horrendous sound and to learn why people were still screaming.

"Don't go!" Naomi called. "It might not be safe."

But the sisters were already gone to see if their husbands were safe.

* * *

How many minutes had ticked by, the screaming growing louder, the air growing thick with dust?

Lemuel himself rode up on a black horse to deliver the news. He and his circle of guards were smiling.

"I bear the most tragic news," he announced. "Naomi, widow of Elimelech, a palace wall has collapsed. Every man assigned to hold it up has been crushed."

Naomi heard his words, but none of them made sense to her. It was as if water were rushing through her ears.

"I regret to inform you that both of your sons have died in the accident."

Naomi collapsed to her knees.

"Of course," Lemuel said, "anyone who dies while employed by the palace receives triple wage for that day's work, so take heart, woman."

The horse whipped around and rode off. *Clip-clop, clip-clop.*

Triple wage? But her sons had been promised that before they had agreed to work for Lemuel today. "I don't believe you!" Naomi screamed after him. "You're a liar, and I don't believe you! My sons were not crushed to death by accident. You are the devil's tongue!"

The black horse stopped and turned around. Instantly, Lemuel was back, looking down at Naomi from atop his tall horse.

"You are free to go see for yourself, but I warn you, it's not a sight you're going to want to remember." And with that, he galloped away.

* * *

It's God's will.

It was the only thing people could think to say. They said it when Mahlon and Chilion were buried together, holding on to each other just as they had when they came into this world.

It's God's will.

They said it when the shock wore off and Orpah cried for nine days and nights, hardly breathing.

It's God's will.

They said it when Ruth gathered all of her husband's clothes and burned them in a fire so hot and close it singed her eyelashes and blistered her chin.

God's will.

They said it when Naomi said nothing, when she refused to shed a tear, when her eyes failed to focus and it took both Sakira and Lydia to force broth down her throat.

How many days and endless nights passed before a group of noisy children dragged the old street preacher on his cart to be left at the gate?

Ruth went to offer Stephen water. Orpah brought him bread.

"Give thanks, for your prayers have been answered," the old man dared cry.

Lydia took the broom to him. "Don't you know we are a house in mourning?" She called to the children to return and take the man away.

"Praise the heavens for answered prayers!" his shriveled mouth cried.

Sakira threatened him. "There are three widows in this house, and your preaching is upsetting them in their time of mourning."

"Send the old one to me," Stephen said.

"Naomi will not come."

But Naomi came. From her hunched position beneath the apricot tree, she lifted herself and shuffled to the gate.

"There you are, Sister, in your rent garments and tattered soul. Give thanks," he said. "Your prayers have been answered."

Naomi lifted vacant eyes.

"It has happened just as I prophesied—maybe not just as you desired, but still. All these years you've prayed to your Hebrew God to make the path clear for your return home. And now no one can forbid you from returning to Bethlehem. Your ties to Moab are forever broken. Praise God!"

* * *

Sakira was drying grapes, hanging them on twine tied between two trees in the small garden. "I hope Chamor won't eat these," she said.

"He's too old to move that far." Lydia chuckled.

"Naomi, would you mind helping me?" Sakira asked.

Naomi put the broom down and slowly lifted her hands to help with the leaves.

"Mothers!" Ruth shouted. "Mothers! It's Orpah. I'm so afraid."

"What is it, Child?" Sakira shouted. "Has she done something to harm herself?"

"Not yet. But we were walking, and she found a small cave, and I can't get her to come out of it. I don't know if there are vipers in it. I don't know if it's a den. Mothers, please, please come help me with my sister."

All three women climbed as rapidly as they could up over the hill, picking their way around sharp-edged rocks.

Lydia was already kneeling at the small, dark entrance when Sakira and Ruth managed to get Naomi there.

Ruth wept. Lydia coerced. Sakira begged.

But Naomi simply knelt down and crawled into the cave with Orpah.

The two of them curled up there together.

"Is Naomi mad?" Lydia asked.

Sakira cast her a hard look. "She knows what she is doing."

Sakira shot out a straight arm to urge the others back, away from the cave. They took refuge on a smooth boulder and waited.

And waited.

And waited.

There was the soft lull of a voice they had not heard in a very long time, a most welcome sound. Naomi was talking to Orpah. What she was saying was too muffled for the others to understand, but it was the first time she had said anything at all since the day Mahlon and Chilion were crushed, enticed like dozens of other Hebrew workers by Lemuel's offer to triple their wages.

It had been a trap.

Everyone knew that now, but there was no punishment for the figurehead king. The only suffering was experienced by the widows and orphans left behind.

The smallest bird, its blue wings fluttering against the blue-sky backdrop, flew in and out of the cave. Soon it began to sing, and so did Naomi.

Naomi sang to Orpah.

No one dared to move for fear the magic would be broken.

She sang a song the others did not recognize, something about a lamb and a shepherd.

When the song ended there was more waiting.

Then Naomi's voice rose for everyone to hear.

"This dark place smells of death, and yet you are not dead, Orpah."

"I feel dead. I feel nothing."

"It is time to feel again. Mourning has ended. Come out into the light and get on with your life."

Naomi rubbed the curve of Orpah's back. "The pain will never go away, but it will find a place to settle."

"Mother, I am now no different than you. I am old and worthless."

Ruth raised herself to go to Naomi's defense, but the others tugged her back.

"Orpah meant no offense," Sakira whispered.

"What am I to do without a husband or a life?" Orpah asked Naomi.

"You have *your* life, Child."

"I wish to die."

"No, you don't. You wish to live."

"I could hang myself from the tree, or I could throw myself off the high ledges above Dibon."

"Yes, you could do those things, and I could do them with you. But that is not what is going to happen. You are still young and very lovely. Though there's no kinsman redeemer here for you, you will find another husband. Perhaps God will bless you with the sons and daughters you've been denied for so long."

As they emerged from the cave, their voices became even clearer to the women gathered nearby.

Orpah turned her head, and the last rays caught in her eyes, eyes that were still big and beautiful. "I should not have worshipped your god. Chemosh is angry with me."

"Chemosh has been melted and turned to armor. If any god is angry, it is the God of Israel, who has seen fit to make of me the most miserable of women. I have no husband, no sons to care for me. I am old, and my God's wrath is all I have."

"That's not true. You have daughters who will always care for you." Orpah waved her hand toward Ruth. "Come help me get Mother down the hillside before darkness falls."

That night the women made a small fire. They ate stew with goat and vegetables. It was not cold, but they huddled around the fire and talked together of Chilion's strength and courage, never mentioning his temper. They wondered at their own sorrow and how they could ever live without the sound of Mahlon's laughter.

When Ruth burst into tears, Naomi said, "It's good to weep. Tears can wash away the pain." And so they let her weep until Ruth was out of tears.

* * *

When the pink light of morning bloomed over the night sky, Naomi stretched and cleared her throat.

"I am leaving," she announced.

Orpah yawned. "Where are you going, Mother?"

"I am going back to Bethlehem."

Lydia shuddered.

"You can't," Sakira said. "The Hebrews will not have you. To them, you are a traitor."

"I am going," Naomi said.

"Then I am going too," Orpah said.

"And I will go also," Ruth said.

"You can't," Naomi told her daughters.

"We must," Orpah said. "You are the mother of our husbands. It is our duty to stay with you."

It was settled, but that did not mean Naomi was at ease. Before the sun rose, Naomi gathered her things and said good-bye to the few neighbors who were friendly to her. When she returned from filling the water skins at the well, she saw that Ruth's head was resting on her mother's lap, and Sakira's skirt was damp with Ruth's tears—tears she had not allowed herself to cry in the presence of Naomi's own grief.

Dan, the man who had been Elimelech's friend and had once shown interest in marrying Naomi, came to the gate. "I have brought a surprise for all of you."

"A surprise?" they asked.

Nathaniel's shaggy head peeked around Dan.

"He is safe now. Chilion had me hide him, but he's needed here now."

The scene was a flurry of love, questions, and reunion.

"Why do you have to leave?" Nathaniel asked Naomi later, his small fists on his hips.

"Bethlehem is my home."

"And it is our duty to go with Naomi," Ruth explained. "We will not leave her."

"I will come and visit you in Bethlehem," Nathaniel vowed, flinging his arms around Ruth's neck. He wasn't even embarrassed to kiss Orpah's cheeks.

"Naomi, I will miss you," he said.

She pressed her lips to the top of his head. "I will miss you, Child. But I will rest better at night knowing that you are here to take care of your mother and Lydia."

"And, if you will allow me, I will do what I can to help you all," Dan said.

Lydia stepped forward, "We will be fine alone."

"No. We will welcome any help from you, Dan," Sakira said.

Dan blushed from the top of his bald head all the way down his neck.

"We are all packed, Mother," Ruth announced. "Even with the three of us, Chamor's bags are not full."

"But our hearts are, aren't they?" Lydia asked, tying the bags to the donkey's back.

"It's been more than ten years since that same poor beast brought my family here to Moab," Naomi said.

"And now, your dream of returning has come true." Lydia turned the reins over to Orpah, who stood stoically, staring into the distance.

"I never dreamed of returning like this," Naomi said. "Oh, please, my sisters, come with us," she begged Lydia and Sakira. "We can make a home in Bethlehem together."

"Bethlehem is not our home," Sakira said adamantly.

"I will stay beside my sister," Lydia said.

Naomi's heart warmed, and she smiled. It was good to see the bond the two women had formed, slowly, hesitantly, but firmly.

Naomi ran her fingers over the smooth olive-wood bench, where she had carved the commandments of God.

"We will sit on it and think of you," Lydia said.

"We will think of you everywhere we go," a grim-faced Sakira added.

"I cannot do it. I cannot take Ruth from you," Naomi said.

Sakira fingered the earring that dangled almost to her shoulder. "You are not taking her; she goes willingly."

Ruth quickly added, "Yes, you know I do. You are Mahlon's mother. I am your daughter. I will never leave your side."

"But Sakira is your mother. What will become of *her*?" Naomi asked.

"I am right in front of you. Don't speak about me. Speak *to* me."

"I fear for you, Sister," Naomi said. "What will become of you if I take your daughters?"

"Perhaps I will marry again."

"Until then, I will care for Sakira," Lydia vowed.

Naomi looked at Lydia, the woman who had entered among them a stranger, but who was now as much a part of their family as anyone.

"I will take care of you both," Nathaniel said. He wore a brave face, but there were streaks down both cheeks where his tears had carved through the dust. He would probably miss his sisters most of all. He was now the age and size that Mahlon and Chilion had been, Naomi realized, when they first arrived in Moab.

"Please, Naomi, go with our blessings. With Orpah and Ruth beside you, soon you will be home," Sakira said.

Home—the word was heavy in her heart. "I once had a home in Bethlehem. I don't even know who lives in it now. Perhaps it has been destroyed," Naomi said.

"Then you will build a new one." Sakira gave her a long, tight hug. "Be on your way while I still have my wits about me."

"What about the journey? It may not be safe for our daughters."

"We will be fine," Ruth said.

"What if my Hebrew people do not welcome the girls?"

"Our peoples have united," Sakira said. "Now be on the road."

Naomi saw their tears. She knew what this good-bye was costing Sakira and Lydia. "Perhaps it will not be forever. Perhaps you will change your minds and come to Bethlehem."

No one said anything because they all knew that once Naomi was gone, there would be no reunion.

"Don't cry now!" Lydia said. "They'll be plenty of time for tears later. You'd better be gone before the sun comes full in the sky and claims your strength."

"Don't look back. Don't look back. Don't look back."

This was the chant Orpah mumbled as they walked away from the home and life she had always known.

Ruth draped an arm over Naomi's sagging shoulders. "No matter what happens, we will not turn back, Mother. We will never leave you."

"Oh, what am I doing?" Naomi silently asked herself. "Why do I feel so compelled? I am leaving Moab and all of my memories. I am leaving the bones of my husband and sons."

Slowly the three widows wound their way down the path, out of their neighborhood, away from trees, and away from the shade of the hillside city to the flatlands of barley and wheat, now in full harvest.

"It's a beautiful sight," Naomi said, "and so much more beautiful because I haven't seen it in years."

Naomi's heart lifted just the slightest. She was going home.

"Tell us of Bethlehem," Ruth said, choking back her tears. "Tell us of our new home and the places where our husbands grew up."

"In the morning, the whole city looks white, but in the evening, especially on windy days when dust hangs in the air, Bethlehem glows as golden as ripe wheat."

"Are the people as kind and loving as you, Mother?"

"I hope you do not judge all Hebrews by the soldiers who have taken over Dibon. The truth is, I don't know my own people anymore. As you know, my parents are dead. My husband's mother is dead and his father is remarried. Elimelech had a sister who was never fond of me. Her daughters are your equals in age. The last I heard, they were living in Jericho. I have no brothers or sisters. There are distant cousins, but they are scattered. I am the only family you'll find in Bethlehem."

"As long as we have each other," Orpah said without conviction. Then, to herself, she mumbled again, "Don't look back. Don't look back. Don't look back."

On they walked, taking turns holding Chamor's reins. When Naomi's hands were free, she took turns holding her daughters', lacing her fingers between theirs, a symbol of unity in the trio.

A few Moabites shouted out their good-byes and warnings to the women.

"Don't go, Orpah! No man in Israel will marry a Moabitess!"

"They'll cut you through like they did King Eglon if they discover you worship Chemosh!"

"They'll mock you, poor Ruth! Stay here and marry a man who will give you the sons you deserve!"

"You'll be plagued with poverty and remain lonely all the days of your life."

Ruth quickened her step and motioned for the others to hurry. They kept moving and did not stop until Hebrew soldiers stopped them.

"I am a Hebrew widow, returning with my daughters to Bethlehem."

"You might be Hebrew, but your daughters are clearly not." The man snatched a necklace from Orpah's throat. It had been turned around so the symbol rode hidden down her back.

"All likenesses of Chemosh are forbidden!"

Orpah wilted in shame and could not make her eyes meet Naomi's.

"I am sorry, sir," Orpah whimpered. "My mother made the necklace for me, and I will never lay eyes on her again. Please allow me to keep it."

"No!"

He waved them on.

Orpah let her hand slip from Naomi's.

* * *

By the time the sun was high, they could see the river sparkling like green-and-white ribbons below them. Above them they could see the roads and ledges of Moab, a rugged place that Naomi realized, for the first time, was truly beautiful.

Naomi stopped. "Please, allow me to rest in the shade. I'm not as strong as I thought."

The girls tended her. Ruth rubbed Naomi's stiff neck and sore hands while Orpah filled their water skins and adjusted the bags on Chamor.

"Thank you, both, but if you will, I need some time alone to pray."

They had seen their mother-in-law pray hundreds of times.

"It still seems strange to me to pray when there is no likeness of a god to look at," Ruth said.

"I don't see Him with my eyes, Daughter. I see God with my heart."

The sisters stepped back and watched as Naomi sought a quiet spot of shade behind the thick trunk of a palm and bowed her head. She stayed that way for so long that Orpah and Ruth finally looked at each other with concern.

"Maybe she has changed her mind," Orpah said, a skip in her voice. "Maybe she has realized that her real life is back in Moab with our mothers, with our friends, and with our people."

Ruth shook her head.

"Daughters!"

They hurried to Naomi, and each gave her strength as they made their way back to the road. Instead of turning toward the great lumbering river, Naomi faced back toward the city.

"Daughters, you have dealt kindly with your husbands, even when they were not kind to you. In death, you have honored them. And you have dealt kindly with me every day that you have known me. Go back now, I ask; return to your mothers' house."

Neither of the women moved.

"The decision has been made, Mother," Ruth said. "We are by your side and are not leaving."

"To stay by my side is to invite the wrath of the Lord against you."

Orpah pulled her veil tight so Naomi could not see her eyes, but Naomi could hear the catch in her voice. "What does it matter whose god is against us, when no god is for us?"

"No! That's not true. I am old. There will be no more sons in my womb. Even if I had a child now, what are you to do, wait until he is a grown man so that you might marry him? Unthinkable!"

"What are you saying, Mother?" Orpah asked.

"Has the heat gotten to your head?" Ruth asked.

She took them to her and kissed their hands, their cheeks, and their foreheads. "I am saying that it grieves me for your sakes that the hand of the Lord is gone out against me."

Ruth said, "But you are such a faithful woman. You've never betrayed your God."

"Haven't I? Then tell me why He has claimed my husband and sons and left me no man to care for me?"

"You have us," Ruth said, "and we have you. Now let's hurry so we can make it to the lowlands before nightfall."

But Naomi would not budge. "I will go on, but you will both return to your mothers. It's the right thing, the *only* thing that can be done. I realize now that I can't take you into a land and unto a people who will reject you. In Israel, especially now, there is no welcome for a Moabite."

"We've heard this already, Mother, and we are by your side," Orpah declared.

"No. I've changed my mind. You must both go back, before we've gone too far. Go now, and let me journey ahead alone."

"No!" Orpah said. "No." But her voice was weak.

Naomi took Orpah by both hands, tilted her chin back, and looked deep into her eyes. "Your soul is full of sorrow. You are afraid, and I don't blame you. But you don't need to fear what will happen if you follow me because I don't want that now. I want you to return."

"I can't," Orpah said. "I have to go on with you."

"That is not true. Hurry. I can offer only sadness and poverty. I know you, Child. You gave your best effort, but now you want to return to your mothers and to your god."

Orpah sobbed. "I can't leave you." But Orpah wasn't looking at Naomi; she was looking at Ruth.

Naomi kissed her cheeks a final time. "You have proven your loyalty to me and I pray you will find it in your heart to find the Lord God Jehovah. Only through Him will you ever know true peace."

Orpah did not attempt to hide her tears. They were tears of both sorrow and joy.

"Look back," Naomi said, and Orpah looked back. Then her feet began to run.

Naomi turned to kiss Ruth good-bye as well, but Ruth did not take a single step back toward Moab.

"Hurry, catch up with your sister."

Ruth shook her head, pulled back her veil, and took Naomi's hand. She refused to let go.

"Oh, Ruth, Orpah has gone back. Go after her."

Ruth clung to Naomi. Her voice rose so that it echoed off the cliffs. "Please don't make me leave you or to return from following you."

"Sweet child, what are you saying to me?"

"I'm telling you, Mother, wherever you go, I will go. Where your home is, there my home will be. No matter how I am treated, your people shall be my people and your God my God."

Naomi's heart burned with the heat of comfort and assurance. "Very well. I cannot argue against a will as strong as yours, Child."

"Only death can part us now," Ruth said. She gave Chamor a slap, and the two widows did not look back. If they had, Ruth thought, they would probably have seen Orpah standing on the ridge, looking down, her tears falling like raindrops.

18

RUTH WAS TOO TIRED AND too hot to weep. Her head hurt, and she blinked at the vision before her. *This* was the holy land that Naomi was forever praising. It was a city built on a hilltop—not unlike Moab—but this one was made of white stone. There were few trees, and the air smelled of smoke and cinnamon.

"It's colorless," she said, licking her parched lips.

"My mother used to say everything in Bethlehem is the hue of a camel's behind."

The humor did not make Ruth feel better, but Naomi felt she was gazing at the most beautiful place on earth. It was rugged, like her people. It sparkled when the sun shone on it, like her people. It was simple and stalwart. She was home, a place where the Spirit of God was invited.

Naomi kept her face veiled.

"Mother, you've slowed your pace. Are you all right?"

"It's just so much to take in. Bethlehem is the same and yet it's not." It took a long moment to realize that one of the missing components was the sight of Moabite guards and soldiers, their detested orange bands waving like victory flags.

A rabbi passed them, and Naomi stepped out of the way.

"Peace, Sister," the man said to Ruth.

Ruth said nothing, and the old man looked up, clearly offended.

"Our peace be unto you," Naomi said, hurrying them along.

"He is your holy man?"

"One of them. Oh, Daughter, there's much for you to learn."

Ruth took a deep breath and tugged Chamor along.

They entered the wide city gates without anyone there to question them. There were no soldiers—only appointed guards who looked at them but did not speak.

"Should I wear a veil too, Mother?"

"It's not necessary. You are out of mourning, and not all the women wear them. It depends on one's husband's wishes."

Leaning on both Ruth and Chamor for support, Naomi scaled the narrow, cobbled road. Houses and shops loomed on both sides. A few people stared over their courtyard walls.

A group of women approached them, stared momentarily, and hurried past.

"Is everyone so unfriendly?"

"I'm surprised," Naomi admitted, "to remember how cold we can seem—distant even. I suppose it's just that people are occupied with their own thoughts."

"You do not greet each other?"

"If we are familiar, we speak. If we are strangers, we usually nod. I'm keeping my veil on so I can recognize faces without being recognized first."

"You're nervous?"

"Very. All these years I've wanted to return here. I've dreamed of it, but now that I'm here, my heart is pounding and my palms are sweaty. Things appear the same, but so much has changed."

The higher they climbed, the narrower the paths became. In many places they had to travel single file, with Chamor in the center. Sometimes they had to step off to the side to allow others to pass.

Naomi walked slower and slower and then suddenly stopped. They'd come to the entrance of the town square with the common well and a gathering of women around it.

Naomi sighed. There it was. The bench, as long and wide and wonderful as she remembered. Tears poured down Naomi's cheeks.

"That's the bench your mother carved?" Ruth whispered.

"Yes, that's the bench I've told you about. Mother took years to carve it from a single tree trunk. The Moabites didn't destroy it. Praise be to the Lord Jehovah!" Seeing the beloved bench made her knees weak, and she reached for Ruth's arm. With her other hand, Naomi lifted her veil so she could get a clearer view. Then Ruth tied Chamor to a post and gently led Naomi over to the bench, where they sat down together, holding hands.

"I'm home," Naomi said so softly only Ruth heard. "I know this does not feel like home to you, Daughter, but it will in time."

Ruth wiped away her own tears.

"I look around and see a memory of Chilion and Mahlon sword fighting with sticks. I half expect to see my Elimelech, marching toward me, eager to help me carry water."

Naomi's head rested on Ruth's shoulder. Her eyes closed to capture the tender memories as long as she could hold them.

"Naomi!"

Naomi knew the voice but did not turn. Not just yet.

She felt Ruth being tugged from her. "Naomi! Naomi! Can it be you? Look, Sisters! It is! It is our Naomi returned from the heathen land."

Kezia flung herself at Naomi and tore the veil back.

"Oh, dear sister, what in the world has happened to you?"

"Call me Mara," Naomi said in a voice void of the joy she'd just expressed to Ruth. "You should know right away that the Almighty has dealt bitterly with me."

"Yes, we've heard. Elimelech was murdered by the filthy hands of the Moabites. And Chilion and Mahlon were crushed to death at the hand of the vile new king. Death to Moab!"

Ruth slid to the end of the bench and went to stand with Chamor.

Kezia went on in a shrill lament. "And Boaz told me he brought you word that my own Salmon died. The Moabites took the lives of our husbands. Woe are we, Naomi. Our woe be forever."

One of the women wailed, making a sound that pierced the air like a forlorn whistle. Another woman joined and then another, until there was a chorus of wailers.

Ruth held Chamor's reins, looking at the scene with a mixture of emotions. Her head turned toward Moab. She could not see even a glint of it from here. All she could see was the unfamiliar. She watched closely to see if Naomi was being treated kindly. She was smothered with women and questions.

Kezia was old, but she flitted about like a dragonfly. "Oh, Naomi! You're once again sitting on the bench made by our blessed Anna. What would she think of you now?"

Naomi tucked her chin, then brought it back up quickly. "Tell me of my house. Tell me of my father-in-law and his wife, Gila."

"They left us years ago. Gila's daughter, the girl Elimelech saved from Chemosh, married a rich trader from the desert. They live in luxury, from what we hear."

"I am happy for Aharon in his old age."

"By now, he too may be dead, for all we know," Kezia said.

"Tell me of the house. Does it still stand?"

"Yes. But it is wrecked. Heber has lived in it off and on."

"It is vacant now?"

"And in shambles. You cannot hope to make a home of it, not in your worn condition."

"I am stronger than I look."

"Tell us of your life in Moab, Naomi. We want to hear every detail."

"My life was hard. My husband died. My sons died."

This prompted more wailing and condolences.

Ruth petted Chamor's neck and led him to the basin for animals. Then, through the din of voices, Naomi's rose, crying, "Daughter!"

Ruth had to weave Chamor through a clutch of women but was at her mother-in-law's side the moment she was summoned. The other women fell back.

"This is your *daughter*?" Kezia asked.

Ruth drew a shallow breath as she felt all eyes take her in.

"She's dressed in the hue of Chemosh!"

Naomi quickly apologized. "I meant no offense. We are used to orange. Please, forgive us for a mistake that is so obvious now."

"She is a Moabitess."

"Yes."

"And you've brought her here, to the land that her people did their best to destroy."

"This is my precious daughter, Ruth. She would harm nothing and no one."

The women's eyes were as daggers, slicing into every part of Ruth. Their glares were so vicious that Ruth imagined she could feel blood run down her back. She imagined how Sakira would have challenged these women, judging her with their eyes.

"Do you have a name?" Kezia asked.

"Ruth."

"She is widow to Mahlon and daughter to me. She is all that I have left in this world to bring me comfort. Please, make her welcome in her new home."

The women became so quiet that Ruth feared they could hear her heart breaking.

It seemed a lifetime had passed since Naomi had been gone from Bethlehem, yet she knew which turns to make without hesitation.

"This is it. This is the home I shared with Elimelech."

Ruth was shocked. "It is huge, and the courtyard is so large."

"And it is all overrun with thorns and neglect."

"I am here to help you, Mother. I know how to work. Together we can make this a beautiful home."

The gate was broken. A parade of mice scampered out of the house. Ruth led Chamor out into a withering orchard.

Naomi squealed. "Look, Ruth! Look! There are tiny green grass shoots coming up from the hard, cracked earth!"

"Yes, Mother."

"You don't understand. I haven't seen green grass grow here in years. Oh, there is hope for us, Daughter. There is hope."

"As long as we have each other."

Naomi swept through the yard and then knelt beneath a huge olive tree.

"Pray with me, Daughter."

Without hesitation, Ruth knelt beside her, the hard earth biting into her knees.

"Oh, Lord, we thank You. We thank You for this home, this land, for the green grass. We thank You for bringing us up out of the land that was once the land of our enemies. We thank You for Sakira, Orpah, and Lydia, and thank You for Your protection over them. We thank You for Your laws that guide us to live better lives. We offer our gratitude to be home."

"Where is your grief, Mother?" Ruth asked, giving Naomi a hand to help her stand. "Where is your bitterness?"

"Gone." A smile stretched over Naomi's face as she explored the house and property more thoroughly. "This house is barren and filled with spiders and rats, but with Heber gone, at least it's free of snakes!"

One of the first things Naomi did was hang the same mezuzah that had hung in Moab.

"This is the first time I've ever really studied it," Ruth admitted, running her fingers over the cherished parchment, then rolling it back into its leather case—a case Mahlon had made and given his mother as a gift—and hanging it on the post by the gate.

"A reminder," Ruth said, then turned to Naomi and surprised her by asking, "Will you consider teaching me what Mahlon taught you? I mean letters? I would like to learn to read and write."

"I haven't practiced for so long, but I will teach you all that I know."

They ground barley and ate enough to quiet their growling stomachs, but not enough to chase away their hunger.

"We have very little food left. We must make what we have last."

"I understand," Ruth said, breaking the piece in her hand and offering it to Naomi. "Eat more, Mother. You look worn to the bone."

"I am. But my happiness at being home is greater than my weariness in getting here."

Because they could not climb the broken stairs to the roof, Ruth gathered the remnants of old, musty straw and made a sort of bed. "If you don't mind sharing with the mice, you should rest now. I'll finish the night's work."

"No. Sit with me a while, Daughter. Let's look up at the moon. The night is so clear you can see the cracks in the moon tonight."

They lay side by side and soon fell fast asleep.

When Ruth opened her eyes, she saw Naomi watching her.

"You wept in your dreams," Naomi said.

"I don't remember what my dreams were."

"Perhaps that's just as well," Naomi said.

"Mother? How can I know your God if I don't know where He is? How do I find Him?" Ruth asked.

"You call for Him," Naomi explained.

"You do that so gracefully. Earlier, when you were praying, I felt like we were not alone."

"The Spirit of the Lord is with those who seek Him."

"How do you know it's there when we can't see Him?" Ruth asked.

"We can feel Him."

Ruth looked up at the moon, a gauzy haze glowing white around it. "Everything is so new here. Maybe if you taught me the words to your prayers. . . ."

"My most powerful prayers have been offered without words."

"You make it sound simple, just like Mahlon used to make it seem," Ruth said.

"True worship *is* simple, Child, as you will come to know in time."

* * *

Three days of hard work and the house was swept and the straw replaced with armloads of dry grass the women picked from along the roadside ditches. Chamor refused to eat the musty straw, so the women burned it.

A few curious neighbors came by to see what was going on, but no one volunteered to help, and no one spoke any words of welcome to either of them. Not even Kezia stopped by. The only visitors they had were some of the local children who wanted to play with Chamor and practice their archery in the vacant lots next to the house.

"I think it's strange that Kezia hasn't stopped by," Naomi said.

"I fear she was upset because of me," Ruth said. "I've changed my orange dress, but everyone in Bethlehem knows that I come from Moab."

"It's nothing that you should be ashamed of."

"I'm not."

* * *

After two weeks the place was tidied but sparse, and the food was all but gone. The joy that Naomi had felt had turned to dust. Some mornings it was difficult to convince Naomi to even get out of bed.

"I don't know what I thought. All I know now is that I've brought you here to starve. We're a pitiful pair—a young and miserable widow in the company of an old and miserable widow."

"No, Mother. God has not brought us here to die but to *live*. I feel it. I know you did too, when we first arrived in Bethlehem."

"That is before I realized how dismal our circumstances are. We are two widows with no men to care for us. I thought Aharon was here. He would be obligated to take care of us."

"We can take care of ourselves."

"Can we?"

"I've been praying, Mother. Not with your words, but in my own way. We are not alone—the Lord is with us."

Naomi tucked her braid back. "It makes me very happy to hear that you've been praying."

"You don't look happy. You look upset."

Naomi took the donkey's tether from a hook on the wall and draped it over Chamor's neck. "I am upset because the only way I can think of to get money for food and necessities is to sell Chamor."

"Oh no," Ruth groaned. "Is there no other way?"

"Not that I can think of."

Ruth's eyes brimmed. "It's just that since Mahlon died, tending to Chamor has brought me such joy. He's a gentle beast, and he's been so good to us."

Naomi clapped her hands. "Please don't worry. It was a bad idea. I see now how much Chamor means to you, and I promise you, Daughter, I will not sell him. I will not take one more thing from you."

"Do whatever you must."

"What we must do is fill our empty stomachs. Let's go to the fields in the highlands. Now that the famine has ended, there will surely be barley we can glean."

"It is lawful to glean in Bethlehem?"

"It wasn't while the Moabites were our overseers. They would prefer we starve rather than let us glean."

"I'm sorry."

"And I'm sorry if I tie you to them. If you, with your kind heart, had been in charge, all of this land would live in plenty."

"Mother, I will go and do it. Gleaning is no work for your back. Please stay and rest."

"But you've never gleaned, Ruth."

"Lydia taught me all I need to know."

"I miss her laugh," Naomi admitted. "If she was here our ladder would be repaired, our roof rebuilt, and—"

"—our bellies full. Lydia could find food in a ditch, in a field, on the limbs of a tree."

"Do you ever wonder how they are doing—the three of them—without us?"

Ruth looked ready to cry. "I think of Mother, my sister, and Lydia every moment of every day. That does not mean I think of returning, because I don't. I am happy here with you, Mother."

"Happy? I don't believe you are happy, Child. But I do believe that you are committed. And I promise things will get better. I don't know how, but they can't get much worse."

* * *

"Naomi! Naomi!"

Naomi peered out from the lower-floor window at a small, shriveled man with a beard that nearly braided itself into a single, thin rope. He wore no head covering, and his tunic was striped, something very unusual in Israel.

"I am Naomi."

"And I am Heber!"

She groaned and wanted to dismiss him without denying him hospitality. Instead she met him at the gate. "I am just now returned to Bethlehem and I have no hospitality, no bread to offer you, not even a drink to quench your thirst."

"So it's true. You've returned in shame and poverty."

She bowed her head and felt her mouth fill with saliva. "Since I've seen you last, both Chilion and Mahlon have died. I am an old woman, and the Lord's hand has gone out against me. What is it you want from me?"

"Perhaps all I want is to greet my poor sister-in-law."

"Perhaps not," she said.

He sneered. "You're living where I took refuge from time to time."

"Yes." Suddenly her chest felt tight. "I returned thinking that Aharon and his family were here."

"Father has probably died by now. And my sister, Berta, that woman has no heart. I went to her and her rich husband, Uriel. I asked for a pittance, really, not much at all, and they turned me away like I was a leper."

"I can imagine. I'm sorry, but I've got work to do, Heber. There are so many things to repair around here."

Just then, Chamor brayed and Heber's eyes twinkled. "I see you have a fine donkey."

"Chamor is a loyal member of our family."

Now Heber laughed out loud. "A beast like that could be a blessing to a man with a weak back like mine."

"Your back seems fine, and I'm not parting with Chamor. He was a gift to Elimelech."

Heber dropped his feigned manners. "I did not mention it before, but now that you are back and your sons are dead and cannot make it right, you must know that before your family first fled to Moab, my brother—your husband, Elimelech—borrowed a great sum of money from me."

Naomi lifted her eyes. "Elimelech never borrowed. We left here with only the earnings he took from his blacksmith shop and what we had left after selling my father's flock."

"No," the man said confidently. "I promise you that Elimelech owed me money. He promised he would repay me upon his return."

"My husband never spoke of such a deal."

"A husband doesn't mention everything to his wife."

"I saw you twice when I lived in Moab. Neither time did you mention that Elimelech borrowed money from you."

"It was a delicate time. I wasn't in such need of repayment. I am now."

"I'm sorry you have fallen on hard times, Heber, but as you can see, my life is not one of luxury."

"Did I tell you that I remarried?"

"No."

"A young wife from Samaria." His face looked sad. "She's recently given birth to a sickly baby—and what with me having my land stolen and my . . ." Heber blinked hard and a real tear trickled from the corner of his eye.

"I wish you and your family well, Heber."

"We need more than wishes, Sister. I will turn around now and go back to the inn where my poor young wife lies hungry and my son lies sick."

"Peace be with you and yours, Heber. I wish I could offer more, but I cannot."

He wheeled around. "I don't mean to trouble you, further, Naomi, but a thought just struck me. You came from Moab, and I wonder if you might have a likeness of Chemosh in your belongings. It would bring me great comfort because I believe faith, no matter where it is put, brings blessings."

"This house and the people in it worship only the Lord of Israel."

"Please don't be upset. It's just that a small idol of Chemosh, especially one made of metal, might be a real comfort to me. My brother designed many of them. Surely one of those could bring me money—I mean comfort."

Naomi wrung her hands.

"Sister, your heart is too old and weak to handle how upset you appear. I'm sorry if I'm the cause. It's just that I have nothing, not even a house to live in."

"Why did you move from here?"

"Look at it. Everything is broken and run down. My wife despised this place."

"It is my home again."

"I see that. And as much as I hate to bring it back up, my brother and I did make an arrangement. I have a contract to prove my claim." From Heber's purse came a document, old and folded and made from papyrus worn to nearly powder.

"Read it," he said holding it out. "Oh, what a fool I am. No woman can read. See how my worried mind has affected me? Forgive me."

She took it from him. "You say this is a contract between you and my husband?"

He smiled. "Yes, yes, it is. It states that he borrowed a large sum and agreed to repay me upon his return to Bethlehem—with interest, of course."

"Of course."

Heber followed her to the small, slanting table, where she sat and stretched the contract out.

"It will do you no good to stare at a document that is only scribbling to you. I can read it for you, Sister, and then perhaps you will see fit to pay the debt your husband has passed on to you."

"Pay you?"

"Not all at once, of course, a bit at a time can be arranged."

"I told you, I returned a widow and childless mother. Aren't you even going to ask about Chilion and Mahlon?"

"I heard already. Pitiful. Must have been a tragic mess."

She looked down at the document. All the hours she had spent practicing her letters in Moab allowed her to make out certain words: "deed" "property" and "schedule." If only she could actually read it! Then she started to understand some of its meaning. All it stated was that Heber was released from debtors' jail last year.

"It looks official," she pretended to concede.

"It is." Heber grabbed the paper, refolded it, and tucked it away. "I hate to think of how much easier my life would have been all those years ago if I had not made such a sacrifice for you—I mean, for Elimelech."

"What is it you want, kinsman? You can see that I have nothing."

"You have this property. With my father gone and Elimelech dead, it rightfully goes to you."

"And you wish to take it from me?" Her tone was incredulous.

"I can sell it to pay the debt I'm owed. Of course, I'm sure there will be something left for you to live on, an allotment perhaps."

"Heber, I feel terrible. You are my first visitor since I've returned home. And I feel horrible that I don't have a drop of wine to quench your thirst or a crust of bread to feed your belly. Add to that, I have no money to pay you this newly discovered debt."

"Yes, well, as we've discussed, you do have this property. All I need is your signature on this contract, and I will sell your home and land, and the proceeds can take care of both of our needs."

"Did you ever resolve your dispute with your nephew, Boaz?" Naomi asked. "You once told me he robbed you."

"Boaz! That man has no heart. He has gobbled up every piece of farming land he can, and all he offers me is grain. The Almighty's hand will strike him. Watch and see!"

Naomi sat on the small broken bench she'd tried to carve all those years ago and decided to act her part as dramatically as Heber was acting his.

"Do you think, Heber, it is possible that God has dealt with me so harshly because of what you claim?"

"What I claim?"

"Yes. I find now that my husband owed a debt he never paid. Is that why Elimelech and Mahlon and Chilion died and I am left a widow with only a broken home to repay that debt? Am I punished because my husband left you robbed just as surely as Boaz robbed you?"

She tilted her head back and began to wail.

He scampered from one foot to the other. "There now. There now. Calm yourself before neighbors come running."

Her head perked up. "Perhaps one of them will be able to read the contract, Heber. The agreement you claim is between you and Elimelech, when really all it states is that you were released from debtors' jail last year and that if you ever set foot in Edom again, you will be rearrested and not set free for a very long time!"

He stammered. "How did you know?"

"My time in Moab wasn't completely wasted."

"But what about the money owed me?"

"I owe you nothing because Elimelech borrowed nothing from you. Now get out and don't come back here."

The tips of his ears and the end of his nose went red. "Is that any way to treat a brother?"

"Yes, when that brother is you, Heber."

* * *

Ruth kept her chin down and her feet moving. She climbed her way up the path that led to Bethlehem's main threshing floor. Already she looked more like a Bethlehemite than a Moabite. Her dress was the shade of "a camel's behind" and her hair was braided and wound in a twist at the nape of her neck. She held the basket she carried tight to her chest; it had been woven by her mother and was one of Sakira's final gifts to her.

The closer she got to the threshing floor, the harder Ruth's heart pounded. She knew she had to seek out someone with the authority to allow her to glean.

In Moab, gleaning had always been forbidden because her father had wanted to control the people and there was no better way to control them than to control their food supply. She saw that now as she remembered slaves being made to do the gleaning after the reapers cut down the barley and wheat.

Off in the distance Ruth could see Bethlehem's reapers hard at work, hacking the bottom of great grain stalks and making bundles. She and

Orpah used to chase each other around those bundles, slicing their bare feet and ankles on the newly cut grain stalks.

This sight was different. She could clearly see women, mostly old widows, picking their way behind the reapers, hoping a loose stalk of grain might fall.

They were the poorest of the poor, and Ruth was ready to beg for a chance to join them.

When she reached the threshing floor she smiled. It was an abundant place of flat white bedrock that gave a full view of the rooftops of the city below. A light breeze whipped around her face and she sneezed from the grain dust in the air.

The threshing floor was abuzz with activity. It was hard for Ruth to believe that for so many years this land had been swallowed by famine.

"Peace," a woman said.

"Peace," Ruth replied.

There were reapers and carriers. Gleaners and overseers.

"Excuse me, sir," Ruth said to a man wearing a blue turban and carrying a whip. "I am Ruth, widow of Mahlon, daughter now to Naomi, widow to Elimelech. Please tell me how I may beg for permission to glean."

The man rubbed his black beard. "You have permission, Sister. By law, you were granted permission to glean the moment you became a widow." He leaned in to get a better look at her. "You are not from Bethlehem?"

"No."

He waited, but Ruth offered no further information. She was terrified he would turn her away if he knew her home had been Moab.

Finally, he smiled. "Peace and blessings to you, Sister. Be certain to glean only in the master's fields."

"I don't know what you mean."

"I oversee only the property belonging to Master Boaz. He is very gracious with the gleaners." And the man's attention was turned to another man who asked a question.

Bedrock. Ruth's bare toes felt its cool and rippled surface. Little bits of grain pushed into her flesh. Two great oxen pulled a dredge across the laid-out stalks. A pack of squealing children rode the sledge for fun and to weigh it down so the grain was knocked from the stalks.

She'd ridden sledges just like this one with dozens of her half-brothers and half-sisters, the king's children in the king's fields.

Men lifted great forks to fan the stalks after the sledges had gone over them. A woman with a broom motioned for Ruth to step back.

When she looked up she saw a man dressed in white cloth and a blue striped tunic. He was on the porch of a tent, and no one had to tell her that he was the master. The way he stood with his shoulders back and a smile on his face gave him away. The man had authority.

For a brief moment their eyes locked. It was Ruth who looked away first. No need to draw attention to herself when all she wanted was to stay invisible.

She could not help staring out at the people who were not her people, at a land that was not her land. Ruth felt so lonely she wondered what it would be like to step over the low stone wall that led to the rocky overlook. She could walk out there and keep walking. Would anyone bother to retrieve her body, to bury it?

No. There was no room in her heart for such thoughts. Naomi needed her, and she had made a promise that she was determined to keep, come what may.

Tightening her hap, Ruth walked around the winnowed wheat and out into the fields where gleaners were stooped over, filling their haps with more than free grain—they were filling their lives with hope.

19

THAT FIRST NIGHT RUTH RETURNED with only enough grain for two cakes.

"You eat, Mother. I'm too tired to chew."

"Oh, Daughter, what have I done to you? Look at your hands. Your knuckles are bloody and your feet are slashed."

"I'm fine. Tomorrow I will glean more grain. I promise. Today I was only learning."

"Let me come with you. Maybe they'll take pity on an old widow like me."

"No." Ruth rubbed the small of her back and winced. "The air is clouded with dust. The sun bakes down. It's no place for you. I promise you that tomorrow I will return with a better harvest."

In the morning rose a pale pink sun.

"It's the color I favor most," Ruth said. "Already the day has begun with a promise of something better."

Naomi yawned and groaned as she stretched her shoulders back. "Let's go to the well and fetch water. I'll boil some tea before you leave to glean."

"I've already been to the well this morning, Mother. There is a full water skin for you. Tonight I'll take Chamor, and we'll fetch water for the cistern."

Naomi kissed Ruth's soft cheek. "God cannot help but bless a child as good and true as you are, Ruth. You will see: in time our blessings of comfort and strength will come."

Ruth smiled. "Have the fire ready. Tonight I will return with enough grain to feed us well."

She kept her word. That night there was enough grain for six cakes. Ruth ate two; Naomi ate two. They split the last two for the next morning's meal.

And so, day after day, Ruth went to glean. By the end of the week, she had enough grain to store some. Every inch of her ached, but she would not stop or even slow down. Later, she walked through their broken gate and saw Naomi waiting there for her. When she saw the woman's face light up as she looked into the hap, Ruth knew she would return to the field every day.

Ruth soon learned that if she left before the sun came up, she was likely to see the master of the field in front of his tent. Most times he stood to survey his crops and his workers. But sometimes she was early enough to catch him down on his knees. She wished she could hear the words of his prayers. What prayer could a man offer that would bring such abundant blessings?

After more than a week had passed, Ruth rose and found her feet hurrying along the path.

"Peace," she said to passersby, sometimes before they spoke the greeting first.

"Why such a hurry?" a woman asked.

"I am going to glean," Ruth replied, as excited as if she were going to the market with a fistful of money; but the truth was, she was anxious to see the master, to know that he was there watching over things. She savored those moments when their eyes met. He never looked away first.

The feelings stirring in her, thoughts of a man so distant and unapproachable, were things she could never share with Naomi. She was sure he was married, maybe to more than one wife. Rich men could do that easily.

They were silly, unexpected feelings that she could never share with anyone, especially not with Naomi. Still, Ruth could not deny that catching sight of the master brought her the smallest sliver of joy.

When she arrived, the master was already out on his porch, and a group of workers and gleaners was gathered around him.

The air was musky, and a small spattering of rain dappled the ground. Boaz lifted his face to the clouds and let the air fill his chest. His land was alive again!

Boaz looked out over his grain fields, all in various stages of harvest. "Look at this miracle!" he called to anyone who would hear him. "All the years that the Moabites took what they wanted, then trampled or torched what remained—those years are gone. No gleaner will be turned away from my fields."

"Sir, we've never seen so many poor widows and orphans benefiting from your generosity."

"Not mine, Micah," Boaz corrected his overseer. "The Lord has been generous to all of us."

"The Lord be with you, Boaz!" someone shouted.

Someone else suggested that he was going to have to build granaries to store the abundance.

Boaz smiled. "God is indeed good."

Suddenly Boaz stopped short. His eyes narrowed and his heartbeat increased. "That woman," he nodded with his chin, "the thin woman with her hair tied up, the one whose hap is light—who is she? I've seen her a few mornings lately."

"And you wish to know her better?"

"Who is she?"

"It's the Moabite damsel. She requested permission to glean here."

Boaz touched a half-moon scar on his forehead. "Not from me."

"No. I spoke with her, sir. She has returned from Moab with Naomi, widow of Elimelech."

"Elimelech—my uncle?"

"Yes," Micah said. "Is something wrong?"

"No. Not wrong." Boaz felt his heart thumping in his chest as if he had run up a steep hill.

He looked at her. She looked at him. Neither of them looked away for a very long time.

At the tent where maids made food for the master and his workers, Boaz hesitated when the wine and sweet breads were delivered.

"I will keep a watch over her, sir. But she stays from sunrise to sunset, so you have nothing to worry about. Go inside and eat and rest."

"You will let me know if she makes any effort to leave here," he told Micah.

"Most assuredly."

Boaz drank and ate. To those watching he seemed in a hurry; he even took his wine back outside with him.

Ruth was still there.

"Do you want me to summon her to you?" asked Micah.

"No, but tell me why she hangs back away from the common gleaners, away from the other maids. She stands out as a lone and sorrowful woman."

"She is a widow."

"And a Moabite." Again, he touched the scar on his forehead. "I do not pity her. Her spirit is as strong as it is graceful."

When Boaz looked again, Ruth was walking from Boaz's field to a neighbor's plot, one of the few he didn't own.

Boaz ran to her—ran like a boy again—saying, "Peace, Sister! Can you hear me?" The wind picked up as the sky darkened. "Can you hear me?" he shouted again.

She spun and stared at him.

He stared back. It was Ruth—Mahlon's wife, now widow—the girl with the golden eyes. Boaz's breath went out of him as sure as if he'd taken a fist to the stomach.

"Sir?"

"Don't go glean in another field."

"I'm sorry?"

"Please," he said. "Abide here."

"Thank you; I have gleaned in your field since morning."

Words jumbled in his mouth, in his brain, and he couldn't think of what to say because he could only look upon her and think that he had never seen a more beautiful yet careworn face: her lips were baked, her nose was blistered by the sun. Her hair was braided and hung long, curving toward him like a half moon.

He did his best to seem casual, but his heart pounded as his eyes took in every detail: How she moved as easily as flowing water. How her hair was braided in dual ropes, wound at the base of her neck. This day tiny yellow harvest flowers adorned her braid and set her face apart as a work of art.

"You are the Moabitess I've heard of."

Her heart sank, fearful he would have her expelled. "Yes, sir. I am come now with my widowed mother-in-law to abide here by her side and with her people."

"And your husband?"

"Mahlon."

"Are you in mourning?"

She looked down at her plain dress, the one Naomi had provided, and said, "The days of mourning have passed. Now my days are spent only to serve and comfort my mother, who has no husband and no sons."

"Naomi's husband, Elimelech, was my favorite cousin. Do you not recognize me?"

Boaz moved a strand of damp hair away from his forehead to reveal a half-moon scar.

Ruth's hand covered her mouth and her golden eyes glistened. She fell to her knees and bowed at his feet. "Sir! You are Boaz, kin to my husband's family. You were with Ehud when my brother was nearly killed by his horse. You saved Nathaniel's life."

"We both saved his life, as I recall." Boaz offered his hand to lift her. "Never bow before me; bow only to the Lord Jehovah."

"I am sorry. It's just that I am overwhelmed with gratitude. I remember that the horse kicked you."

"Yes," he said, as if his thoughts were elsewhere. "And I remember that your eyes are golden, the color of ripe wheat."

For a long moment, the two of them fell into an easy silence. Ruth knew they were being watched. She had heard the comments and judgments of others the entire time she had been gleaning. She was a Moabite, an enemy. What right did she have to take anything more from Bethlehem?

Suddenly, there were tears in her eyes. "I'm sorry," she apologized. "I can put on a stalwart face when people are unkind, but you have shown me nothing but kindness, allowing me to glean in your fields. Thank you. And I know Naomi thanks you."

He looked away from her trembling lips and asked, "How is Naomi?"

"She is very grateful to be back home, where she belongs."

"And you? How do you feel, Ruth, about being here in Bethlehem?"

She batted back a tear. "I promised my mother that I would lodge wherever she lodged."

"I am sorry that such great loss and sorrow has entered your family. I want you to know that Mahlon was a good and brave man, like his father. Our people would not be free if it were not for their loyalty and bravery— Elimelech, Mahlon, and Chilion all played roles in the death of—"

"King Eglon was my father."

Beneath Boaz's black-and-gray beard, his face went red. He shuffled his feet and cleared his throat. "Yes, I knew that. I'd just let it slip my mind."

She stepped away, and the silence between them now took on a sharp edge.

"Thank you again for allowing me to glean. You are a generous man."

"Are you thirsty?" he asked.

"No, your maids were kind enough to fill my water skin."

He snapped and whistled, and two young men came running. "This maiden will be offered only the best and freshest water, drawn from the spring well. She will eat in the shade of our tents anything she asks."

"Thank you, but I cannot do such a thing. I am a stranger in this land and in these fields," Ruth said.

"You are kin," Boaz said, his face suddenly reddening. "Come and take your meals in the tent where I eat. Eat the bread; dip your portion in the vinegar and enjoy."

"Thank you, sir."

* * *

The fire was going when Ruth returned home. It was hardly more than a single flame, but the sight made Ruth smile.

"I'm glad the fire is burning," she said, "because I've brought two ears of corn in addition to our grain. And Mother, you must drink from my water skin—the water is sweet. It came from the high spring."

Naomi drank and took the hap. "Every day you manage to gather more grain. You work so hard, Ruth."

"The master of the fields is generous to gleaners. Boaz says that the Lord expects him to share what he's been given."

"Boaz! My kinsman is the master of the fields where you glean?"

"Yes."

Her eyes went heavenward. "Forgive me. I've been so focused on Heber that I've neglected to even think of Boaz."

"Heber hasn't returned again, has he? I know he torments you."

Naomi spread the grain out, picking the chaff from the kernels. "Yes. He was here again today. Heber didn't come to the gate, but kept walking back and forth in front of the house, whistling. I tell you, that man bothers me as much as any viper. But let's not talk about Heber. Tell me of Boaz. Is he as wealthy as I imagine?"

"He owns many of the high fields. He spoke with me today."

"He spoke directly to you?"

"Yes. I told him you were my mother now. I think, perhaps, that is why he is so generous with me."

Naomi rubbed her eyes. "Boaz is a scribe. He is a wise man."

"Is he married?"

"Why do you ask?"

"He resides in a tent that overlooks the threshing floor, but I have not seen a wife beside him."

"And you've been looking, Ruth?"

She blushed. "It's just that a man who owns so much land and has so many men in his employ . . . you would expect to see him with his wife and sons, but I have seen nothing of Boaz's family."

"Kezia is his mother."

"The woman who was so unkind to us on our first day here?"

"Yes. The woman who has not once stopped to visit me."

"Maybe you should pay her a visit, Mother."

"Perhaps I will."

* * *

The harvest became busier, and every day Ruth brought home a heavier hap. Naomi grew stronger, and she rejoiced when she saw that Ruth's thin frame began to fill out again as her sunken cheeks took shape.

Ruth left so early each morning that she had to walk in complete darkness, but she knew the way now. Once Naomi heard Ruth humming a melody that Orpah used to sing to them.

"The curse is lifted," Naomi said. That day she rebraided her hair, put on the only other dress she owned, and went to pay Kezia a visit.

She found Kezia in the garden of her courtyard sorting spices into various baskets.

"Peace, my sister."

Kezia looked up and squinted. Her white hair looked like cotton in the sunlight.

"It is Naomi, your kinswoman."

"Peace, Naomi. Enter the gate and sit with me."

Naomi entered. The courtyard was three times as large as hers. The cistern was three times as deep and twice as wide. There were fig trees and palms and benches for both sitting and reclining.

"Your garden is lovely," Naomi said.

"Your heathen daughter-in-law is not with you?"

"Ruth is gleaning that we might eat."

"She's gleaning in my son's fields, no doubt."

"Boaz has been very generous. He is a good man."

"Yes, my son is a good man. Sit, Naomi, and breathe in the scents of the spices. There's cinnamon and cardamom and rosemary." She held different baskets, so small they fit in Naomi's palm.

"They are delightful."

"Boaz bought them in Egypt. I have an entire collection in the house if you would like to see it."

"Yes, later. Right now I just want to look upon you and remember your kindness to me. You were there when my sons were delivered."

"I remember that time. God was good to you, Child."

"He has never left me."

"Not even in Moab?"

"Especially not in Moab. I know that I was bitter when I first came back. I felt I'd been punished."

"You were punished. You were left with no man to provide for you, not even one of your sons."

"But I no longer feel punished. I feel blessed."

"Blessed? How can you say that when you have nothing?"

"I have Ruth. She is my blessing. She provides food for me, keeps me company, and, at night, she listens to me as I teach her about Jehovah."

"She wants to learn?"

"She's been immersed. She prays. She honors the God that we honor, Kezia. I have come to ask that you lead the other women to treat my Ruth with openness and to show yourselves in a friendly way toward her."

"She is from Moab."

"Yes, but she has forsaken the ways of her youth for new ways—our ways."

"I make you no promise," Kezia said. "I am old. My husband died at the hands of the Moabites."

"So did mine."

The pause between them could have turned hard, but Naomi was determined to win the woman's favor.

"Kezia, tell me all the gossip I've missed these past years." Naomi chuckled.

So did Kezia. "Go get that chair over by the house. It's more comfortable. If I'm going to go back that far, we'll be here awhile."

* * *

Ruth's back was stooped and her hap was already half full though the sun had not yet climbed to a midday height. She noticed a mother and her five daughters, some so small they trailed far behind, gleaning in front of Ruth. When two of the children veered among the sheaves and came back with their baskets full, a young man ran toward them.

"Drop what you've stolen!"

The mother hurried and put herself between the man's wrath and the children. "Forgive us," she begged. "My girls did not know."

"You should have taught them better," the man scolded. "You know the area where you are permitted to glean, and you also know where you must not venture. If your children wander off the row again, you'll be escorted from Master Boaz's fields and made to glean elsewhere."

"Thank you, sir. I understand."

Ruth felt pity for the mother. What sorrow had befallen her to bring her to this place at this time? From her own gatherings, Ruth filled the daughters' baskets.

"You are too kind," the grateful mother said.

"Kindness has been shown to me and to my mother. The Lord your God would expect nothing less from me."

Afterward, Ruth waited, taking only what the mother and children did not glean. That night was the first night she returned with less rather than more.

The next morning when Ruth arrived in the field Boaz himself came down to greet her.

"Master."

"I heard what you did yesterday."

"I did nothing that you have not agreed to. I took less, in fact."

"Yes, I heard. One of my servants gave me a report that you showed great kindness and generosity to a widow and her children."

"I did less than what you've done for me."

"Walk with me," he said.

Ruth walked beside him. They walked without saying anything until Ruth was next to him on the porch of his tent. She saw the view of the fields, the workers, and the city below them in the distance.

"All of this is yours."

"God has blessed me abundantly."

"Your family is surely proud of you."

"My wife is dead. I have no sons."

"I am sorry," Ruth said, but in her heart she was glad he had no wife.

* * *

Micah came to Boaz at the end of the day.

"You seem distracted, Master. Is anything wrong?"

"No. No. I want you to let the Moabite woman search among the sheaves. Let her take all she can. If fact, see to it that handfuls of grain slip to the ground that she covers."

"Master . . ."

"At the end of the day when she beats out all that she has managed to glean, how much grain does this woman take back to my kins-woman?"

"Almost an ephah of barley," Micah reported.

"That's not sufficient. See that she receives more and that she receives from every harvest: barley, corn, and wheat. Be generous with her."

"Whatever you say, Master. It will be done."

Boaz suddenly lost half of his confidence. He lowered his voice and looked away from Micah. "Tell me if you can—does the woman, Ruth, the Moabitess, look with favor on the young men working the fields?"

"Master?"

"The fields teem with young, strong men. Does Ruth look at any of them?"

"No, Master. You and I are the only men she has spoken to; other than that, she speaks only to women. She looks upon no man with favor."

"Good."

"Sir, is there anything more?"

"No. Go now and see that Ruth's hap is full by the end of every day."

* * *

Naomi baked more than bread. She baked small clay vessels to store their surplus now that Ruth was bringing home more than sufficient grain for their daily needs. The small, crude jars would not suffice for a wet season, but for now they kept the mice and insects out of the grain.

While Naomi was falling into a fast and easy routine, sitting with Kezia or walking around the market, Ruth became worried when Boaz was not on the porch looking down at her. He did not seek her out or even wave to her.

At the end of a long day Micah approached Ruth.

"Have I done something to displease the master?" she asked, afraid.

"No. Boaz has sent me here to tell you to stay with the maidens and let his young men watch over you as they do for the young innocents. Boaz worries when you are out here alone, so far from the others."

"Please pass my gratitude along to your master. Assure him that I won't wander away from the others."

"It's not safe," Micah said. "He wants to protect you."

"Thank you."

She watched Micah walk away and saw the scars that tracked across his shoulders. The man had been flogged, and she knew without anyone telling her that the Moabites had done it.

They had left in this land many scars, seen and unseen, and she realized how difficult it must be for Micah to show favor and kindness to her, knowing who she was.

20

Even from a distance Ruth could see by Naomi's expression that something was wrong.

"What's wrong, Mother?"

"It's Chamor."

Ruth's heart broke. "He's dead?"

"No. He's gone. I was with Kezia at the well. When I returned, he was gone."

"He probably just wandered away."

"I've searched for him all day. He's gone."

Ruth supported Naomi and walked her up the street to their home.

"Chamor was a gift from Aharon. He means as much to me as family."

"I know," Ruth said. "We will find him."

Naomi clasped her hands to her heart. "No! Chamor did not wander off. He wasn't led away by neighborhood children. Heber stole Chamor. He probably sold Chamor already." Naomi sobbed.

"I will go and search for him."

"You can't. It will soon be dark, and it's not safe out there. Anything could happen to you, and then I would truly be alone, with no one to keep me alive. Oh, Ruth, there are no words to tell you, dear daughter, what you mean to me."

Ruth did not glean the next day—or the day after that. She spent her time searching for Chamor. The thought of the donkey being afraid, hungry, or mistreated broke Ruth's heart. Chamor was just a donkey, but he had been her friend. He had carried her burdens and listened to her unload her heartache.

When she did not find him, she returned to the fields without a smile and with only a feeble wave for Boaz.

He came straight to her. "Are you ill?"

"No."

"You haven't been here to glean for the past two days. You did not glean in another field, did you?"

"No."

"Then tell me, please, what has you so sad and troubled? It's not Naomi, is it?"

"No. It's Chamor."

"The donkey?"

"Yes." Ruth burst into the tears of a sorrowful child.

"You're crying over a missing donkey?"

"Yes."

Boaz put his hand to his mouth to hide the twitch of a smile. "If you are in need of a beast of burden, we have more than we need. You are welcome to borrow any one you wish." He waved a hand over the expanse of his field dotted with donkeys, camels, and oxen.

"You don't understand," she said, wiping hot tears from her cheeks. "Chamor is not just a donkey—he is family."

The next day it was Boaz who abandoned the harvest to accomplish a mission. Naomi was home alone when she heard a whirlwind of noise and rushed into the courtyard to see a man, a horse, and a cart laden with pots, cloth, food, and household items. Two milking goats were tied to the back.

"Peace be unto you, Sister."

"I'm afraid I have no money to buy your wares."

"And I'm afraid my favorite aunt does not recognize me."

"Boaz!" Naomi greeted him as if he were the most important person on earth. "The water I can offer you comes from your own spring. The bread I can bake you comes from your generosity to my daughter. Thank you, Boaz. You are an instrument in the hands of God, whether you know it or not."

"I came by because I've heard rumors."

"Rumors? About us?"

"Yes. Disturbing rumors that all have to do with my uncle Heber."

Naomi sighed. "*That* man."

Boaz made himself comfortable on the bench in the courtyard. His eyes took in the broken ladder, the unhinged gate, and the sparseness of the property and he felt a twinge of guilt.

"My men heard Heber boasting of how he nearly took advantage of you. He almost fooled you into signing over your property to him."

"That was his plan."

"I'm here to tell you that, as a scribe, I know there are records in the treasury of Bethlehem, records my grandfather left. Those records state that upon his departure from Bethlehem, this parcel—homes, orchards, and courtyards—was given to Elimelech. With his death and the death of your sons, for which I am so truly and deeply sorry, the land is yours. You are free to sell it or to live here."

"I want only to live here," she said with a relief he could not possibly understand.

"Heber has squandered his inheritance many times over. He accuses me of stealing his land outright, but I assure you it was a fair contract."

"I have no doubt."

They sat and talked for a long time, each sharing good memories and revealing hard times.

"I am so sorry about the death of your wife."

"I wish you could have known her."

"I wish so many things were different," Naomi said. "But the unhappiness I thought would be mine forever has lifted. It's all because of my daughter-in-law, Ruth. You know her, I believe."

"Ahh . . . yes. Ruth. Ruth is . . . a kind and lovely woman."

His red-tipped ears and the twinkle in his eye did not go unnoticed by Naomi. Immediately a thought formed in the front of her mind, a thought that made her grin.

When Boaz's horse whinnied, he said, "I hope you will not take offense, but I have brought a humble offering of things your newly settled household might use."

"Oh, Boaz, I could weep tears of joy and gratitude on your shoulder. I don't question why the Lord turned His wrath on me. I'm only grateful that your hand has managed to turn it away."

"I am just your humble kinsman. If you tell me what more you need, I'll see that you're taken care of." He walked through the orchard and around the house, glancing inside. "Tomorrow my workmen will be here to repair your cistern, your stairs, and anything else that is in need of repair."

"My heart is being repaired by your visit."

"And you have repaired my mother's heart with your visits. She told me how kind you have been to keep her company."

"I feel the same about her. It is a lonely life—the life of a widow in Bethlehem."

At the gate Boaz hesitated. "We should have your orchard replanted, and I'll have my men dig new furrows so the trees can be watered more evenly."

"That will be a blessing to this household for generations to come. But I suspect that's not what your tongue wants to tell me."

"No. I mean, yes. I want to inquire about Ruth. Is there anything you can tell me about her?"

"I can tell you that she is most grateful every day for your care and concern. She speaks very highly of you, Boaz."

"She does?"

"Yes, indeed she does."

"She is a kind woman."

"You said that earlier."

"Um, well . . ."

"And you are a kind man. Is there something more you would like to know about my daughter?"

"Is she betrothed?"

"No. What man would have a Moabitess for a wife? It would take a confident man of God who was strong and in a good social position to protect her from judging lips."

"Yes, I suppose it would."

Naomi grinned.

"Oh, there is one more gift I'd like to give you before I take my leave." Boaz put his fingers in his mouth and made a shrill whistle. A young lad leading a donkey came loping down the road.

"Chamor!"

"Just as you suspected, Heber stole the donkey and sold him to a caravan company. Thankfully they had not yet left, and I was able to buy him back for Ruth—I mean, for you, Naomi—*and* for Ruth, of course."

"Of course."

Boaz took his leave. When Naomi turned around, she realized that she was far richer now than when he arrived.

* * *

Ruth was overjoyed at the sight of the old donkey. She was equally surprised to find a table set with bread and fruit and cheese and fresh goat's milk.

"Where did all of this come from?" Ruth questioned.

"It seems the generosity of Boaz knows no boundaries."

"Boaz was *here*! I wondered where he was today; I didn't see him at all."

"So you watch for him?"

Her cheeks went the color of a spring rose. "He is the master, and I am a gleaner."

"Well, I doubt that he is so thoughtful of all gleaners. He asked after you."

"He did?"

"Yes."

Ruth couldn't hide her happiness. "What did he want to know about me?"

"Everything."

* * *

Bandits on fast horses from the desert came in the night and tried to steal the grain from Boaz's threshing floor. They were caught, but after that Boaz hired extra guards and seemed much more occupied with his harvest than he had been with Ruth.

Then Naomi began feeling ill and came down with a fever. While she was sick, Ruth refused to glean. She hardly left Naomi's side except to gather yarrow and meadowsweet, two herbs that came straight out of Kezia's garden.

Ruth approached the gate nervously. "I am sorry to trouble you, but my mother has fallen ill and asked that I request your advice and a few herbs to break her fever."

"Come here, Child."

Ruth hadn't thought of herself as a child in many years but entered Kezia's gate as timid as a girl.

Kezia's wrinkled face smiled into another wave of folds. "Don't be afraid. I was unkind to you that first day only because I was wary of your people. You have proven loyal to Naomi. That tells me all I need to know about you. Come help yourself to whatever you need."

Kezia had shelves lined with baskets and bottles and jugs, all containing herbs and spices.

"I've collected them over time," Kezia explained. "My husband, Salmon, was an important man. My son, Boaz, is also important. They both travel and bring me the flavors and medicines from near and far."

"Boaz is your son?"

"You didn't know that?"

"I suppose Naomi has told me, but I wasn't thinking of anything except how to get Naomi well."

"Let me come with you. I'll know what to do."

Naomi's illness did not last nearly long enough, at least for Kezia, who seemed delighted to have someone ill to tend. When Naomi had recovered, the three women sat in the shade of Naomi's courtyard and talked.

Kezia told tales of a Bethlehem unfamiliar to even Naomi.

"It was a place where the Spirit of God was invited. Children did not go hungry and men did not go to war. When I was a girl, Bethlehem looked out on the great river, on the Sea of Death and across the valley like it does now, but now it is broken and just beginning to heal. Then it was strong and whole. Bethlehem is named *House of Bread* because it began as a land of abundance."

"And it will be again," Ruth said, "now that the fighting has stopped."

"At least it has paused," Kezia said, taking a drink from Naomi's cup. "Our people will always fight with each other. A truce is not the same as peace."

Ruth felt her shoulders tense. "I truly am sorry for the pain my people have caused yours, but I think of myself as God's daughter now. He has adopted me into His family. He has said that what I bring is sufficient."

"I have never seen greater faith than Ruth's," Naomi said. "She has not looked back since she covenanted with our people—her people now, Kezia."

Kezia clucked her tongue. "I'm not saying I am among them, but there will always be people who do not accept you. They will hold your past against you."

"That's not Ruth's fault!" Naomi's voice rose higher than she meant it to, and she drew back.

"It may not be her fault, but it is her problem," Kezia said.

With that, the conversation ended, and Ruth volunteered to walk the old woman home.

"I'm old, but I can walk myself home."

"It will soon be dark, and I'd feel better if I knew you got there safely."

"Or you can stay the night with us here," Naomi offered.

"No. I'm most comfortable in my own bed."

On the way to Kezia's house, Ruth did not know what to say, so she said nothing—just crooked her elbow out and let Kezia hold on to her for support.

They were halfway between homes when two stray dogs rounded the corner in front of them. There were low walls on both sides of the narrow street. The animals looked wild and hungry, their dark fur matted.

One of the dogs let out a fierce growl.

Kezia screamed.

Then the larger of the two beasts bared its yellow fangs and came at them with such force that Ruth did the only thing she could think to do—she put herself in front of Kezia and took the full impact.

Somehow Ruth did not fall down but stayed upright; she used her arms and legs as the best shield she could muster to protect a terrified Kezia.

The larger of the two dogs barked and bit into the hem of Ruth's dress, shaking the fabric violently and ripping off the bottom corner of her skirt.

"Go away!" Ruth shouted. "Get away from us!"

Kezia kept screaming.

The dogs barked. They bit. They tore with their claws.

Ruth felt a sharp, hot pain in her leg. The air filled with the scent of fresh-butchered meat.

"Kezia!" Ruth kept putting herself between Kezia and the vicious animals.

Then there were others, men and boys with sticks. The dogs yelped and ran away with a band of stick-waving children behind them.

Kezia's screams continued.

"Are you all right?" someone asked Ruth.

"I am all right," she said. Then, in an instant, she collapsed on the cobbled street.

* * *

By the time Ruth was strong enough to glean again, barley and wheat season was at an end and corn was in full harvest.

The wounds from the dogs were not as deep as they looked, but by the second day a swollen red ring circled every bite mark. On the third day, when Naomi began to feel strong enough to sit beside Ruth, a fever set in.

Yarrow root tea did nothing.

Meadowsweet only upset Ruth's stomach.

"My son will pay for a physician," Kezia said.

"Your son?"

"Boaz."

"*My* Boaz?"

"*Your* Boaz?"

"She's out of her head," Naomi said, trying to hide a smile.

By the fourth day she truly was out of her head. Ruth's thoughts seemed melted into a puddle. Her leg was double its size and constantly on fire. When she managed to get her eyes open she thought she saw Boaz standing across from her. She thought she heard his voice. She thought he was praying.

A week passed before the fever broke.

"Praise the Lord," Kezia said. "We've all been praying for you, Ruth."

"We?"

Naomi leaned down and kissed her forehead. "You've got a whole army on your side, Daughter."

"Naomi speaks the truth," a man said—a rabbi. "We all know what you did to save Kezia. We know how you've been a faithful daughter to Naomi. May the Lord be with you so that you can walk without pain and continue to serve your sisters of Bethlehem."

* * *

One night, when the wind was blowing and smoke was in the air, Naomi woke to the sound of their new nanny goat rummaging around.

"Are you all right, Ruth?" Her voice cut through the night.

"I'm feeling much better. Tomorrow I will try to go back to the fields."

"No. It's too soon."

"But the barley and wheat season is nearly over and the corn is nearly harvested. I've got to go and fill our storage vessels."

Naomi followed the goat into the orchard and then looked up at the hills. She could see the torchlight from the men guarding the threshing floor. She knew Boaz would be there with his harvest, and she thanked the Lord that He had brought such a wonderful man into their lives.

Then a powerful impression struck Naomi; she could not say whether it was her own idea or pure inspiration, but she knew what she had to do.

"Ruth! Wake up. Please, Daughter, wake up and hear what I have to say."

"Mother, are you all right?"

"What I'm going to ask of you may not sit well. It may not make sense to you, but I ask that you do as I say."

Ruth wiped the sleep from her eyes.

Naomi guided her out into the orchard and pointed up to the high hills where the threshing floor was lined with flaming torches.

"The flames of Chemosh were the colors of fire. You once laid sacrifices on that altar. I am going to ask that you lay a different kind of sacrifice on a very different altar."

"Mother, I don't understand."

"I want nothing more for you than what I believe the Lord wants for you, Child. Already, you have sacrificed your own life to make mine more comfortable."

"Mother?"

"I pray the Lord will open your eyes to see what I see. Now look up on the hillside. This night and the next, Boaz will sleep on the threshing floor to keep thieves from stealing the harvest. I want you to prepare yourself. Go with me and we will immerse you completely in the mikveh, anoint you with the sweetest perfume. Wear your freshest dress. Then wait, my daughter, wait until he has finished eating and has found his sleeping place. Go in without being seen by the others and uncover the feet of Boaz."

"Mother, what are you telling me to do?"

"Lie down next to Boaz."

"Mother! Then what shall I do?"

"Then he shall tell you what to do."

Ruth could not catch her breath.

"I know what I am asking of you, Daughter. Do you know *why* I am asking it?"

"You don't want me to remain a widow," Ruth stammered. "You don't want us to have to glean until we die."

"All that is true. But I am asking this of you because I love you. There are few men on this earth as truly good as Boaz. There are even fewer women as truly good as you, Ruth. We have little time to waste. Do you understand?"

Ruth nodded. "Isn't it best to wait and let Boaz take action?"

"Boaz was married for years. His wife never bore him a child, and still he took no action, though he was advised to divorce her. A man whose wife does not bear him children has every law in his favor to rid himself of her."

"I know that, Mother. I know that because I failed to give Mahlon a son or a daughter. I failed to give you a grandchild."

"I don't mean to injure your feelings, Daughter, but the truth is, not every flaw in the plan is a woman's fault, and there comes a time when a woman has to act first to get a man to take the action he should."

Ruth slowly said, "I understand."

21

STILL LIMPING, RUTH RETURNED HOME early from the fields. She had seen Boaz only briefly and from afar. He lifted his chin but did not wave at her. He seemed especially busy counting and measuring.

Ruth's heart did not stop hammering all day, and by the end of the work, her hap was only partly filled.

Naomi and Chamor met her in front of the gate.

"How was the day?" Naomi asked.

"Everything is just as you said it would be—very busy."

Naomi gave her a tight embrace. "Are you hungry? I have your favorite cheese and honey."

"I'm too nervous to eat a bite."

"My nerves are frayed too. If this goes wrong, and it well could, we will lose everything and be forced to leave here shamed."

Ruth started to say something, but Naomi cut her off.

"But if it goes right, you will have a husband who is worthy of you," Naomi said. "That's all I want. I cannot bear to see you come from gleaning one more day, your knees and hands raw and bloody and your spirit broken. Even though Boaz has been so generous, there is no guarantee another woman won't wedge her way in before you and stop his flow of kindness to us."

"Mother, I know you mean well, but I have so many doubts."

"You had doubts about moving with me to Bethlehem, yet you felt it was the right thing to do, and you did it. Trust me, Ruth, you deserve Boaz and Boaz will be blessed by you. I feel it is the Lord's will."

"How do you recognize what is the Lord's will and what is simply our own desire?"

"It is often impossible to distinguish between the two. When my husband announced that we were leaving Bethlehem for Moab, I was caught between staying here where the commandments were honored and moving to a place of idol worship. If I stayed, I would defy my husband, which was against the Lord's laws. If I went, I would defy my faith. Sometimes we have to do something not because we are certain it is the Lord's will but because we believe He will work it out for our good *if* our hearts are right."

"He wants us to choose?"

"Yes. Once the harvest season is over, there will be no more gleaning. Boaz will leave Bethlehem for a time to sell his surplus harvest. We have to act now, Ruth."

"Tell me what to do, Mother, and I will do it."

* * *

The water felt cold to Ruth.

"The only other time I've been completely immersed was at the time of my conversion," she admitted.

"Now it's not just to clean your soul, Child. Before you can present yourself to Boaz, we've got to scrub your skin and your hair and wash every part of you."

"Boaz has no idea what is about to happen to him."

"That's just how we must keep it."

"Kezia knows nothing?" Ruth asked.

"Nothing. I could not tell her because she could not keep from breathing out our secrets."

"I don't think she would approve," Ruth said.

While Ruth cleaned herself, Naomi explained, "Now that you're in Judea, where mikveh are plentiful, this is what must be done whenever a woman is unclean."

"I understand."

Naomi had sewn Ruth a tunic from a swatch of cloth Boaz had given them. They cleaned Ruth's teeth with sand and oil. When she was clean and dressed, Ruth sat on the bench in the courtyard. Naomi took her place behind her and anointed Ruth's head with sacred oil. She then pronounced a blessing of guidance and dedication.

"Smell that scent?" Naomi asked, wafting the oil beneath Ruth's nose.

"Its aroma is citrus."

"It smells of hope."

Finally, Naomi braided her hair and put flowers in it the way Ruth liked.

"Chew some mint, Daughter. Elimelech always used to like to kiss me when my breath smelled of mint."

"I feel like a girl again—a girl who has never been married and is at a loss about what to do with a man."

"You were a good wife to my son; it will all come back to you, trust me."

The stars were only beginning to brighten against the blackening sky when they finished. It was too early to leave, so they sat at the table and waited. It was hard to tell which one felt more anxious. Their feet bounced. Their fingers tapped. They kept starting sentences without finishing them.

Naomi gave clear instructions over and over.

Then it was time and they went, arm in arm, Naomi walking Ruth as far as she could.

"Go back now and rest, Mother. I'll be all right no matter what happens."

Naomi kissed her. "I always wanted a sister and never had one; I always wanted a daughter and never had one. In you, God has given me both."

Dusk slowly faded into darkness. The breeze that always blew had calmed as Ruth approached the tent. Food tables around the tent were cleared, and Ruth watched as the men said good night to each other, the guards took their places, and the torches were set aflame.

Ruth had just made her way onto the threshing floor when Micah saw her. She was grateful her face was not an uncommon sight here—but even so, this was late for her to be in the threshing area.

"Is there something you desire, damsel?" he asked. "Something I can do on behalf of my master?"

Could he see her forehead bead with sweat? "Thank you," she said, doing her best to keep her voice steady, "I wanted to express my gratitude to Boaz."

Micah looked to his left. "I am afraid Master Boaz has taken his leave for the night. I'm certain he will be glad to accept your gratitude at sunrise."

"Yes, yes. Thank you."

And Micah held the torch for her as they made their way off the floor and back into the stubbly fields.

"Can you see your way under the light of the stars, or do you need my torch?" Micah asked.

"I can see by the stars, thank you." She panicked. Ruth broke into a lope and then into a full-blown run; the sharp grain stubble sticking out of the ground cut her feet and jabbed at her legs. She limped worse than she had in a week as she ran past the fields, down the beaten dirt pathway to the cobbled walks, up to their street, and back home to Naomi.

Ruth stopped before reaching their gate, heaving for breath.

Naomi had warned her to wait, to be careful, and to not allow herself to be seen. She'd violated all of those instructions. She'd failed.

Out in the street, Ruth fell to her knees in the dark and prayed to God, who felt as far away as the farthest star.

"Please give Boaz the knowledge to do what is right because I don't know what it is, but I am willing to obey. I do not recognize the whisper of Your voice the way Naomi does. I will trust her, Father. Please stop me if what I am doing is wrong."

The night thickened, and Ruth waited and tried to listen for a voice, a prompting, or a warning. All she heard was the sound of night birds and bugs combined with the whinny of a horse and the whispers of people who would soon be sleeping on their rooftops.

When Ruth felt her breathing calm and peace in her heart, she crept back up the street. She continued up the hill and through the fields, the moon rising with her.

A group of women passed her without greeting. She knew that bands of harlots came at night to offer themselves to the harvesters. What if she was mistaken for one of them?

So many things could go wrong.

"I trust You, Lord," she whispered, then she hid between piles of corn stalks and waited.

"Let me not be seen," she prayed when the guards made their rounds. "And don't allow me to make a mistake and lie down at the feet of the wrong man!"

After the guards had left, she entered Boaz's tent. At the end of a corn heap she found Boaz, snoring evenly. His sandals and head cloth were there at the base of his bed.

Ruth had never been so nervous and was glad for the cold night air because it stopped her from perspiring. She had been married, so a man's body was not unfamiliar to her, but she felt awkward and afraid as she leaned over and uncovered his feet. Boaz kept on sleeping, breathing deeply. She could smell wine on his breath, but she didn't think he was drunk—just worn out.

Now what am I supposed to do? she wondered. She felt her knees go weak, so she bent down and knelt on top of his sandals. The leather was worn smooth. Where had these sandals taken Boaz? She let her fingers touch the material of his head cover and felt its richness—thick and expensive.

Her heart thundered. She decided to curl up at the foot of his mat, like servants did, lying opposite their masters.

He stopped snoring and she held her breath, afraid he had awoken. But then his snoring started again.

Ruth felt another wave of panic. What if Boaz kept right on sleeping and didn't wake up until morning? What if he cried out and everyone saw that she'd lain by him? She could be stoned for doing so. What would happen to Naomi then? If Sakira could see her now, what would she think? She had never missed her sister, Orpah, more.

What was she supposed to do? She slid closer slowly until she felt Boaz's heartbeat, slow and strong. He was probably old enough to be her father, but the man was young in muscle and enthusiasm.

He loved life. He loved the Lord. Could he ever love her?

Ruth noticed now that there were other sounds too. The threshing floor was sleeping quarters for at least a dozen other men. Their sleeping sounds surrounded her and made Ruth remain as quiet as the flutter of a moth's wings.

When the moon had rounded its way to the center of the sky, Boaz turned over, and his bare leg brushed hers. He sat up like he'd been slapped.

"Who are you?" he demanded through the darkness.

"I am Ruth, thine handmaid," she said, her voice shaking as if she were a pillar about to crumble.

"Ruth? Ruth!"

She wanted to run away and keep running. But she did not move. What had Naomi told her to say? "Please, sir, spread your skirt over me, for as Mother explained it, you are my near kinsman."

"Ruth," he whispered, saying her name softly with something more than hospitality. "Ruth, I understand. Don't be afraid."

She trembled.

"Ruth, it's all right. Naomi is right. I am your near kinsman. And you, my maid, have shown more kindness in this moment than you can know. You could have followed after one of the young men during the harvest, but here you are with me."

She felt nervous, her thoughts frantic. What if Boaz thought she wanted to lie with him only for the night, when what she really wanted was to become his wife?

"Fear not, Naomi's daughter. I will do what you've required of me. I will not harm you or your reputation. Tomorrow, the entire city will know that you're a virtuous woman."

He pressed his lips against the back of her hand, and Ruth wished that moment would last forever. She felt safe again, cherished in a way that she had never known. Mahlon had been a boy, she realized, but Boaz was a man.

"What is it?" she whispered when he pulled back from her.

"The law states that your kinsman redeemer has the right to marry you and to father sons in your dead husband's name and honor."

"Yes, Naomi explained your law to me."

"But did Naomi tell you that there is a nearer kinsman than me?"

"Who?"

Boaz groaned and turned away like he might be sick. When he looked back at her there was fear in his tone. "My uncle, Heber."

Boaz held Ruth that night while they whispered of the memories and lessons they kept closest to their hearts. He asked many questions about her, so she told him about growing up in Moab, of being raised in and out of the palace, of learning to love her father, a man most people despised.

She talked of her love for her mother, Sakira, and younger brother. She did her best to describe their basket shop, the temple of Chemosh, and the gardens and pools of the palace. She wept when she talked of Orpah and how Orpah had protected and guided her all of her life.

"I cannot begin to understand the sacrifice you've made for Naomi," he admitted.

"She is my mother just as if we shared the same blood."

"Sometimes the bonds that love forges are much stronger than the ones made by blood."

Ruth pressed her lips together and waited for her body to stop shaking, then she spoke words she did not think she would ever say. "You said something one day to me about Mahlon and his bravery. Tell me the truth, Boaz; did my husband help to murder my father?"

"In a way, yes, we all did."

"We?" she tried to ask, but the word stuck in her throat.

Boaz filled his lungs with air then released it slowly. "I need you to understand something you cannot possibly understand. Under Moabite rule, we were treated as dogs, less than dogs. Our men were beaten, sold, and killed. Our women were abused. Our children were kidnapped and sold or taken as tokens to appease Chemosh."

Ruth hardly dared breathe.

"We are not a people made to cower. Years and years ago Ehud came to my father and to my uncle. He was gathering a secret army to fight to free our people." He paused, taking another deep breath. "Mahlon was young, but already he was a swordsmith; the child had a gift from God for a very special purpose. You see, Ehud knew the only way to bring down the Moabites was to kill the king—your father.

"He asked my uncle Elimelech to craft him a short sword to fit his left hand. The sword had to be very, very special. It had to be made over time—years even—with scraps of metal that would not be missed by the overseers appointed to watch my uncle at his blacksmith shop. It also had to be small enough to be concealed and sharp enough to kill on the first attempt."

"I understand all of this," Ruth said, looking down.

"Do you understand that Mahlon was the one who ended up designing and making that sword?" he asked. Then, lifting her chin so their eyes met again, he said, "I was the one who hid the sword in a tribute basket and brought it across the river." Sighing, he continued,

"Elimelech was the one who hid it in Moab, waiting for just the right time. Mahlon concealed it after his father's death. But your sister's husband, Chilion, the man so conflicted, finally joined our forces by hiding the sword in your father's sleeping chambers so Ehud could use it when the time came."

The reality of what Boaz was telling her hurt like a sword in her back. She knew bits and pieces, but now the whole picture became clear. "Naomi? Did Naomi know the plan was to kill my father?"

"No."

He pulled Ruth toward him and held her shaking body. He kissed her tears from her cheeks and whispered, "One day, I will answer all of your questions, but this is not the time—or the place—to tell you how many, many men worked for years to dethrone your father and free our people."

Boaz's honesty made Ruth want to open her entire heart to him.

"I understand why he did it," she said. "I forgive Mahlon. I forgive you—all of you."

He held her gently as she cried silently. They were tears she could not shed in front of Naomi, for it would hurt Naomi if she knew how deeply Ruth missed Sakira and Orpah and Nathaniel and even Lydia.

When the tears stopped, he asked about her injured leg and told her how much he appreciated the way she had protected his mother from the vile dogs.

He told her of his days as an apprentice in Jerusalem.

"Why did you not stay there and work as a scribe?" she asked.

"I had a boyhood dream," he admitted, "to own the land I now own. I had a dream that one day Bethlehem would be free from Moabite rule and I would be wealthy and important."

"It seems all of your dreams came true."

"Not all of them," he said, and he talked of his wife's death and his endless pain at losing her.

"What about the pain caused by her not bearing you children?"

"It caused us both great sorrow."

"But I was a wife to Mahlon, and I never bore a child, never even had a miscarriage."

"God willing," Boaz said, clutching her to him, "our fortunes will change."

"How can we speak of marriage when it's Heber who is the nearest kinsman redeemer?" She shuddered at the thought of marrying that man.

"I will see to Heber. Let me have time to pray and ponder. You need not worry about my uncle."

As the sun began to rise, Boaz reluctantly walked Ruth to the edge of the threshing floor. When the guards saw him with a woman, they turned their heads.

"I don't want this to be well known—that you were here," he said. "People won't understand. But before you go, hold out your veil, for I will not send you home to your mother-in-law empty-handed."

* * *

Naomi was pacing by the gate when Ruth appeared. She looked as though she had not slept at all.

"Tell me," she urged. "Tell me what transpired."

Ruth gave her a hug and then laid out the bounty that Boaz had given her. It even included corncobs for Chamor.

"Boaz is that thoughtful," Ruth said. "I have never imagined such a man."

Naomi sighed. "So, it went well?"

Ruth took a deep breath, not sure where to begin.

"There's joy in you, but there's also dread. Tell me, Ruth, tell me what happened."

"Boaz is a man of honor. He pledged his feelings for me and told me how he would make me his bride if he could."

"What do you mean *if he could*? He can. He must!"

"He can't—at least for right now."

"Why not?"

"Because there is a closer kinsman redeemer."

"Who?"

"You did not tell me of a nearer kinsman redeemer, Mother." Ruth pressed her hands to her cheeks and shook her head.

"Who?" Naomi repeated, the color draining from her face.

"Heber."

Naomi moaned like she had been stabbed. "Oh no. Of course. Of course. Oh, dear child, this news could cost us our home and our lives. It could ruin everything. Heber *is* the nearest kinsman redeemer."

"Why didn't you consider him when you were making all of your plans?" Ruth wept.

"I don't know," Naomi said, trying to comfort Ruth. "I suppose because I don't think of Heber as family."

22

MICAH PRESSED HIS HANDS OVER his throbbing temples and strode up and down the threshing floor, kicking dust from the stores of corn and grain that rose around them like small hills.

"Pardon my boldness," he said to Boaz, "but what could possibly be so important to the lord of the fields that he has to rush off on the very day the harvest is counted?"

Boaz smiled a brilliant yet nervous smile. "I trust you, Micah, to be fair with both my purse and those of the buyers."

"But you are the lord and master, and it is your first harvest settlement since the Moabites were driven from Bethlehem. You have to be here for the counting."

"I don't. I've got you, my trusted friend, to take care of my business."

"We have anticipated this harvest for a generation," Micah argued. "The famine is over and the harvest is in. Today, above all others, is the day when every hand is needed in the counting and measuring. I beg you, Boaz, stay with us to see that all things are done according to your desires."

Boaz looked out at the coming dawn. He stretched and yawned and said, "Micah, all these years I've held a dream to be the largest landowner in Bethlehem."

"And you are."

"What has it brought me—my wealth, I mean?"

"You own the grandest house in Bethlehem. More servants bow to you than to any other man in Judea."

"But am I happy?"

"You seem happy to me. Why ask such questions now?"

"Because now I know that my Lord wants happiness for me. He has opened my eyes and my heart, Micah. Look around, friend, look at the abundance of our efforts."

"They are great indeed."

"And with no one to share them, what happiness do they bring?"

"You always share what the Lord has given you, Master. Even when the harvest was scant, you shared."

"The Almighty willing, by night's end the Lord will share with me a portion of happiness I long ago abandoned my hope of ever having."

"Forgive me, Master, but your words make little sense to me."

Boaz laughed. "Of course things could go terribly wrong and I could come home with a heart broken beyond repair."

"Master? Are you ill? Have you slept?"

"Hardly a wink." Boaz laughed.

"Master, I beg thee, tell me what's more important this day of days than counting your own harvest."

Boaz's face lit up as the sun peeked over the horizon. Suddenly everything that had been gray was golden—the houses, the hills, and the fields.

"This is the color of her eyes, Micah. Her eyes are golden."

"Ruth's eyes?"

Boaz turned to Micah and grinned. "What's more important than counting? Catching a rat, my friend. That's what's more important this day."

Boaz had not seen Heber since the day he bought back Chamor from the traders. Then he'd paid his uncle for information. It was always about money with Heber, and, if that's all it came down to, Boaz would spend his last farthing to buy the hand of Ruth.

At the time he and Heber last parted, Boaz had hoped to never lay eyes on his uncle again. But now he sent paid men in every direction to bribe anyone for information about Heber's whereabouts.

"I have to find my uncle this day," he told the men. "It can't wait."

Heber was not at the inn where his wife and new son were staying.

"I haven't seen my husband in days," the woman said bitterly. She was young. Her skin was dark and her eyes darker. Her hair was dyed the purple of eggplant, and both of her hands were stained in intricate patterns with the henna desert women were so fond of. The babe in her arms looked small and sickly. "Spare me money, sir. Heber left us destitute."

She thrust the tiny, crying baby into Boaz's arms. He hesitated, but once the child was tucked between Boaz's elbow and chest, the boy calmed down and closed his eyes.

"Does he have a name?" Boaz asked of the child.

"Delshad."

"I've never heard that name."

"The desert people, my people," she added, "would call him Happy Heart. But tell me, Boaz, does my son look happy to you?"

There was nothing happy about the woman or the child or the place of poverty in which they were staying.

"What name are you called?"

She looked indignant. "You are my husband's nephew, and you do not know my name? Into what kind of family have I married?"

"We are not close to Heber. I'm sorry to tell you, but we are not."

"I am called Nunah—for *this*." She pointed to the dimple in her chin.

Boaz listened with patience as the woman told a story that had been told too many times already. Heber had swept into her life with claims of great wealth and promises for a better life. But everything he said turned out to be a lie. Now that she had been left, she wanted only to go back to her people.

Boaz gave the mother enough money to pay for passage back to her desert land and to purchase food for herself and supplies for her child. Then he paid the innkeeper their back rent and more to finish out the rest of the month.

"You are not the evil dragon Heber painted you to be," a relieved and grateful Nunah said. "May your god favor you this day."

In spite of a frantic and widespread search, no one found Heber all that morning.

Boaz went to the synagogue and told a priest his dilemma, then vowed to the holy man, "I am afraid he has fled again, maybe to Moab, maybe all the way to Aharon in the desert. It doesn't matter. No matter how far I have to go or however long it takes, I will find Heber."

"And if Heber refuses to accept your proposal?"

"He won't. I know my uncle." Boaz spoke with confidence, but there was the slightest tremor in his tone. "I am counting on his greed."

The priest looked thoughtful. "Put a few coins in my hand, and I will pray for you, Boaz."

Boaz paid the holy man to pray for him. He also prayed for himself. All the while his head and heart were filled with memories of the previous night. It was like a dream, reliving Ruth's brazen courage to do what she had done, and it swelled his heart with love for her. What kind of woman would risk everything to be with someone she loved?

Twice—Ruth had done it twice now. Once, in moving away from Moab to a foreign land and a foreign god. Then last night. By following Naomi's pleas, Ruth could have met with a very different fate.

"I thank Thee, Lord, for the faith of a good woman. Bless our union now, before it even begins, and bless it always." And, as in all of his other prayers, Boaz vowed to serve the Lord God of Israel and to put no other gods before Him.

It was late afternoon before one of Boaz's searchers reported that Heber had been found at a small brothel close to the city gates.

"Stay by the door and do not allow my uncle to leave."

"He won't leave. Heber has been holed up in there for days."

"Go now and see that he doesn't escape. I will be there shortly."

Boaz immediately sent word to his other searchers: "I will pay you double if you will leave now, go directly to the threshing floor, and offer my overseer, Micah, your services. He will be relieved for the added help. And tell him that I'll be by his side as soon as my business is concluded."

He paid each messenger well, and the men hurried off happily.

Next, Boaz went back to the priest and paid him to gather more priests and judges and men with authority. "I need ten," he said. Then Boaz gave him directions to meet at the brothel.

From street vendors on his way, Boaz gathered ten meals of roasted corn and grilled fish. Soon, ten elders sat around outside the brothel, talking and eating and waiting for Heber to emerge. Boaz explained about Ruth and Naomi, but he mostly talked about his uncle's devious dealings, including how he had attempted to swindle a widow out of her home.

"Uncle!" Boaz cried an hour later, when a dazed and drunk Heber finally emerged.

"Boaz?" Heber staggered toward him, half curious and half afraid. "What do you want with me?"

"Sit, and I will tell you."

Heber saw the ten elders and quickly sobered up. He rubbed his bloodshot eyes and spat foul waste on the ground.

The chief priest motioned for Heber to follow; all the men got up and walked to an awning where they had both shade and partial privacy.

"This is a matter of haste," Boaz said with growing confidence. "Our Elimelech's widow has returned from Moab."

Heber stared at him sideways. "I am aware. You bring me no new news in telling me of Naomi. The woman has returned bitter and unpleasant." His eyes shifted from elder to elder. He looked like a rat, suspicious and ready to run. "Is it any wonder? God struck her husband and sons dead. His hand is against her."

Boaz stepped in front of Heber and looked right into the man's small, dark eyes. "Naomi tells me you wish her to sell her home and the land on which it sits."

"We had a conversation about the possibility. I did nothing to threaten her or to coerce her, if that's what she is claiming."

"She said you told her that you have a contract to prove that Elimelech owes you money, money Naomi cannot pay."

Heber seemed to feel the elders' eyes boring into him, and he scratched himself nervously. "Is that what Naomi told you? Are you going to pay her debt, Boaz?" His worried look softened.

"There is no debt, is there, Uncle?"

Heber stammered but could not manage a straight yes or no.

"May I see the agreement you struck with Elimelech before he left for Moab?" Boaz asked, holding out his hand.

Heber scampered backward. "I have no such deed, and if Naomi said so, she's—"

"She's what?" Boaz cut him off.

"You did not show her a contract?" demanded one of the priests.

Heber's lip quivered.

"You did not try to trick her with a contract?" the priest demanded again.

"Trick? No. No. You're mistaken. I showed her a contract, but it was only as a likeness. The contract I had with Elimelech was verbal, a bond between an uncle and a nephew. It's something you know about, Boaz."

Boaz sighed. "Naomi is in need of care and provisions for the remainder of her life, Uncle. As her family, we must do all we can to provide for her."

"Yes, well . . . you are in a position to provide for Naomi. I am not."

The chief priest stood and arranged his robes, righting his tilted headdress. "Heber, are you the only surviving brother of Elimelech?"

"Yes."

"Then we must advise you that as Naomi's nearest kinsman redeemer, you must lawfully buy the land from her."

"Buy?"

"As her kinsman redeemer, it is your lawful duty."

"*I* am Naomi's kinsman redeemer?" His voice squeaked.

"You just admitted as much."

Another elder stood. "As the brother of her husband, it is your lawful duty to marry Naomi and buy her property. She must be provided for immediately."

"Marry Naomi? *Buy* her property?"

"Are you unfamiliar with the law?" the priest asked Heber.

"I am unfamiliar with this law," he said, his eyes still darting, searching for a way out, but the men surrounded him.

"It is unfortunate for you that you have not learned the laws. Ignorance, however, does not excuse you."

Heber shook his head. "Naomi? She's old and weathered."

"Yes, she is," Boaz said, trying to keep himself from grinning.

"I do not marry old women. In fact, I have a young wife now—very young. And she has just given birth to my son. My duty is to her."

"We are aware of how you have honored your husbandly duties," the priest said, pointing to the brothel door.

"And Nunah never wishes to see you or to speak to you again," Boaz said.

Heber's head jerked up at the mention of his wife's name. "How do you know my wife's name?"

"She told me," Boaz said. "She also told me how you've treated her and your sickly baby boy."

"I have no money to provide properly for them," Heber argued.

Again, the priest pointed to the brothel door.

"How many times have you been married, Heber?" another priest asked.

"Six, maybe seven."

"Nine," the priest said. "You have been married nine times."

"Yes, Nunah said she is your ninth wife," Boaz said.

"Do you or do you not wish to claim your rights as Naomi's kinsman redeemer and make her your tenth bride?" the elder asked.

Heber shifted his bones uneasily. He looked at each face, narrowing his red-rimmed, watery eyes. "Are you telling me I *have* to buy Naomi's property and take her as my wife?"

"You know the law, Heber."

He squirmed and scratched his head.

Then Boaz half smiled. "Don't look so distraught, Uncle. The law says you do not have to marry Naomi."

"What? You just told me—"

"You can pass the obligation on to the next kinsman."

"Who is that?" Heber asked.

The elders all nodded to Boaz, who sighed and bowed his head like a great burden was being shifted to his shoulders.

"You? Of course you would want her property. You want to own all of Bethlehem."

"We all know the accusations you have leveled against me in the past, Uncle."

"They've all proven to be false," one of the elders said. "Now you must make a decision, Heber—do you wish to claim your lawful right as Naomi's kinsman redeemer?"

"When you buy the property," Heber said to Boaz, "will I receive any of the money Elimelech owed me?"

"How quickly your stories change, Uncle. One moment there's an agreement, then there's not, and now there is again."

Heber ignored Boaz and looked to the eldest of the priests. "Sir, tell me, as Naomi's kinsman redeemer, as creditor to her dead husband, may I lay claim to her property without paying her now?"

"No. You must buy her property *now*, and you must marry her without delay."

Heber hunched his shoulders and scrunched up his nose. His voice went high like it did whenever he got excited. "Maybe I will marry Naomi and buy her property. Maybe I'll grow grapes for my own wine in her back orchard."

Sweat trickled down Boaz's temples, and his fingers balled into fists.

"Yes," one of the elders said, "but you lived in that house and tended to that orchard for a long span while Naomi was in Moab. You know the state of disrepair the property is in. It will require a great deal of money and work to make it livable."

Heber gulped. "Naomi lives there now with a Moabitess who was married to one of her sons."

"Yes," the priest agreed, "the law states that you must also buy Ruth."

"Ruth?"

"The Moabitess, widow of Mahlon."

"I met her once—in Moab—but how can you expect me to marry someone I do not know?"

The priest went on. "And the law says you must bring up children with her, all in the name of Mahlon."

"More children!"

"Yes, more children to your credit and to Mahlon's eternal inheritance. So are we in agreement—you wish to claim your rights as Naomi's kinsman redeemer?"

"I cannot do it," Heber said. "I have nothing for my own inheritance." He grabbed his head and tugged at his hair, swaying and wailing like a man suddenly gone mad. "Elimelech took my generosity! Boaz, you stole my property and destroyed my altar to Baal. Now I am a lone man with nothing and no one."

The elder stepped in front of Heber. "You have a wife and newborn son."

"Oh, spare a man some money, will you, Boaz? You're the richest man in Bethlehem, and I am a pitiful beggar with nothing to offer my poor hungry wife and sick newborn daughter."

"Son, you mean."

Heber stopped wailing. "*Son* is what I meant to say."

"Enough of this show," the presiding priest said. "Do you or do you not wish to decline your lawful rights to Naomi and her property?"

"Yes. I decline."

"Then pluck off your shoe and hand it to your neighbor," the elder said, "and let this agreement stand as your testimony in Israel."

Heber looked at Boaz, not with suspicion but with relief. "Gladly, if it will get me out of the obligation I have to marry an old woman and take on another wife and more children." Heber removed his dusty sandal and handed it to the man beside him.

Boaz ran his fingers through his hair and looked first to heaven, then at the elders, and finally at all of the people who had gathered to stare. "Ye are witnesses this day, that I have bought all that was Elimelech's, and all that was Chilion's and Mahlon's. Today I vow to care for the widow of my uncle. Naomi will never go without. Moreover, Ruth, the Moabitess wife of Mahlon, have I purchased to be my wife, that the name of the dead be not cut off from among his brethren and from the gate of his place: ye are witnesses this day."

"We are!" the people shouted.

"We are," the elders agreed.

With all the shouts of joy came prayers and blessings. A moment into the celebration, Heber sneaked forward and tugged at the cloak of his nephew.

"Boaz?"

"Yes, Uncle?"

"Can you spare a poor man money for a cup of wine? I'm parched."

23

THE BETROTHAL OF BOAZ AND RUTH was quick and the wedding simple, though all of Bethlehem turned out for the celebration. Boaz offered to bring Sakira and Orpah and the rest of Ruth's Moabite family to Bethlehem for a stay.

"Perhaps someday," Ruth said. "I do not know that my mothers could be happy for me and my new life. Their god is not my god."

"And Orpah?"

"We've received word that she remarried—one of Lemuel's guards. I pray for my sister's happiness."

"Nathaniel?"

"He is needed to stay with my mothers." She reached for Naomi's hand. "I am completely content right where I am now—with my mother and with you."

Somewhere in the crowd were two sisters, grown women now, married with children of their own.

Naomi recognized them right away. "Jola and Edna!"

"Auntie Naomi. We heard you had returned to Bethlehem and we wanted to come and see you."

"Where are Berta and Uriel? I've wondered about them for years."

"They are in Jericho," Edna said. "Mother says if you wish to see her, you must make the effort." Edna smiled uneasily.

"Mother has not changed," Jola said.

Naomi draped an arm around an old woman's shoulder. "Surely you two remember your auntie Kezia. She was the wife of your grandfather's brother, Salmon."

Kezia looked at the women through her old, clouded eyes, then said, "Tell Berta she never returned my shawl."

The women burst into laughter.

"Come, Nieces," Naomi said, her voice faltering slightly. "I can't wait to introduce you to Ruth and Boaz."

"What's wrong, Auntie?" Jola asked.

Edna reached over and wiped Naomi's cheek.

"It's just that the Lord has been so merciful to me. Look how He has blessed me with a family that is not as sparse as I had feared. I am not alone."

"No, you are never alone," Kezia said. "God is with you."

And then Naomi stretched her arms wide and tried to fit them all into her embrace.

* * *

In the months that followed, people flocked around Anna's bench, where Naomi liked to spend her afternoons basking in the sun and the memories. Most afternoons Ruth joined her, and they sat together and prayed silent prayers of gratitude, their fingers intertwined.

One day when Ruth arrived, Naomi was not there. She hurried to Naomi's home and raced through the new gate.

"What are you doing, Mother?" she asked.

Naomi was down on her knees, a blade in her hand, a small, worn, wooden bench before her.

Ruth read the intricately carved letters that ran along the bottom of the bench, just below the artwork. "Thou shalt have no other gods before me."

"When my mother carved the commandments," Naomi explained, "she was only copying designs that she could not read. But I can read and so can you, Daughter, and that's a miracle in this land."

"I'm grateful for the lessons of my youth," Ruth said. "Tell me more about this bench. It's not a replica of your mother's bench. It's unique."

The corners of Naomi's lips curved upward, and her eyes sparkled. "Long ago I started to carve beauty into this bench. But I lost heart because I will never be the artist that my mother was. I thought I was not good enough, so I feared that my work would not be accepted."

Ruth ran the side of her thumb over the vine that Naomi was carving. "It's beautiful, Mother."

"Look how each leaf, each petal is different, yet we are all connected to the vine. That's how it is, Ruth: God is the vine, and we are the petals, the flowers, and the fruit."

"Different, yet all one." Ruth smiled. "The gospel seems so simple through your eyes, Mother."

"It makes me happy. And speaking of happy, you look radiant this morning."

"I've brought an apple to feed Chamor," Ruth said.

The donkey had already recognized Ruth's voice and was looking around the corner of the house, his neck outstretched. While she fed Chamor, Ruth could not stop smiling.

"I already know what has brought such radiance to your face," Naomi said, "but I long to hear the words come from your own mouth. Tell me, Daughter. Tell me the good news."

"This is the third month I have missed the red tent, Mother," she said.

Naomi shouted with joy. She interlaced her fingers and held them to her face in a humble, thankful prayer.

"Does Boaz know?"

Ruth nodded. "His smile was even wider than mine."

* * *

When the sickness came and Ruth was forced to lie still and could not lift her head, it was Naomi she called for and it was Naomi who came.

"Mother!"

"I'm here, Daughter," Naomi said.

She held Ruth's head. She rubbed Ruth's feet. She sat beside her and never ceased to pray until Ruth could keep down a cup of broth and until the color returned to Ruth's pale cheeks.

"You are more than welcome to come and live in this big house with us," Boaz offered. Then, turning to Ruth, he said, "Mother takes only one room, but there are many."

Naomi kissed Boaz's cheek. "Someday, Son, I will accept your offer. But for now, Chamor and I enjoy our home, which you've so graciously repaired for us. It is more than comfortable."

* * *

Almost every morning that summer, Naomi and Ruth took turns sitting first on Anna's bench at the well, then moved to the shade of Naomi's bench, sitting close together in the afternoon.

"I haven't just carved vines," Naomi said one afternoon. "I've carved our family. The vine is the Lord; without Him, we would have no life. We are the leaves and branches. Look . . . there's one for Elimelech, one for each of our sons, and even one for our tiny daughters, whose spirits still find me now and then."

Ruth's smile seemed tender at the thought of Naomi's daughters. Naomi realized that it had taken her a long time to even be able to talk about her lost daughters. She sighed, then said, "This leaf is for you, and this one for Boaz, and this stem will grow leaves for the children that you will have."

"Where does the vine end?" Ruth asked. "I see no beginning and no end."

"It doesn't end, Daughter. It will go on forever and ever."

Ruth took Naomi's hand and placed it over her swollen stomach. She felt the baby kick, and that kick brought tears to Naomi's eyes. As she thought about all they had been through together, tears seemed to rain down from Naomi's eyes like great drops of water on a land that for so long had been dry and barren.

* * *

In time, the boy was born, plump and blessed with mighty lungs. After the midwife severed the cord, she handed the baby to Naomi, who washed his body, then rubbed it with salt to close his pores and toughen his skin for the harsh climate of Bethlehem.

Kezia was there, handling the swaddling cloth. She and Naomi wrapped the baby in it.

"You were at my side," Naomi told Kezia, "when my twin sons were born. They would not have lived without your care."

"Who would ever have imagined that we would share a grandson?" Kezia whispered to Naomi. "God is so good."

Finished swaddling him, Naomi passed the baby to his mother's outstretched arms.

He nursed right away.

"That is a sign from heaven, if ever there was one," Naomi said. "There is milk for our children!"

As Naomi spoke, they heard someone approaching the door. When it opened, light poured into the room, with Boaz casting a long shadow as he stepped through the doorframe.

"You may enter," Naomi said.

As Ruth placed their son in the crook of Boaz's arm, Naomi asked, "What will you call him?"

Boaz could hardly get the name out. Tears filled his eyes, but his smile was wide. "Obed," he finally managed to say.

"Obed," Ruth repeated.

"I know that name," Naomi said. "It means *servant of God.*"

"Yes, and he will be," Boaz vowed. "All the days of his life, our son will serve only the true and living God."

In a very real sense, Naomi realized later, the child's birth signaled all of Judea's rebirth. Men, women, and children came to see the baby, a baby that Naomi knew had been denied to both of his parents for so long, a son born of faith.

When Boaz reluctantly returned to his fields, Naomi stayed beside Ruth. She held the baby until his little pink mouth yawned and he fell asleep. Then she laid him in a cradle at his mother's bedside.

"Is he all right?" Ruth asked.

"He is perfect," Naomi said, and she bowed her head and prayed her favorite prayer of only gratitude.

"Mother," Ruth said, "I want to share with you something so tender I haven't even told Boaz yet."

"Yes, Child, I'm listening."

"I want to tell you that I've prayed too. All this time, I've prayed for the strength to abandon my old beliefs. I've prayed for protection for us. I have even prayed for Chamor." She laughed and continued. "I have prayed that the Lord God of Israel would accept me, a stranger, a convert, and that He would find it in His heart to adopt me as His own."

Ruth smiled so brilliantly that it seemed to make the shadows scamper from the room. Then she said, "And He has, Mother. God has heard the prayer of one so common and foreign."

Naomi clasped her hands and nodded.

"I loved my father," Ruth admitted, "but he was not a good man. I see that now so plainly. But my Father in Heaven has found me, claimed me, and treated me as a good and faithful father treats his own daughter."

Naomi's heart felt ready to burst. "All of these years I have borne so much sorrow," Naomi said. "My heart was so heavy at times that I did not understand how it could have kept beating—but it did. And now, when its chambers are worn thin, I wonder how it does not burst with all of the happiness it holds. Oh, Ruth, my daughter, I am a blessed woman."

"Accept it as God's gift to you, Mother. Embrace the joy."

For a long moment the two women wept tears of joy together. Then Naomi said, "Ruth, you're worn out. Treasure this chance to sleep, as every new mother should."

Sitting in a chair near the cradle, Naomi watched as Ruth's eyelids seemed to grow heavy and finally close. Naomi vowed to stay awake, to rock the cradle where Obed slept, but she yawned, and soon her chin dropped to her chest.

When Boaz returned, he found the three of them asleep. His son slept softly on lamb's wool. His wife slept on their bed, her face turned toward her mother, who slept on a nearby chair.

Boaz smiled as he saw Naomi's hand, her fingers interlaced with Ruth's. Even in sleep, he realized, this mother and daughter reached out to each other for comfort and support.

He thought of waking them to explain how much their example of selfless love meant to him, but he realized that he'd only be pointing out the obvious. Instead, he crept over to the cradle, but the sounds of his steps woke the baby. Quietly, he lifted Obed and, stepping into the golden light that streamed through the window, her looked out at the town that glowed the color of his wife's eyes.

So Boaz took Ruth, and she was his wife: and when he went in unto her, the LORD *gave her conception, and she bare a son.*

And the women said unto Naomi, Blessed be the Lord, which hath not left thee this day without a kinsman, that his name may be famous in Israel.

And he shall be unto thee a restorer of thy life, and a nourisher of thine old age: for thy daughter in law, which loveth thee, which is better to thee than seven sons, hath born him.

And Naomi took the child, and laid it in her bosom, and became nurse unto it.

And the women her neighbours gave it a name, saying, There is a son born to Naomi; and they called his name Obed: he is the father of Jesse, the father of David.

—Ruth 4:13–17

About the Author

Toni Sorenson was in fourth grade when she won her first writing award. The *Salt Lake Tribune* named her an "Aspiring Author." In seventh grade she won top honors as Utah's Young Author in creative fiction. In college she was named one of America's most promising writers and the Nashville Songwriters new-song-of-the-year winner for lyrics she penned.

Her nationally published works have sold more than a half million copies. Her alliance with Covenant Communications has yielded more than twenty published works, including *Master* and *Messiah*, accounts of the life of Christ. She won the prestigious Association of Mormon Letters novel-of-the-year award for *Redemption Road*. In 2013 Covenant honored Toni with the Making-A-Difference award.

Ruth and Naomi is the heart-wrenching story of two Biblical women whose hearts lead them on one of the most harrowing adventures told in scripture.

Toni is the mother of six. She spends her time writing, traveling, public speaking, hiking, and just "hanging out" with her children, grandchildren, and friends.